I0592717

Spinner's
Lake

End Haven
Regional
Airport

Idle County
• Fairgrounds

Old Mill
Historical
Site
• Old Mill Roa

Greifenberg
Manor •

Birmingham Road

12

The Place
with
No Name
•

H ◉
End Haven

Main Street

Hunter Avenue

The
Mo
Wo

Comp

Lemon
Avenue
Library

Elijah •
Bryce's
House

The
• Knoll

IDLE COUNTY

Fing
Lake

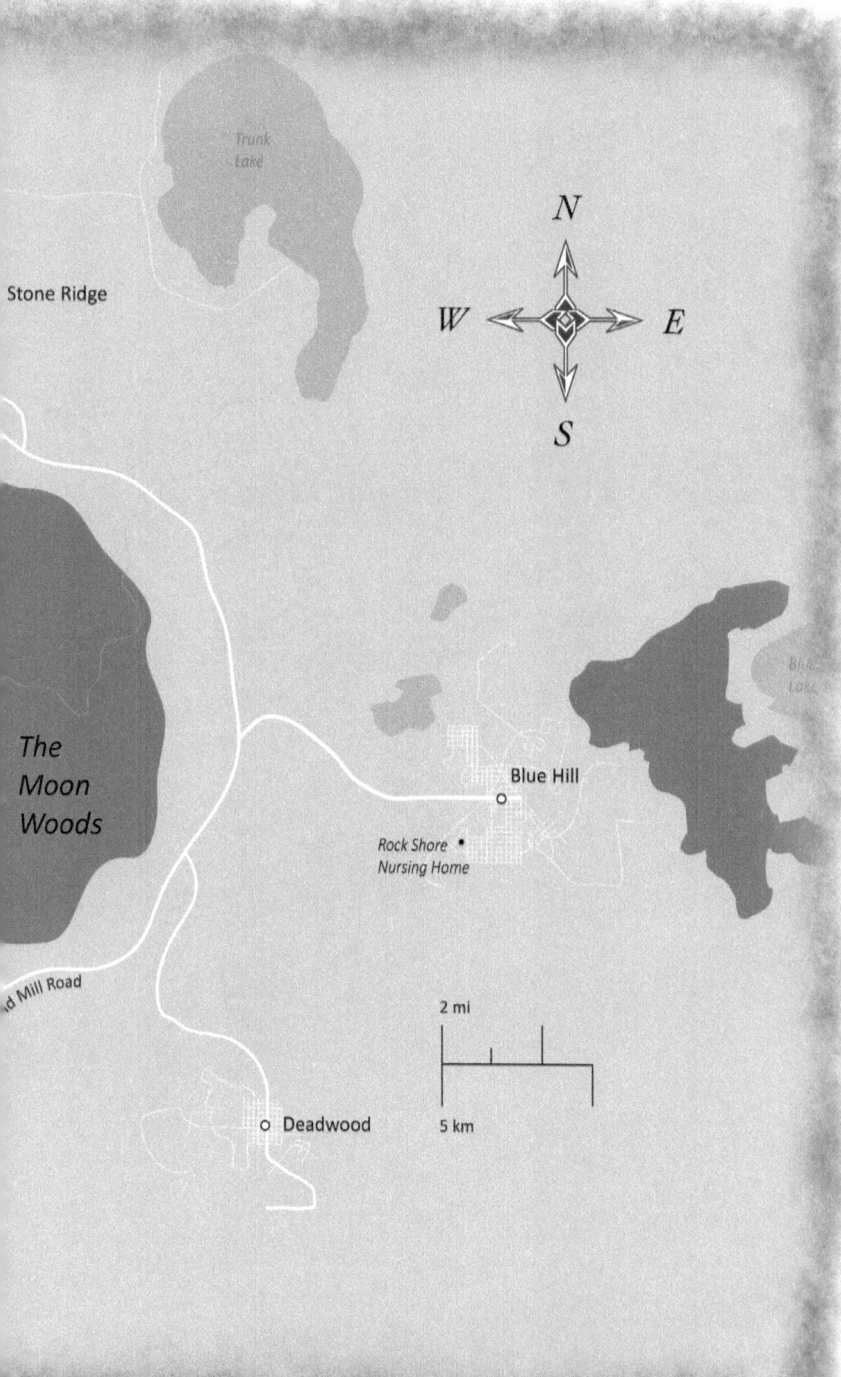

THE

RELEASE

OF

JONATHAN
FLITE

ALSO BY MATTHEW J. BEIER

The Breeders
The Confessions of Jonathan Flite
The Rise of Jonathan Flite

THE

RELEASE

OF

JONATHAN FLITE

BY MATTHEW J. BEIER

AN EPICALITY BOOK • EPICALITY BOOKS

San Francisco

Library of Congress Control Number: 2016953948
Paperback Print ISBN-13: 978-0-9838594-7-5
E-Book ISBN: 978-0-9838594-8-2

FIRST HARDCOVER EDITION
Also available in e-book format
Epicality Books, 2016
www.epicalitybooks.com

For Mike Shay, who, despite thinking everything is meaningless, gave me the time to get this series off the ground.

1910

April 29, 1912 - *William and Anna Villard, parents of Simon Villard, commit suicide in Connecticut; Simon moves to live with his uncle in Idle County.*

February 3, 1918 - *Simon Villard, at age thirteen, is seen by his neighbor crushing a sparrow under his heel.*

1920

1930

April 20, 1930 - *Simon Villard is ordained a priest.*

May 6, 1933 - *Elizabeth Parker, while still infatuated with Simon Villard, meets Joshua Grime at a dinner party.*

March 2, 1936 - *Suspecting Simon Villard isn't what he seems, Joshua Grime actively begins courting Elizabeth Parker.*

June 2, 1938 - *Elizabeth Parker and Joshua Grime marry.*

1940

October 2–12, 1947 - *Joshua Grime goes missing; Simon Villard vanishes after being confronted by Elizabeth.*

November 16, 1948 - *Joshua Grime is declared dead.*

1950

1960

March 2, 1964 - *Victor Zobel is born.*

January 31, 1966 - *Max Pope is born.*

September 1, 1969 - *Elizabeth Grime begins teaching at Benedict Wise University.*

1970

1980

September 5, 1983 - *Max Pope starts premed degree at Benedict Wise University.*

1990

September 10, 1992 - *Cynthia Foster and Elijah Earnshaw give up their son for adoption.*

June 30, 1995 - *Nicolas Leandro Rim is born.*

2000

June 3, 2005 - *Elijah Bryce meets Molly Butler.*

February 26, 2008 - *Max Pope moves to Palmer, Alaska.*

July 4, 2010 - *The Idle County Seven vanish without a trace; Victor Zobel organizes search of the Moon Woods.*

2010

April 12, 2014 - *Kara Butler is born.*

March 14, 2020 - *Jimmy Barber is born.*

2020

May 30, 2020 - *Jonathan Flite is born.*

2030

August 19, 2033 - *Judge Barry Wallace tries Jonathan Flite as a juvenile after the murder of Ellen Graber.*

November 30, 2037 - *Nicolas Leandro Rim breaks into Crescent Rehabilitation Center.*

May 31, 2038 - *Jonathan Flite is released from Crescent Rehabilitation Center.*

2040

PART 1

BURIED TRUTHS

1982

"NEW AGE MUMBO JUMBO." That was the label people slapped onto any unorthodox hint that life was anything beyond the subatomic particles that gave it a means to exist. Staunch atheists scoffed at every attempt to reconcile such hints with real science, and organized religious flocks dismissed them with equal fervency, sometimes deeming them misunderstood (or even demonic) manifestations of their own particular objective truths. As such, both sides adopted extreme closed-mindedness, and anything that didn't fit within their worldviews got slapped with this dismissive term and shoved under a rug. In the shadows, however, where individual experiences mattered, indications of some deeper meaning to life kept coming.

For a random example, take Patty and Doug Chillings. They were an everyday, slightly overweight couple living in Nampa,

Idaho, in 1982. One night, at 3:13 a.m., both of them awoke to the sound of their golden retriever, Clarence, whimpering. In a sleepy daze, Patty sat up to shush Clarence, who was sitting at the foot of their bed. When her eyes cleared, however, she saw a small boy standing next to the dog. Quite sure it was a dream, she blinked five times. The boy neither moved nor disappeared.

"Doug." She nudged her husband, her gaze glued on the boy. "*Doug. Wake up.*"

Doug jumped awake, propping himself on his elbows. His first thought was that there was an intruder in the house; he would realize later that a sense of it had already crept through his dreams, into his bones, just moments before his wife's voice woke him.

Patty pointed at the boy.

Doug saw him.

Clarence whimpered.

Then, the boy disappeared in front of their eyes.

Sunrise came without another wink of sleep for either of the two people. They had searched the house high and low for any sign that a child had broken in during the night, but there was no sign of an unexpected visitor. All the doors were locked, and the windows were unbroken. Neither spouse could call the other's vision a subjective hallucination, because they had both seen a boy in their bedroom, and they had done so without telling the other what they were seeing. Only when the boy disappeared and Clarence stopped whimpering did they confirm with each other the shared apparition. Patty, who was sterile and who had always wanted a son, secretly wondered during the nights that followed if the boy had been some distorted reflection of her barrenness, an apparition of undecided probability.

She never realized how close this was to the truth.

2015

F AR MORE RELEVANT ON A BROADER SCALE was Professor Banner Tate, a doctor of physics situated academically and comfortably among the redwoods at the University of California Santa Cruz. He was an atheist as a rule (because what sense was there in speculating about things beyond the feasible lens of science?), and, despite adhering to the widely accepted tenet of quantum mechanics stating that the very act of observation played a role in dictating the physical world as human beings knew it, he was perfectly happy adhering to Niels Bohr's Copenhagen interpretation and not asking further questions. Sure, some considered this idea to be a skeleton in the closet of modern physics, but for all practical purposes, quantum theory predicted reality with extreme accuracy. That was all that mattered.

In 2015, however, Professor Tate served as faculty advisor for a wheelchair-riding graduate student named Dorothy Garland. (It wasn't a joke—the professor often wondered but never asked what her Oz-riddled parents had been smoking when they named her.) All he knew about Dorothy's background was that her family was dead, and she was a student at UCSC by way of some wealthy benefactor. She made an impression on Professor Tate, because she always had to settle her wheelchair just right in front of the desk in his cluttered office, and she always had her blond hair pulled back behind her heart-shaped face in the same simple way. Not wanting to upset Dorothy by asking the reason for her wheelchair, Professor Tate learned of it by whispers among two fellow faculty members: agenesis of the corpus callosum, a full absence of the band of neural fibers connecting the right and left hemispheres of her brain. Because she had trouble communicating through speech, she typed out her part of any conversation using a keyboard-equipped tablet connected to her wheelchair.

Yet the whispers went further than just her peculiar health condition. A fellow faculty member named Julie Kendrick, while marveling one morning at Dorothy Garland's performance in her nonrelativistic quantum mechanics course, claimed there were rumors that the young woman could "read minds." This of course amounted to heresy in their physics department, but Professor Tate saw the genuine unsettledness in his colleague's eyes.

"I heard it from Audrey Pell," Professor Kendrick said one day as she accompanied him across the tree-lined bridge outside the Interdisciplinary Sciences Building. "She was a TA when Dorothy was in undergrad. Quantum Field Theory Two, I think. Apparently one of the other students saw Dorothy at a student meet-up at Global Village Café. She was telling people she could read their thoughts. And you know how she types everything out on that little tablet?" Professor Kendrick glanced left and then right before descending into a whisper. "*She was typing out exactly what they were thinking.*"

Professor Tate wasn't the type of man people played jokes on. He tried to look into his colleague's eyes, but they were turned toward the bridge's weathered boardwalk.

"And she's in the physics department of all places," Professor Kendrick pressed, adding the most uncomfortable chuckle Professor Tate had ever heard.

"No joke?" he said.

"No joke. But there's more. She's brilliant in class, but she's got ideas. Pretty crazy ideas. We're talking New Agey crap. Tells people they all have 'spirit guides' and that Earth is just a school created by souls who use it to learn. She even told one girl, some undergrad, that her 'spirit guide' wanted her to know she should 'make amends with her mother sooner rather than later.' And guess what? That girl got a call two days later from a sibling. Turned out their mom had metastasized liver cancer. The girl just moved back to Iowa."

Professor Tate knew better than to entertain the sprig of interest forming in his gut. He laughed off Professor Kendrick's story as some sort of prank, even made *her* laugh it off, but on the night before his next quarterly meeting with Dorothy, he remembered the story and began devising potential methods to test her mind-reading abilities. He was quiet all through dinner at his house on Bayana Drive, near the university, and despite joining his wife, Catherine for an evening walk under the ocean-bound sunset, he couldn't shake the tremble of discomfort in his chest as he pondered ways to elicit a psychic statement from the disabled woman—or prove her a fraud. His racing mind kept him awake well into the night, long enough so that Catherine woke up at 2:34 a.m. and said, "All right, Ban, you're doing that loud stress breathing again. Can you sleep on the couch?"

The next day, Dorothy Garland rolled into his office. She jerked her wheelchair to a stop, then looked at Professor Tate with a blank expression when he choked out, "Good morning." Dorothy continued staring at him as her fingers crept slowly over the keyboard mounted to her wheelchair. She then rotated the tablet toward his desk. On it was a simple message typed in an exceedingly boring Courier font:

> *You don't have to manipulate me into reading your*
> *mind. I can do that on my own. I'm sorry your wife*
> *made you sleep on the couch. Now can we focus on*
> *my research?*

For the first time since learning the nature of quantum mechanics, Professor Tate felt the very foundation of his world shake. His own defenses caused a half smirk to contort his expression, and when he looked at this young woman—at her heart-shaped face, her black glasses, and the glint in her eyes that suddenly looked like a mixture of amusement and exasperation—he experienced a flutter of intellectual vulnerability.

In the following weeks, Professor Tate checked his email every morning, expecting to see a message stating that Dorothy had requested a new, less manipulative faculty adviser. But she never did. Every quarter until the completion of her doctoral dissertation, she wheeled into his office, and they discussed her research relating to high energy theory and quantum gravity. Never again did they discuss the fact that she could read his mind. Dorothy Garland earned her PhD, did postdoctoral research for a few years, and then—for a time—faded into academic obscurity.

2033

CONNECTED TO DOROTHY GARLAND with an almost
humorous lack of obscurity (though nobody realized
it yet) was Judge Barry Wallace of Providence, Rhode
Island, whose life changed forever the day he met Jonathan Flite,
the so-called nurse killer. The dirty-blond boy was just thirteen
years old when he first entered the man's courtroom in August
2033, staring with his heavy, steely-hazel eyes at the daffodils
sitting on the judge's bench. The flowers had come from Judge
Wallace's wife, Marilyn, that morning, in honor of their thirty-
fifth wedding anniversary. He had brought them out from his
office on purpose, sure that Jonathan Flite, whose case file had for
some reason plucked his emotions, would be nervous about his
preliminary hearing.

Except it wasn't Jonathan's first collision with the Rhode
Island Family Court. He had already severely injured a girl named

Melinda Berry at summer camp when he was just ten years old. Did this mean he was a hopeless case? That the subsequent killing of his nurse, Ellen Graber, was just another burst of violence in what would soon become a trend toward lifelong incarceration? The severity of the crime had been enough for Rhode Island's attorney general to call Judge Wallace personally with a warning that she would be sending a formal request for Family Court jurisdiction to be waived so Jonathan could be tried as an adult.

But the boy was just thirteen. *Thirteen.*

Judge Wallace had seen ruthless, wayward youths, and this boy did not fit the description. Nor had his initial statements to police at Hasbro Children's Hospital the night of Ellen Graber's murder lent themselves to signs of senseless malice.

"Nobody believes me," he had sobbed over and over after apologizing profusely for what he had done. And then came the most questionable comment of all: *"I just needed somebody to believe me. She was actually nice to me. I wanted to show her I wasn't crazy."*

Ellen Graber's husband, Craig, now a heartbroken and single father of two, had gone on a rampage against Jonathan Flite. Publicly denouncing the boy's previous judge with the Melinda Berry incident, his childhood psychological care, and of course his "careless" mother, Winifred, Craig Graber had even garnered airtime on Providence's local news channels—a brown-haired widower in a sweater vest, pausing on-camera to wipe away tears, calling for the permanent removal of this thirteen-year-old boy from society. What Judge Wallace noticed, and what finally inspired mercy in him, was that nobody was paying attention to the boy's story.

That he had memories in his head.

That they belonged to seven teenagers.

All of whom disappeared from Idle County, a region along the southwestern edge of Minnesota, in 2010.

Not once had anybody ever bothered to take the boy seriously. When he had finally begun speaking on his eighth birthday, claiming he had spent his life in a state of confusion, out came an alarming number of references to those seven teenagers: Molly Butler, Elijah Bryce, Lindsay Thorsen, Gabriel Creed, Pauline Gilbert, Clayton Graf, and Jillian Pope. Jonathan Flite claimed not just that he knew details about these kids' lives but also that his head had been swarming with what he claimed were their memories, fully formed, even before he was old enough to understand them. Of course the seeming absurdity of the claims outweighed any chance that people might ever consider their merit, even momentarily.

After setting aside his initial skepticism over young Jonathan's mysterious declarations and considering how deflated, dejected, and desperate the boy looked the first day they met, Judge Wallace grew dissatisfied with the case's legal trajectory. The fact that Jonathan could describe buildings in Idle County that had been torn down before his birth? Discounted. That he had insight into thirty-year-old police records that had been sealed when they were first reported? Overlooked. That he could speak French, supposedly because a girl named Jillian Pope's memories of the language were ingrained in his head? Ignored. *"Learned it from Clarette the nanny"* had been the explanation given by his psychiatrist, Dr. Glenn Coyle.

It became clear, too, that Jonathan's mother, Winifred, wasn't really careless. If anything, she cared too much. Not about Jonathan, though—about herself. She had spent the last thirteen years worrying about her son and how his "psychosis," as she referred to it (and how doctors vaguely described it), would make her look. Judge Wallace could see through the woman's flimsy attempts at feigning the type of concern a good parent might have. She caked her face in makeup, never left the house unswathed in designer clothing, and always discussed Jonathan's problems only in context of her own life.

"I was about to leave for Greece."

"I never thought I'd have to deal with something like this."

"Always. He always keeps up his games. Just to spite me!"

When Jonathan whispered Jillian Pope's favorite French lullaby during his hearing (because Judge Wallace had asked for a specific example of his so-called psychosis), the closed courtroom had been silent. When he described how Molly Butler's brain tumor showed its first symptoms during a protest to save Idle County's Lemon Avenue Library from being torn down, Craig Graber shifted uncomfortably in his seat. When he described how Elijah Bryce had his genitals cut with a knife by a bully named Damon Jacoby, one of the incidents that was still on file with the End Haven police department but had never been made public, nobody had a solid explanation as to why Jonathan's claims had been ignored his whole life.

And Judge Wallace had a secret.

When he was a boy in North Platte, Nebraska, up until he was eight years old, he had two friends that his parents (who never shied away from beating him, even for the smallest grievances) called imaginary. Except these friends weren't imaginary. Their names were Achaikos and Sarah, and they looked as real to him as any other people. He saw them whenever he called for them, and they told him things his parents never would: that he would go far in life if he trusted his feelings, that he would make a difference in other children's lives, and that he would, after escaping the farm in Nebraska, be happy.

Achaikos and Sarah also called themselves his "teachers."

Whether they were ghosts, figments of his imagination, or something even more ingrained in the fabric of the universe, Judge Wallace didn't know. All he knew was that, when Jonathan Flite talked about a few of the Idle County Seven knowing a disabled girl named Rebecca Sparks who could read minds—and who also talked about "past lives" and "spirit guides"—his body broke out in goose bumps. Not only was it an alarming matter of public record that Rebecca's family had died in a house explosion in 2007, but Jonathan also claimed that Gabriel Creed, who lived on the other side of Idle County and who later went missing, had helped save Rebecca from the house after being warned of its gas leak by his then-six-year-old sister, Eloise. The house had apparently exploded moments later. Little Eloise, according to Jonathan, had been "psychic," similar to disabled Rebecca.

It seemed such talents and their associated mysteries were commonplace in Idle County. Upon hearing Jonathan Flite discuss them, Judge Wallace remembered Achaikos and Sarah, his special childhood friends. Rarely since leaving Nebraska had he given them more than a moment's worth of thought. Yet this young nurse killer, whom Judge Wallace ultimately decided to try as a juvenile based on what he could only describe as empathy, had triggered in him a need to know more, to ponder the bigger life questions underlying their rapidly crowding, increasingly troubled world. When he allowed Winifred Flite to enroll Jonathan at Crescent Rehabilitation Center, a for-profit juvenile detention facility on the Atlantic coast, the judge knew, despite the public backlash it would bring from Craig Graber, that he was doing the right thing. Why?

Because he had a heavy sense that the boy was about to shed a glaring, public light on all of life's most unsettling questions and that, when it happened, it would give society a much-needed kick in the pants. For that, Judge Wallace wanted front-row seats.

2038

WINIFRED FLITE BLINKED TWICE when Dr. Colin Freede slid the opened blue envelope toward her, across his new, glass-topped mahogany desk. They were at Crescent Rehabilitation Center on May 26, 2038—four days before her son Jonathan's eighteenth birthday. It would mark the point at which Jonathan could return home, with one year of probation and monitoring until the Rhode Island Family Court deemed him a regular citizen once again. Since last November's break-in and triple homicide at Crescent, however, the trickle of reporters knocking on Winifred's door to ask about her nurse-killer son had become a near-daily rush. Most were from Rhode Island, Massachusetts, Connecticut, New Jersey, and New York, but some were independents from the Midwest and West Coast. Considering the range of media coverage thus far, it wasn't ex-actly surprising that an anonymous stranger had begun sending

Jonathan letters; people liked to attach themselves to notoriety any way they could these days. The nature of the letters' content, however, left Winifred's mind buzzing at some depth just below reason. It silently screamed of something bigger, as if Jonathan's fame and reputation had yet to reach their full bloom.

The envelope in front of her now wasn't construction-paper blue but, rather, something warmer, perhaps closer to the color of a robin's egg. Wearing latex gloves, Winifred lifted its unsealed flap to find another letter inside. This made four. Today would be her only chance to see the hard copy, because an FBI agent from the Providence resident agency was already scheduled to pick it up within the hour. On the strip of plain stationery were two paragraphs addressed to her son Jonathan. This message had been postmarked in Tokyo—surely by some sort of mailing service.

Dear Mr. Flite,

Listen to your dreams. Understand that, in them, on levels your physical brain can only interpret and convert to you as symbols, you test out probable choices you might consciously make in your waking life.

Your ambition has always been to open people's minds, and now is the time for action. Elevation of the collective consciousness will soon mark the difference between humanity's progress and its decline. When you help blow open society's perception of itself, don't forget that you have allies all around. There are no coincidences.

Signed,
Have You Guessed Yet?

"Same sender as the others, obviously," Dr. Freede said. "I haven't shown it to Jonathan yet."

"You might as well. He'd just accuse us of conspiracy if it went to the FBI first. Even though it doesn't say a word about Christian fanatics or Geneva."

Dr. Freede ran a hand through his graying black hair and sighed, as if to pass off the gesture as continued stress over the ongoing global investigation into last year's nuclear terrorist attack in Switzerland. Winifred knew, however, that it was simply an attempt to show off his right arm's newly built bicep. His open-collared shirt today was coral, Winifred's favorite color, but for some reason it looked incredibly garish against the stone-gray walls of his office. Perhaps it was the ever-present flirtation in his eyes, which he had failed to douse since she had stopped sleeping with him in December. He seemed not to have noticed that Winifred, against all her willpower, had begun to accept a world beyond him, beyond his pathetic wife, and beyond their little sex game that had amounted to nothing at all. Not only had her son Jonathan recently outlined for the FBI a list of names he claimed aligned with Jillian Pope and her celebrity stepfather Victor Zobel's time in Geneva, but he had also proven to Winifred, as much as she hated to admit it, that his mysterious memories were legitimate. And here this licensed psychiatrist was, still acting like a hormone-dripping fifteen-year-old.

"'Blow open society's perception of itself.' What do you suppose that means?" The words left Dr. Freede's mouth through a sharky grin.

"I've stopped trying to wonder," Winifred said. She snatched the letter and its blue envelope off the table. "I'm showing it to Jonathan. I need another pair of gloves."

"You sure it's a good idea? You could just show him the photo."

"You sure your wife doesn't want to know about our affair?"

Dr. Freede handed Winifred the new pair of latex gloves, and she swirled in her white Galli Ricci dress while turning to leave his office. She knew the effect this would have on the man; she had no intention of giving up her power card, not until Jonathan was out of Crescent for good. In the past six months, every sane aspect of her life had dissolved into fairy dust. No way in hell was she going to shed her superbitch personality, even if every rancid corner of it screamed of some great misunderstanding of what truly mattered in her life and world. Maintaining the self she knew was the only mechanism she had for keeping her existence in check.

After exiting Dr. Freede's office and turning right, Winifred passed the security desk. Her son's favorite guard, Sounder, gave her a cautious smile and nod.

"Afternoon, Ms. Flite."

"Hi."

Short. Not sweet. Sounder knew all about her facades, and he knew she knew it. Even so, she had somehow talked herself into hiring him to be Jonathan's private bodyguard for the foreseeable future. They were about to become as close as family, despite all intentions she once might have had for her life. "Where's Jonathan?" she asked.

"Out by the water, studying for his calculus final. I can go get him if you'd like."

Winifred walked straight past Sounder's offer, clip-clopping through the sunny main hall of Crescent Rehabilitation Center and turning left when she reached the common room. There, four boys were seated around a coffee table playing poker. She recognized one of them by more than just his face. It was Aubrey Carlyle, one of the two boys who had corroborated her son's story after the break-in six months ago. Jonathan, along with Mason Witzel, his waifish friend who had been killed that night, had warned Aubrey and his style-obsessed friend, Jimmy Barber, that Paul Simpleton, the nighttime security guard, had been planning something underhanded. It had been the day Dr. Thomas Lumen, the psychiatrist from Minnesota who was now unwittingly her friend, visited Jonathan to ask him about the Idle County Seven. Mason, Paul, and a second security guard named Kenneth Tilton had been found dead in the wee hours of the following morning, and even now details surrounding the incident were murky. The police had found a zealously Christian note in Paul Simpleton's front shirt pocket, one that appeared to implicate him in his own suicide and the other two murders. News reports had speculated that Simpleton had merely been a faith-fueled copycat of Cardinal Jean-Claude Apostol, the Catholic fanatic who had bombed Geneva, but this hadn't aligned with the boys' stories.

"*The killer wasn't Paul. There was somebody else here that night. Way bigger than Paul.*"

"*He had a mask on and talked with an accent.*"

"*Jonathan sprayed him with a fire extinguisher.*"

Just as Winifred sniffed a bit of acknowledgment toward Aubrey, a much smaller boy appeared from behind his shoulder. It was Jimmy Barber, the one who dressed like a fashion designer and who had been the second boy to back up Jonathan's story. He was now enrolled in Crescent's day program, according to Dr. Freede's gossip, and while he no longer lived at the facility, he attended tutoring and therapy there five days a week. Before Winifred could pass, Jimmy stood up and gave her a slight bow. "Hi, Miss Flite. I sure hope you're well."

Careful not to catch her heel on the blazing-red shag rug under their feet, Winifred nodded to Jimmy but was far from mustering a smile. "Very well, thanks. But I don't have time—"

"Jonathan's outside," Jimmy continued. "He wanted to be alone."

Winifred upped her pace, and she noticed Jimmy's gaze fall on the blue envelope as she passed. His eyes widened, and as she stepped outside, onto Crescent's back patio, the boys descended into a fit of whispers.

She peered down the rocky coastline. The last time she had been in Crescent's backyard had been six months ago, for the December funeral of young Mason Witzel. Mason had been shot three times—twice in the face and once in the chest. Today, one would never have guessed that such violence had happened here. It was sunny, warm, inviting. The growing flock of reporters converging on Newport still made a martyr of Mason whenever they could, despite the boy's having shot his abusive father in a premeditated manner. His death had fed all possible channels of controversy, and while the media had taken what they knew of the surface details and painted the security guard Paul Simpleton as the killer, the police and FBI had made no such final assessment. Winifred had few insights into the details of their investigation, but considering how they had questioned Jonathan about his supposed past-life memories involving Victor Zobel, the neurosurgeon-turned-celebrity-atheist, she had deduced that they were working on a theory much different than the ones being perpetuated by the public at large. Internet gossip mills had reported on rumors concerning Zobel's childhood connection to Cardinal Jean-Claude Apostol, Geneva's bomber, but so far, he was still a public darling, and nobody prominent in the media had investigated the rumors with any seriousness. The FBI's dire urgency regarding Victor Zobel made Winifred guess that they were thankful for this; their investigation was still operating in the shadows.

In the light, however, was Craig Graber, husband of the nurse Jonathan had killed. While the man's public outcry had begun to reach national news outlets, few media personalities had posed any serious questions about Jonathan beyond his supposed Idle County Seven delusions. Graber perpetuated the "nurse-killer" angle every chance he could, citing Jonathan's "insane" spiritual claims as attention beacons for further copycat religious extremists who would fight against anything that challenged their belief systems. This, Graber said, had already resulted in the loss of three more lives during last year's attack at Crescent. "That's four deaths Jonathan Flite is responsible for," the man had recently told ABC's local affiliate. "*Four.* Are we seriously going to let him walk the streets with our children?" Reporters' questions were now flying at Winifred closer, hotter, faster. Just this morning, she had driven through a crowd of at least twenty journalists, photographers, and camera operators turning from her street onto Wellington Avenue. Was this how life was going to be now? Or would these people eventually tire of Jonathan's story, once something bigger and better came along?

The Atlantic inlet danced in choppy sparkles today, and seabirds arced and dove amid their piercing calls. Sitting on the shore's edge with his back to her, a mere silhouette against the sunny reflections, was Winifred's teenage son. Jonathan's dirty-blond hair had grown unruly since her last visit three weeks ago; it was blowing backward in the eastward wind, hinting at his impending freedom. Winifred's high heels dug into the grass as she balanced down to the rocks where he was sitting. When she cleared her throat, his shoulders jerked in surprise. Without turning to face her, he said, "I didn't know you were coming today."

"Dr. Freede called. You got another letter."

Jonathan half turned his head. Out of habit, Winifred stepped backward, almost falling, until the drive to keep her dress clean somehow willed her to stay upright.

"Same as the first three. Dr. Freede did the video thing while opening it, and we sent it to Agent Prescott. He has an agent from the resident agency coming over to get the hard copy."

"Of course." Jonathan turned fully around, noticed the latex gloves on Winifred's hands, and then reached for the extra pair she had brought him. He donned them before grabbing the letter, which almost hurtled into the wind during her handoff. Winifred studied Jonathan's face as he read it, but he offered nothing—not even a hint of what he might be feeling. She had trained him well, apparently.

"*Do* you know who's sending these?" she asked.

For a second, Jonathan's eyes twitched in a near-squint. "Not sure," he said. "Let the FBI figure it out."

Winifred sighed, and when Jonathan's sharp, knowing gaze made fleeting contact with hers, a wave of the embarrassment rushed through her, one she now felt whenever they inched toward intimacy. "Jonathan, if this is somebody you know about from Idle County, you need to say so."

Jonathan turned back to the water. "Nope. I'm done. Look at what's already happening. Reporters everywhere. It's a damned circus."

It was just the type of nonanswer Winifred had come to fear since Jonathan received his first blue-enveloped letter two months ago. While each one had been steeped in pseudospiritual language beyond Winifred's mental scope, the second to last had encouraged him to start telling the public his story—and sharing his memories of the Idle County Seven—all in order to beat to the punch anyone who wanted to silence him. Once his story was known to the masses, any such attempts to hide the truth would be futile. He had discussed the fate of the Idle County Seven with only one person Winifred was aware of: Kara Butler, the younger half sister of Molly Butler. Whether what he told her was true nobody could say, but ever since their video conference last December, the gut instinct about Jonathan's condition Winifred had always tried to ignore had crossed a threshold into the realm of unwelcome trust. That day, she had been faced with proof of her own connection to Idle County, one she couldn't deny. It had come in the form of an obituary photo from 2004— that of Elizabeth Anne Grime, an old librarian Jonathan claimed to remember.

Four times before Jonathan's birth, Winifred had seen this woman. Never had the woman spoken to her, but never either had she aged. Always, too, she had appeared at some sort of crossroads in Winifred's life, wearing an expression to complement or offset Winifred's current mood. It was now clear, however, that this woman had been dead. *Long* dead. That this fact aligned with stories Jonathan told about the Idle County Seven—ones about ghosts—now made each of Winifred's already-crooked footsteps feel as if they were happening in a pool of shoulder-deep glue. She could barely move forward. Everything was holding her back, and everywhere she looked, the facts were dripping in on her, showing loopholes only an open mind would allow her to maintain. But her mind was too cluttered to be open, too fragmented to be strong.

Jonathan's ropy triceps—made of pushups out on the grass ever since spring rolled around, Dr. Freede had told her—flexed as he adjusted himself on the rocky shore. "You know what I want to do when I get out of here?" he said.

Winifred stared past him, at the choppy Atlantic. "What?"

"Disappear. I want to disappear."

"You and me both."

Just as the sun passed from midday into golden afternoon, Winifred stood behind her son, sharing (perhaps for the first time ever) a commonality. *Someday*, she thought. *Maybe someday this will all be behind us.*

Yes.

Someday.

2038

THE SMELL OF LEMON-SCENTED PLEDGE drifted into Nicolas Leandro Rim's nose as he sank onto his squishy, microsuede couch and gulped down his chocolate protein shake. It was May 27, 2038, and he had just returned from Ripple Fitness to his sunny apartment on Babcock Street in Hartford, Connecticut, all while under the watchful eyes of the city police. They had been keeping him under surveillance in unmarked cars ever since the FBI agent, Ethan Prescott, visited in January. That had been just five weeks after Nicolas's botched attack on Jonathan Flite at Crescent Rehabilitation Center in Newport, during which the young man had practically blinded him with dry chemical foam from a fire extinguisher. Now, at the end of May, the bureau's local-law-enforcement counterparts were still watching him, which meant they had gathered nothing concrete since the beginning of their investigation. It was, as his favorite

English-language expression said, a pity. Getting caught would, in almost all ways, be a relief.

The lemon Pledge. Nicolas smelled it again. Had he forgotten his cleaning lady, Loretta, was scheduled for today? Yes, by the look of it. The dust on his bookshelf was gone, his glass-topped coffee table glistened, and his love seat, perpendicular to the couch, had vacuum lines across the microsuede. How funny that his life continued to go on, day by day, when every bit of waking, conscious acknowledgment of the world had become to him an exercise in disenchantment.

The FBI had known he was an employee of Carey Developments (an offshoot of Zobel Enterprises' Grand Natural Development Corporation), that he owned and managed a number of apartment buildings under his own company, Hill Properties, LLC, and that he had, on more than one occasion, partied with Paul Simpleton, one of the two security guards he had killed at Crescent Rehabilitation Center that snowy night last November. They had even tried to solicit a confession from him by claiming that Jonathan Flite had identified him as the perpetrator with a "high amount of certainty" in a photo lineup at the Providence resident agency. At this, Nicolas had simply shrugged, wearing his best innocent expression. He had been wearing a black mask that night, so facial recognition would have been impossible. The mysterious part of it all was that they seemed to have no irrefutable evidence against him—just his name, identity, and whatever else their court orders and subpoenas had entitled them to. This made him wonder if Jonathan Flite really had come through, if his supposed memories of Jillian Pope's childhood were somehow real, and he had successfully recalled Nicolas's family from their days in Geneva.

From what Nicolas could tell, the FBI knew only that he was a squeaky-clean Swiss immigrant. They hadn't yet discovered his other two identities, both of which were legitimized by fraudulent Swedish birth certificates created by God knew which corrupt Stockholm city official. Their existence was a testament to the strength of his shadow community. He had grown to trust those who provided him with the means to be a criminal, because all their lives were on the line.

At the moment, however, he was being watched too closely to use his fraudulent identities and bank accounts. He couldn't return to his home country without looking suspicious. He had even ceased all use of his quantum key proxy server connections in the chance that ActoFiber, his internet provider, had ways of unencrypting his activity for the FBI were they to get a subpoena and check his records. Nicolas had never done anything questionable under his own name except feign friendship with the security guard Paul Simpleton. All aspects of their "friendship" were, by all provable accounts, normal. For the first time in what felt like eons, he was living solely under the identity that God— and the country of Switzerland—had given him at birth. This felt refreshing in a way that threw the guilt of his past actions into horrendously jagged relief.

Nicolas rolled his head back, onto his couch's plush, pillowed cushions. He was about to drift away to the sound of *Bless Us, Father* reruns when there was a knock on his front door. He recognized the rap pattern at once.

"Nick? You in there?"

It was Aurora Demark, his tenant from unit 302, two floors above. She hadn't come calling for his gentle touch in months, since around the time the FBI started sniffing around. She had always loved the sound of his accent during their romps in bed, especially when they got loud enough for the neighbors to hear. He eased off the couch and shuffled toward his front foyer. When he pulled his creaky front door open, there Aurora stood under the afternoon sun, which was making a glowing halo of her wavy blond hair. He had to squint to see her face.

"I thought you didn't like to cheat on your patrons," he said with a wry smile. "And I just worked out. The way you like."

But Aurora wasn't smiling. "Giving my two-month notice," she said. "I figured I'd give you the courtesy of an actual visit. But I found a new place closer to work."

Nicolas straightened his posture, trying to reconcile Aurora's cautious expression with the rush of melancholy washing through his heart. He readjusted his stance, raising one of his muscled arms against the doorframe and leaning in on it.

"Would you like to come in?" he asked. "I was just about to take a nap, but—"

Aurora cocked her head with a smile that appeared to be made purely of politeness. "No thanks. Just letting you know I'm leaving. I really should—"

"Did they talk to you?" Nicolas's gaze flitted toward the unmarked police car just long enough for Aurora to notice. He watched as she shifted her stance from one curvy leg to the other and crossed her arms. Instead of looking away, she looked straight into his eyes. She had the face and body of a Hollywood starlet, which probably helped her sell lap dances at Mermaid Corner, but what Nicolas loved most about her was her ability to be direct.

"Yes," she said. "And I haven't felt safe being near you ever since. Is that what you want to hear?"

"No."

"In that case, I won't ask you if you're involved in some big crime. And considering you're from Switzerland, I *really* won't ask what big crime that might be, because I think everyone on Earth knows. But I'll give you the benefit of the doubt. Because you once told me you hate liars. If that's true, I don't want to hear your answers."

"And what if I hate myself?"

Disappointment glinted across Aurora's face. She stepped back, her silver heels clicking on the paint-flaked wood of their building's front porch. "I hope the best for you, Nick. You'll get my rent check. Send whatever's left of the damage deposit to the bar." A second later, she was skipping down the sidewalk, her purse slung over her shoulder and her golden locks sailing behind her. She passed the unmarked Hartford police car without a glance.

In shock, Nicolas stood in the doorway, leaning against his raised arm. This was yet another coil in his life's downward spiral, because he would never hurt Aurora. Never.

But what did it matter anymore? Certain he now looked conspicuous, he leaned off his arm and stood upright, glancing at the unmarked car. The officer, whom Nicolas recognized as one of the usuals, was watching him. Nicolas raised an arm in a polite wave. How was it that the wave felt genuine? That he actually wished this officer luck in bringing him down? Why, if he really wished this, didn't he simply walk across the street and turn himself in?

Nicolas had found that killing people could unhinge the human mind, chasing out all logic and happiness and, hell, even pain. It was a nightmare knowing that all the shameful acts he had committed over the years still existed, hidden in the past, ready to be exposed as soon as somebody—anybody—connected enough dots to discover them. Every waking breath had become an effort to run, to hide, to escape the life he had chosen for himself. And why? To survive? What was the point of survival after it became misery in an existence barred from redemption?

It had all become a waiting game, because Nicolas Leandro Rim was guilty. When he thought about the life he had lived and the different choices he might have made, he wondered why he continued to breathe at all. The image of Aurora high-heeling it down Babcock Street (and soon it would be one of those forever memories) suddenly hit him like a ghost made of forsaken opportunities. Brightness lost, because he had allowed his life to go so, so wrong.

Instead of going back to the couch, Nicolas went to his office, a rather dank room at the rear end of his first-floor unit. There, among all the digital records and paperwork that told the world he was an upright resident of the United States, was the flimsy plastic shelf that held his blank computer paper. The piece on top was covered with dust (Loretta had clearly not thought to remove it so he could be greeted by a fresh sheet), and he shook it off as he grabbed a pen and headed toward his kitchen table. There, under the warm-tinted LED light, he made the heading for a note.

To Anyone Who Cares I'm Gone

Shame. It was a most powerful thing. A tool to change a life or destroy it, brought on by others, by the self, or by beliefs that aimed to keep a person in line before being flagrantly disregarded. Nicolas closed his eyes. Through his mind's eye darted the scrambling little figure of Mason Witzel, Jonathan Flite's young friend at Crescent Rehabilitation Center—the boy had been preparing to take that first bullet in the face just as Nicolas shot. And then had come Jonathan Flite himself, that mess of bullets, the dark images of the fire extinguisher swinging through a haze of dry chemical foam. Through the story's cracks came two mysteries Nicolas now cowered under: the memories Jonathan Flite supposedly had in his head and the reason Victor Zobel wanted those memories erased from the world.

If the boy really did have the memories of Victor Zobel's stepdaughter, Jillian Pope, however that might be possible, he would remember the Rim family. Yet Jillian had moved back to the United States and disappeared by the time Victor sponsored Jonas Rim, Jonas's wife, Genevieve, and teenage Nicolas in their move to New Jersey. Even in a worst-case scenario, there was no way Jonathan Flite could know anything truly incriminating about the family. There was also no way he could know the extent of Victor's deceit and manipulation.

Tears dropped from Nicolas's eyes when his pen returned to the paper lying on the table in front of him. As he wrote, the words came out in German, the language of his childhood.

WHEN PEOPLE THOUGHT OF IDLE COUNTY, the nastier little dramas usually appeared in their memories first. The vanishing of the Idle County Seven was of course the event that brought a bit of fame to the otherwise sleepy, obscure region, but even that had petered out after police found evidence that the teenagers had somehow ended up in Dallas. People here had a way of filling in their own blanks, of making unpleasant stories tolerable so that they didn't have to acknowledge their nagging, collective feeling that Idle County was somehow different—that life here was, for whatever reason, not as entangled with the world as it was everywhere else. The lesser dramas of the region still had their impact, though, and with its being a small, insular place, very few could escape tragedy without being connected or somehow affected.

Damon Jacoby, after his run-in with Elijah Bryce in the

summer of 2005, had been one of those tragedies—a small one for some. But when it made news, people had found out and spread the word (in slightly judgmental whispers) that Damon had been a "troubled kid" whose birth parents had "died of AIDS." His Uncle Ed and Aunt Marion had raised him, telling him only that his dad had secretly "been a fag" and had given his mother the "gay disease" that killed her. Damon could see and appreciate the whole story now, all the pieces that had been only mental snippets during life, but he was still afraid of facing whatever was coming next.

The beauty of being dead was that he could see forward and backward on his own private spectrum of probabilities. He could see where his own collisions with Elijah Bryce had changed the boy's life, and he could see where Elijah's own choices had done the same for him. The physical universe, Damon now knew, was a cooperative endeavor, a testing ground for growth. He knew there was more to it than that, much more, but he was still blocking it out. He would progress when he was ready.

Right now he was flying over the Moon Woods.

From above, through a few clouds, it was a vast circle of dark pine trees, far enough away that the pointed green needles swaying at the treetops looked soft, like an inviting carpet on which to rest, were one to descend and sink in. But Damon knew they were sharp, in the physical dimension where they mattered. He wasn't affected by such things anymore, but he would stay high up, where it was comfortable.

The Moon Woods were finally attracting attention. Damon now lived in a place where time couldn't be measured, where the spacelessness of the mind, what he now understood to be the *real* universe—stretched forever in an endless array of unique, ever-changing potentials. He had known for a long time now (sometimes it felt like an eternity) that the conscious energy creating Idle County had a freer flow than most other places on Earth. It transferred in and out of its physical time and space like air through a screen. Here, however, the camouflage created by the outer senses of the living was thinner. More apparent to some. Sometimes it drove people mad.

Damon liked to replay the final moments of his life over and over. There he stood, on the jagged rock bridge linking the shore of Spinner's Island to the shore of Spinner's Lake, watching Elijah Bryce and Molly Butler as he fell out of their view. It had been a choice—to tumble backward, to hope that a rock would crack open his skull and release him from what he had perceived to be the burden of life. Elijah had sprung for him, tried to grab him, but it was too late. There, under the golden sunrise, Damon, the bully, had died.

Despite having been young, his regret was deep. He had found as he watched Elijah and Molly sob over his body and ultimately carry it back to shore that he had absolute freedom to experience this regret as long as he needed to. His focus now was still on Earth; behind him (mentally but not spatially, if there could be such a sensation) was a very pleasant fog that dazzled white and made a joke out of his old eyes' concept of brightness. He would enter it at his own pace. There were loved ones waiting for him, he knew, and while their identities were still ambiguous, the sensation of familiarity they radiated felt like the best kind of tears. He had seen hints of them in human form, which of course was their way of letting him know all was well.

Watching the world and seeing its array of probabilities from this vantage point was like watching from backstage a play that had no script. It was a display of all the conscious intersections that formed the meat of life. He had been the person to glue Elijah Bryce and Molly Butler together, and he had watched them mourn his death, watched as kids at End Haven Middle School called them "the Murderers" the following year, and watched as the kick-boxers Lindsay Thorsen and Alan Sparks became two of the few who mustered the courage to befriend them. So many tangles, so many junctures. He had even watched as Elijah, Molly, Lindsay, and Alan began volunteering in Blue Hill—at Rock Shore Nursing Home (as people in Idle County still called it, even after it had been transformed into an accredited and licensed medical research facility). That was in mid-2006, by their measure of time. It was also the thing that set them on their ultimate collision course with Maximilian Pope and Victor Zobel.

While Damon was still blocking certain things out, it was clear now that he and Elijah Bryce had both chosen the circumstances of their births and the souls they would intersect with while on Earth. They had even devised cues during life—events or junctures that came across as coincidences, déjà vu, or heavy bursts of intuition—that would remind them of possible choices that would lead toward their most ideal developmental paths.

Elijah's cue had been an **X** shaped of stones in the Moon Woods. Neither he nor the woman who had buried her dark treasure almost thirteen years before had been outwardly aware that they were simply carrying out a track of possibilities they had already set up before adopting physical form. Many potential paths for Idle County had been set, and because of how it had all ended up—even because of what Damon had done to Elijah Bryce in 2005, and then to himself—he now recognized the part he had played. It had been small but significant, and what Damon had come to realize was that the game was still going. The souls involved in the drama of Idle County had come into life wanting to change the world. One of them, who had chosen to be born this time in Rhode Island (into a most unique body and brain), was finally beginning to achieve his goals.

Now, on Old Mill Road, far below Damon, a white rental car circled the southwest corner of the Moon Woods. In it was a young woman named Kara Butler, who was the biological half sister of Molly, the girl he had almost killed the day before he died. In this version of today, Kara had come to Idle County to see what all the fuss was about. To see if the story about the boy in Rhode Island might be true. To see if the unique characteristics of the Moon Woods could heal her father's ailing brain, or at the very least explain why Victor Zobel, the owner of the property, might have plotted last year's catastrophic bombing of Geneva, Switzerland, to keep the truth about the place a secret.

So many twists and turns. So many crisscrossed souls. So much life. Damon Jacoby—if he could even go by that name anymore—marveled at all of it.

Just as he began to wonder yet again if there might be some way to take back all his interactions with Elijah Bryce, he heard a voice. Then a burst of laughter. Yet they weren't real sounds; they came to him like thoughts, except they felt more real and intimate than any thoughts he'd had while alive. As always, they were familiar, coming from the fog behind him. He hadn't yet dared to follow.

"Hurry it up," came the voice again. "You're not going to change that life. You don't need to."

There was no fear of death on this side, but there was embarrassment. He had made a mess of his life, which had culminated during the summer of 2005. Damon realized now that his physical body, his brain in particular, had contributed to his behavior. It had been sensitive to the patterns of energy in Idle County, but he had been unable to control it. He hadn't just bullied Elijah Bryce; he had genuinely tried to kill him, leaving their chosen, intertwined life challenges unresolved.

A reckoning would come. It had to. What Damon dreaded, however, was the task of owning up to his own failures and finding a way to right his wrongs.

2005

I T WAS ONLY THE SECOND DAY OF SUMMER VACATION, and Elijah Bryce was already miserable. Damon Jacoby, with two minions in tow, was riding across the Lemon Avenue Library's yard, heading straight for Elijah as he approached his bike.

"Hey, faggot, why don't you put those books down and come behind the library with me?" Damon yelled. "I need to take a piss, and I thought you might want to watch!" Balancing on his bike, the bully lifted his Green Bay Packers jersey, exposing his abdominal muscles, before dropping it again and sneering.

Beet red, Elijah had just shouldered his backpack and begun to struggle with his bike lock when Damon's ridged tire ground into his soft calf muscle. "Get away from me!" he screamed, hating the sound of his own voice. Any normal boy would get angry, puff himself up, and fight back, but no, not Elijah. Even the thought of defending himself just sparked more humiliation, because there was no way in hell he would ever win against these boys.

"Little faggot boy is trying to get away so he can go kiss his boyfriend! Isn't that right, faggot?" Damon said, wheeling his front tire back, then forward again toward Elijah's leg.

This time, Elijah stepped away to avoid it, but Damon just advanced the bike further, causing him to trip over his own pedal. The hard rubber footrest dug into Elijah's shin. He regained his balance but still looked like a fool, and if this was what seventh grade was going to be like in the fall, he would just as soon die.

"I heard you were looking at Alec Pent funny one day when he wasn't wearing a shirt. His sister, Natalie, said you and him were in the Moon Woods last summer, camping in the same tent, and you were staring at him when he was taking his shirt off. He thinks you're *gay*, and so does everyone else."

"Alec Pent is a jerk," Elijah said, knowing any effort he made to defend himself would, as always, burn the label of "gay" even deeper. He turned away from Damon again, hoping Nolan Snagsby and Tyler McFadden had perhaps allowed some space for him to get through. Instead, they were even closer, chuckling as Damon mocked him.

"Oh, Alec Pent is a jerk now, huh? I heard he was your best friend until last summer, when you freaked him out. Natalie told everyone about it, 'cause Alec told his parents at the dinner table. You were *staring* at him. Boys don't stare at boys, faggot. Hell, you'd probably like it if I dragged you behind the library and whipped out my dick!"

Elijah was trembling and grasping his handlebars, forcing the tears lining his eyes to stay put. "I'm not gay!"

"You're *gay, gay, gay*—"

"Shut up! Let me out!"

"What, so you can go touch your—"

"*Leave him alone.*"

Elijah was staring at the ground through a glaze of tears when a cold voice cut through Damon's torture. It belonged to a girl; he knew that immediately. Even so, she had the same vocal authority as Mrs. Kemberton, last year's English teacher, who had no trouble whipping even the rudest bullies into line. Elijah looked up. When the tears dropped from his eyes enough to offer a clear view, he saw a small dark-haired girl standing in the middle of the library's front sidewalk. Despite her manner, she didn't look a day older than any of them. Her eyes, dusky and hawklike, shifted from Damon to Elijah, then back to Damon.

The tormentor forced a deflated chuckle, but it came out as a stammer. "What, the little fag is being saved by a girl?" Something behind the newcomer's glare had cornered him, as if it were threatening to expose the very secrets of his soul.

"Get out of here," she ordered.

Damon had already backed his bike away and was now turning the handlebars toward the street. "And why do you think you can tell me what to do?" he said.

The girl's eyes narrowed. "Because you're a coward, and cowards doing stupid things can only argue by running away. You don't deserve to be at this library. Now *leave him alone.*"

A particular seriousness behind the girl's character pierced the triangle of bullies in a way that would have made Elijah uncomfortable were it not his saving grace. For whatever reason, Damon appeared to take her at face value, and he gestured with his head toward the street and began pedaling away. Nolan and Tyler followed, laughing and chiding him. Just before their voices faded, Elijah heard Damon yelling at them to shut the hell up.

Elijah turned to his bike, not quite trying to mount it but not quite able to look the dark-haired girl in the eyes.

"Are you okay?" she asked. Now her voice was far gentler, nothing like the piercing one that had driven Damon away.

Elijah took a deep breath, sure his face was pulsing red. He still couldn't look at her. "I'm okay, yeah." He steadied his bike for departure but stopped when, from the corner of his eyes, he saw the girl approaching a light pink bike parked two slots down from his. She was now right next to him.

"You know, those boys are just being dumb," came her gentler voice again.

Elijah finally mustered the courage to look up. What he saw framed under the girl's straight black hair was a circular but lean face devoid of makeup yet positively burning with maturity and what he could only describe as spirit. It was almost as if she had stepped out of some other realm, having been waiting in the wings to catch him as he was falling. "I know they're dumb. I go to school with them. They're a year older."

"End Haven Middle School?" the girl asked.

"Yeah. They're going into eighth grade. I'm going into seventh."

The girl let out a sudden, nervous sigh. "Me too. Seventh grade. I go—well, I *went* to Saint Andrew's school since kindergarten, but that only goes up to sixth grade. I guess my whole class is pretty much going to End Haven Middle School, but I'm still kind of nervous. It's big."

"It's not that bad," Elijah assured her, realizing only after the words left his mouth that the recent display of his popularity might beg to differ. "I've been there since fifth grade. There's more switching classes in seventh grade, but we still have homeroom every day for ten minutes."

"I'm going to miss Saint Andrew's," the girl said, still standing next to him. She stuck her hands in the pockets of her jeans and made no attempt to rush away on her bike. Elijah didn't know what to say, so he offered her a grimace and what would hopefully appear to be an understanding nod. She regarded him for a moment, as if considering his worth. "I'm Molly Butler, by the way," she finally said.

"I'm Elijah Bryce."

They surveyed one another, and when Elijah looked into her shadowy eyes, his heart fluttered with hope.

The feeling began to fly when they started riding home together. Molly was heading toward Exeter Avenue, which was north of Lemon Avenue by one block, while Elijah had to continue another two miles, toward the long, southbound stretch of Windsong Road. His house was second from the last at the end, on the fringes of End Haven, near the Moon Woods.

"You go to that library a lot?" Molly asked as they rode along Lemon Avenue. The afternoon's light breeze sent her dark hair backward in delicate wisps.

"No, not usually," Elijah said. "I mean, I go when I need books. I buy a lot of them, though. Paper route money. I do that in the mornings."

"The *Wind Prairie Tribune*?" Molly asked, referring to the newspaper from Wind Prairie, the nearest larger city to Idle County. It lay an hour southeast of them, but its newspaper had long since replaced Idle County's more provincial *Circle Gazette* as the standard record for daily happenings both locally and in the wider world.

"Yep, the *Tribune*," Elijah replied. "I was stocking up on books today, though. Not much to do now that school's done, and I can't afford to buy *that* many." He grinned at Molly. For the first time since last summer—since the dreadful incident of his staring at Alec Pent's shirtless chest (which had been more confusing than it had been purposeful), Elijah remembered what it was like to feel comfortable with another person. "I do like that library, though," he continued. "I miss the old librarian. She always remembered my name when I came to get books, even though I didn't talk to her much."

"Mrs. Grime," Molly said quietly. The old librarian, who had owned and managed the private library for as long as Elijah could remember, had died late last summer. A number of kids in his class had attended her funeral, but he had simply read about it in the newspaper. She had been somewhat of a town legend, revered by all who made it common practice to borrow books from her.

"She really was nice," was all Elijah could bring himself to add, for Molly had suddenly hushed after saying the woman's name.

They reached Donahue Street, and Elijah decided to take a detour and follow Molly left, toward her house on Exeter Avenue. A minute passed before Molly spoke again. "Do you stay home alone in the summer, or is someone there with you?"

"Babysitter," Elijah said. "I actually just live with my mom, but she works all day. Pretty sure she pays Selma way too much to make sure I don't die or whatever. I usually do stuff by myself. Selma just studies for grad school." He glanced at Molly with a sheepish smile. She smiled back, appearing to understand him perfectly. It was on the tip of his tongue to tell her that he was adopted, that his adoptive father had run out when Elijah was just three years old, and that his mom had only recently gotten over the divorce by finding religion again. But his better sense made him swallow the urge. *Too much information*, he thought, aware of how desperate he'd look if he allowed the girl's kindness to fill in his emotional gaps too quickly.

"So, do your parents both work, then?" Elijah asked.

"Just my dad," Molly said. "My mom is dead."

Elijah's heart did a double take as they turned right, onto Exeter Avenue. At first he was frazzled by the immediate shock of imagining the pain this girl must have gone through, and then he settled on an awed sort of compassion. Molly sounded strangely matter-of-fact about it, but when he turned to look at her, she was staring at the pavement racing under her tires. Her expression was somehow both somber and serene.

"This is me," she said as they approached a tan, medium-sized house on the left. She slowed at her driveway, veered into it before stopping, and then turned to him. "I hope those jerks leave you alone. Their parents obviously did a bang-up job of raising them. If they keep picking on you, though, you know who to call." Molly did a cool, rhythmic dance with her head, purposefully being overzealous about her own awesomeness. "I'm at that library a lot, so I'll keep an eye out. You know, to shoo them away if they get too close."

Elijah could only smile at her blunt reference to having been the hero of his library skirmish.

"Hopefully I'll see you around," Molly continued. "At school in September, at least. I'll be the one eating lunch all alone."

Elijah grinned, hoping his euphoria wasn't as obvious as it felt. "That makes two of us. I'll keep an eye out for you."

With a wave good-bye, he resumed his bike ride, redirecting himself toward home and trying to forget Damon Jacoby and his friends. Molly Butler, whether she was to be a momentous presence in his life or a fleeting one, had made a difference, at least for today. But he'd be lying if he were to say he didn't want desperately to see her again. Because friends made life better. Everyone knew that.

2038

ATONEMENT. That was how Jimmy Barber had first labeled his friendship with Jonathan Flite. It was, at the time, an attempt to make things right, because the night of the attack at Crescent Rehabilitation Center, he had failed as a human being on a grand level. A viral WPRI news report had now made sure the world knew it, too. Everyone had seen his quivering face and teary eyes (perfectly backlit by the morning light) as he admitted that he had not stood up for Jonathan Flite when it really mattered. Jimmy typically enjoyed grandiosity, but this level of it had come with an odd mixture of shame and intrigue that he didn't know how to classify. Laced throughout this feeling was some underlying need to make amends and change his path. This was why he was in downtown Newport, shopping for a birthday gift that would mean something to Jonathan. He was alone, still unaccustomed to the freedom (and sometimes near-obscurity) of no longer being a full-time resident of Crescent.

Jonathan Flite's eighteenth birthday was on Sunday, May 30, just two days away. Jimmy wanted to send him out of Crescent in style.

The scenario held two problems. First, like himself, Jonathan Flite had family money, enough to buy anything he wanted once he was released from Crescent. Second, he knew nothing about style, nor did he care about it. A five-hundred-dollar scarf meant as much to him as a four-dollar tube of toothpaste, which was why Jimmy had bought the five-hundred-dollar scarf as a gag gift so that he could wrap inside it something Jonathan would actually like: a book, the old-fashioned paper kind, a variety of which could be found at Scripted Corner, the old secondhand store on Thames Street.

"Can I help you, sir?" came a crinkled voice from behind him. It was the white-haired cashier, a man who looked too old to be working anywhere, let alone in retail. But Scripted Corner was slow, museful, and dusty. Perhaps it suited him.

Jimmy turned on his sharp Giuseppe Zanotti shoes. The old man was taller than he was, so with as much poof as he could muster from his skinny chest, Jimmy marched forward and knocked the counter with both knuckles when he reached it. "Hello there, sir," he said. "I'm looking for a book. For somebody smart. It's a present, and I want him to, you know, *like* it. I stick to *trends*, not books, so I'm basically clueless."

With a quick glance up and down Jimmy's tiny, smartly adorned frame, the old man stuck a finger in his ear to itch it, then raised his eyebrows. "Somebody smart, you say? Hmm. I would say science. Does he like science?"

"For certain," Jimmy said.

"Upstairs, and to the left. There's a sign at the end of the aisle."

"Grand. Thank you." Jimmy turned around and swished off toward the stairs, wondering if (and almost hoping that) the man had recognized him just a *little* bit. There wasn't a person under sixty-five in Newport who hadn't seen his news interview, he reckoned. Of course once his ex-friend Kevin Stimmey tipped reporters off to the flashier aspects of Jimmy's history—particularly the ten-thousand-dollar Gucci watch he had tried to steal from Macy's when his mother, Kendra, hadn't been looking, and then the subsequent attempted robbery of Three Golden Apples at gunpoint—people had become cautious.

That part of Jimmy had changed now, but it had been replaced by something potentially more troubling. Mason Witzel's death last November, as violent and unjust as it had been, had become the most exciting thing ever to happen to Jimmy. The drench of emotion pervading Crescent after the break-in had fed him from all possible angles. He had treated Jonathan and Mason like insignificant bits of trash just hours before the tragedy happened, when they had tried to give warning that Paul the night guard was up to something fishy. Acting dismissive had been the best way to keep things interesting—make fun of the outcasts, stay on top of the game by giving them just enough attention to let them know they were inferior, and be knowledgeable of all things popular and fashionable in a way *nobody* would have the courage to emulate. That had been Jimmy Barber's social strategy since his enrollment at Crescent, and it had served him well. Until that night.

He had been sleeping soundly in his bedroom when the gunshots woke him up. Four muffled ones initially on the first floor, then three more on the second floor—this time louder. His first impulse upon waking was to fix his pillow hair so he would look presentable if something really was happening that would force him out of bed. His second impulse was to realize how stupid this was, if something bad really was happening.

When the masked intruder had ascended to the floor Jimmy shared with Jonathan Flite and begun spraying bullets around (and when Jonathan screamed, "Get in your room! This guy has a gun!"), Jimmy had slammed his door shut and sunk straight to the ground, the way characters did in movies, so that bullets flying through the wall would have less of a chance of hitting him. For the first time in months, however, his heart had been pounding with excitement. *Real* excitement, the type he hadn't felt since the night he had attempted gunpoint robbery of Three Golden Apples. What Jimmy realized the night of November 30, 2037, however, was that excitement didn't have to come from breaking the law. It could in fact come from being a good person, like Jonathan Flite was.

The boy had seemingly attracted terrorists. *Terrorists.* Jimmy's foray into juvenile crime had (according to therapy) been a result of his intense desire to experience a sense of ambition and excitement that his parents' money couldn't satisfy. When he had then very nearly been caught in that intruder's spray of bullets, fearing for his own life and suddenly realizing he *liked* being alive, he had also realized that Jonathan Flite, the nurse killer, had made an attempt earlier that evening to warn him. To *save* his life.

Put simply, Jonathan Flite had been the bigger person. He had also opened Jimmy up to an entirely new type of experience: that of feeling bound to somebody, of actually appreciating that another person had acted selflessly for the greater good—or at least tried to. In the course of a single night, in a whirl of police cars and detectives and relocation to temporary housing at the Rhode Island Training School, Jimmy had experienced a mental shift. He decided that Jonathan Flite was a most potent leader, a generator of excitement. Even if it meant that his life might someday again be in danger, he wanted to follow.

Now, at Scripted Corner, he scanned the secondhand science books, wondering what all their authors would say about the mysterious drama surrounding Jonathan. The young man had gained people's attention because of his so-called memories of those kids who disappeared in Minnesota ten years before his birth, yet he had spoken very little about them to Jimmy. Apart from the person who had broken into Crescent last November, only a handful of peripheral spiritual bloggers and the weirdo sending him the letters in blue envelopes had taken these peculiar, past-life memory claims seriously. So far, the media was still focusing on the prospect of having a violent killer walking the streets. That Jonathan had attracted the attention of at least one violent religious fanatic seemed still to be a less important tangent.

Here were some book titles that seemed to do him justice:
Neurological Coherence: Quantum Effects in Biological Systems.
Copenhagen: A Debate to Define the Cosmos.
Our Elegant Universe.

Jimmy picked up *Our Elegant Universe*. Its cover was a glossy black, and it depicted a peculiar magenta shape that looked like a sheet of paper folded in more ways than its two sides should allow. It looked far too complicated for Jimmy, but when he flipped through the contents and saw the phrases "M-Theory," "holographic principle," and "Many Worlds Approach," he knew it was the right gift. He grabbed *Neurological Coherence*, too, for good measure.

When he paid for the books and exited Scripted Corner (receiving at least four skeptical glances from the old man at the front counter), a woman in a cheap, brown pantsuit was standing on the sidewalk. Her loosely braided brown hair clashed with her outfit, and she was holding herself as she might at a bus stop, except for the fact that she wasn't facing the street. Jimmy gave her a once over, and just as he turned to the right, she took a quick sidestep to block him.

"Jimmy Barber?"

Jimmy's heart fluttered with exhilaration, but he immediately adopted an air of exasperation. "Excuse me. I'm just trying to shop here. Leave me alone."

"Is that why you told your 7,453 ActoHub followers that you're browsing at Scripted Corner? For used books? You don't seem like the type."

With flair, Jimmy spun to face the woman. "What do you want?"

"My named is Lydia Clark. I'm a writer for the news blog *Providence Today*, and I was checking your feed. I'm wondering if you'd like to tell me a bit about your friendship with Jonathan Flite."

"And why on earth do you think I'm going to blab about that?"

Lydia scrunched her nose into what she seemed to think was a cute smile. "Well, you sure didn't seem to have a problem spreading your news interview about Jonathan Flite all over the internet. The tears were a nice touch, by the way."

"It was a difficult time," Jimmy said. With an operatic sigh, he turned and started down the sidewalk.

Lydia's flats scraped the cement as she shuffled after him. "So, can you tell me if Jonathan is nervous about his impending release, considering all the public smears from his victim's husband?"

"Craig Graber has no respect," Jimmy said. He upped his pace and was thrilled when Lydia did the same.

"But Jonathan? Is it true he's become even more reclusive since Mason Witzel's murder? That his doctors think he might snap again?"

This time Jimmy's theatrics burned with near-actual rage, and he stopped in his tracks. He slowly turned his head toward Lydia, registering just enough that his delivery would have made for a great shot in a film. "I've heard nothing about that. And you're cheap for wanting to exploit him. He's a minor!" He spat on the ground in front of Lydia's shoes, then broke into a run with Jonathan's gift clutched in his hand.

"He'll be eighteen on Sunday!" chided Lydia Clark, who remained standing on the sidewalk, smiling over Jimmy's childish retreat.

2038

SHELLY BRYCE HAD ALWAYS considered herself a star at Common Ties Senior Community, End Haven's poshest independent living center (if she did say so herself), and until recently, she wouldn't have had it any other way. Despite losing neighbors almost every week to the assisted living branch down the street (or sometimes more often to a hole six feet underground), she had always looked on the bright side, trying to radiate Christ's love to every shadowy corner of her world possible. She was always the one to buy new puzzles and books to put in Common Ties' social area (because everyone loved leisure), bake pies for residents even when they didn't ask for them (because who didn't like pie?), and even sometimes offer to help the facility's cleaning staff (why was it that they sometimes missed the most obvious of dust bunnies?). All these things she did in Christ's name with just enough obscurity to escape the judgmental eyes of people who thought religion was for the birds. New Naturalists like Victor Zobel had all but destroyed Christ's kingdom here on Earth.

Until two months ago, very little of this had affected Shelly. Even after last summer's unspeakable nuclear terrorist attack in Geneva committed by the fanatical Catholic Cardinal, Jean-Claude Apostol, she had been perfectly content lighting up her small corner of the world and showing people what religious faith *really* was. It was the job of Christians everywhere to prove both the crazies and the atheist New Naturalists wrong—one person at a time if necessary. Shelly had embraced this task with pride.

This past May 31, however, everything had changed. Jonathan Flite, the nurse killer in Rhode Island, whose very nature reeked of Satan's stench, had been released from juvenile jail, only to become a news sensation and turn her life upside down.

Up until last year, very few people had known or cared that Shelly once had an adopted son named Elijah. If ever asked, she had whisked his very name under the table and hidden behind an expression of love, heartbreak, and what guilt remained of her less-than-satisfactory mothering job. Her gray hair made it very clear just how much a thing of the past Elijah was.

"Yes, my little Elijah. God bless him. But who wants cookies? I just baked some chocolate chip!"

Now Shelly could barely trace how the pieces of her own inconsequential, faith-based life had intersected with a story making international news.

It was 10:02 a.m. on Tuesday, August 3, 2038, two months since Jonathan Flite's release into normal society. She was sitting on her couch alone, staring out the windows of her spotless, white-carpeted apartment at what promised to become a very warm morning. She had as usual readied herself for the day—showering (holding the support bar to avoid falling on her bad ankle), putting on a modest denim blouse and matching shorts (who cared if they were out of style yet again?), and finally finishing her ensemble with a soft layer of makeup and a spritz of perfume (because she still liked to feel like a woman, thank you very much). She was all dressed up with nowhere to go, however, because leaving her apartment would mean fighting through a flock of reporters and getting her face splashed across the news. Delia Jones, a friend from Common Ties, had already left a voice mail two hours earlier.

"Shelly," she had started in a truly frightened whisper, "The Flite boy's mother is in critical condition. I don't know if you saw the news about what happened last night. There are a bunch of reporters outside asking about you and your son, Elijah, and even his biological mother. Don't go out today. I know you said you needed some eggs and spinach, but I'll go out and get them for you if need be."

Click.

Shelly quietly blessed Delia. The brown-haired eighty-year-old always had an eye out for her. And no, Shelly had not seen the news. She couldn't bring herself to watch, because all it did was make her anxious.

In the eight weeks since Jonathan Flite's release from juvenile lockup in Rhode Island, the tension in her heart had been building more and more each day. She had heard the boy's name peripherally in recent years (always relating to his claims of having "past-life" memories of the Idle County Seven), but she had ignored the ridiculous story as a rule. Reincarnation wasn't real, and nobody claiming it was had any business dragging her late son back into the limelight. Even so, all the drama surrounding young Mr. Flite over the last two months had forced her not just to pay attention but also to spend every waking moment with her guard on high alert. It had started with a trickle of independent-journalist calls last December, after somebody had made an attempt on the boy's life. Now, in the eight weeks since his release, it had turned into a near-daily barrage. Just last Tuesday she had finally changed her cell phone number and given it only to three close friends at Common Ties—Delia Jones, Patrice Delgado, and Casey Fitzgibbons.

As far as Shelly could tell, the media swarm had started because of Jonathan Flite's claims about having past-life memories involving Victor Zobel, the secular world's rich, influential, atheist darling. Zobel had of course been the stepfather of Elijah's friend and co-vanisher Jillian Pope, but what of it? Why did Shelly have to be roped into all this new, meaningless speculation?

Zobel's name had been linked last year to Cardinal Jean-Claude Apostol, the Geneva bomber, and rumor had it that even the FBI had taken an interest in what Jonathan Flite had to say about it. Despite the bureau's absolute silence regarding these rumors, journalists of all persuasions—media-conglomerates and independents alike—were now wondering (under the guise of legitimate "news") why such a reputable government agency would take this teenage boy's assertions seriously. Not only that, but they were starting to acknowledge the assertions themselves: that he knew things about the Idle County Seven, whose disappearances remained to this day one of the most peculiar cold cases in Minnesota's history. Reports claimed that, as far back as age eight, Jonathan Flite said the teens vanished in the Moon Woods, just five miles east of End Haven. And all this mattered *why*? Because the man who now owned that forest was the same Victor Goddamned Zobel Shelly once knew. Not only had he personally funded local searches for the teens after they vanished, but he was now also connected, at least via internet gossip, to the Roman Catholic zealot who bombed Geneva.

Shelly had come to accept that her son and his friends had driven on a whim to Dallas, where something deplorable had happened. It was all the evidence ever implied. Same with the death of Elijah's biological mother, Cynthia Foster, later that year—it had been the product of coincidence, a freak hunting accident in Alaska two months after his disappearance. It hadn't even made front-page headlines. Shelly, while forever grief-stricken over the loss of her son and silently relieved after Cynthia's death, had come to be selfishly content with the stories' explanations, because how else was she supposed to get on with life? Now all these things were bubbling to the surface again, along with a degree of regret she would not have expected. In the last twenty-eight years, she had somehow settled for accepting the mystery and moving on with her life, but now this Jonathan Flite boy—a random and troubled stranger—was saying Elijah disappeared right here in Idle County. What did it say about her that all she wanted was to preserve the mystery and never again let it touch her life?

Such old hands I'm getting, Shelly thought, eyeing her wrinkles as she sat on the couch, her arms resting on her legs. What could an aging woman do when all she had was a small apartment and the buzzing world closing in on her? If all this hoopla didn't die down soon, her life would become misery. It seemed sacrilegious to pity one's self when Christ had hung on a cross, bleeding from nail wounds on his hands and feet, but Shelly couldn't help thinking that—

Her old cell phone buzzed. It was sitting two feet away on the couch's leather armrest, looking woefully unused since receiving its new number last Tuesday. She picked up the phone without answering. On its display was a nonlocal number. 212. New York City. She hadn't had a call from that area code since 2010, the year Elijah and his friends disappeared.

It was a reporter. It had to be. How could they have found her new phone number?

With a hint of rage (because this was the last time she would ever do a stranger the courtesy of answering a phone call—and yes, she would have to switch her number again), Shelly answered the call with a very sharp "Hello?"

Through the earpiece came a rustle of paper and then a very young female voice. "Hi. My name is Clovia Bell, and I'm with CBS's *WorldLine*. Is this Shelly Bryce?"

Shelly swallowed air. She didn't even bother asking the young woman how she found the number. She already knew. "Yes, this is me. I mean, I'm Shelly. You said *WorldLine*?"

"Yes, that's right. The streaming newsmagazine?"

"I know the show."

"I understand that you also met our host Alice Winterblume once or twice? Back when she was starting her career at WCMP news in Wind Prairie? She interviewed your son Elijah in August of 2005."

For a moment, Shelly responded with silence. Alice Winterblume was the cream of the news-journalist crop, and she always had ways of getting her story. Perhaps it was worth listening to this Clovia Bell girl, if only to avoid being painted as a heartless crone on the most popular news documentary program in history. "What can I help you with?" Shelly finally said.

"Well, I'm calling because . . ." More paper rumples. The girl had to be some sort of intern. ". . . Ms. Winterblume is in the preliminary stages of putting together a full-season series that involves your son Elijah and his friends. They were known as the Idle County Seven?"

Of course they were known as the Idle County Seven. Shelly Bryce closed her eyes, then leaned back quickly so she could smell her own perfume. She tried to cover her unrest with a cough. "Yes. They were. I do recall Ms. Winterblume interviewing my son."

"I have here in my notes that it was back in 2005, after the death of a boy named Damon Jacoby," young Clovia Bell said. "Anyway, we're wondering if you would be willing to be part of our news investigation of the Idle County Seven case this coming October. Ms. Winterblume always liked your son. Thought highly of him, I mean."

"Well, thank you," Shelly replied, peering at her chipped pinky fingernail.

"Would you be willing to speak with our segment producer over the phone? His name is Grayson Roberts, and he's handling all the interview scheduling for when Ms. Winterblume comes to shoot in Idle County."

"She's coming here?"

"She is."

Shelly's legs were shaking. No, she would not speak with CBS. That part of her life was finished and long behind her. If she were to end up on *WorldLine*, what would everyone at Common Ties think? That she was trying to capitalize on the Jonathan Flite case and get famous? Trying to embrace the limelight instead of live out her life in service of the Lord? Her son was a memory best left alone, thank you very much. As much as she hated to admit it, he had also been—or at least would have been—an advocate of homosexual depravity, the sort society had yet to recover from. There was nothing in this lost mystery that Shelly wanted revealed to the world. It was her responsibility to make this clear.

"Ms. Bryce?"

Shelly almost growled into the phone. "I'm not interested."

She ended the call before Clovia Bell could say another word. Knowing these news people, they'd let somebody more powerful call back, recruiting begging services all the way up to the classy, ravishing, sea-parting Alice Winterblume if necessary. These people liked a good story; it was all they ever wanted. Shelly thought they would have learned a lesson after last summer's nuclear attack in Switzerland, not to mention after the copycat attacks on Jonathan Flite. Some stories were just too serious to be made into entertainment for the masses—and yes, that was all news programs were these days. With the streaming independent channels, it was all cheap, uneducated commentary by people making homemade news reports; with the big online stations, it was bombastic music, fast cuts, and any type of deplorable, on-demand drama to tug the heartstrings.

Shelly stood up, walked across her spotless living room, and stopped at the kitchen's cookie-cutter bar, a granite counter under a wall cutout from the living room that looked in on the stove and microwave. She laid her veiny hands flat, supporting herself against the wave of fury boiling up inside her. It was fury at everything—all those hurts and embarrassments and irritations that had no right to rear their ugly faces now, after so many years. Elijah's disappearance was behind her, and these days, she *liked* it that way. Deep down, at a level she didn't like to acknowledge, she knew she'd have to explain this relief to Jesus once he finally came to take her.

Screw it. I need to get out of here.

Whatever had happened to Jonathan Flite's mother last night, Shelly didn't want (or need) to know. If there were reporters camped at Common Ties' front doors thinking she might somehow contribute to the charade, she would go on a drive instead of her usual walk. That way, she could leave through the garage. So be it if people around town saw her and stared.

It was August, but a cool one so far. Shelly donned a light coat before leaving her apartment. End Haven's weather could never be 100 percent predictable. Even summer temperatures could drop drastically when low pressure in the jet stream sent cold air from Canada down across South Dakota, through Idle County's distant hills, and into town. It rarely happened just like that, lickety-split, but Idle County was unpredictable enough to jolt people into preparedness at the slightest intuitive whim.

True to form, when she exited Common Ties' garage and rolled her blue Ford Sanctuary's windows down, Shelly shivered. The sun was out, however, and it really was quite warm—exactly as the weather report on her phone had predicted. The pine trees lining Brookings Street were swaying in a light breeze, but only just. The aging digital sign on the US Bank building at the Main Street intersection showed a comfortable seventy-six degrees. A mosquito buzzed through the window just as she halted at the driveway's stop sign and glanced back at Common Ties' front doors, where there was indeed a group of reporters waiting.

Alice Winterblume.

That was why she was shivering.

Shelly Bryce was still a Christian, regardless of society's bullying of religious people, and while she didn't like to admit that anything could break through the power of Jesus Christ and scare the living daylights out of her, the call this morning had. Last year, she had turned down flat any sort of interview with that psychiatrist from Wind Prairie who was writing the Idle County Seven book (Dr. Lumis, was it? Or Lumen?), and that had been *before* all the recent Jonathan Flite hoopla. Until now she had avoided any direct resurrection of her son's unpalatable bit of history. Today's call from *WorldLine*, however, had officially put her on the field with people who clearly cared more than she did about finding out what happened to Elijah. Alice Winterblume was a class-A journalist, one who had successfully ridden up the tide of on-demand news media and internet-based networks. Her investigative journalism, the chops of which were cut and shaped with the original Idle County Seven case in 2010, was now streaming television's gold standard for quality. To deny her, especially after she had painted such a heroic portrait of Elijah in 2005, grated on Shelly's conscience.

Yet who was actually caring about *Shelly* in this situation? Nobody. It was the Idle County Seven mystery. It was all anybody ever wanted to know about, no matter how much familial pain they stirred up in the process.

Elijah had disappeared and never been found. For all the scant clues the police and FBI had found—and they truly had been scant—nothing had yet explained why her adopted son would have chosen to do something so garishly drastic. He may have identified himself as *gay*, but he had just been "coming into his own," according to people who supported that lifestyle. He was even in the process of forming an antibullying group at End Haven High School, which he had planned to spend his senior year running. The biggest clue anybody had found were two cars in a suburb of Dallas, the first belonging to Molly Butler's druggie boyfriend, Clayton Graf, and the other belonging to Jillian Pope, whom Shelly had always secretly thought of as "the abortion girl." These kids had been sick, a reflection of an increasingly Godless society, and it seemed they had all thought it well to secretly drive toward Mexico for some last hurrah, before Molly succumbed to that brain tumor.

Somewhere along the way, they got lost. Or taken. Or killed. That was all anybody could ever piece together, wasn't it? Even Elijah's precious, perfect, and sin-stained biological mother hadn't been able to uncover anything substantial before her death.

As far as Shelly Bryce was concerned, it would have never happened had Elijah not met Molly Butler. The girl might have had cancer, but Molly always was, Jesus forgive Shelly, a rather *unnerving* girl. Those dark eyes, that way of looking at people as if she knew something they didn't—everything about her had screamed "questionable influence." Apart from having helped land Elijah in the hospital after that dreadful Spinner's Island incident the first summer they met, the girl had pushed his mind away from God, which remained (as far as Shelly was concerned) her greatest fault.

Shelly scoffed at it all, scoffed at herself. Life never quite seemed to fit in a box, did it? The Bible made it seem so easy.

As she turned left onto Brookings Street (with nowhere in particular to go, though she was considering the Younkers jewelry section at Skydale Mall, where she always looked but never bought), the loudest yell she had mustered in years—probably weak by most people's standards—escaped her mouth. "*Damn you*, Elijah. *Damn you.*"

For this, again, she would someday answer to Jesus.

2010

I T HAD BEEN EIGHT DAYS. Eight days, and no word from Elijah. Cynthia Foster was rarely a nervous woman, but for Elijah and his friends to be gone this long was not normal at all.

She had been working her tarot booth at the Fourth of July fair as always, hoping to see her biological son (and maybe even Molly Butler, if the poor thing was up for it) sometime before the lightning on the horizon turned into a full-fledged storm. With her freshly dyed, blazing-red hair flowing over her starlight-subtle blue dress, Cynthia had waited, glancing up every so often as new fairgoers passed by, anticipating that at least a few of their legs would eventually lead to those faces she had grown accustomed to seeing every year. Time was limited now. Elijah had just one year of high school left, as did most of his friends. And Molly? She was an old soul, ready to fly as soon as that dratted tumor took her.

Except Molly was missing, too. Just like Elijah and the others.

Now Cynthia stood in her seventies-yellow kitchen, looking out the window at her neighbor, old Mr. Child, as he struggled to mow his lawn. Her first inclination was to go out and help, but she had a tarot appointment with Vivian Miller at ten o'clock. That was six minutes away, and Vivian was always early.

The doorbell rang.

"Coming, coming," Cynthia said, mostly to herself, wondering just what it was that made her clients keep coming back. She wasn't the most legitimate of psychics. She could read people with her own intuition and insight, yes, but seeing their future or glimpsing their past lives or talking to their spirit guides? Nothing close. She went by the cards—*and* by the bits of intuition they sparked when juxtaposed with people's immediate reactions to them.

Her cat, Miles, was lying in front of the door. He meowed when Cynthia nudged him with her foot so she could pull it open. The moment she saw graying blond hair, she knew the person standing on her porch wasn't Vivian Miller.

Shelly Bryce, looking sleepless and lost, was holding up a tarot card, glaring at Cynthia through the screen door. On the street out front, her new Ford Focus gleamed red under the sun. Cynthia said nothing at first, because she recognized the tarot card right away.

Death.

She had given it to Elijah five summers ago.

"I thought I could accept you in his life," Shelly Bryce said, shaking her head. Looking closer, Cynthia saw that the woman was trembling with rage.

Here it was, the explosion they both had been waiting for since Cynthia entered Elijah's life five years ago. She opened the screen door and then stepped back after Shelly took hold to steady it. "Do you want to come in for tea?" she said.

"*Screw* your tea!" Shelly screamed, throwing the Death card in Cynthia's face. It flew past the front door's threshold and fluttered to the living room's worn beige carpet. "You got him into all this! I knew the summer he met you that it was just a matter of time before I lost him. Whether it was your goddamned *AIDS* or your goddamned New Agey *bullshit*, I knew he was lost. Because of *you*."

The words hit Cynthia across the face. She let them sting on every curve and corner.

"And now I thought you'd want that heathen card back," Shelly continued. "Found it in his sock drawer. He obviously got it from you. Tell me, Cynthia, are you happy now? Because mark my words, you'll end up in hell if you don't start giving a damn about the effect you have on people around you. First you bring a child into the world that you can't even take care of, and then you guilt your deadbeat cousin and me into adopting him, and then you twist your way back into his life and mess him up completely. Did you *really* think you were capable of being a healthy presence?"

Bracing herself on the doorframe, hating the trickle of belief seeping from Shelly's words into her heart, Cynthia bent down to pick up the tarot card from the floor. She had mailed it to Elijah five years ago, when he wasn't even thirteen years old. God, how inappropriate that had been. Cynthia knew she was open-minded and open-armed, but boy oh boy, did she ever know how to cross boundaries that eventually blocked her into a corner. "Thank you for bringing the card back," she said. "But it belongs to Elijah. He'll want it when he gets back."

"*Gets back*?" Shelly seethed. "Tell me, oh psychic wise one, since when do you think those kids would just leave for eight days without saying a word? And without running a single credit card? Not to mention Molly Butler. She's not going to be able to . . ." The woman was crying now, full-on tears. Until this moment, Cynthia had been tethering herself to hope, because the alternative was unthinkable. The certainty in Shelly's eyes, however, was like a quaking red drum.

From the corner of her own eyes, Cynthia saw Vivian Miller's blue Honda approaching. "I have a client at ten," she told Shelly, whose face contorted in disgust at the very mention of her tarot and palm reading business. "But I want to be with you on this. If that's possible for you. I love that boy. You know I always have."

"*Death*," Shelly whispered. Her expression cracked, then quivered as if it might shatter. "You might want to close your psychic shop if you really don't feel it." She turned on her scuffed tennis shoes and marched back up the sidewalk.

Cynthia let the screen door swing shut in her face. Vivian Miller was toddling down the sidewalk, her white hair bouncing back and forth as she glanced repeatedly between Shelly and Cynthia. Had Vivian seen Shelly on the news during the press conference two days ago? Had she made the connection to what Alice Winterblume, that reporter from Wind Prairie, was now, as of this morning, calling the "Idle County Seven Mystery"?

Cynthia welcomed Vivian in, and they settled into a tarot reading that could not have felt more artificial. All Cynthia could see as Vivian drew her cards was young Elijah's sunless round face and sandy, buzzed hair back in 2005, the day he drew his Death card. She had read it as a message of crumbling and rebirth, not literal death. Except that summer had progressed in a way that, in retrospect, made her think she should have done a better job reading the signs. What was it Elijah had whispered to her as he was lying in the hospital, after he and Molly returned from their near-deadly excursion to Spinner's Island? Something about Idle County being strange. That it messed with people's heads and made them know things they shouldn't be able to know.

"And . . . see things they shouldn't be able to see."

Cynthia remembered the hospital discussion with crystal clarity. Looking back now, it wasn't the only time she had heard this. What about Maximilian Pope, father of young Jillian Pope, who was now supposedly a resident of Alaska but also nowhere to be found, according to police? He had been accused of purposefully ending the life of an eighty-four-year-old patient named Josiah Marple during an Alzheimer's drug study at the research facility built on the bones of Rock Shore Nursing Home, but hadn't he also been accused of illegally looking for anomalous brain activity in his patients? Evidence of some sort of higher-consciousness activity as they approached death? Cynthia had given Max Pope the benefit of the doubt when his questionable activities began making local news headlines. Now she wondered if he had performed his study in Idle County for a reason, if perhaps he had seen patterns of human psychological experience here that he had deemed worthy of investigation.

"What do the cards say?" Vivian Miller asked, rapt at Cynthia's mask of concentration. There was nothing in the cards for Cynthia to work with, but thankfully, Vivian was the type to grasp at any psychic spin thrown her way.

"I see rebirth," Cynthia said. "New beginnings."

Inwardly, Cynthia recalled Elijah's beautiful, lightly freckled face the last time they had spoken. He had come to mow her lawn just twelve days ago, as usual in a tight white T-shirt to show off the muscles he had begun to grow. After downing a glass of raspberry-flavored Crystal Light, he had rushed off with a quick "Love you," probably to some social event with his friends. Four days later, they had all vanished.

Vivian Miller's eyes were wide, and she was already nodding at Cynthia's mention of "new beginnings." Another line came to Cynthia's mind, one that sounded not just like one Vivian would eat up but also one that might be wise all around. "New beginnings," she said. "They always come when you least expect them. But you also have to *let them*."

Vivian gasped with a spellbound nod. Cynthia swallowed the grief welling in her throat and continued the session as if nothing at all were the matter—and as if Elijah were perfectly safe, perfectly happy, and perfectly still rooted in the trials of the world.

2005

ON JUNE 17, 2005, Elijah Bryce was sitting comfortably—yet alone—in his house on Windsong Road, on the new leather couch his mother Shelly had just purchased from the Slumberland outlet next to Skydale Mall. He sat carefully in socks so that he didn't scuff the soft brown leather with his toenails, which probably needed a cut. Shelly Bryce rarely had money for new things, but this couch (and its matching chair) had been a treat, a living room upgrade she had been saving up for since last fall. Their house was by no means cramped, but nothing in it had ever really matched, and save for Elijah's bed, nothing had ever quite been comfortable. For the first time since school had let out, it was cloudy. The air billowing his living room's white curtains was thick, almost electric, hinting perhaps at a storm.

Since the couch had been delivered four days ago, Elijah had spent almost every waking hour on it, reading the books he had brought home from the Lemon Avenue Library two weeks ago—the day Damon Jacoby attacked him. He was halfway through a hardcover called *In God We're Dust* by a neurosurgeon named Victor Zobel. It had been sitting on the library's "Popular New Releases" table, and its beautiful blue and yellow cover, designed against imagery of clouds, had drawn his eyes immediately. It had turned out to be a beautifully written atheistic manifesto by a man who saw potential for peace in three main things: science, rational thought, and the dismissal of ancient concepts like God, heaven, and higher consciousness. Elijah had hidden the book from his mother, because it went against everything Pastor Linus at Lake Gospel Church told her. But he was hooked.

Elijah heard the creaking of the dining room chair his baby-sitter Selma always sat in while studying for her GRE. After a few paper rustles and some footsteps, the young woman was standing in the living room archway. "Elijah, it's time to get off your butt. It's almost one o'clock!" As usual, her blond hair was tied up in a messy knot around her tall, oval face, and she was wearing a fit-ted, salmon-colored T-shirt over boyish exercise shorts, as if she were ready for something fun and outdoorsy at a moment's notice. Selma was what his mother called a "go-getter." An "active person." A girl who "had a lot going for her." She was planning to become a nurse anesthetist.

Elijah laid *In God We're Dust* pages-up, on his stomach, to hide its cover.

"It's been almost two weeks," Selma said, sauntering through the living room. She sank onto the new leather couch. "You haven't once left the house on your own volition. What gives?"

Elijah scratched his nose, then looked out the window at the empty house next door. Seeming too small for the two lots it was built on, its "For Sale" sign, which had been standing in the yard for almost a year, had just recently been switched to "Sold." Right now, staring at the house's chipped white siding seemed far preferable to telling Selma about why he couldn't leave the house. "I just like reading," he said.

"Bull," Selma replied. "I mean, not *bull*, but I know you like doing more than that. What happened to Alec and Natalie Pent and Pauline Gilbert? Last summer you guys were attached at the hip. Didn't you even camp in the Moon Woods one weekend?"

Elijah could feel the humiliation rising in his face for the millionth time since summer started. He shifted his gaze from the house next door to the line of trees behind it. Windsong Road ran north and south on the eastern edge of End Haven, and about a mile through the trees in Elijah's backyard was Old Mill Road, which circled the Moon Woods.

Last summer, just two weeks before news about the murderous priest, Simon Villard, and the sheriff's department's religious cult broke out, he had camped on the inner edge of the Moon Woods for a night with Alec, Natalie, and Pauline. The girls had shared one tent; the boys had shared another. Elijah had been holding a switched-on flashlight as Alec took his shirt and shorts off before climbing into his sleeping bag. The sight had paralyzed Elijah—he hadn't been able to keep from staring at Alec's rippled abdominal muscles, his perfectly shaped chest, and even the outline of what lay beneath his boxer shorts. Alec had noticed him staring. For a second, their eyes locked, and then Elijah had clicked the flashlight off. The next morning, Alec had barely spoken to him. They had left the Moon Woods with a bare minimum of exchanged words.

The entire reason for their trip, though Alec had made him keep quiet about it around the girls, was to dig at a special spot that some of the other boys at school had been whispering about—a patch of ground marked by an **X** formed of small stones. Word had trickled down from two boys in the grade ahead of them that something was buried there, and no, it wasn't treasure. The way they had talked about it, whatever was buried under the **X** seemed to be a well-controlled secret, something sought out and unearthed only by the bravest of boys. Alec had planned to find the spot with Elijah, and Elijah knew his intent had been to join the ranks of the daring—possibly to have social leverage with the boys on his new soccer team. They had found the spot upon arriving but saved any digging for the next morning, when they could escape the girls' attention before sunrise.

After the flashlight incident, however, Alec had wanted to leave the Moon Woods first thing, even before breakfast. He hadn't talked to Elijah all school year. Natalie had been snide. Even Pauline, usually gentle, had looked embarrassed every time they crossed paths. Two weeks later, of course, news about Simon Villard and the Moon Woods cult exploded in Idle County. Elijah had heard no whispers of the **X** since. Perhaps the very real horror of the serial-killer priest, his mass grave site, and his homicidal devotees had rendered the boys' little mystery both innocent and inert.

Elijah stood up from the couch, wanting to hide his blush from Selma. "Maybe I'll go for a bike ride," he said. "I'll take my phone." Before his babysitter could give him any other bad ideas, he grabbed *In God We're Dust* and marched out of the room—anything to escape her concerned eyes.

He sure didn't want to head west, toward downtown, but east? He could go east. Through the trees, toward the Moon Woods. They were always empty. Hell, maybe he could even take a shovel and dig at the mysterious **X**, if it was still there. This summer, the thought of doing it alone seemed like a symbolic nail in his social life's coffin.

Knowing Selma was watching and feeling sorry for him, he refused to look her in the eye as he filled his bike's water bottle and threw three granola bars, a banana, and Victor Zobel's book into his backpack. "I'll be in the Moon Woods," he said. "There's a better spot to read there. Nobody to bug me."

Sinking under the weight of his own rudeness, Elijah entered the garage through the kitchen, pressed the button to open the main door, and walked to his bike. Just before backing it out into the driveway, he remembered the stone-marked **X**. He grabbed one of his mother's gardening trowels and threw it into his backpack.

2038

WINIFRED FLITE, still trying to shed the thick coat of anxiety that had enveloped her at Crescent Rehabilitation Center two days ago, sat in her therapist's Zen-green waiting room, trying to drink a mug of hot tea as her cell phone rang for the hundredth time that day. Her personal number was unlisted, but somehow, either through one of her lukewarm acquaintances or through the fearmonger Craig Graber, it had been leaked to the press, just like everything else in her life.

Winifred was here to make sense of it all, or at least try to, because on May 31—just three days away—every bit of comfort she had would disappear. Jonathan would be restricted to the state of Rhode Island and enrolled in Crescent's day program for one year following his release, but otherwise, for the first time since 2033, he would be her responsibility. Fortunately, he had been the one to ask if she could hire Sounder, his favorite security guard, to live with them on the premises of her Columbus Avenue home. If Winifred were to tell anybody that she wasn't thoroughly relieved at the prospect, it would be an outright lie. Sounder was a divorced father of one, and his daughter, Tiffany, lived with her mother most of the time. Winifred had offered him a hefty sum to walk away from his position with Sparrow Security—well over triple his regular salary. But wasn't that what having millions of her parents' dollars and hundreds of moneymaking investments was for? Hell, giving Sounder the freedom to put little Tiffany through college and grad school felt like some stale attempt at philanthropy, one Winifred's own mother, Julietta, might even be proud of, were she to give a damn what her daughter did these days. Ever since Jonathan's incarceration in 2033, Julietta had kept even more distance than usual, citing her "endless line of commitments." Winifred's father, Stanley, who lived on his yacht on the Mediterranean whenever he wasn't touring Earth's golf courses, had been downright silent. His grandson, Jonathan—and by extension the boy's failure of a mother—had become a most severe blight on his family name.

As if to punctuate all Winifred's issues, the door behind her swung open, and there she stood: Kate Crookston, the bright-eyed and blond-haired psychotherapist who for some inexplicable fashion reason liked to wear brooches shaped like sea creatures. "Winifred!" she said. "Sorry! My video session ran late. How are we today?"

"How are we." Boy, did Kate Crookston like those inclusive, plural personal pronouns. Winifred smoothed the top of her hair bun.

"Come on in! Have a seat," Kate continued, ushering Winifred toward her plush office couch. "So, how's the week going?"

"Is it okay if I say 'worse'?" Winifred asked. She glanced out Kate's tall, sunny second-floor window on Long Wharf. Outside, mocking every idea Winifred ever had about what it meant to have a normal life, were the boats of the Newport Yacht Club, rocking back and forth in the sparkling harbor. "Jonathan's birthday is Sunday. We have his release hearing Monday. It seems so damned fast. I can't even imagine what it's going to be like having to . . ."

To what? Be a mother? Winifred recognized the heat seeping through her chest as guilt.

"To have him home?" Kate offered.

Winifred gave a willy-nilly shake of her head, worried the guilt might mix with her pride and make her combust. It was Dr. Thomas Lumen, Jonathan's mousy Minnesota savior, who had suggested last December that she consult a therapist following the shock of seeing on his reading tablet the portrait of Elizabeth Grime, that silly old librarian from Idle County. In April, after she had called the man to pour out her concerns regarding Jonathan's looming release (and even invite him to a welcome-home dinner scheduled for the same night), she had finally realized he might have a point. Even so, Kate Crookston had come highly recommended by nobody in particular. Winifred had called her based on an internet search, liked her casual tone, and decided they were to be a match—even though they had yet to discuss anything lurking beneath the surface of Winifred's situation with Jonathan.

"Maybe it's about him coming home," Winifred finally said. "But Craig Goddamned Graber broke the *law* five years ago by talking publicly about Jonathan's case, and I didn't sue him soon enough to beat the statute of limitations. Now we're being swarmed by reporters. I have no goddamned recourse. Everyone's concerned about having a killer running around the neighborhood, and let's face it. My son's a *killer*. I can't change that. I can't even bring myself to feel safe near him. I want to give him his own apartment, maybe down here near the water, but then he'd be all alone with the reporters every day, and I'd be up at home feeling guilty, like an even worse mother than I've already been. How's that?" Each word had a deflating effect on Winifred. Before she knew it, another burst of them escaped her lips. "And then there's these weird-ass letters with the blue envelopes Jonathan is getting. No idea who's sending them. They make Jonathan sound like some sort of messiah, which freaks me out, because it makes me worry that people *won't* eventually get bored with his story—because of his memories and their implications, you know? And if they ever find out the FBI talked to Jonathan about *more* than Paul Simpleton's crazy, Christian suicide note, it's going to be a nightmare. I'm talking national news about some supernatural teenage wonder boy. I don't know how I could ever deal with that."

"I'm hearing a lot of you, you, you," Kate said.

"Well, isn't that why we're here?" Winifred snapped.

Kate didn't so much as bristle at her tone. The woman knew how to deal with bruised egos, apparently. "You're talking about the memories your son claims to have," Kate continued. "And yes, I've been following the news just like everyone else. I'm picking up, though, that you're afraid of what might happen if the more mysterious part of him starts hitting the media lens more than it already has. Am I right?"

Winifred crossed her legs and placed her cold hands atop her exposed knee. "I have no idea what to think of his memories. Why on *earth* he would have been born with them."

"Do you think they're real?"

In her mind's eye, Winifred saw her own finger swiping across

Dr. Lumen's tablet and Elizabeth Anne Grime's obituary photo popping up. "I have reason to believe they are," she now said—curtly, to make it clear she was still in charge of whatever sanity she had left. "And let me be blunt. I'm a New Naturalist. Which means I don't believe in any of that past-life, religious hoo-hah garbage. Except . . ."

She wished the window were open, so she could hear the seabirds.

"Except?"

Did Winifred dare tell Kate Crookston, who was only a non-stranger because health insurance paid for their conversations, about the old woman she had seen?

If there's one person who won't go to the press, it's Kate Crookston.

"I've seen a ghost," Winifred said. "Four times, before Jonathan was born. Same ghost. I didn't realize what I was seeing until last December. And it was a woman my son has memories of. A goddamned librarian whose obituary photo I saw for the first time after the attack at Crescent. There. You wanted to know what's really wrong. That's what's really wrong. I'm afraid I'm losing my goddamned mind."

For the first time, the facade of patience Kate usually wore cracked to show what appeared to be real clinical intrigue. Nowhere in her expression were incredulity, judgment, or poorly hidden traces of humor. "Now, let me ask you something," Kate said. "Do you think you're the first person in our planet's history to see a ghost? Or to think they saw a ghost?"

"Of course not," Winifred said. "But I've always considered people like that to be crackpots. Obviously."

"So it's your *belief* that's making you afraid. You believe ghosts should never be anything more than proof of some sort of psychosis. Is that correct?"

"Sums it up. Yes."

"But what if they're not?"

"Well, *clearly* they're not."

"But you just said you're afraid you're losing your mind."

"Damn it, *yes*. But I know I wasn't crazy back then, when I saw this woman. I was just a stupid kid. I had no idea what I was seeing or what I was doing with my life."

Kate sat up and adjusted herself in her chair. "And do you now?"

"Do I what?"

"Have any idea what you're doing with your life."

"*My life is a fucking nightmare*!" Winifred screamed. "That's why I'm here, for Christ's sake!"

Again, not even a bristle from Kate, who was simply leaning her face into her hand, with her pointer finger resting upward against her temple. "Are you done?" she said after Winifred's anger huffs dissipated. Boy, was she good.

"I'm stuck wondering what's even *real*," Winifred hissed. "If ghosts are real, it means everything I believe in is false. Everything the *world* believes in is false. That science is a joke, and we're all just deluding ourselves."

"You may be pleasantly relieved to know that science has a long way to go before it has all the answers," Kate said. "Are you aware that physicists are still arguing about whether the universe we see and live in is even solidly *there* before it's consciously observed or measured? That the particles creating it are seemingly dictated by a system of probabilities whose origin nobody has a good explanation for?"

The heat of exposed ignorance blushed on Winifred's face. "No, I didn't know that."

"How about the fact that scientists don't even know what consciousness actually is, and that a bunch of them are saying New Naturalism is an incomplete thought fad for the masses that doesn't even begin to answer this major question?"

At this, Winifred's blush verged on scarlet anger. She had embraced Victor Zobel's so-called thought fad almost immediately after reading *In God We're Dust.*

"My point is that there might actually be some comfort in realizing we don't know everything," Kate continued. "We don't have enough information about reality for *any* rigid belief system to be rational. If you really start thinking about this, it might help you shed the anxiety that suffocates you every time your preconceptions are challenged."

Winifred's heart thawed just enough for Kate's point to land and start to burrow. After a moment, the courage to utter an honest response crept slowly into her bones. "That still doesn't tell me why Jonathan is the way he is. Not knowing scares the hell out of me."

"Understandable," Kate replied. "But there may be ways to pursue answers. You might be interested in a doctor named Malcolm Stephenson. He was a psychiatrist in the late 1900s who spent the last thirty years of his career studying kids who claim to have past-life memories. He even started an organization for psychological professionals before he died, and they're still continuing his research today, mostly through regression hypnosis. Point being . . . there *are* routes toward pursuing answers if you're open to trying."

"Why do I feel like trying would make everything worse?"

Kate shrugged. "I think you're afraid of what you don't know, and of embracing questions that might reshape your outlook.

When beliefs change, or even encounter hints that they might *need* to change, it can feel like a lifequake. That's what I like to call it."

"A lifequake. Sounds about right." Winifred had not even the slightest desire to chuckle.

"So, the question becomes: How do you deal with it? What pieces of the problem are you going to tackle first?"

"You're making a pretty big leap," Winifred said. "I've only been here twelve minutes."

Kate was the one who chuckled at this. "It's what I'm here for. We could either deal with the root of the problem or the surface—that being Jonathan's release. Dealing with the surface stuff could help your current, tangible life, and attempting to deal with the possibility that he might actually have these memories could lead us down the rather daunting road of trying to figure out the secrets of the universe. I can definitely tell you what we'll get to the bottom of first."

Winifred glanced at the clock. Forty-seven minutes left.

To embrace this new direction in her life was to embrace a change of heart, which presupposed she had a heart to begin with. This more than anything became a flutter of fear she had no context for dealing with. She had feelings, oh yes, many of them, but they were tightly kept secrets behind the grand fortification decorating all sides of her psyche. When she thought of herself, she saw a woman so overwhelmed that the events coloring her life had become walls, and she had allowed them to rise, hard as steel, around her. Yet she had listened to Dr. Lumen, had somehow found wisdom in his suggestion to start the work of escaping, of breaking through.

Winifred had always believed her consciousness to be epiphenomenal, in Victor Zobel's terms—a truly meaningless by-product of the electrical and chemical processes of her brain. Now, for the first time ever, that belief was not enough to cover the breadth of her life experience. "I need to know why it's possible for Jonathan to have these memories," she said.

"The root of the problem it is," Kate said, settling into her chair. "The secrets of the universe await us!"

Winifred pursed her lips.

2005

WHEELS ON THE BUMPY DIRT. Green blurs wisping past Elijah Bryce's eyes. One pedal pump after another, harder and harder, as the trail behind his house led him east.

The last time Elijah had biked this route, he had been following Alec Pent, Natalie Pent, and Pauline Gilbert. Like everyone else in town last summer, they had been completely oblivious to the cult activity happening in the Moon Woods. Their camping trip had simply been an attempt to do a real "grown-up" activity alone. Tim Pent, Alec and Natalie's father, had been a hardcore backpacker before having kids—he had even climbed to one of Mount Everest's base camps. So, when Alec had the idea to go camping alone in the Moon Woods (partially to dig at the mysterious stone-marked **X**), the man had helped them plan it with a level of enthusiasm Elijah had rarely seen in a grown-up. Two weeks later, the FBI had swooped into town and exposed the mass grave site and the sheriff's-department cult that had been worshipping the serial-killer priest from the 1940s. Since then, the concept of spending time in the Moon Woods seemed almost taboo, despite the FBI's having made it a much safer place.

The trail carrying Elijah veered left, dipped downward into a dark patch of drying mud, and then hit a short but steep incline as the trees broke. There it was: Old Mill Road, the circular, two-way motorway separating the Moon Woods from the rest of the world. Its cracked pavement had crumbled along the edges and sunk toward the ditches lining either side. Across Old Mill Road was a patchy layer of young birch trees that acted as a shield to the Moon Woods' Outer Ring, a wide halo of grassland surrounding the actual forest itself. From what Elijah had seen the few times he had ever driven the full loop with his mother, the Outer Ring ran all the way around the forest.

He pedaled slowly across the road, passed through the thin layer of birches, and found the spot where a slight trace of a bike trail ran straight ahead, toward the towering pines. The Outer Ring's grass was almost two feet high in the spots where the ground was less gravelly, but almost all of it looked yellowed, as though it couldn't quite tap into the energy of life. Elijah pedaled faster and faster. Behind him, a wind was building. He saw a strip of lightning zigzag across the gray clouds just as the first of the Moon Woods' conifers engulfed his field of vision. A few seconds later, he heard its roll of thunder.

Maybe I'll get struck by lightning, he thought. *Might be better than facing seventh grade.*

About three hundred feet into the Moon Woods, Elijah came to the spot where he and his ex-friends had set up camp the previous summer. Even in today's dimness and despite the deflating memories it stirred in him, it still aroused a mild sense of magic.

Pauline Gilbert had dubbed this site "the Knoll," because rising from the forest floor's carpet of dead, brown pine needles was a ten-foot hill severed down the middle, from top to bottom, by a wall of flat gray rock. The inclined slopes of the small mound fell around the edges of the stone face, leveling out with the earth in front of it. Last summer, he had lain with Alec, Natalie, and Pauline atop the Knoll, looking at the treetops and discussing the mysteries of life. Back then, those mysteries had to do with aliens, ghosts, heaven, and hell, things Elijah no longer had any good reason to believe in.

After leaning his bike against the Knoll's vertical front, he gulped some water, then took out his library copy of *In God We're Dust* and climbed to the top. Standing at the edge of the rock face, he surveyed the forest. It smelled damp, if there was such a smell. Great pines jutted out of the ground at random intervals, creating a series of pillars that lent the woods a cathedral-like solemnity. As usual here, according both to town legend and to Elijah's experience last summer, there were no obvious sounds of animal life but his own.

Using his backpack as a pillow, he lay atop the Knoll and cracked open *In God We're Dust*. The first paragraph his eyes found, buried on whatever page of Chapter Seven he was on, seemed to grab him by the brain with a wrenching twist.

> *Philosophy cannot prove the existence of God, nor can our conscious experience of feeling that we're a meaningful part of something bigger. The latter*

is simply a result and a demand of evolution, an experience created by our neurons to give us meaning while we are alive. Programmed into our DNA is a drive to survive, made obvious not just by the proliferation of our species but also by the recklessness with which we have encouraged it. At the expense of our society and habitat, we have created philosophies to flesh out these animal inclinations, because they continue to feed not just our survival and evolution but also our sense of value and purpose. Were we simply to find value in our very existence, independent of some destiny mandated by an invisible deity, wouldn't that create meaning enough?

If this viewpoint was legitimate, it would mean that nothing in Elijah's life—neither his joys nor his miseries—would actually matter in the long run. He couldn't tell whether the idea made him feel worthless or defensive. By Victor Zobel's logic, one of those lightning strikes he had seen on his way into the Moon Woods could hit him and kill him, and nature would still go on. Even if people were to care about his death, their care would simply be a result of their brain's programming to value life so they could survive another day. Once *they* died, his existence wouldn't matter at all, in the universe's grand scheme. The sun was going to burn out someday anyway, right?

Elijah set the book on his chest and closed his eyes.

HE AWOKE, HAVING NO IDEA HOW MUCH LATER, from a dream in which he was digging at the stone-marked **X** he and Alec Pent had planned to incorporate into last summer's adventure. Had Alec been with him in the dream? *Yes*, Elijah thought. *Either him or someone else who felt like a friend.*

He sat up, and after a second of reorienting himself, he got to his feet. It wasn't storming yet, but a low mist was creeping into the forest from the Outer Ring. He dug his cell phone out of his pocket and saw that it was just past 3:00 p.m. Glancing over his shoulder, toward the heart of the Moon Woods, Elijah tried to locate the **X**, assuming it was still there (though he had decided upon waking that, if so, it soon wouldn't be). It had been somewhere off to the left—behind the Knoll by a couple hundred feet, near a large, circular boulder.

There the boulder was. Behind his turned neck, at ten o'clock.

Elijah's feet were moving before he could have his final say. Within seconds, he was circling the boulder. Resting freely on the carpet of dried pine needles was the **X** formation that the elite boys of End Haven had repeatedly dug up and, with care, rearranged. Elijah dropped to one knee, checking over his shoulders in a burst of self-consciousness, as though someone might be watching him. All he saw was the low layer of mist creeping through the trees.

The **X** in front of him was made of twenty-one stones, one in the center and five spaced alongside each other, jutting out in four tangents. It was definitely a man-made mark, but why would anyone have made it in the first place?

*Because **X** marks the spot, silly.*

This was what Elijah told himself as he carefully removed the stones from their arrangement and, using his mother's gardening trowel, began to dig. The trowel was about six inches long and three inches wide, and he could scoop only one small portion of damp earth out at a time.

Elijah had just begun to consider using his hands when the trowel's metal tip struck something solid. He tried another spot close to it. Again, something stopped the trowel from delving deeper.

Soon, he had uncovered what appeared to be a small wooden box. It was square in shape, perhaps ten inches on all sides, and buried a foot and a half down. Elijah lifted it out of the ground. On its back edge were rusted metal hinges. Opposite them was a single metal latch—also rusted—where the top opened. Below it, on the side of the box, was a rose, carved into the wood and painted pink and green. The receptacle looked as though it might have once been a jewelry box. Elijah tried the latch. With a high-pitched creak, it opened.

The box was full of sand.

Elijah frowned, wondering if all the boys' speculative whispers at school had been a prank. He dipped his fingers into the sand. It was fine, like the sand along the southern edge of Spinner's Lake. He extracted his fingers and dipped them again. This time, he dug down farther and touched something hard. It was circular and ribbed. After securing a firm grip on it, Elijah pulled, and a hard object came forth. The sand in the box fell into place around it, only to reveal a second object that had been covered in the box's corner. Elijah made a note to examine this second object more closely once he had inspected the most unexpected one in his hand.

It was a small glass jar filled with something powdery, some of it layered in vaguely different shades. Elijah felt something crinkle, like paper, under his fingers on the rear side. Turning it around, he saw an old white sticker label filled with five lines of cursive handwriting. Elijah had to squint to read the words.

Tracey Lee Earnshaw, Miscarried, April 1990, 26 weeks

Alex Jason Earnshaw, Miscarried, February 1989, 30 weeks

Kasey Andrew Earnshaw, Miscarried, November 1987, 18 weeks

Taylor Jordan Earnshaw, Miscarried, July 1985, 21 weeks

Michael Lawrence Earnshaw, Miscarried, May 1982, 32 weeks

When it dawned on Elijah what he was holding, a sudden and irrevocable guilt snaked through his gut. He had dug here to be brave, on a half wish that correcting last summer's botched Moon Woods excursion could make it right in some small way. But **X** had not marked the spot; it had likened him to a grave robber. Except this was almost worse, because the ashes in the jar had once been somebody's hope for children.

Elijah surprised himself by realizing he was holding back tears. It wasn't exactly that he was face-to-face with the remains of somebody's lost hopes; it was a glaring reminder that the first thing he had ever done in life was be unwanted. Not only had he been thrown out to the dogs for adoption, but he had also become an unspoken burden on his adoptive mother the minute the man she had teamed up with to raise him dumped her for the sunny state of Florida.

He blinked away a set of tears and placed the jar of ashes delicately back into the box. They rested peacefully on the sand. It was then that Elijah noticed again the second buried object. It was only partially exposed in the sand, but it was unmistakable: a row of teeth jutting out, into the day's fresh air.

It was a jawbone. Judging by its gold rear molar, it appeared to be human.

PART 2

COINCIDENCE
AND
INTERSECTION

2010

CYNTHIA FOSTER HAD NEVER TAKEN COINCIDENCE at face value. Not since she had conceived Elijah Bryce, not since his healthy birth in 1992 free of the HIV virus threatening to overtake her system, and not since his discovery of the jawbone—and the ashes of her previous miscarriages—in 2005. That he had been the one boy in End Haven curious enough to investigate the box she buried in the Moon Woods made her wonder just how much of a fluke it had all really been. And heavens, she couldn't forget Elijah and Molly Butler's discovery of the rest of the jawbone's skeleton later that summer. Despite all the violence, heartbreak, and unpleasantness it involved, it had all been *too* perfect, as if life had set the game up to make or break them. Now, five years later, since he and his friends had seemingly driven down to Dallas on a whim and been victims of some accidental misfortune, Cynthia was looking for patterns—or unlikely coincidences—that the police might not be thinking of.

What kept rising in her mind were thoughts of Max Pope, Jillian Pope's publicly shamed father. He had been all but chased out of Idle County in 2007, after news broke of his questionable human testing endeavors at the retrofitted Rock Shore Nursing Home. He hadn't been heard from since his daughter's disappearance four weeks ago, which seemed too strange, too unlikely. Max had loved his daughter more than anything, according to snippets of conversation Cynthia had picked up from Elijah and his friends. This didn't jibe with the man's recent radio silence.

She sat in her car now, under the pouring August rain, in Rock Shore Nursing Home's old parking lot in Blue Hill. Here, after transforming the building into a licensed research facility, Max had begun conducting a study of a new Alzheimer's drug called Dasparta with patients who had volunteered to live out their dying days as participants in the research. His supposedly double-blind study, funded by his private Gateway Project organization, had been approved under the guise that it would be measuring effectiveness of the drug in relation to patients' life spans—essentially to see whether it could prolong life. According to Rock Shore's employees, however, Max had also secretly been searching for anomalous brain wave patterns during the process of death.

Elijah and his friends Molly Butler and Lindsay Thorsen had met Max in 2006, at Benedict Wise University's First Annual Ghost Symposium in Wind Prairie. Somehow, they had learned about his Gateway Project and become volunteers at Rock Shore, visiting the dying patients in whatever ways mattered. During this period, the three had met the awkward, lumbering, but sugar-sweet Gabriel Creed, who had become their close friend. From what Elijah had told Cynthia, they had sometimes read books to the residents; other times, they had brought in puppies and kittens from Claw and Kibble Animal Shelter to cheer everyone up. All that ended, of course, when Max was accused of killing his patient Josiah Marple on purpose, in order to inquire—and measure—if the brain behaved any differently under such circumstances. He had left Idle County legally innocent but under intense scorn. As had recently been reported by the *Wind Prairie Tribune*, the Minneapolis *Star Tribune*, and now even CNN, sources claimed he had changed his name to Michael Johnson and moved to Palmer, Alaska.

It wasn't so much what Max had done, but what he had been aiming to do. Why had he run his medical experiments in Idle County in particular? Why were these seven kids, some of whom were known to have supported his belief in parapsychological phenomena, still missing?

Cynthia was far enough from the vacant research facility's main awning to look inconspicuous if someone were to glance her way. The shrubbery lining the parking lot was overgrown, but the paved roundabout at its entrance was still smooth, without even a crack, despite the three icy winters that had passed since its last use. Cynthia didn't want to be caught here, sitting in her rusted turquoise Ford Escort, particularly considering that Gabriel Creed's parents—who lived nearby—might stone her if they saw her due to their fear of anybody who didn't believe in Jesus Christ's saving grace. Even so, all her instincts had told her to come here—to look at Max Pope's old experiment site, to think, and to let her mind see the ideas and patterns. She had always felt, perhaps like Max, that Idle County was a place where people could break through the camouflage of life, perceive the game, and maybe even start to understand its rules.

Cynthia opened her car door and stepped out, onto the roundabout's smooth pavement. Her fifty-four-year-old knees creaked as the rain trickled down her red hair, past her graying roots, and onto her scalp. She walked toward the shuttered building's main awning and to the door. She pulled. It was locked. Of course.

Damn it.

But what had she really expected? For a supposed psychic, she was flying unbelievably blind, even if her specialty amounted only to tarot readings.

When she turned around, however, a child was standing in the rain, behind her car. It was a girl, and her brown hair was dripping wet and hanging on the contours of her bony face. She was wearing a faded green rain jacket and sopping-wet flip-flops. At first, Cynthia hesitated—even wondered if the little girl might be a ghost—but then she realized that such apprehension was ridiculous. She walked closer. The girl looked about eight or nine, and her wide eyes were gray-blue, shrouded in a peculiar weight that was rare for a child.

"Can I help you?" Cynthia asked.

For a moment, the girl just stared at her. Then she said, "What are you doing here? Nobody's in that building anymore."

Cynthia gave her the warmest smile her running makeup would allow. "I'm actually just . . . trying to think of answers. I know that probably won't make sense to you. I must look pretty silly, huh?"

"It makes sense," the girl said. She readjusted her stance, stepping with her sandaled feet into a puddle.

"Aren't you a little bit cold without proper shoes on? Or rain boots?"

"Can't afford rain boots," the girl replied.

"Are you alone? Do you need help of some kind?"

"No."

Cynthia grimaced.

"I live over there," the girl continued, pointing to a row of rundown two-story houses that lined a tree-canopied street perpendicular to Rock Shore's own Kendall Lane. "My dad used to work here. My brother Gabe disappeared four weeks ago."

Cynthia suddenly forgot how wet her hair was getting. Gabriel Creed was one of the kids who had disappeared along with Elijah. Hank Creed, his father, had been one of the research facility employees who accused Max Pope of murdering Josiah Marple in 2007. "Excuse me?" Cynthia said. "Your brother is Gabriel Creed?"

The girl nodded. "And I'm not supposed to say anything that Jesus doesn't want me to say. But I knew you were out here."

"You *knew*?"

The girl lifted a rain-slicked arm and tapped her right temple with her pointer finger. "Yeah, I *knew*. And I wanted to tell you something. They're saying to listen to your *dreams*."

Cynthia chuckled. "Who's saying that?"

"The people behind your shoulder. I think they're your guardian angels. But Momma might say they're the devil's children."

A shudder took Cynthia by the spine, bottom to top. Around them, the rain pattered the pavement, rustling against the low hedge lining the parking lot to their right. Gabriel Creed's sister stared right into Cynthia's eyes. Then, for a moment, she glanced upward and to the left, as if trying to catch some sound above her hearing frequency's range.

"Now they're saying that all the . . . that all possibilities . . . are set up before we're born," the girl continued. "Dreams are where you practice all your choices. Then in normal life you actually make them. Life's all about learning to make the realness you want. I mean . . . learning to make the *reality* you want."

Cynthia stared at the little girl for a long time. Far behind her, along the tree line of Blue Hill—the actual bluff on the town's east side—a snake of lightning lit the sky. The girl was either extremely imaginative or yet another product of Idle County's uncanny tendency to promote psychic activity. Or both. "Can I drive you home? Cynthia asked. "What's your name?"

"I'm not supposed to get in cars with strangers," the girl said. "But my name is Eloise. Please don't tell my Momma that I'm out here. She says Jesus sends people to hell if they can talk to the devil's children."

"There is no devil, honey," Cynthia said, for the millionth time in her life stepping over inappropriate boundaries. But skinny little Eloise Creed didn't deserve to be raised under such a horrendous shroud of fear. "I just want to make sure you're all right and you have a place to go home to. Nobody likes being stuck out in the rain, right?"

"I do, sometimes," Eloise said.

Cynthia had to smile at this, though she was sure her sopping, rain-sagged hair made her look like Pennywise the frightful dancing clown. "Well, honey, I should be off then. I was just—"

"It's a dream about Alaska," Eloise interrupted. "That's what they're saying."

Silence between the pitter-patters of rain.

"You had a dream about Alaska last night. They're saying it matters."

A clap of thunder sounded around them. Tingles ran across Cynthia's neck as she mentally examined her dreams from the night before. Had there been one about Alaska? There had been mountains, she knew, and . . .

Suddenly, she chuckled. Eloise chuckled, too, as if trying to follow along.

"Palmolive dish soap," Cynthia said. "And I remember Russia being close. I dreamed I was washing dishes, worrying about an avalanche in the mountains. I did dream that last night. Is it *Palmer*, Alaska? The thing I'm supposed to pay attention to?"

Young Eloise smiled. Then she turned and started racing back toward her house.

"Wait!" Cynthia screamed. Her heavy, wet clothes bounced on her body frame as she ran after the girl. "Honey, wait up a second!" In the middle of Kendall Lane, standing once again in a drop-dotted puddle, Eloise Creed turned to face her. Cynthia was huffing and puffing like an old bat. "Eloise, I need . . . I need to ask . . . Do you know what happened to your brother and his friends?"

"Momma says they're all going to hell," Eloise yelled from the middle of the road.

"But do *you* think they're going to hell?"

The girl paused, as if waiting for information to filter into her brain. It was a classic psychic mechanism, so often used by fakes, tricksters, or people like Cynthia herself, who simply had gifts of clear intuition. "Nobody's telling me," Eloise finally said. "But I talk to angels sometimes. And I saw Gabe in mine and Sandy's bedroom the night of the fireworks. He was smiling in the doorway, like the angels do. Momma says talking to angels is the only way to talk to dead people without going to hell."

"And how did you know to come say hello to *me*?"

"*They* told me," Eloise said, once again gesturing to a point just over Cynthia's shoulder, where nobody visible was standing.

A pair of headlights, along with a swishing noise of tires driving in the rain, curved around the bend of Kendall Lane behind Eloise. Without waiting for Cynthia to ask any other questions, the girl turned and ran toward the perpendicular row of rundown houses.

Cynthia turned back toward the abandoned research facility. *Palmer, Alaska.* It was the town news outlets said had been Max Pope's last rumored whereabouts, after a name change. The FBI had apparently been alerted to the questionability of his move to Palmer after the Gateway Project fiasco. Their Anchorage field office was already working with the Palmer Police Department to check all leads with that angle, though most were considering it a dead end since Jillian Pope and Clayton Graf's cars were found outside of Dallas. Still, possibilities were possibilities.

When Cynthia climbed into her car, she grabbed the steering wheel, then leaned forward and rested her head on it.

Elijah wasn't your boy to begin with. You have no right to play any role but that of a witness in the investigation of his disappearance.

She had buried that wooden box and marked it with **X** the same week she had buried Elijah's birth father and namesake—the husband she had truly known only at the end. The virus inside him had caused him to develop AIDS and scrapped him like refuse for a junkyard, even before Samuel Jacoby, the secret lover who had passed it along to him, succumbed to it as well. They had been two men playing secretly and unknowingly with fire, and now Cynthia was the only bit of that flame left burning. Today, her HIV virus count was undetectable, but back then, the day she had buried that box, it had been high enough to bring her CD4 cells down near the three hundred mark. She had been readying herself for her own curtain call, hiking into the Moon Woods eight weeks after Elijah's adoption, her tears invisible in the forest's shadows, to bury what remained of her old life. The irony of his healthy birth after five inexplicable miscarriages had almost unraveled her, because it had come, she had thought, too late.

It was a spear in Cynthia's heart to know she could have

raised her son after all, that she wouldn't have died and made him an orphan. But Shelly Bryce had done a good job, despite some bumps along the way. Cynthia had often wondered in the years since Elijah had come back into her life if she would have managed quite so well. Her late husband's cousin, Kevin—the one who had offered to adopt Elijah to begin with—had run out on his wife and the boy after just three years. Shelly, who hadn't even been a biological relative, had stepped up to the plate. Perhaps the woman had done Elijah a favor by severing him from Cynthia's long line of bad judgment calls.

Except Idle County was a very small place where people's secrets intertwined, wove their ways to the surface, and created what had become a most troublesome tapestry. Today, young Eloise Creed had become not just a reminder of this but also a new thread. She seemed to be proof of something Max Pope had been trying to study, something Elijah and his friends had also shown interest in.

And this is just the beginning.

Cynthia realized she was crying when she felt her steering wheel grow sticky with tears. She started her car, rolled through the roundabout, and began her slow drive back to End Haven.

2038

WINIFRED FLITE STOOD at her marble kitchen counter with a vodka tonic, sliding its crystal glass back and forth between her fingers just gently enough not to let the drink spill out. It was Saturday, May 29, 2038, the eve of her son Jonathan's birthday. The sun had set, and exactly eighteen years ago, she had been pampering herself. Jonathan's birth had been a scheduled cesarean, timed perfectly, the way she had tried to do with everything back then. The evening before, she had gone to the spa, got a facial, pedicure, and manicure, and then ate the seared sea scallops at Café Zelda. It had been the perfect precursor to what she had envisioned would be a grand success in proving herself.

Tonight, she was facing the reality that she would soon be living with a killer. It wasn't just that her son had actually committed acts of violence; what troubled her now was that his arms, hands, and brain—products of her own flesh and blood—had been capable of such a thing to begin with. She had allowed it to happen. She had ignored his personality, ignored his needs, and ignored the fact that he was unusual. In her attempt to have the perfect little life, she had closed herself to the possibility of it being challenging, unique, or spontaneous. Her fear of anything other than the expected had made Jonathan a ticking time bomb. What she now wondered was whether the bomb had truly yet exploded—or if perhaps his attacks on Melinda Berry and Ellen Graber, not to mention the fiasco at Crescent last November, had simply been mere clock ticks toward the detonation.

At least Sounder would be with them. He would keep Jonathan in line and keep him safe. What the man lacked, and what they all lacked, really, was experience with the media. There were ways entirely nonviolent in which Jonathan could be targeted, ripped to shreds, and thrown out to the dogs. Now that the larger news establishments had caught wind of Jonathan's story (though they were still spinning his Idle County Seven claims as being the result of some psychosis), Winifred sensed it was only a matter of time before somebody would start asking the right questions and shed light on the story's implications. Beliefs about the nature of life, when put up for debate, had the power to destroy entire civilizations. Cardinal Jean-Claude Apostol, the Catholic cardinal who had detonated the bomb in Geneva last August, had become the world's most recent poster boy for such destruction.

It was 8:30 p.m. "ActoVid call," Winifred said into her new phone's microphone. "TV connect, kitchen. Call Tom Lumen." She wasn't wearing her pixel-equipped contact lenses, which of course had no way to record her face anyway, so the television on the kitchen wall sprang to life. She saw herself in a small screen window to the right as the panel blinked with a shimmering graphic reading "Calling Dr. Thomas Lumen."

She'd be lying if she were to say this wasn't about to be the high point of her day. Did it show vulnerability that she was the one calling first? They had devised a system of checking in twice a week, mostly for Winifred's sake (though neither of them had said this outright). Yes, she had started therapy. Yes, she was trying to make strides. Mostly, however, it felt good to have a friend.

It took only eight seconds for Dr. Lumen to answer. The graying, mousy man was wearing a white V-neck undershirt with his chest hair just visible, and he was sipping his usual Scotch. Adjusting his glasses to fit better on the bridge of his nose, he said, "I'm sorry, ma'am, but you've interrupted me in the middle of a very important drink."

"Did you fix your flight schedule?" Winifred asked, taking a sip of her vodka tonic. "Jonathan will be happy to see you. Surprised, too, I think. I'm still not sure what kind of food we should cater. I don't even know what he likes these days."

"Have you thought about *asking* him?" Dr. Lumen said, chuckling.

Winifred scoffed, but a smile underneath the expression broke through. "Yes. Right. 'Jonathan, we're having a "Welcome Home, Nurse Killer!" dinner for you to make up for all my years of calling you crazy! What would you like to eat?'"

"You sure have a way of putting it into perspective."

"Is that your way of telling me therapy was a bogus idea to begin with?"

Dr. Lumen laughed. "I'm pretty sure you're not beyond saving. Even if those reporters are hounding you."

"I'm just ignoring the calls now. At least three of them want exclusive interviews with me and Craig Graber. Like, live in the studio and streaming. A 'face-to-face battle.' They want to see me defend Jonathan's honor."

"And would you?" The psychiatrist's smile waned as he asked the question.

Winifred gave him a desperate shrug. "Would *you*? I guess the question is, 'How bad will all this be once Jonathan gets out?' There've already been threats called into the juvenile courthouse for Monday. And messages left on my phone. Like stupid, cliché breathing-but-no-talking crap. People who have seen too many movies." At this, she could see Dr. Lumen's expression contort with an attempt to mask his own concern. Yes, they both knew what happened at Crescent last November. It had been a drastic move by people wanting to shut her son up. Ironically, it had also put Jonathan on the map much more thoroughly than before, in a way that had drawn the attention of at least a few super-religious crackpots in the shadows.

"You must know I'm not entirely gullible enough to think you're not worried," the psychiatrist said.

"Well, what can I do?" Winifred asked. "Except for moving to a desert island, I'm sort of stuck where I am. And Jonathan can't leave Rhode Island for a year, assuming all goes well. It's a nice little target for anybody who wants to off him. Can you believe I seriously have to consider these things?" In her head, she heard her therapist, Kate Crookston, saying, *"I'm hearing a lot of you, you, you."*

"I take it you've called the police."

"Not about the calls this morning.

"Christ, that was just this morning?"

Winifred dismissed Dr. Lumen's concern with a flutter of her hand and another sip of her vodka tonic. "It's nothing new. We'll have an officer outside for the first week. And Sounder is moving in. God, who would have thought?"

Dr. Lumen swirled the melting ice in his Scotch glass, then furrowed his eyebrows as he took a sip. He didn't need to say what he was thinking; Winifred could read his body language without much effort. He was attempting to wrap his mind around the fact that the news story was Jonathan's and her *lives*. All the personal details people around the country were reading safely behind their ActoLenses, computer screens, or tablets were the concerns she had to breathe through every moment. The media hadn't yet latched onto the fact that the FBI had used Jonathan's statement to isolate Nicolas Leandro Rim, a man who had grown up in a family Victor Zobel had once befriended in Geneva. If that were to become public knowledge, and if Nicolas Rim were to become a famous criminal linked to her family name, it would sink her reputation even further.

"Let's just finish our drinks and talk about you," Winifred said. "Are you still an alcoholic?"

Dr. Lumen raised his glass. "Probably a little." He took a bigger sip this time, then said, "And wait, before we start psychoanalyzing me, I wanted to tell you something. It's a bit unexpected. I got a call from Kara Butler today. Molly's sister from the videoconference last December. She's pondering a trip to Idle County. Hasn't bought her ticket yet, but she wants to go sometime in the next month or two. She thinks maybe August."

Something shivered in Winifred's bones as Dr. Lumen said this. "Do we know why?"

"To check things out, she told me," Dr. Lumen said. "I'm guessing it has to do with whatever Jonathan told her that day on the phone. She still won't say what it was. But every time we've talked since then, she's sounded kind of . . . shaky."

Winifred and Dr. Lumen drank together after this, neither one speaking for a long time. Whatever Kara Butler now knew, it had been enough to drag her interest away from Portland and toward Idle County, the birthplace of her dying father and long-lost sister. It all felt like pieces of a moving, ever-shifting puzzle with no predictable completion point. Perhaps all they could do was place their pieces in whatever way fit best at any given time. Tonight, for Winifred, that meant sitting back and embracing the rare comfort of another human being. And neither of them once tried to tackle (or even mention) all the cosmic questions underlying the fact that they had been brought together at all.

2005

*E*ARNSHAW. *EARNSHAW. EARNSHAW.*

The name repeated itself in Elijah Bryce's head. He was reclining on his bed with his clunky Dell laptop open in front of him, listening to the *Star Wars* soundtrack through the machine's paltry speakers. In the two hours since he had returned from the Moon Woods, all he had been able to think about were the ashes and the jawbone. The jawbone was real—it had to be, because what kind of plaster model would have a gold tooth? Whoever buried it with the ashes had probably been named Earnshaw, and it was possible they still lived in Idle County, perhaps even in End Haven.

Elijah brought up the DexOnline telephone directory. He typed in the last name "Earnshaw" and the city name "End Haven, Minnesota," then pressed "Enter." It brought up zero matches. He next tried the towns of Stone Ridge, Blue Hill, and Deadwood.

Again, no Earnshaws. Finally, he brought up Google's homepage and typed "Earnshaw" and "End Haven." It brought up a number of matches, the first two of which were separate news pages from the *Circle Gazette*. Elijah opened them, only to realize they were obituaries. The first was dated Sunday, October 15, 2000.

> *Louise Gertrude Earnshaw, 83, beloved wife and mother, died Thursday, October 12, after a short battle with pancreatic cancer. She is survived by her husband, Daniel, and preceded in death by her son, Elijah Charles Earnshaw. A wake will be held at Bell Brothers Funeral Home on Monday at 6:00 p.m., followed by a funeral at Emmanuel Lutheran Church in End Haven on Tuesday at 2:00 p.m. Burial will take place at Rutgers's Field Cemetery immediately thereafter.*

The next obituary was dated February 2, 2001.

> *Daniel Elijah Earnshaw, 81, died Wednesday in his home. He is preceded in death by his wife, Louise, and son, Elijah. A funeral will be held at Gloria Dei Presbyterian Church in End Haven on Monday, February 5. Burial will take place at Rutgers's Field Cemetery immediately thereafter.*

Elijah Charles Earnshaw and Daniel Elijah Earnshaw. The names pummeled Elijah's heart, because both of them shared his own name. There had been one time during his childhood, just one, when his mother Shelly mentioned in passing that he had been named after his biological father. It was staggering that, of all the boys in End Haven who had dug up the box buried under the stone-marked **X**, he might be the one for whom it had some grander significance. Yet the ashes and jawbone were bound to have affected one of the local diggers eventually. The fact that it might be him was almost comforting. For the past year, his sense of mattering at all in the world had been fragile at best.

He glanced at the third website that had generated Google results. It belonged to an IT consulting firm, whatever that was. Elijah skimmed it and saw that it was a business in Wind Prairie naming one of its employees as Hillary Earnshaw, who had a client in End Haven called Steelhead Printing. Neither this nor the following listed sites seemed relevant, so he closed the web browser and sat back in his chair.

Earnshaw.

Whoever these people in the obituary were, they were all dead now. If they were indeed related to the miscarried babies buried in the Moon Woods, the deceased son, Elijah Earnshaw, might have been the father. The parents, Louise and Daniel Earnshaw, would have been too old based on the years scribbled on the ash jar's label.

But who had the mother been? Was she dead, too? And why would she have buried ashes with a human jawbone? Perhaps she hadn't buried the box herself. While the writing on the jar had looked like that of a woman, Elijah couldn't be sure.

Over the tinny orchestrations coming through his laptop speakers, he heard the cautious footsteps of his mother ascending the stairs. Shelly Bryce was a short but solidly built woman, and she had never quite mastered the ability to sneak silently through the house, despite her greatest efforts.

"Elijah?" she said, opening his door a crack without knocking.

He looked up from his laptop and saw the slit of hallway in which his mother stood. It was nearing eight o'clock, and the sunset's golden light was shining through one of the windows behind her, backlighting her blond but graying curls in a fiery glow.

"Hi," Elijah said. It was the blandest of salutations, but having three things to hide from her now—Damon Jacoby's torture, the reason for it, and the unutterable truth about what he had found in the Moon Woods—made feigned apathy the only option.

Shelly opened the door farther and crept into his room to the best of her ability. She had let her hair down after a long day at her nursing job, but she was still wearing her scrubs. As usual, the general exhaustion in her face inspired conflicted gratitude in Elijah. Perhaps it was because he was getting older, but the reality of what this woman had done for him was getting clearer and clearer. When his adoptive father, Kevin Bryce, ran off, Shelly had stayed and raised him the best she could. Despite her overzealous embracing of religion, it meant everything to him; it meant his life.

"I'm a tired old bat, I must say," Shelly said, easing herself onto the edge of the bed. Elijah brought up his feet to make room. The bed squeaked.

"You watching your shows tonight?" he asked.

"I am. About the only relaxation I feel anymore. But I guess that's just grown-up talk."

"I can handle grown-up talk."

Shelly smiled, scrunched her nose, and shook her head. "You don't want to have to handle that yet, honey. But I do want to ask you something. Selma says you've been hiding in the house all summer. How come you're not out with Alec and Natalie and Pauline? I talked to Alec and Natalie's Aunt Julie at Bible study the other day. She told me Alec has a *girlfriend* already. You know her?"

Elijah's heart raced, and the awful shame now accompanying Alec Pent's name burrowed in his chest. He had seen but never met Alec's girlfriend, Lindsay Thorsen, only now it was "ex." "They broke up already," he told his mother. "She went to some kickboxing camp in Washington, DC, I think."

"Oh well, romances at your age are always short-lived. But what about the Pent twins and Pauline Gilbert? Did something happen?"

Elijah suppressed a deep breath that would have given his anxiety away. "Alec's in soccer all the time, and Natalie and Pauline got in a fight at the end of the school year. I don't want to be hanging out with just one of them, because then the other might feel bad."

Shelly shrugged as if there were words she could say but chose not to. Elijah saw pain in her eyes, the secret kind she would never admit to. Part of it seemed to be that of a mother for a son, even an adopted one, but another part seemed to be identifying with his loneliness. Just as the silence between them was about to become uncomfortable, she forced a bright expression. "Well, aren't there *any* friends you can spend time with?"

Elijah fished for something, anything, to get her off the subject. "I met a girl at the library who seemed kind of nice."

Shelly lit up. "A girl? Was she pretty?"

Elijah's chest tightened, and now his only concern was hiding the fact that he hadn't thought of Molly in that way at all. "*Mom*," he groaned, pasting a smile on his face, trying to harken back to the days when it really would have been proper to groan about such things. As usual, his mother would think he was simply acting shy and embarrassed about girls when, in actuality, he couldn't escape the worry about why they had failed to catch his eyes the way boys like Alec Pent had.

"Well, I'm just *asking,*" Shelly said, beaming. "But that's good you met someone new, huh?"

"She's one of the Saint Andrew's kids. She'll be at End Haven Middle School in September, she said."

"Oh, a *Catholic*, huh? Just be careful of *that.*" Shelly took a deep breath, then heaved herself off the bed. Her feet hit the floor with a light thump. Facing the door, she turned her face toward Elijah. "Anyway, Selma says you're reading, at least. You should be due back at the library any time now. What's this pretty girl's name?"

The anxiety in Elijah's chest tightened even more. "Molly. I think."

"Well, maybe you'll see Molly again one of these days. Can't hurt, can it?"

"I guess not."

"Elijah Christopher Bryce"—Elijah knew his mother was about to be serious when she used his full name—"Have you thought about praying? For things not to be so lonely? I know you haven't really taken to Lake Gospel yet, but I think if you just open your heart to . . ." She shook her head, as if satisfied that her trailing off would have planted some life-changing idea in his head.

What, open my heart to a God who wants me to burn in hell?

If he wasn't careful, this conversation would turn into one of their church fights—not the way he wanted to end this strange day. Nine years ago, his mother's divorce had caused her so much angst and embarrassment that she had stopped attending Emmanuel Lutheran Church, where she had once been an active participant. Last year, however, a coworker had invited her to Lake Gospel Church on the west side of End Haven, and she had been dragging him there every week since. It had not been that bad until two months ago, when Pastor Linus delivered a raging sermon saying that homosexuals were the spawn of Satan and had spots reserved for them in hell. Thinking of the shirtless Alec Pent, Elijah had sunk into the church pew, hoping nobody would notice his flushing face. Now, if his mother were to see the copy of Victor Zobel's *In God We're Dust* stuffed in his open backpack, she'd likely force him to ride back to the library and drop it off that very night.

Shelly sighed. "Okay. At the very least, I want you spending time with friends this summer. No more sitting around the house or going off alone. I'd think your room would get kind of boring after two straight weeks, even when you have your *Star Wars* posters to look at."

A shred of bitter sarcasm lined her voice. She hated *Star Wars*.

"I've been sitting on the new couch mostly," he replied.

Even though he was staring at the back of his tilted-shut laptop, he saw his mother's gaze linger on him. He imagined that, perhaps just for a moment, she was realizing the truth about him, understanding why nothing would ever be able to fix his problems. Finally, she spoke, almost in a whisper.

"Goodnight, hon." She turned and crossed his bedroom. This time, her footsteps almost managed to be silent. Elijah looked up as she eased his door shut. She was looking at its knob, so she didn't see him notice the pained expression on her face.

"I want you spending time with friends this summer."

Last Elijah checked, he had only one friend, and she was almost a complete stranger. If motherless Molly Butler visited the Lemon Avenue Library as often as she said she did, however, perhaps she'd be there tomorrow. Maybe she could even usher him toward the old phone books, if the library still had them, because there was an essential question he needed answered: Who else had the last name "Earnshaw" in 1991?

2038

THE BRIGHTLY LIT DISPLAY of Younkers jewelry sparkled before Shelly Bryce's eyes, as it always did when she came to browse. It was therapy for her, browsing over things she would never buy, partially because it put her life into perspective. She prided herself on her ability not to let these expensive material objects lure her into the trap of buying, buying, buying, because what was it but useless temptation? Idolization of objects did not gain anybody the keys to heaven. Today, however, her anxiety about the seriousness of the Jonathan Flite situation on the East Coast, not to mention the call from Alice Winterblume's people this morning, was too strong. Perhaps buying a pearl necklace— retail therapy—really could help get her mind off it all.

"Can I help you, ma'am?" came a woman's voice from behind the counter.

Wanting to avoid recognition, Shelly looked up just enough

to see the woman's name tag. No matter how bad a mood she was in, she knew it was *always* important to address service workers by name, because they sometimes had the hardest (and lowest-paying) jobs.

Eloise.

Before the name could make its impression in Shelly's psyche, she said, "Thank you, Eloise, but I—"

Then her gaze accidentally found Eloise's face. Shelly's blood might as well have run cold, just like it did for characters in mystery novels. Standing in front of her was Eloise Creed, sister of Elijah's old friend Gabriel and one of the few people she had hoped never to see again. Eloise had been a child the last time they crossed paths, but oh, what a frightening child she had been. She looked almost the same these days, despite having a more womanly shape to augment her lankiness. What age would she be now? Thirty-five? Thirty-six?

"Ms. Bryce," Eloise said. "How have you been?"

The rising Jonathan Flite drama fluttered wordlessly between them. Shelly clenched her jaw and ran a hand over the back of her head, despite the hair spray holding her gray locks in place. Could she run? Simply leave the jewelry counter without a second glance? No. That wasn't the Christian thing to do. Jesus would have embraced his enemies. Eaten dinner with them. But this woman? Shelly was certain that if she looked too closely into those eyes, she might find the devil and become mesmerized. "I must be going," she managed to say. "Lots to do today, and I was just passing—"

"Wait!" Eloise said. "Just a second, please?"

Shelly stiffened, but she kept her feet planted on the ground and her gaze glued to the glistening jewelry in the case before her.

"Seems most everyone in our group has either left Idle County or died," Eloise continued.

Our group. The statement sent a shrieking tingle up Shelly's spine. It was as if Eloise Creed thought Elijah's disappearance with Gabriel somehow made them friends.

"I just wanted to ask . . . are you following the news about this Jonathan Flite kid out in Rhode Island? I suppose you must be. Crazy what happened to his mother last night."

Shelly pretended to know how Winifred Flite had ended up in critical condition, not to mention how everything else in the Flites' lives had spiraled downward since the beginning of summer. She had no desire to hear the details, but she now dared to look at Eloise Creed. "I'm not sure what to think." Then because she couldn't help herself: "Shouldn't *you* have known all this crazy stuff would happen? Aren't you some kind of psychic?"

The younger woman adopted a nervous smile and glanced over both her shoulders. They were alone, which meant Shelly couldn't escape without breaking God's rule against rudeness. But her stomach was churning.

"That was just something that happened when I was a kid," Eloise said in a low voice. "I stopped seeing and hearing stuff when I left Idle County. Mostly. I was in Minneapolis until a few weeks ago. Moved back here to take care of my mom. She went a bit off her rocker after Jonathan Flite hit the news again back in May. I think the press conference last night made her think the End Times are officially here." Eloise let out a worried chuckle. "Probably just mental illness. But my dad's in Arizona now, and none of my siblings wanted to come back and help."

Shelly had to offer the young woman an apologetic head dip at this. Everyone knew Abigail Creed was crazy and gave Christians everywhere a bad name. According to rumors around town, she had even left her evangelical church in Deadwood a few years back to form her own church—of one. "I'm sorry to hear," Shelly now said, though in actual fact, Idle County would be far better off the moment Abigail Creed was gone. She started to take a step toward Younkers' exit. "I really must be going—"

"Mom got a call from Alice Winterblume last night," Eloise said. "You met her back when your son found that skeleton, right? Was that in 2005?"

The hairs on Shelly's neck stood on end. She ignored Eloise's question and instead said, "It was actually Alice who called?"

"Well, a segment producer or something. They're doing a show. I got the idea it was a preshow, because they're waiting to see what happens with the Jonathan Flite stuff out east. But now that his mom is in the hospital and the whole world is watching, I think *WorldLine* wants to step in and start asking the big questions. Like, the ones the reporters started asking last night before the explosion."

Explosion?

A bloom of humiliation rose from Shelly's heart to her wrinkled face. Her willful ignorance of what had just occurred in Rhode Island was now glaring. Was she the only person who *didn't* want to hear how the dramas of Idle County were ruining even more lives? Was it no longer good enough simply to love Jesus and have faith in his saving grace? "I *did* get the call," she told Eloise, "and I can tell you I'm not going anywhere near a show if they do one. Whoever this Jonathan Flite boy really is, he's obviously just out to make trouble."

Eloise Creed had the manners to let Shelly go this time. Shelly left the store, squinting as the sunny spring day met her eyes. Was nothing sacred here in Idle County? It was a small enough place where one could never go out in public without seeing another familiar face, but why did everyone find it so perfectly agreeable to dig into private feelings and personal business? Not to mention that of all the people who had ever frightened Shelly Bryce, Eloise Creed was at the top of the list. Despite her height, the now-grown woman looked and acted normal enough, but nothing pleasant could ever replace the memory of that evening in 2010, when she had quietly tapped on Shelly's shoulder at the Idle County Seven's candlelight memorial service, right as Shelly had been wondering where on earth Cynthia Foster was and why she was absent. Eloise, just an eight-year-old string bean, had made Shelly lean over so she could whisper something.

"Oh yes, and what might that be?" Shelly had politely said, not yet realizing that this child's nature rested in darkness.

"You and Cynthia have the same guardian angels. And they're saying she's dead up in Alaska. And that she wanted to let you know you did a good job. Oh, and . . . something about Elijah. You don't have to worry about him."

Cynthia Foster had died from a hunter's stray bullet in Alaska two months after Elijah's disappearance; the hunter who shot both her and the man she had been found dead with had turned himself in to police that very night. No questions; no mystery. Yes, Cynthia had been in the same town Jillian Pope's father, Max, had lived in, and she had left one voice mail that Shelly had deleted out of spite without even hearing, but there had been nothing to suggest her death was at all related to the drama consuming Shelly back home. The Idle County Sheriff's Department did question Shelly about a call they had received from Cynthia that same day, but from what Shelly could tell, the department had considered the call a product of paranoia, as it hadn't offered any concrete leads. Coincidences were coincidences; Cynthia had simply been in the wrong place at the wrong time, trying to dig her fingers into work that belonged to the police.

Today, on the sidewalk just outside the front doors of Younkers, Shelly's shivers had returned, despite the seventy-degree morning. How was it that her attempt to escape the day's toils—and that damned phone call from *WorldLine*—had led her straight into the jaws of Gabriel Creed's younger sister and all these unwelcome memories? How was it that every time Shelly thought of Elijah's biological mother, she felt a rush of defensiveness?

For all her mistakes, Shelly had done her best with Elijah. Cynthia Foster had known this. Their intersection and reunion in 2005 had been almost too coincidental, as if some demonic force driven by Cynthia's New Age heresy had twisted its way into what should have been Elijah's peaceful, Christian existence. Jesus was the way, the truth, and the life.

"Excuse me, ma'am? Can I help you?"

A parking lot attendant holding a broom and dustpan was standing to her left, head tilted forward, as if he were assessing her lucidity.

Shelly was staring off into space in front of everyone. Thankfully, nobody seemed to be putting together who she was. "No, no," she said in as sugar-sweet a voice as possible. "I'm just all aflutter today!"

Before the attendant could even smile, she hopped into the crosswalk, forcing an approaching car to stop, and walked across the parking lot's roadway. The twinge in her gut pushing her to ponder Elijah's disappearance again was growing stronger every moment, after all those years she had spent trying to move on, to build a life free of mystery and grief. What did it say about her care as a mother that she wanted to keep it all buried? That she had relegated her adopted son to the past and moved forward happily?

When Shelly reached her car, she turned it on, backed out of her parking space (without checking to see who might be standing behind her), and decided to drive east. Only after she reached Hunter Avenue, turned left, and passed the last intersection of End Haven did she realize she meant to continue on, toward the Moon Woods.

2038

J UVENILE PROBATION. It sounded so *official*. Jimmy Barber had been through the hearing process himself (and recently), but it had involved very few flashing lights, crowds of reporters, and screamed requests for details. It was Monday, May 31, and Jonathan Flite was now eighteen years old plus a day. He was wearing an ill-fitting suit with a light blue shirt and gray tie. His pants hung at least an inch too high over his dress shoes, but he seemed not to care. Jimmy, of course, had already begun formulating a plan to take his friend suit shopping once he was finally free—today's look was strictly temporary.

He had offered to join Jonathan at his release hearing at the Garrahy Judicial Complex in Providence, with full intent of waiting in the hallway during the probation and parole hearing. Jonathan had rushed through his own birthday celebration at Crescent yesterday evening, blushing through the boys' mostly tone-deaf rendition of "Happy Birthday" and eating only a sliver of cake before hurrying upstairs. Jimmy had not found a good time to present him with the scarf from Nordstrom and the two books from Scripted Corner, so he had brought the gifts to his math tutoring session at Crescent this morning; they were hidden in his favorite leather satchel. But his friend had come downstairs looking clammy, pale, and altogether unready to accept something as flighty as a birthday gift. Instead, Jimmy had asked if he wanted company at the courthouse. Jonathan had smiled faintly and, with only a trickle of hesitation, nodded.

Jimmy had hoped Deputy Clark Keedlesby, the dapper young sheriff's deputy who was driving Jonathan to Providence, would allow him to ride in the police car as well, but it took only a raised eyebrow from the man to let Jimmy know that he would have to drive separately. "We'll be going through the security entrance anyway," the deputy added. Jimmy, thanking his lucky stars that he had received a flashy BMW for his eighteenth birthday on March 14 (despite the plethora of self-driving taxis available for his use), left Crescent ten minutes ahead of Jonathan so he could scope out the courthouse scene.

It was a fifty-minute drive to the brown-brick judiciary complex. Sure as always that he probably looked miniature behind the wheel of the BMW, Jimmy approached the building via Friendship Street so he could check the status of the rear security entrance. Lining the sidewalk on the left side of the gate was a flock of at least fifty reporters and cameramen. Despite the fact that they weren't even supposed to know about this confidential juvenile hearing, they were standing there like birds waiting to be fed. To the right of the gate were about twenty-five protesters holding signs. The first one Jimmy saw read "**NO KILLERS ON OUR STREETS**." The one next to it read "**FLITE DESERVES THE BITE.**" There was one sign higher than the others on the far right whose holder was obscured in the crowd. It read "**BLASPHEMERS WILL BURN.**"

Jimmy drove to the opposite corner of the complex, parked, and then walked back around on Dorrance Street, past the six-story courthouse's front doors. The elevated patio preceding them was empty, save for a lone woman sitting on the surrounding stone ledge sipping a cup of coffee. She didn't even glance up as Jimmy passed. Parked to Jimmy's immediate right, however, facing him along the street's nearest lane, were seven electric vans decorated with news-station logos. Because their crews were currently at the rear security entrance, they were empty and quiet, but Jimmy knew they would later be poised for Jonathan's eventual exit from the main doors following his hearing.

Jimmy walked left, back onto Friendship Street, and started down the sidewalk, toward the reporters and protesters who were waiting for Jonathan to drive through the rear entrance. As sickening as it generally was that these reporters' livelihoods depended on creating drama for the masses out of other people's lives, he couldn't help but shiver with anticipation at the prospect of their noticing him in the crowd and descending upon him with questions he would refuse to answer. He had already promised Jonathan that he wouldn't make any unplanned statements, and Jimmy was nothing if not true to his word. Even so, he adjusted his collar, exaggerated his overly compensating posture, and approached the fray.

Both the reporters on his end of the gate and the protesters on the far end were calm, whispering among themselves, waiting. No sign of Jonathan yet.

Jimmy hovered at the back of the flock. A few of the reporters and cameramen glanced at him without a second thought, as if he were simply some kid looking to get on television. When nobody's gaze lingered on him with even the slightest bit of intrigue, Jimmy coughed and faux-fixed his already perfect hair. This garnered only a few more sideways glances.

Deflated, Jimmy began pushing through the crowd. "Excuse me. Excuse me, please," he said. "I'm trying to get through! This is a sidewalk, not a side*stand*." Gaining a few more miffed glances, Jimmy aimed himself toward the security gate. Around him were microphones and cameras of all varieties, from garden-variety, independent journalists with wannabe-official blog names labeled on their cameras to full-on, streaming conglomerate subsidiaries from far beyond Newport—ABCs, NBCs, and CBSs, many with station names he didn't even recognize. He did recognize the city names on some of their microphone and camera decals, however: Boston, Manchester, Hartford, New Haven, Albany, Buffalo, White Plains, and even one from New York City.

Just as he emerged at the front of the crowd, murmurs arose, first from the reporters behind him and then from the protesters on the far side of the unblocked driveway. Approaching them on Friendship Street was Deputy Keedlesby's squad car. As the man began turning toward the closed security gate to await its opening, Jimmy saw Jonathan Flite in the back seat. His friend was red-faced, looking straight ahead with an emotionally naked expression.

The reporters and protesters were already screaming. Jimmy joined in the fray, waving to hail Jonathan's attention through the squad car's window. Jonathan continued to look forward, as if fighting all urges to glance out either side of the vehicle.

Jimmy rushed forward to the window and knocked on it. "Jonathan! It's me!" he yelled. "Ask the cop if I can follow you through!"

As the vertically barred gate began opening with a mechanical whine, Jonathan glanced out the window. The moment he saw Jimmy, his face scrunched into a slightly troubled expression, but then he smiled and shook his head, yelling something to Deputy Keedlesby that Jimmy couldn't hear.

Behind Jimmy, the news crews were closing in, pressing him against the car. Inside it, Jonathan seemed to notice that his stylish friend was in danger of being trampled, perhaps even thrown under the car's tires. Jonathan once again yelled something to the driving deputy. Jimmy turned around as much as he could, breathing in every waft of the crushing body heat, every molecule of perfume, every dose of light from the camera flashes. Tingles ran up and down his spine as the reporters screamed from his side of the driveway.

"*Jonathan, are you afraid of what might happen if you walk free?*"

"*Mr. Flite, do you plan to stay in Newport?*"

"*We have reports that City Hall has received bomb threats if they let you walk today! Do you have anything to say about this?*"

Filtering through from the other side were even louder screams from the protesters.

"*Jonathan Flite should have the death sentence!*"

"*Get this killer off our streets!*"

"*You think Ellen Graber would want him walking free around her kids?*"

The squad car began easing through the gate. Jimmy turned back to the vehicle's window and saw Jonathan pointing toward the windshield. Deputy Keedlesby had slowed to wait for the gate to finish opening, so Jimmy fought his way to the man's window and knocked on it. The deputy took a moment to recognize him and then, with an eye roll, gestured with his head toward the security lot. He accelerated toward it, and Jimmy trotted along with the car. As they crossed the threshold, the reporters and protesters fell away.

Jimmy glanced through Jonathan's window as Deputy Keedlesby pulled ahead to park. Through the glass, Jonathan gave him a quick nod. If he was exasperated by Jimmy's desire to be on the front lines, he showed it only by holding back another smile.

He'll thank me one day, Jimmy thought. He turned around to face the reporters and protesters, who for the moment seemed confused as to why a random boy from the sidewalk had followed Jonathan Flite into the lot. Then, to Jimmy's surging relief, one of the reporters screamed, "It's Jimmy Barber!"

Jimmy recognized the voice, even as the rise of yells from other reporters threatened to consume it. It belonged to Lydia Clark, the blogger who had ambushed him at Scripted Corner. She was waving from the front of the crowd, somehow content to be dressed in a terrible lavender pantsuit that looked as though it had come from a 1990s thrift store. "Jimmy! Lydia Clark from *Providence Today*! We met the other day! Can I have a word?"

Just as the gate began to close, Jimmy fluttered his hair back, hoping it was long enough to catch a bit of wind. He adopted a glare for Lydia and remained silent. In his pocket, his ActoPhone suddenly began vibrating at uneven intervals. Message alerts.

"Are you here to support Jonathan Flite today?" Lydia Clark asked, leaning sideways to beat the gate. The reporters around her hushed as they waited for an answer. "Jimmy? Can we have a statement? Do you know anything about the rumors that the FBI is taking Jonathan Flite's past-life-memory claims seriously? That they're even confiscating his fan mail? Does he really have credible information linking last November's attack to Victor Zobel and the Geneva bombing?"

Jimmy froze, momentarily losing control of his aloof expression in favor of wide-eyed concern. Of all the people connected to Jonathan from the rehabilitation facility, he was the one most likely to have let those FBI details out of the bag. He had not, though; the bureau had been very serious about maintaining the secrecy of their investigation.

The gate had closed, but his ActoPhone was still alight with vibrating notifications. Jimmy dug into his pocket and looked at the slew of ActoShouts now dominating his hub.

> *Keep fighting for your friend, @JimmyBarber.*

> *You're stupid for trying to save him from the electric chair, @JimmyBarber.*

> *Sweater tied around your shoulders? It's almost summer, @JimmyBarber.*

> *@JimmyBarber – Rot in hell with your boyfriend, you faggot fashionista.*

Jimmy flashed what he hoped was an incredulous glance at the cameras and crowd. Is that what these people hoped to report on? Speculation about his quite legitimate bisexuality, which Jonathan most definitely (and comfortably) did not share?

He glanced at the next shout.

*Jesus Saves, @JimmyBarber. To follow Jonathan
Flite is to be a minion of Satan. Do you see my sign?*

Ignoring the new screams that had drowned out those of
Lydia Clark, Jimmy glanced up and through the gate again, this
time at the signs bobbing up and down on the driveway entrance's
left side. After reading six of them, his eyes fell once again on the
tall one reading "**BLASPHEMERS WILL BURN.**" Whoever was
holding it was obscured in the crowd, but the text seemed to align
with the "Jesus Saves" ActoShout.

Jimmy looked back at his phone and clicked on the shouter's
Acto name: @WestonCarrow. When the profile loaded, he saw that
it belong to a pale, long-faced man with bright and beady blue
eyes that almost rattled off the phone's screen. His graying red hair
was thin and receding, and his mouth was pulled back in what
looked like a perpetual wince. The fine print of his ActoProfile
read, "Preacher, Healer, Prophesier, and Founder of the Children
of God—Eastern Chapter—Americas." Jimmy wondered if the
Children of God had other chapters, or if this man had simply
deluded himself into thinking his singular point of view had somehow achieved a legitimate global presence.

"Jimmy! Can you tell us anything at all?" Lydia Clark continued, yanking Jimmy's gaze back to the crowd. Beyond the gate,
she and her competitors were waiting like salivating dogs. On the
left side of the driveway, the protesters had begun chanting "Flite
deserves the bite!" over and over. Somewhere among them was the
pallid, taut-skinned Weston Carrow.

Jimmy took a step backward, shaking his head at Lydia,
hoping the morning light was catching him at a good angle. He
had a duty to Jonathan, and doing it would probably drive these

reporters and protesters crazy. Which would, of course, inadvertently feed their frenzy.

"Have a most pleasant day," he said through the gate's bars. Then he turned around and rushed toward Jonathan, who was being escorted by Deputy Keedlesby toward the courthouse's rear door.

2005

ELIJAH BRYCE BIKED SLOWLY down Lemon Avenue, dreading the prospect of hearing Damon Jacoby's bike pedals zipping out from some side street or driveway, ready to make his life a living hell. It was Saturday morning, June 18, and a perfectly agreeable one—birds chirping, sun shining, and just enough of a breeze to remind Elijah why people liked to wake up every day. Yet his last trip to this library had started out the same way and then turned into a nightmare. Caution was his rule now.

When he reached Lemon Avenue's intersection with northbound Main Street, he saw a small, nimble figure in the castle-like library's front yard, near the grayish-tan bricks lining the building's base. It took only a second for Elijah's heart to leap with luck. It was Molly Butler. Today, her black hair was pulled back in a ponytail, and she was wearing red shorts and a loose fitting white T-shirt. In her hands was a large watering can. Elijah approached the steel bike rack and made a rattling sound as he parked. Molly looked up, focused her eyes through the sun, and smiled.

"Hey!" she said. "I was hoping you'd come here one of these days. I'm just watering the flowers."

Elijah grinned. "Wouldn't it be easier with a hose?"

"Yeah, if it reached," Molly said. "I tried already. At least it's been rainy lately." She followed Elijah toward the mahogany front doors. "Library closes early today, in about an hour. Miss Peabody's going through the computer to see how many books are being checked out lately. I guess the city owns this place now, and they're thinking about shutting it down."

"What? This place is awesome!" Elijah said, holding the door for Molly as she stepped into the medieval-looking foyer. "Didn't the last librarian own it herself before? Mrs. Grime?"

"She left it to the city when she died, I guess with enough money to keep it going for a while," Molly said. "But the new librarian, Miss Peabody, says Mayor Havisham is a tool and wants to close the library and put the money toward something else. I guess Mrs. Grime didn't 'stipulate' how long specifically the money was supposed to go toward the library. The mayor is a lawyer and is trying to screw us all out of it."

Molly grimaced as they walked past the empty front counter, which was circular and lay on the left side of the main floor under a large, centered atrium. A second floor of bookshelves rose on either side of it, forming two opposing balconies. On their right, a large, wooden staircase spiraled upward. If Elijah remembered correctly, there was another staircase somewhere off to the left, on the far west side, buried amid the rows of books.

Just as he was about to part from Molly and go seek out anything resembling old phone directories, he heard footsteps approaching from the shelves along the back wall. Miss Peabody appeared, and she was holding a hand to her nose, attempting to stifle a sneeze. Good morn—" she started, but she could not hold it any longer. She covered her nose and exploded. "Oh, man, that always happens back there," she said after grabbing a Kleenex from the counter. "I swear, it must be the dust, even though I've been trying to keep this place as clean as possible."

"I like the smell of old books," Molly said.

Elijah smiled. It was also one of his favorite smells.

Miss Peabody nodded with an irritated expression that indicated she was still upset about the sneeze. "Don't we all? But unless Mrs. Grime kept a cat in here that I still don't know about, I must be severely allergic to it."

Molly chuckled. It seemed she and Miss Peabody were already on unusually friendly terms. This librarian was young compared to Mrs. Grime, perhaps in her early thirties. She wore wiry glasses and a heavy ponytail, always held back with the same flowery clip.

"You're new," she said to Elijah after making sure the sneezes had abated. "I mean, I recognize you, but you're not usually here with *this* one." She raised an eyebrow at Molly, but with a snarky grin. "Are you guys new chums or something?"

"Actually, we sort of just met," Elijah said, glimmering at the chance to be part of their small circle of friendship. When Molly smiled and opened her mouth to speak, however, he held his breath. The last thing he wanted was for Miss Peabody to know about Damon Jacoby.

"Yeah, we've sort of been here randomly at the same times," Molly said. "He has books to return."

"Well, have at it then," Miss Peabody said, circling to the back of the counter. "I'll get them checked in while they're fresh."

Elijah took the books from his backpack and handed them to her. "Hmm, *In God We're Dust*," she continued. "A lot of people are talking about this one."

"It was pretty cool," Elijah replied, glancing at Molly, who was staring at the book with narrowed eyes.

Mrs. Peabody looked at Molly as well, shrugged, and then said, "Can I help you find anything else today, Elijah Bryce? Or is that it?"

Elijah took in half a breath. "I'm actually wondering if you have any old phone books here," he said slowly. "Like, ones from a while ago. The late eighties or early nineties, I mean."

Miss Peabody surveyed him with a curious expression, and whatever she wanted to ask, she didn't. Molly also gave him a sideways, inquisitive glance.

"I'm just trying to find out about a name," he said in a quiet voice.

"We do have a row of phone directories, actually," Miss Peabody replied. "Mrs. Grime kept them back by the old newspapers. Most of the papers from before the digital age are on microfilm, though."

Elijah had seen detectives trolling through microfilm on television, but he had never looked at it himself. He glanced at Molly before following Miss Peabody. For a moment, it seemed as though the dark-haired girl wanted to follow them. Just as Elijah was about to invite her along, however, Molly raised her arm and offered them a slight wave of her fingers. She turned and headed toward the spiral staircase.

"Here are the Idle County directories," Miss Peabody told Elijah when they reached the northwest corner of the library, gesturing toward the bottom shelf on their right. "You'll find both the white and yellow pages in each directory, and they go back pretty far. 1944 is the oldest, I think." She put her hands on her hips and observed the shelf for a moment, then turned to Elijah with a matter-of-fact face. "Is this what you're looking for?"

"It's perfect. Thanks."

"No problem," Miss Peabody said. She turned and walked away, making a rhythmic, snapping sound with her tongue on the roof of her mouth, as if to the beat of a song. She wasn't exactly the same brand of welcoming as Mrs. Grime had been, but Elijah liked how no-nonsense she seemed.

He glanced down at the row of phone books. They were nearly identical to the ones he found on his front porch every summer. They got progressively yellowed and tattered as his gaze moved right to left, from the most recent ones toward the very oldest. Miss Peabody had been correct; the first directory was from 1944, it being by far the thinnest and most faded of the bunch.

Elijah grabbed the one from 1990. He opened it and began scrolling through the "E" names. "Earnshaw" would be toward the beginning.

Eagan, Eaglebrown, Eagleton, Eaperpie . . .

Then he saw it.

Earnshaw.

There were two entries, as he had expected there would be, based on the internet obituaries. The first one read "Earnshaw, Daniel and Louise," followed by a street address. Elijah's pulse raced as he read the second set of names: "Earnshaw, Elijah C. and Cynthia L. Foster."

Elijah C. Earnshaw was dead according to the obituaries, but Cynthia L. Foster? The jury was still out on her. The address next to the names was an End Haven address.

408 S. Cage St.

Having come prepared, Elijah grabbed a pen from his pocket and scribbled the woman's information on the back of his hand. Either she and Elijah Earnshaw had been married while she kept her maiden name, or they had been unmarried and living together. Had they a son? One they hadn't wanted?

Elijah shut the directory, placed it back on the shelf, and walked toward the library's main atrium. Miss Peabody must have been off working under some mountain of books, because the space was empty once again. Surely Molly Butler was still somewhere upstairs. Seeing as she was spending her sunny Saturday in a library without anyone her own age, Elijah figured she could use a good-bye just as much as he could. He ascended the staircase, wondering if this somehow meant he was starting to like girls the way all the other boys did. Wasn't this the sort of thing somebody with a crush would do?

The stairs ended in front of a long aisle that stretched toward the easternmost side of the library. On both sides of it were rows of tall wooden shelves that extended left and right, each holding a ladder that was connected on a sliding track line.

Elijah walked down the aisle. His light, sneakered footsteps made the wooden floor creak. He looked left and right, hoping to find Molly among the books. Three rows down, he glanced left and saw her. She was sitting alone at a small table under a giant, circular stained glass window. It was made of a million bright and colored pieces, as if it belonged in a cathedral, and soft, coral-colored light shone through it, making the visible dust sparkle. At the sound of Elijah's footsteps, Molly looked up.

"Hi," she said.

"Hey," he replied.

"Did you find your phone books?"

She was still about forty feet away from him. He walked slowly down the aisle, confident enough that he wasn't intruding. "Yeah, I did." After a glimmer of curiosity from Molly threatened to expose his secrets, he said, "Weren't you going to help Miss Peabody?"

"She's almost done for today, apparently," Molly said. She looked at the stained glass window, then seemingly at the very air between her and Elijah. "I found this spot last summer and kind of love it. Makes me feel peaceful, I guess." She sighed, then glanced downward. "What's that on your hand?"

Elijah froze, and he could tell by the heat rising in his face that he was blushing. He had forgotten how obvious the street address inked on his hand would be. "Nothing," he said. "Just an address."

"For . . . ?"

A year ago, Elijah would have had friends with whom to share the secret of the Moon Woods, the ashes, and the jawbone. Now it seemed to be his alone. "I'm not sure who to tell," he said. He gestured questioningly at the chair across from Molly, and she extended her hand toward it with an encouraging nod. He pulled it out and sat down. "I dug up something in the Moon Woods that a few kids at school were obsessing about last year, before all that cult stuff happened. It's kind of . . . weird."

Molly's eyes ignited with fascination as Elijah relayed the story of his bike ride to the Knoll, the stone-marked X, the ashes, and the jawbone. At his mention of the possible human remains, Molly gasped, but at the same time, she leaned closer over the table. When Elijah finished, his arms and hands were sweaty, and his legs felt shaky and numb. "If it's a real human jawbone," he said, "it could be important. Like, something to call the police about. But I wanted to go to this Earnshaw house first to see if I might be missing something."

"When are you going?" Molly asked.

Elijah shrugged. "Sometime before this ink washes off, I guess. I was thinking today."

After a moment of hesitation, his new acquaintance said, "Want company?"

2038

WINIFRED FLITE FOUGHT HER WAY through the flock of reporters, photographers, and cameramen as she left the Garrahy Judicial Complex. Their questions didn't even matter to her anymore; they were all the same, and there were no new answers she could give. Jonathan was free. Despite being confined to the state of Rhode Island until his nineteenth birthday, this was it. Either the media would tire of his story, or they'd start asking the questions that really mattered.

Mr. Chase, the sixty-year-old driver Winifred had hired for the day, was parked in a pickup zone between two of the news vans. He was waiting by the car's closer rear door, looking more nervous than she would have liked. She had decided against driving her own Jaguar or ordering a self-driving car, because neither would have assured successful maneuvering in the event the crowd became unruly. Behind Mr. Chase, directly across the street, were the sign-wielding protesters who had earlier been stationed outside the rear security entrance. They seemed to have doubled in number since the start of the hearing, and now two police officers were patrolling their front line.

When Winifred was about ten feet from Mr. Chase's black Mercedes limousine, she heard the reporters hush. Taking a split second to jerk her neck back toward the doors, she saw that Jimmy Barber, with Jonathan standing behind him, had stopped at the top of the steps.

Oh, please, no.

Jimmy clear his throat. "You people need to realize that you'd be better off leaving Jonathan Flite alone," he began. "You also may want to start asking *why* somebody would have taken the time to plan a break-in at Crescent to silence him. . . ."

Winifred stopped listening and rushed through the crowd of distracted reporters. Based on what had transpired during Jonathan's probation hearing, she now felt—with truly cemented inklings of dread—that the media circus had only just begun. Judge Wallace had demanded as a condition of Jonathan's probation that he begin sharing his story in a more transparent fashion so that the public might better understand why the court saw fit to try him as a juvenile and release him at age eighteen. Based on her son's posture now, which looked alarmingly acquiescent, it had taken just ten shaky steps out of the courthouse for him to start complying. Adding to the nightmare was that he was allowing Jimmy Barber to be his "voice."

Judge Wallace had also taken much care during the hearing to impress upon Jonathan the seriousness of his decision to allow the boy to walk free. He had also reiterated his belief (a continued belief, since the incident with Ellen Graber) that Jonathan's recorded instances of violence had been the result of living under the stress of having divulged a worrisome secret, only to have nobody believe him.

"You, my friend, need to learn to express who you really are without caring what other people think," the man had told Jonathan in a flat, matter-of-fact tone. "I'll leave the nitty-gritty up to your therapists, but what I want to see from you in one year's time is a sense of confidence in your place in society. It's going to be a challenging year, because the vultures outside may not leave you alone, and they may try to dictate your place themselves. You're going to have to buck up and stand up for yourself."

Jonathan had been seated at a white table and staring at its scuffed surface, listening to the judge with a bowed head.

"Do you understand what I'm saying, young man?" Wallace had pressed. "Your mother says you've made some new friends since the incident last November but that you've been hiding out and keeping silent about all the things you claimed troubled you in the first place. I'm here to say that it's time for you to deal with whatever truth is behind it all. And next year, I want to see progress. I need to see proof that I made the right decision with you. What are your thoughts on this?"

The judge's gaze had bored into Jonathan, whose face remained bowed.

"Please look at me, Jonathan."

Slowly, Jonathan had raised his eyes and looked at Judge Wallace. "I'm scared to deal with it," he said. "All the times I've tried, nobody has listened."

At this, Winifred had of course blazed under a hot rush of guilt. Yet that guilt, ever-present now, had been addressed. She wanted no part in her son's mysterious link to the missing Idle

County Seven kids, because any acknowledgment of it meant she'd have to follow through on that impossible task of attempting to solve the mysteries of why they somehow shared a link to begin with. This could open doors of thought she wanted to keep closed. Her therapist, Kate Crookston, had recognized almost immediately that Winifred's inner discord was connected to her resolute fear of facing the reason for her son's condition. Even the New Agey, hoo-hah stories about other kids being born with memories of other lives (yes, Winifred had begun to read up on the subject) didn't explain why Jonathan would have been born with *seven* sets of memories. Nowhere out there was a recorded case of this, not even in the work of Dr. Malcolm Stevenson, the now-deceased psychiatrist who had spent his career traveling the world studying past-life memory claims. When Winifred had finally Googled the subject, she realized almost immediately that some of the pages detailing the man's work were ones she had found in Jonathan's internet history long ago, after he had finally started talking at age eight. Oh, how the past liked to mock her.

Now four reporters and their cameramen had turned their attention back to Winifred, positioning themselves between the sidewalk and the Mercedes. Mr. Chase rushed to the far side of his limousine, opened the back left door, and beckoned for her to enter that way. As Winifred rushed to the protesters' side, the pursuing reporters assaulted her with a barrage of questions, but only the usual ones: Was she afraid of Jonathan? Afraid that he might be a threat now that he was free? Afraid that the world would blow up in her face? Check. Check. Check. All of the above. Hiding her terror behind an unsympathetic, makeup-caked grimace, Winifred ducked into the simply adorned limousine.

"I'll go get your boy and his friend," Mr. Chase said, glancing at Jonathan and Jimmy. He slammed the door behind Winifred.

No sooner had the door locks clicked into place than Winifred glanced up, out the left window, and noticed one of the protesters walking slowly across the road. It was the person holding the sign reading "**BLASPHEMERS WILL BURN**." He was moving straight past the closest patrolling officer, who was dealing with the fanatical woman on the far left side holding the sign reading "**FLITE DESERVES THE BITE**."

The red-haired, middle-aged man walking toward the limousine was tall and thin, and his pale, shiny skin was pulled taut over his high, sharp cheekbones. He was wearing a constricted, partial smile, and he approached with an eerie calmness, seeming to pause time, because nobody was noticing him.

"Mr. Chase, there's a man out—" Winifred started, for a second forgetting the driver hadn't entered the car after closing her door. She glanced right, out the window facing the courthouse, where Jonathan and Jimmy were fighting through the camera-wielding harpies. They were still ten feet away, and Mr. Chase was standing with his back to the right-side door, waiting for them.

Please let the door locks work, Winifred thought, turning left again to look out the window. When she peered through it, however, her body seized, and her stomach rushed to her throat.

The high-cheekboned man had reached the limousine and was crouching down in front of its tinted glass, still holding his sign upright with one hand. He was staring straight at Winifred, wearing a white, flowing shirt whose top two buttons were undone. Winifred was a foot away from him, through the narrow pane. When she looked at his pale neck, she could see an organized pattern of scars. Knife slits? Burns?

"Jesus," Winifred whispered. She forced her arms to move, to grope blindly around the back seat for her purse, in which lay the can of pepper spray she now carried everywhere. If the man were somehow able to open the door, it would be her only defense. In what seemed like slow motion just as her fingers clasped the canister, he raised his free hand and pressed it to the window. On it was another scar, this one a branded burn mark in the shape of a Christian cross.

"Those who lead us toward the End Times must be destroyed!" the man shouted through the glass. His voice was low, but it had a reedy quality that made it sound like an anxious whine. Winifred had the sudden inkling that she was face-to-face with a madman, the kind people always heard about in the news and saw in movies. In his eyes was the same blazing (yet somehow disassociated) look she had seen in serial killers' mug shots, terrorist beheading videos, and, most recently, Cardinal Jean-Claude Apostol's ActoVid upload just moments before he blew the city of Geneva to his precious kingdom come.

The limousine door to her right opened, and Jonathan jumped into the back seat next to her. "Get in and shut the door," she said immediately, gesturing suddenly to the left window, where the man still stood with his hand pressed to the glass. Mr. Chase had now closed the door behind Jimmy Barber, who was climbing to the lengthwise seat on the far side. Upon finding his place, he immediately turned around to look at the man with the scars.

"That's one of the guys who ActoShouted me," Jimmy said. "He's the founder of some group called the Children of God. Why the heck are they letting him so close?"

He scoffed in a way that sounded much too dramatic to Winifred, as if he were playing the role of "supportive friend" in some B movie. She couldn't pinpoint why this made her even more nervous.

Jimmy shook his head as he turned back toward Winifred and Jonathan. He then thrust his phone in their faces. On it was the ActoProfile of a man named Weston Carrow. Winifred grabbed the phone and looked closely at his photo. It was indeed the man outside, and since the start of the court hearing, he had already posted nine ActoShouts about Jesus, hell, and Jonathan Flite's being a harbinger of the Antichrist. Outside, two police offers were escorting him back to the line of protesters.

Winifred was shaking. For the first time, she felt truly threatened by those who hated Jonathan. Carrow, second in vitriol only to Craig Graber, had posted his most recent shout just seconds before approaching the limousine.

> *Jonathan Flite's New Age claims are a threat to Christ's Kingdom of Peace here on Earth. Be on your Soul Guard, for we are on ours.*

Weston Carrow was the first person since last year's killer at Crescent to acknowledge publicly the inherent ideological threat in Jonathan's claims about having memories of the Idle County Seven. It appeared the man thought the story's non-Christian, reincarnation-related implications were even worse than the fact that Jonathan had strangled Ellen Graber to begin with. How was it that religion could so crushingly derail people from rationality?

Jonathan, sitting next to Winifred, put a hand on her arm. "It's okay, Mom," he said. "The cops are taking him back to the protesters."

"Yeah, to the *nut jobs*," Jimmy added from the lengthwise seat.

Then, with a relishing sigh, he said, "I think I need to have the driver drop me off at my car in the back. I can't fight any more reporters today!"

Winifred wanted to snap at Jimmy for having jumped into the limousine in the first place, but she refrained. Glancing at her son and handing him Jimmy's phone, she said, "You really think it was a good idea for Jimmy to have made that statement?" Her vocal tone hinted at the old bite with which she used to accost him, except now it took only five seconds for tears to follow. "I just . . . I think it might draw even more attention. I'm not sure I can handle that."

"Me either," Jonathan said. "At least Sounder'll be there when we get to your house. He's already behind us." He sat back in the limousine's side seat, staring at Jimmy's phone and reading through Weston Carrow's ActoProfile. "I was just testing the waters with those reporters. Trying to do what Judge Wallace said."

"And they *loved* it," Jimmy added. "If we keep giving them nothing gossipy and telling them to investigate *why* someone wanted you dead, it'll keep us classy. Trust me."

Winifred glanced at her son, who shrugged just as the driver's door opened. Mr. Chase entered the limousine and was finally free to take them away.

"Quite the crowd out there," he yelled through the front divider with a quick inhale, skirting the obvious issue that he was about to drive Rhode Island's infamous nurse killer home for lunch. When they pulled away from the courthouse toward Clifford Street, leaving the journalists, protesters, and Jonathan's juvenile delinquency behind them, Winifred reached into her purse, pulled out the flask she had bought on her last trip to Morocco, and took a drink.

2005

4 08 SOUTH CAGE STREET both was and was not what Elijah Bryce had expected. Slowing on his bike with Molly Butler at his side, he read a sign that stood in the yard.

Psychic Cynthia
Palm and Tarot Readings
~ First Readings Are FREE ~
Walk-Ins Welcome

The words were painted in lavishly colored letters that reminded Elijah of 1960s hippies he had seen on television. Sure enough, when he glanced toward the house's large veranda, he saw a ceramic peace symbol hanging where other people might usually have secured flowers. Off to the left was a porch swing, its back support just visible beyond a row of flowers blooming from a planter. From what Elijah could tell, it, too, was painted with bright, rainbow colors. A tangle of cedar bushes and an ailing flower garden lined the front of the house, and ivy crawled up its side. On the left edge of the yard was another strip of cedar bushes, separating the lawn from that of the next-door neighbors.

"Well, I think that's her," were Elijah's first words.

"You're sure her name was Cynthia?"

"The phone book said Elijah C. Earnshaw and Cynthia L. Foster."

Molly wheeled her bike forward so that she was directly at the head of the front sidewalk. "Well, then, I guess you know she's still living here. Do you think she works on Saturdays? It says 'first readings are free.'" She started wheeling forward.

"No, I can't! My mom wouldn't like—"

A female voice interrupted them from across the yard.

"Can I help you two?"

A middle aged woman with flaming red hair was ambling around the far corner of the house, toward them. In her arms was a basket of what appeared to be gardening tools. She walked slightly unevenly, as if neither foot ever quite found the right spot on the ground. The tone of her voice made Elijah wonder if she thought they were there to cause trouble.

"Are you here for readings?" Psychic Cynthia Foster asked.

"N—"

"Yes," Molly cut in.

"Do your parents know you're here?"

When Elijah fumbled to find words, Molly took charge with a polite smile. "Well, no, but they wouldn't mind if we were. We're just curious—that's all."

"Curious, huh?" Cynthia Foster regarded them with her lower

jaw thrust outward and her mouth slightly open. Through his fear that she might somehow get them in trouble, Elijah noticed how beautiful her face was. A tremor of familiarity emanated from her, and as Elijah's heart latched onto it, he fluttered with nerves. If his mother were to find out about his quest to see if he had any biological relation to Cynthia the Psychic, she would never forgive him.

"We've never had our fortunes told before," Molly continued. "I mean, if you call it that. I've only seen it done in movies."

The woman considered them for another long moment before raising her eyebrows.

"Okay, then." She beckoned to them and walked toward her house. "We'll set down a spread for you and see what the cards have to say. Which one of you wants the reading? How about one tarot reading, one palm reading? How does that sound? And I'm Cynthia, by the way. I'm sure you've guessed that already. What are your names?"

Again, it was Molly who spoke. "I'm Molly, and this is Elijah."

For a moment, Cynthia's face froze, as if one of their names had caught her off guard. Her gaze darted quickly to Elijah, and she looked him over head to toe, almost too quickly to be noticed. Had the woman just officially recognized him?

She seemed to waver between hesitation and enthusiasm. Then she walked toward the house. "This way." She led them through a light screen door into a dimly lit dining room and ushered them to sit down at a small wooden table. There, on its flat, scuffed surface, was a deck of cards. They looked almost like regular playing cards, but when Cynthia sat down and started shuffling them, Elijah saw they were decorated with pictures that looked nothing like the ones on the cards he and Alec Pent had played War with when they were still friends.

"You," Cynthia said, pointing to Elijah. "I'm getting the feeling that you need this more than she does. But I'm not going to ask why." She ran a finger along her forehead and cleared a long strand of red hair from her eyes. "Have you ever had a tarot reading before?" When Elijah shook his head, she continued, "Of course you haven't. That's why you two showed up today, right?" There was a glint of disbelief in Cynthia's eyes, as if she knew they hadn't come here expecting to find a psychic—or at least somebody pretending to be one.

Cynthia fanned the cards in a horizontal row and waved her left hand slowly over them. Elijah had no idea what a tarot card reading was, and he could barely fathom how his ambition to dig up the stone-marked **X** had landed him in the house of a woman who might be his biological mother. He was playing with fire, and if he wasn't careful, his life at home might go the way of his social life: a fast, depressing spiral downward.

The psychic pulled a card from the spread. "The Eight of Cups," she said, setting the card in front of her. It was upside down to Elijah, but from what he could see, it depicted a landscape of sorts, which included a strange sun and moon in the same circle and eight chalices stacked in two uneven rows. "Now, Elijah, and—forgive me—what is your last name?"

"Bryce," he said, with a trickle of hesitation.

Molly, who was intensely watching the tarot card, did not see Cynthia flush.

"Bryce, huh?" It was obvious to Elijah now that his name meant something to the woman and that she was making light of it. It was almost aggravating the way some adults thought young people couldn't pick up on anything. When Cynthia continued, however, it sounded forced, as if her throat were tight. "Now, Elijah

Bryce, we have the Eight of Cups. This first card represents you at present—and the heart of whatever matter is currently affecting you most." She glanced at the card. "Not exactly surprising for someone your age. You're at a point in your life where you're focusing on your own personal truth and looking for answers. You're trying to find the facts in the midst of a very confusing time. How old are you?"

"I'm twelve, almost thirteen," Elijah said.

Now even Cynthia's smile tightened. "Again, not surprising. You're realizing your childhood is coming to an end, and adult issues are about to become *your* issues. I wouldn't be surprised if you've been worrying about a lot of things as of late. Am I right?"

Elijah glanced at Molly, who seemed to be taking Cynthia very seriously. The girl glanced right back at him, and he saw an odd, almost terrified look in her eyes.

"Don't worry if this feels strange," Cynthia assured him, letting out a sigh. "Most people feel weird about it their first time. Life is like that with a lot of things." She smiled to herself, then drew another card.

"The Two of Swords." She lay it horizontally over the first card to form a small cross.

Elijah swallowed. His throat was completely dry.

"This, Elijah, is what opposes the matter at heart. You're denying truths in yourself that only you can know. Because of this, you've lost people, but only because you've driven them away out of your own fear."

When Cynthia flashed him what he construed to be a knowing glance, Elijah thought about Alec Pent, Natalie Pent, and Pauline Gilbert, the friends he had grown up with but now no longer spoke to. After his peculiar encounter with Alec Pent's shirtless chest, he had been too embarrassed to look any of them in the eye, even the two girls and their parents. Pauline in particular had continued to invite him places, but after a few months of sixth grade and no success, she had given up. Only after they were no longer speaking had Elijah realized the only alternative was utter loneliness.

"Strength," Cynthia said in a lighter voice, drawing a third card. On it was a woman who appeared to be taming a lion. Above her head was a strange figure **8** symbol. Cynthia set the card directly below the first two. "This, your subconscious mind knows, is a key part of who you are. Even if you can't always recognize it, you are a strong person, and you can endure hardships with the best of them. Not only can you deal calmly with frustration, but for you, getting angry is rarely the answer. You're a compassionate person, Elijah, and you have a strong sense of what others are feeling. You're kind to them without question." Then, in a surprising gesture, she winked at him. "I don't need a card to see that in you."

Elijah's heart raced faster as he realized part of him was wishing for a connection to this woman. She wouldn't judge him for feeling attracted to other boys; he could see this already. The allure of having that type of support sent him into a fit of nerves.

"Ah, yes, the Moon." This card depicted a large moon with a scowling face and two doglike creatures barking up at it. Cynthia placed it to the left of the center two. "This is the past. You were feeling fear, Elijah. Lacking courage. That truth you're still now trying to deny was, until recently, something you wanted so badly to be false that you tried to make it so in your mind." Elijah felt himself turning red as he remembered the feelings he experienced with Alec Pent last summer. "You were confused, scared, and at a loss for where to turn. And thus, you tried to convince yourself this aspect of you wasn't really there. Typical, for any of us experiencing feelings like that."

Molly broke her gaze from Cynthia's spread and glanced with wide eyes at Elijah. Her expression was hard to read; he would have welcomed a less serious one, because all he wanted to do right now was chuckle off the eerie accuracy of Cynthia's reading. If every problem in his life could be solved so easily by a deck of silly cards, he had a lot more to worry about than just Damon Jacoby.

Cynthia drew a fifth card and placed it above the two criss-crossed in the center. This one showed a man standing with a long branch in his hand. In the background were eight other branches against a blue sky. "The Nine of Wands," she said, straightening the cards in the spread and seeming to consider her next words carefully. "You'll remember what we said about your subconscious mind being strong, Elijah. This could be a reflection of that, but with a more negative bent. You have strength and stamina to get through the difficult parts of life, but you still expect the worst in things. Everything from family, to friends, to your own future. You think people don't like you—that people *won't* like you—but that's only a flaw in your conscious mind. That's where confidence lives, and that's what you're lacking, because you're too busy trying to plod through your difficulties. Mind you, this is just a general reading of your current state, and all these things can change if you want them to."

Molly sat back with cool eyes, as if weighing Cynthia's words against her knowledge of Elijah so far. Elijah, still trying to convey nonchalance, finally tried to force a meager chuckle. It died at his lips, because Cynthia was watching him with a grin that was difficult to read. Elijah felt naked, but somehow, the woman's beauty in the late morning light soothed him.

She drew another card. "This, the Page of Cups, is your near future, Elijah. This is the road you'll find yourself on as the days progress."

Nervous tingles ran down Elijah's back. He noticed goose bumps on his arms.

Cynthia placed the card to the right of the center cross, completing a larger cross with the four surrounding cards. "Don't you worry, honey, this is to be embraced. Your heart is going to lead you in the right direction. Still, Elijah, forgiveness is where you will face a choice. There are unresolved imbalances in your life. The opportunity is coming for you to understand someone who has hurt you, perhaps someone who left you, and you never knew why. Mending broken relationships is one of the great joys of life that too few people ever experience enough. I think you're going to be a bit angry about something, but if you choose to forgive, you'll be given a gift beyond what you can understand now."

Elijah wondered if either Molly or Cynthia could hear his pounding heart. He was suddenly sure that this trip to 408 South Cage Street had just changed his life. If this woman was his biological mother, she now seemed to know it, to already be asking for his forgiveness.

"The Six of Swords represents how you see yourself," she continued, placing another card to the right of the completed cross. "You're experiencing a general sadness as of late. Am I right? Depression is what most of us call it, myself included." Finally appearing to be more at ease, Molly surprised Elijah by chuckling with Cynthia. These two, it seemed, were no strangers to sadness. "You're still trying to pick up the pieces, though, which is hopeful. You know deep down that you'll someday be able to find a happier place, so you keep plodding forward. This is a good thing, in my humble opinion. Keep it up.

"Others, however, trust you," Cynthia continued, drawing an eighth card and setting it above the seventh, forming the start of a column. "You are a friend, Elijah, and that is evident to people when they meet you. You set people at ease in ways you don't even know, and they're drawn to you because of it. You're not as invisible as you think you are."

Yeah, maybe because I'm shaping up to be the class fag, Elijah thought. He considered Molly but didn't look at her. She had noticed him, and she was now sitting at his side as he met the woman who had likely given him up for adoption. Perhaps the comfort this roused in him was something he had to trust in return.

Cynthia placed a ninth card above the one previous. "Your hopes and fears are found in the Tower. You want your world to crumble, to be torn open raw, because then you'll be able to start new. At the same time, it's probably a little bit terrifying, because it means you'll have to reshape yourself based on your own understanding of the world, of other people, and of life." The woman brought a hand to her lips. She rubbed the lower one gently with the tip of her pointer finger. "I think you're the type who is smart enough to know that this is coming anyway. This is *life*, Elijah, and you're about to jump into it head-on. Don't you *ever* listen to those people who still tell you that you're just a child, because you're almost thirteen. You're about to experience one of the most difficult phases of life—adolescence. Everything you've known from childhood will be tested, and much of it will come crashing down. But this Tower card tells me you're already prepared for it. You're expecting it, even, both in your fear of it and your hope *in* it."

For the first time since his reading began, Elijah spoke. "You're not exactly making me excited to grow up."

Molly laughed, and Cynthia smiled through musing eyes. "Yes, yes, it's a scary thing, puberty. Not just that, but growing up. You'll have to create yourself, and that's sometimes a *really* difficult thing to do. But now your last card will show your future, the outcome of this stage in your life—"

She drew another card, then stopped and frowned.

"Well, that's interesting."

She set it at the top of the column. Elijah squinted to make out the details.

It showed a skeleton riding a horse.

"Death," Cynthia said, not without a chill in her voice.

"*What?*" Molly demanded, her voice almost as piercing as it was the day she chastised Damon Jacoby.

A pit formed in Elijah's stomach. Suddenly, the stark reality of his circumstances caught in his chest like thick, black tar. He thought back to the ashes and jawbone he had uncovered in the Moon Woods. If this woman really had discarded them—and if she truly was his birth mother—perhaps their connection was best left buried. What had she been doing with a human jawbone in the first place? Elijah imagined the fury his mother would brandish if she were ever to find out about this.

"I think we should go," he said to Molly.

She turned to him, biting her lip. "But Elijah, there's something—"

"I want to go."

Cynthia stood up abruptly and gathered the cards from the table. "You know what, kids?" she said, visibly agitated and in a more motherly tone than the one she'd just used to explain the cards. "It might not have been a good idea for me to invite you inside for this. I guess I didn't stop to register how young you both are." It was as if the Death card had scared her, too, because her bringing up their young age contradicted what she had just said about Elijah no longer being a child. She picked up her deck of cards, which were all in a pile now. "These are just"—Elijah thought she was going to say "fun and games," but instead, she said—"tools. Often more complicated than most people can really understand."

"Thanks," Elijah said briskly before walking toward the door. Molly followed, still appearing caught between leaving with Elijah and staying to hear the Death card's explanation.

It seemed pretty darned clear to me, Elijah thought, trying to ignore the fear, grief, and humiliation crawling up his throat.

Death.

As he and Molly mounted their bikes, the red-haired psychic watched from the door, looking guilt-stricken, maybe even heart-broken. It was difficult to tell, because Elijah glanced back at her only once before riding away.

"You both take care now," she called after them in a tone that was far too cheerful to be genuine.

As Elijah pedaled, all he could see was that skeleton riding the horse. Today's trip to 408 South Cage Street had been more than he bargained for, and as he and Molly rode away, the fact that he had been the one boy in End Haven to care about investigating the ashes and jawbone made him wonder at the chances of it all be-ing related to his biological family. Coincidences happened all the time, but this one had left him shaken in a way that Victor Zobel's *In God We're Dust* had no method of explaining.

When he arrived home, he ran straight past his mother and to his bedroom. This terrible year of 2005 already belonged to

Damon Jacoby, the nightmare of a bully. If fate was about to throw death into the mix, Elijah wondered if there would be any way to escape it. He lay on his bed with a whirling gut, staring at the ceiling, until he heard the call for dinner at six o'clock.

PART 3

IT'S ALL IN THE CARDS

THIS IS WHAT DAMON JACOBY EXPERIENCED after he died in the summer of 2005: painlessness, a curtain pulling up, and a view of his life—the choices he had made and all the ones he didn't. He saw in vast, inhumanly splendid detail how connected he was to a much grander picture than he ever imagined, how the teeming Earth, the universe it sat in, and the sensations of the physical senses were all simply part of a camouflage projection created by the very threads of consciousness that intercepted them. So intricate was the web of events leading to Damon's death that all he could do was review the web again and again and wonder if he could have done better.

Elijah Bryce had not been his brother, but they had been close in a way that few among the living would consider pleasant, helpful, or even remotely valuable. Now Damon saw the value. He could feel the ramifications of his having been the bully; he could also recognize Elijah's growth at having played the victim. It had taken a long time for Damon to experience the glimmer of recollection that life worked this way and that time itself wasn't really a way to measure existence at all. He saw now that time was simply a gradation, a slowed-down measure of action between any two arrays of possibility. Life—a particular body, a particular set of circumstances, a particular family—was merely a stage play of conscious focus set amid those arrays. To experience, to *act*, was to develop.

Damon and Elijah had been playing this game in the dark, the way it was supposed to be. Yet there had been one link physically connecting them, a secret long buried with a history not even its burier had been aware of. The jawbone Elijah had uncovered, perfectly human and perfectly set to change their lives, had garnished and tarnished the events that had led to his and Damon's births in the first place.

It had been a prize exchanged between their biological fathers at the Idle County Fair—an object that eventually became a symbol of clandestine love, a harsh reminder of their shame, a shadow of horror whose depths neither was truly aware of.

Young Samuel Jacoby, eventual father of Damon, had been working a dice game stand at the fair in 1986, and he had received the jawbone as a gag prize from his manager. "A good luck charm from India," the manager had said. "Give it to someone special."

Elijah Earnshaw, eventual biological father of the adopted Elijah Bryce, had won the jawbone as a prize while visiting the fair with his then-wife, Cynthia Foster. They had been in the unsuccessful throes of attempting procreation that year. Elijah Earnshaw would never have told Cynthia that he hadn't wanted a child; the only reason they eventually conceived successfully was because, on a level even deeper than his subconscious, he knew he wouldn't be living much longer.

Samuel Jacoby clearly considered Elijah Earnshaw special, because later that night, after their jawbone exchange, they met face-to-face once again at Pete's Bar in north End Haven. This time, they were each other's only company, and they went on to finish the evening in the natural privacy of Saint Andrew's Grotto, doing deeds that had made them feel ashamed but alive—both in ways they had scarcely taken the time to understand.

Cynthia Foster—after she had given her healthy son up for adoption following her husband's death from the HIV infection passed to them by Samuel Jacoby—had found the jawbone buried in the man's sock drawer. Remembering the fair, the person who had given it to him, and the life dream of having children that was now never meant to be (because her CD4 cell count had grown alarmingly low), she had buried the jawbone along with the ashes of the babies she had tried so hard to bring into the world. She had given her one healthy child up, because her life had fallen to pieces, and she had been absolutely sure that she wouldn't survive to raise him.

Life was action.

Its development was a chain.

Everywhere, in all directions, there were links.

Damon knew he needed to move on. To unplug himself from this chain of probabilities that had so consumed his focus. He had long since realized he was what many living people would call a ghost, but he now knew that he had simply shifted his focus from that physical system of life and that the patterns he created while experiencing it would always be part of him. From certain points of view, he had now been dead a long time.

2038. He was hovering over the Moon Woods.

Now he was on Windsong Road, early morning, watching somebody—Elijah Bryce—deliver newspapers. It was 2005.

A few weeks later, still 2005, the night after his death. Standing at the foot of Elijah's bed, as always feeling naked without the cloak of time to give him a context.

The Lemon Avenue Library crumbling under a wrecking ball. 2009.

Unnamed human beings—two of them—hunting for deer along the north edge of what would eventually become Idle County. Before year measurement began.

2091. Three girls named Theory, Clara, and Ruth, huddling in End Haven Middle School's most private hallway before the start of history class, crestfallen over the recent death of a young Asian girl known worldwide—though whom none of them had actually met.

Back to 2038. Damon was again following Kara Butler, the younger half sister of Molly Butler, as she drove her white rental car down an unmarked road leading toward the center of the Moon Woods. She parked in front of a heavy gray gate about six blocks into the forest. Hanging on it was a sign reading, "**NO TRESPASSING. PERIMETER IS MONITORED**." Above her were towering pine trees; the partly cloudy day above them could barely reach through.

What day was it, from her time perspective? Damon had only to wonder to get an answer. August 3, 2038. Kara's thoughts were racing about Victor Zobel, the man who now owned the Moon Woods and who had been responsible for Elijah Bryce's death, though the anomaly in the underground cave there may have led to it anyway. Interlaced with her thoughts also were worries about

Jonathan Flite, the teenager in Newport, Rhode Island, who had been released from his juvenile facility two months ago. The release itself—to say nothing of the young man's peculiar memories of Molly, Elijah, and five others who had gone missing in 2010— had sparked a rash of extreme violence by religious radicals and attracted nationwide attention. Jonathan was halfway across the country from Kara Butler, but as of last night, his mother, now a victim of a violent Christian fanatic, was at a hospital in critical condition. Damon now saw that all these souls were linked, much like he had been linked to Elijah Bryce.

"Are you ready to let them play out their lives?" came that voice from behind him—the same one as always, again as if it were nothing more than a thought. Damon now recognized that all thoughts were perceptions. All sensory experiences on Earth were simply filters of such perceptions, and on this plane of focus, those filters no longer existed. The vital energy that drove his conscious development—the same force behind all reality—could now operate much more freely.

He adjusted his focus in a way that felt like turning around. In front of him were three figures—one close, and two distant. The close one he recognized immediately as his father, Samuel Jacoby, from this previous life.

"I'm afraid of what comes next," Damon said. The figure of his father shimmered, and for a moment, he took another shape, one that Damon immediately recognized. Now it was clear that this life hadn't been their first together. The entity in front of him had been developing with him since the beginning, if there had even been a beginning.

"There's nothing to fear here," his father said. *"You're creating all your experiences."*

Behind him, the two murky figures began taking familiar shapes—ones that reverberated first as fear in Damon's heart and then as joy. One of them was Elijah Bryce. The other was Molly Butler. These personas, too, were just two personalities of many that they had once embodied, meant to remind him of the lives they had shared. Seeing them like this made Damon more comfortable, and they knew it.

As quickly as it took for him to think it, Damon was inside their minds and personalities, sensing thoroughly all the unique patterns of energy they had ever adopted. They were sharing these patterns with him, and the knowledge of their endlessness came as easily as yet another shift of attention. Conscious energy, he now saw, sought to know itself. That was why certain souls created the physical experience to begin with. Elijah, Molly, his father—they were all safe, they had all lived meaningful lives, they were now simply helping Damon realize he was free to construct anything he wanted.

Within moments he was racing toward a light he had before perceived as fog, allowing himself to fall into the joy of realizing that none of his fears had ever mattered. It had all been a game, and each of the players, in their own ways, had won. In the real universe, struggle, rivalry, and sorrow never endured.

2005

ON Tuesday, June 28, Elijah Bryce was in his front yard, hosing off his mother's cheap patio chairs, when the frail but tan mailman, Phil, roamed into his yard from the newly sold house next door. Elijah shut the hose off and met him halfway across the grass. "Good morning, Mr. Bryce," Phil said, peeling through his stack of mail and grabbing about a centimeter's worth. "Finally having a neighbor move in, I noticed. You met him yet?"

"Nope," Elijah said. "Is he there already?"

"Don't think so, but he's already getting mail. Probably illegal for me to tell you that."

As Phil did a final check of the mail stack, Elijah glanced at the small house on the next lot. It was still covered in chipped white paint and sat at least a hundred feet away. The house had been a foreclosure, and the rumor on the block was that it was a major fixer-upper, possibly the cheapest house in End Haven. Molly, who had come to Elijah's house for lunch and a game of Monopoly after the tarot card reading (they had even exchanged cell phone numbers when she left, finally), had noticed the house with an uneasy, lingering glance. "Not sure why, but that place gives me bad vibes," she had said. Elijah had never thought of it that way before, but after Molly said it, he couldn't disagree.

Now Phil stopped his sifting on the last piece of mail—a bright red envelope—and frowned. For the first time since Elijah could remember, the middle-aged man paused before handing over the small pile. He took another glance at the last envelope, then handed it all to Elijah. A weak smile followed. "Have a good day, son," he said before cutting across the lawn toward the neighbor's house.

Elijah flipped to the bright red envelope first, the one Phil had stopped to look at before handing it over. It was addressed in cutout letters.

ELIJAH THE FAG BRYCE

Mortified, he turned toward the window to make sure Selma couldn't see the envelope. It was from Damon Jacoby. He knew this despite there being no return address.

Embarrassment and fear pulsed through Elijah as he tore the envelope open. Inside was a picture of a grown man, printed off a computer—surely a photo from a gay porn website, probably one Elijah himself had visited on some lonely night or another, when his mother was long asleep and the dark house was quiet. He looked at the picture just long enough to hate himself for wanting to keep it to look at later, in his room, alone.

Red with humiliation and sure that Selma would come out any second and see the picture in his hand (and, worse, find out that people were making fun of him for being gay), he raced for the garbage can, which stood in the open garage. He ripped up the picture and the envelope as fast as he could, lifted out one of the older kitchen garbage bags, and threw the shreds underneath it. It was gone for now, but what if Damon were to send another? What if Elijah's mother were to find it?

Elijah hoped this had been the bully's last stamp.

He approached the yard again in a light sweat, still fending off his beet-red face and too humiliated to make sure Phil wasn't looking back to check on him. If there was anything worse than being embarrassed, it was knowing that someone was feeling pity for him because of it. Trying not to vomit, he sat on the front steps and scanned the rest of the mail. There was a second letter addressed to him. This time, there was a return address, and no name could have surprised him more.

Cynthia L. Foster.

Sweat formed on his palms. Two letters in one day, both from people he was terrified of. What were the chances? Slim to none, even in a town the size of End Haven.

Again fearing Selma's attention, Elijah went inside, threw the rest of the mail on the couch, and ran upstairs to his bedroom.

"Hey, Elijah. . . ." he heard Selma say from the dining room.

"Hi," he replied just before shutting his door and ripping open the second envelope. Inside was a tarot card and a letter. First, he flipped over the card and saw that it was the Death card that had driven him away four days earlier. Fear trickled through him again at the sight of that skeleton on horseback. *If it's not one piece of mail, it's got to be another,* he thought. He then dared to read the letter.

Dear Elijah,

I found your address in the Idle County phone book, just as I believe you must have found mine, seeing as it was written on the back of your hand (I do notice such things). Perhaps we think alike? Anyhow, I must apologize for Saturday's encounter. I did not want to stop by your house unannounced; hence, this letter. You left before I could explain the last card in your tarot spread, and so, I will explain it now. First and foremost, you must know that the Death card is not what you seemed to think it was. If the other cards all seemed to tell you something true about yourself, I can see why you must have been afraid. You should know, however, that Death most usually does not signify the actual physical death of a person. It is typically read as being more symbolic of an ending, perhaps to an era of life, as would be when one is going through a transition. Again, as I said during your reading, you are growing up, and that in itself is going to be a huge transition, one that you'll see the grandness of only once you're through it. The Death card also represents the entanglement of a person in forces he or she cannot control, such as fate. Whether it's a matter of fate you're tangled up in or something even more powerful, I could not tell just by your cards. After all, they're only cards, and between you and me, I'm living off two life insurance policies, not my palm and tarot reading business. That should tell you something. Even so, I would be much obliged if you would stop by for tea sometime—no cards involved—to discuss life. Something about your reaction to the reading on Saturday made me suspect that there's more going on under your skin than you'd like to let on. Just a thought.

Yours sincerely,
Cynthia Lynn Foster

Elijah's heartbeat seemed to be doing two things at once. Half of it seemed to slow with the comfort of Cynthia Foster's words, and the other half seemed to be racing with the knowledge that this sort of interaction between adult and child felt forbidden. Surely it wasn't normal for an adult to invite unknown children into her house for a tarot reading, and even more surely was it irregular for one to write a child a letter and, in it, invite him over for tea. If she really was his biological mother, however, did that make it okay?

The coincidence of receiving both pieces of mail on the same day rattled Elijah. Perhaps Cynthia really was psychic. Perhaps she had sensed he would need some comfort today to offset Damon's letter. Or—and this would be even more ridiculous—what if Damon had been the one to psychically sense that his letter might rain on Cynthia's parade? Elijah alarmed himself by suddenly wondering whether this might be possible, and whether every argument in Victor Zobel's *In God We're Dust* was misguided.

Molly Butler, he knew, was a girl who had "vibes." She had been engrossed in Cynthia's tarot card reading, and afterward, she hadn't been able to stop discussing the strong possibility that perhaps the woman really was Elijah's biological mother, and maybe life had thrown them together for a reason. She had also hesitated when attempting to tell him something else during their Monopoly game.

"I also saw something in the living room that I think was a—" she had started, but then she had shaken her head and chuckled.

"Wait, what?" Elijah asked, rolling the dice. "What did you see?"

"It was probably nothing. Never mind."

Elijah had furrowed his eyebrows and given her his best "*You can't just start saying something like that*" look.

First with a sigh and then with a deep breath, Molly whispered, "Sometimes I see things. Or think I do. But seriously, it was probably nothing. It looked like an outline of a person, though."

"Like, painted on the wall you mean?"

"No, like a ghost. But again, it was probably nothing."

Unsure how to proceed after this strange statement, Elijah had forced out a laugh and then shaken his head. Molly in turn had blushed and dropped the subject completely, veering them back toward surface-level observations about Cynthia. They had whispered about the tarot reading over Monopoly as Shelly Bryce toiled away in the kitchen, cooking a casserole for a potluck at Lake Gospel Church. Now that Elijah thought about it, however, Molly hadn't yet called him to plan their excursion to the Fourth of July fair on Monday. Had he offended her? She definitely had a different life outlook than he did, but she was also the only person who seemed capable of being his friend. Perhaps it was his duty to make the call.

Elijah tucked Cynthia's letter—and the Death card—into his underwear drawer, a place where his mother would surely never look, and ran back outside to resume rinsing her patio chairs, some of which were now dry and only half clean. He switched the hose nozzle back on. The minuscule drops glistened in the sun and became a sparkling, colored tapestry before Elijah's ruminating eyes. They hinted at a gentle yet orderly beauty to the universe, something his own life had yet to reflect with any clarity. Seeing the blue and yellow cover of *In God We're Dust* in his mind, he wondered if any of it would ever matter at all.

2010

Cynthia Foster clutched her most prized white crystal in her hand as the Boeing 737 she was sitting in roared to full power outside her row's window. She was in seat A14, on the runway at Minneapolis-Saint Paul International Airport. As the plane began racing toward takeoff, she wondered just how crazy this Alaska trip to investigate Max Pope really was. It was September 3, 2010, and the high temperature in Palmer today would be a balmy fifty-two degrees. She sensed deep down that the comfort provided by the crystal in her hand was just a placebo comfort, but then again, the placebo effect was a powerful thing. Maybe that was all that mattered.

From Anchorage, the drive to Palmer would be just over an hour.

She had spent $792 on the plane ticket, clearing out a fourth of her "for emergencies" savings. All of this was on a whim, but her run-in with Eloise Creed last month had inspired her to consider the trip to Palmer to see what she could find out about Max. Had he somehow been involved with Elijah and the others' disappearances, or was he truly still up there? In the two months since that fateful Fourth of July night, neither the police nor Victor Zobel and his crew of volunteers had found any substantial clues about what had happened to the seven teenagers. It continued to appear as if they had been driving toward Mexico and somehow been sidetracked. By hoodlums? By a drug cartel? By something even more sinister? Nobody knew.

Cynthia knew, however, that Occam's razor didn't always provide the correct line of reasoning—that reality didn't always work in the simplest of fashions. She had spent days putting together the story of Max's tenure in Idle County, but just last week, after already booking her ticket to Alaska, she had remembered an aspect of it police didn't seem to be applying to any current investigation: the Sparks family house explosion in 2007. They had been a local family tragically lost that year due to a gas leak in the middle of the night; their house on Lefton Street had blown up on November 13, just four weeks after charges against Max had been dropped in the Josiah Marple case.

The explosion incident had involved two peculiarities. First, the sheriff's deputy who initially arrived on the scene had apprehended fourteen-year-old Gabriel Creed, who was standing outside the blazing house, sobbing and screaming about the burning bodies inside. Gabriel had been friendly with fifteen-year-old Alan Sparks (not to mention Elijah, Molly Butler, and Lindsay Thorsen) via their joint volunteering at the revamped Rock Shore Nursing Home, and he had claimed he arrived early enough that night to help Alan start evacuating his family from the house. After

Alan had run back inside to get his younger brother, however, one of them had switched on a light, and the house had exploded. The police ultimately released Gabriel, but whispers later circulated around Idle County that the boy, whose parents were known for being fanatical fundamentalist Christians, had claimed during his questioning that his "psychic little sister" had warned him about the gas leak. After forensics analysts concluded that a loosened nut on the family's dryer had caused it, Gabriel had been absolved from official suspicion. While the boy's claim of taking a cash-paid taxi to the Sparks household that night had not checked out with any local drivers or street cameras, it remained unlikely that he had somehow broken into the house earlier that night to loosen the dryer nut. In the end, investigators had declared the explosion to be an unfortunate accident.

The second peculiarity surrounding the case had seemed far less significant, but it had recently plucked the back of Cynthia's mind. The sole survivor of the Sparks family had been eighteen-year-old Rebecca, the family's physically disabled oldest daughter, who had been confirmed alive that very night by Max Pope. Max had said, and it was quoted in the *Circle Gazette*, that she had "stayed late at his house to talk about theories of the universe." It was whispered, of course, that the man, whose reputation was already tarnished by the nursing-home murder accusations, had manipulated the young, wheelchair-riding woman into having a sexual affair.

When Cynthia met Max, she hadn't sensed that he was any sort of predator. A man ruled by his zealous beliefs about consciousness, maybe, but not someone who would ever truly endanger another person. Still, was anybody looking at this link? Elijah had mentioned Rebecca to Cynthia in passing only a few times, but always in a dismissive, nonchalant tone. Had that dismissive nonchalance been covering for something?

The police were looking at evidence and hypothesizing likely answers, but they didn't seem to be questioning these murky factors in between. If nothing else, today's trip to Alaska would provide Cynthia alone some comfort. The alternative was to spend the rest of her life wondering if she could have done more to find Elijah. That simply wasn't an option.

She lightly brushed shoulders with the man sitting next to her, in B14. He was middle aged but leathery and handsome, dressed in jeans and a Carhartt jacket. She had noticed him glancing at her in the terminal as they were waiting to board, and because men so rarely showed her attention despite the fact that she still had what she considered to be a pretty face (even at age fifty-four), she had assumed he was judging her for her flaming red hair and cheap clothing. Of course he had ended up next to her.

"You look like a nervous flier," he said when Cynthia braced herself following the plane's slight dip after liftoff. Without waiting for her to acknowledge him, he continued with, "I always just tell myself that a crash would probably be a better way to go than cancer. Right?"

Cynthia glanced at the man, noticing at once his scruffy gray stubble and pleasant smell. Deodorant, not cologne. "I don't fly much," Cynthia said, making fleeting eye contact. The man had one of the most soothing smiles she had ever seen, and nothing in it suggested perversion or malice.

"What's bringing you to Alaska?"

A crinkle of emotion intensified the crow's feet around Cynthia's eyes. Her expression became neither a smile nor a grimace, but when she considered the reason for her trip, she had to fight to hold back tears. "I guess you could say I'm going to check somebody out," she said. Then she shook her head. "Sorry. Long story."

"Six hours' worth?" the man said, exhaling as he looked back toward the front of the plane. "Unless of course you hate plane talkers. I can shut up."

Cynthia grinned. "I don't hate plane talkers. It's just that . . . we're on a crowded plane." She glanced over the man's lap. In the aisle seat was a suited businessman who was already asleep with his mouth hanging open. "I'm headed to Palmer, though. Do you live in Anchorage?"

"Wasilla here," the man said. "That's where I have my home sweet home. Sometimes doubles as my hunting shack if I get lucky."

An animal killer, Cynthia thought. When he glanced at her again, however, a glint of humor in his blue eyes made her want to continue their exchange.

"I've never been to Alaska," she said.

"Well, then, you're missing out. I like to think of it as the clearing at the end of the path. For people who like mountains, anyway."

"'Clearing at the end of the path.' I like that."

"Read it in a book once," the man said. "I'm Frank, by the way."

Frank. Simple, to the point. Probably a Francis. Cynthia felt the familiar sensation of intuition pushing her toward comfort, were she to allow it. How come it was that life always presented fleeting doses of human interaction that could color plans and expectations in the most unexpected hues?

She looked back toward the front of the plane and quickly said, "I'm Cynthia." Her day's agenda was strict, but she could already feel herself being lured by distraction. Her initial plan for the afternoon was to ask around local businesses in Palmer to see if people knew or had seen Max Pope (going by "Michael Johnson"). It was a town of only five thousand people, and as Max was now linked to a national news story whose public appeal had not yet petered out, perhaps he would be a hot topic. He had carried himself like a movie star the one time Cynthia had met him; she was hard-pressed to think that anybody in Palmer who knew of him wouldn't have something to say. Would they also know anything about Max's connection to Rebecca Sparks? Unlikely, but one could hope.

All Cynthia remembered about Rebecca was that she had moved to California to live with some long-lost uncle after her family had perished in the gas explosion. Internet searches had uncovered a number of old Associated Press news articles, many of them syndicated repeats of the house explosion story reported locally around the state of Minnesota. A few of them went as far as linking Rebecca, the sole survivor, to Max Pope and the closing of his "experimental guinea pig hospice." Otherwise, their unusual friendship seemed to have lost steam in the wake of the explosion tragedy.

There had been no online records relating to Rebecca after her move to California. Cynthia had put in a request to the Idle County Sheriff's Department to see a copy of the explosion incident's police report, but due to the fact that Gabriel Creed had been found sobbing outside the Sparks house that night after trying to help evacuate the family, they had refused to release a copy to Cynthia. Police history involving any of the Idle County Seven was now locked. Despite being encouraging, it had also left her own little investigation at a dead end.

But Rebecca Sparks had spent time with Max Pope. Enough

to conveniently miss being incinerated with the rest of her family. Had nobody ever questioned this? Had any traffic-light cameras snapped photos of Max's car that night, and had Rebecca truly been with him the whole time? There seemed now, in retrospect, to be so many possible holes in the story. Cynthia knew she might be imagining all of them, but seeing as the police and FBI seemed to have so few clues as to the whereabouts of her biological son, it didn't matter. A stone left unturned was a possible answer tossed into oblivion.

The plane jolted in the air. Cynthia braced herself, taking in a fast breath and holding it. The last time she experienced turbulence had become the reason she hated flying.

"It's just like riding a wave," her rowmate Frank said, noticing her anxiety. "The pilots barely notice bumps like that."

Cynthia's grimace involuntarily turned into a smile. "What, do you fly?"

"My brother-in-law is an air traffic controller up in Anchorage. He used to be in the air force." He smiled and raised his eyebrows up and down quickly. "We'll get there safe. Don't worry."

"It's been a long time since I've flown anywhere."

"I do this flight twice a year," the man said. "Where again did you say you're from?"

Without considering the weight her words now carried, she said, "Idle County. Southwest Minnesota." She looked out her window, then quickly back into the plane again, because the vision of Earth creeping backward far below set off her anxiety bells and whistles.

Frank tripped up on his own response after her mention of Idle County, as if it had caught him off guard. "Like *Idle County* Idle County? Making news lately? I hadn't even heard of the place until this year. Sad about those kids. My mom has been following the story like it's some *20/20* special. Is that still a big deal down there then?"

"I'd say so," Cynthia replied, trying to keep her face stony. Yet she couldn't stop herself from talking about Elijah. Doing so would be an insult to his memory. "I'm . . . my son was . . . biological, I mean . . . he . . . Christ."

Frank's face lost its ruggedly flirtatious flair, and he was staring at her now in a way that made his leathery skin stand out like a relief sculpture. Looking straight into her eyes, he said, "One of those kids was your son?"

Cynthia took a deep breath as if it might stop her urge to cry. "I put him up for adoption when I had him. My husband and I . . . husband at the time, I mean—he's dead . . . we tried and tried to have a baby for so long. I guess I should say *I* tried and tried . . . I'm sorry, this is just way too much information. I have problems with oversharing and crossing boundaries. People avoid me because of that, I think."

"Six hours," Frank said, glancing at a shiny silver watch on his wrist. "Not leaving this seat."

But Cynthia shook her head. "Maybe later. Maybe over dinner, if you're really that curious. I don't know anybody up in the Palmer-Wasilla area."

Frank cocked his head with half a smile, as if wondering the obvious: Had Cynthia just asked him out on a date? Replaying the statement in her mind, even Cynthia couldn't quite answer that question. Chalk it up to her tendency to be repellent to strangers. Her HIV-positive status would likely be a detractor from further frivolity anyway, because most heterosexual men had little to no education on the subject.

Frank suddenly looked straight into her eyes. "Dinner would be great. I'll come to you."

Cynthia laughed, shaking her head. "I'm sorry, I just—"

"You say 'sorry' too much," Frank interrupted. "Don't be sorry."

"I'm from Minnesota. I can't help it. We're sorry about everything there."

Now Frank was the one to laugh. "So, you're going to Alaska to check up on somebody. Relating to your son?"

A shade of desperation escaped Cynthia in a sigh. "A man who knew my son at one point apparently lives up there, but he seems to be missing, too. People say he was crazy, but maybe he was just trying to get off the grid. I'm flying up to find out whatever I can. The FBI and police don't seem to be asking the questions I'm asking." Cynthia squeezed the crystal in her hand, which she hoped Frank had not noticed. "Elijah's adoptive mom would kill me if she knew I was doing this."

"You didn't tell her?"

"I didn't tell anyone."

For almost a minute, Cynthia and Frank the stranger sat next to each other, imprisoned in their airplane seats. She had just started to wonder if her oversharing had silenced him for good when he asked, "Did you and your son always know each other? Or did he find you? I had a friend who knew who his birth parents were but was always too scared to meet them. Fear of being disappointed, I think. Always made me a little sad for him."

An animal killer who's sensitive. Gotta give him a few points for that, Cynthia thought. She chortled at the memory of how she and Elijah had met. The jawbone. The tarot card reading. And then of course the acknowledgment of their biological relationship and her turning in of the jawbone to the police. That, however, was what had sent Elijah and Molly on the little summer investigation that almost got them killed. Damon Jacoby, in his madness, had been the resulting casualty.

"Sometimes I wonder if he would have been better off never having met me," Cynthia said. "I guess we can't really control how we all bounce off each other in life, right?"

Frank smiled in a way that made Cynthia feel the weight of her own loneliness. She smiled back, unsure whether she was desperate for friendship or genuinely sharing a moment. However troubled her smile was, he seemed to accept it at face value. Whether he was a fleeting link in her life's chain or one that would alter its direction, she didn't know. She sat back in the airplane seat and thought about all the inappropriate things she had done in her life. After the tarot card reading, she had lured Elijah back into it, plain and simple. Hell, call it what it was: she had *ambushed* him, and at one of his most frail, vulnerable moments—at Idle County's Fourth of July fair in 2005, just after his first truly violent run-in with Damon Jacoby on the bumper-car platform.

"Pretty sure I would have made a bad mother," she now said to Frank.

Instead of laughing this off, he gave her an uncertain shake of his head. "Doesn't seem true to me. You're on this plane, aren't you?"

Cynthia closed her eyes to block a rush of imminent tears. Yes, she was on this plane. It counted for something. And if Palmer, Alaska, led to nothing, she would try to track down Rebecca Sparks. If there was one thing that made her a good mother, it was this: until her dying day, she would never stop looking.

2005

THE SUN WAS TURNING GOLD when Elijah Bryce and Molly Butler arrived at Idle County's Fourth of July fair, which was a colorful but somewhat rickety whirl of game stands, rides, and people eating food on sticks. Elijah wasn't partial to fairs—he didn't like the smells. In some places, it was exhaust from generators mixed with farm animals; in others, it was fried foods mixed with the stench of outhouses. This fair had been around every Fourth of July since Elijah could remember, and for some reason, he went every year. Last summer, he had come with Alec, Natalie, and Pauline.

Tonight, he and Molly walked amid the tents and watched enthusiastic guests playing trivial games. Elijah witnessed one man toss three large rings over moving targets in an elevated pool of water. The woman standing next to him, dressed in tight jeans and a wide-open black blouse, giggled and removed a cigarette from her mouth before kissing him on the cheek.

Behind the man and woman were two boys whose athletic shoulders and muscular, tan arms drew Elijah's attention and didn't seem to let it go. Just as they finished tossing their rings, Molly tapped his shoulder. "We might want to get out of here." She gestured with her head toward the two boys. Elijah flushed when he finally shifted his gaze from their muscles to their faces.

It was Nolan Snagsby and Tyler McFadden, Damon Jacoby's friends.

"Damn it," Elijah said. "Act like we didn't see them." Just as he was turning away, however, he caught Tyler's gaze. The boy simultaneously nudged Nolan and pulled out his cell phone, which he immediately began dialing with a vindictive laugh.

"We can hide in the crowd," Molly said. "They wouldn't try anything around this many people."

Elijah rushed with her into the sea of Idle County residents—old ones, young ones, families, lovers—and for a few minutes, it seemed they had escaped. Was Damon at the fair and just separated from Nolan and Tyler, or was he at home? If he wasn't even here, Elijah had nothing to worry about.

He and Molly approached a wall of rides along the north edge of the fairgrounds, near their entrance. "How about bumper cars?" Molly suggested. "It's only a dollar. No line."

"Sure," Elijah said.

They paid their money, then walked up the wooden ramp toward the bumper cars' metallic platform. Elijah was just strapping himself into a gold car when he heard footsteps running up the wooden entrance ramp and then a voice that turned the evening's warmth to ice.

"Found ya!"

It was Damon Jacoby. He, Nolan, and Tyler were already

strapping themselves into three of the cars across the platform. Damon's was a bright, garish red. Molly, who had just strapped herself into the pink bumper car, seemed to recognize his voice, too, and she flashed Elijah a wide-eyed glance.

The operator directed them to fasten their seat belts. The next moment, the bumper cars roared to life. If Elijah jumped out of his car now, Damon would beeline it for his legs.

Elijah started driving, following Molly, who was leading him to the corner opposite Damon Jacoby. She bounced off the wall, turned, and headed straight toward Elijah. Elijah decelerated before bumping into her, but the concerned expression on her face told him she was only trying to find lemonade in the lemons.

"How's End Haven's favorite little fag? Did you like your letter?" Damon was yelling at the top of his lungs, but the cars were too loud for anybody beyond the platform to hear. He was speeding toward Elijah. "You think you could hide from me here? I had a dream last night that I kicked your ass on the bumper cars. I knew *exactly* where you'd be."

Damon crashed into him. The impact of his car jolted Elijah's neck in four different directions at once.

He pressed his foot to the pedal and started flying toward Molly, whose car was caught between two strangers. Dislodging her with another bump, Elijah gestured behind him with a panicked look. Molly saw Damon. Anger ignited her eyes. Now Nolan and Tyler were fast on Damon's trail, and all three were heading toward Elijah, Molly, and the two strangers.

"Turn, Elijah! Step on it!" Molly yelled.

Elijah turned and rushed toward another corner just in time to hear Damon's car bump into Molly's. She screamed at the impact, and the two strangers yelled angry obscenities at

Damon. It took him only a moment to turn, and soon, he was chasing Elijah. The whirring sound of the bumper car became high pitched as Elijah started driving in wide circles as fast as he could, all while trying to drown out Damon's jeers of, "Gay boy, gay boy, gay boy!"

Nolan broadsided Elijah from the left, forcing him against the platform's sidelines.

"Good one, Nolan!" Damon said. He pummeled Elijah from the rear, and again, Elijah's neck jerked painfully.

"Stop it!" Molly screamed from the other side of the platform. But her voice was moving closer. "Get away from him!"

"Your little girlfriend can't save you this time, Bryce," Damon said. "Oh wait, she *can't* be your girlfriend, can she? Because you like *dudes*! Do you two talk together about boys you like, huh? Talk about Alec Pent's muscly chest?"

Tyler had finally caught up with them. It was three against one.

"Why did you come to the fair, Bryce? You going to stand in the tent for all the deformed weirdos so people can make fun of you? I think I saw one for that by the outhouses—"

"They do *not* have that sort of thing here!" came Molly's scream just before she collided with Damon's car. It appeared she had been moving at top speed, because this time, it was Damon's neck that wrenched uncontrollably.

"Oh, you're going to get it," he said, trying to turn his car around.

But Molly was forcing him against the rail, and the car didn't budge. "So," she started with a scathing glare. "Why exactly are you making fun of Elijah?"

"Because he's a *faggot*," Damon replied, laughing. Like last time, however, Elijah saw his terrorizing demeanor flinch under Molly's gaze.

"Oh, he's a *faggot*, is he? What would it matter to you even if he was?"

"Because faggots just die and rot in hell," Damon said. "Trust me, I know."

"Oh, ho hum," Molly pressed on. "Is that what your parents told you or something? If so, they seem pretty stupid!"

"My parents are *dead*, you bitch."

Elijah, who had been watching their interchange from between Nolan's and Tyler's cars, widened his eyes in surprise. They, too, were subdued at Damon's words, but Elijah could tell they had already known the truth. Like himself whenever Molly mentioned her dead mother, they looked as if they had no idea what to say.

It was Molly who seemed most surprised at Damon's words. "Oh," she said, her voice suddenly empathetic. "I didn't know. I'm sorry."

"Yeah, you don't know anything about me, so stay the hell out of my business."

A loud buzzer sounded around the platform, and Elijah heard the cars automatically disengage. It was a slow, surreal few seconds as he and Molly, joined by Damon, Nolan, and Tyler, unbuckled themselves and walked across the platform, toward the wooden exit ramp.

Just as Elijah stepped onto it, thinking he was home free, he felt two hands ram his back. He fell onto the wooden walkway that led back down toward the fair, and the side of his head hit the metal railing's vertical support. Damon leaned down and grabbed Elijah by the hair.

"Hey, kid, you stop that!" the bumper car operator yelled, but

Elijah could only hear his voice as if from a distance. His neck was contorted at a terrible angle, and through the guardrail, he saw three of his classmates: Tessa Silverman, Brian Jarrod, and Travis Moran. They were watching the scene, pointing. Travis was laughing as if it were some comedy television show.

"You get in my way again, and I'll *kill* you," Damon whispered in Elijah's ear before kicking him in the stomach and running off the platform. Elijah heard Nolan's and Tyler's footsteps as they scampered after Damon. They were whispering to each other in nervous voices.

Molly, who had walked ahead and realized something was amiss only after the bumper car operator's yell, rushed to Elijah's side. The operator was five feet behind her.

"You all right, kid?" the heavyset man asked. "Those guys hurt you much?"

"They've been bullying him ever since summer vacation started," Molly told the operator.

"I'm okay," Elijah said, but his forehead was throbbing. The operator examined the spot where it had made a direct impact against the metal pole.

"You're going to have a bruise there, I think," he said. "But nothing's bleeding. How're your knees? Any slivers?"

It was his stomach that hurt the most, but Elijah sat up completely and examined his knees. He saw a number of long, wooden strips sticking out of them. "Yeah, looks like there are. But I'm okay. Really." He could feel the embarrassment swelling his face.

"There's a cop stationed right close to here," the operator said. "I'm going to go on and bring him over."

"No," Elijah croaked, deflating at the sound of his weak, pathetic voice. "I'm fine. It was just—"

But the operator had already left to fetch the policeman.

"Elijah, Damon just assaulted you!" Molly said. "This time it was *worse*. You can go to juvenile jail for that! I saw it on a talk show once." She glanced over her shoulder. "Here comes the cop."

The policeman approached, speaking into his walkie-talkie. ". . . a kid in a green shirt with two friends, who're both wearing red," he was saying. He finished his brief overview, sank to his knees to look Elijah in the eye, and introduced himself as Deputy Eli Thropp.

Molly did most of the talking. She told Deputy Thropp everything, starting with the bullying at the library. Elijah's heart sank further and further with every passing word. A few people walking by had stopped to watch them, including a few more kids he recognized from End Haven Middle School.

"Anything else?" Deputy Thropp asked.

Damon's words echoed in Elijah's mind. *"You get in my way again, and I'll kill you."*

"No," Elijah replied. "I just want to go home."

"We'll follow up with the boy's parents then. Jacoby, you said his name was?"

"Damon Jacoby," Molly answered. "But he said his parents are—" She stopped, now appearing unsure whether the policeman could benefit from knowing what they had learned on the bumper car platform.

"Yes?" Deputy Thropp asked, waiting for Molly to continue.

She finished in a downhearted, almost betraying voice. "He said his parents are dead."

"Well, he's got to live with somebody. We'll follow up just to make sure they know what he's been doing."

They waited with Deputy Thropp for another five minutes,

until other security deputies began reporting that they hadn't found anybody matching Damon's description. "Well, you kids be careful," the policeman said. "I'm sure he was just out to cause trouble and didn't mean for it to get violent."

As Elijah walked with Molly back into the fair, he felt a pang of anger at the deputy's nonchalance. It was Molly who voiced it. "'Didn't mean to get violent'? Yeah, right. *That's* total crap."

"Yeah, probably," Elijah said.

Molly was watching him from the corner of her eye as they walked along a row of game tents. "Are you okay?" she asked. "Like, for real?"

He grimaced and shrugged, hoping his fight against tears wasn't as obvious as it felt. The humiliation was worse than any he had ever experienced, and it felt as if everybody at the fair were watching him and whispering behind his back.

"You don't have to be embarrassed," Molly told him in a low, consoling voice. For the second time that summer, she had guessed his emotions to a tee, despite the barriers he was trying to hold up. "Everybody who saw what happened was concerned about you, and they were all glaring at Damon. Just so you know."

"Not my classmates who walked by," Elijah replied. The coil of humiliation in his stomach had forced out tears against his will. Instead of dripping, however, they rested along the edges of his eyes.

"You saw people you know?"

"Well, not people I *really* know—just ones I go to school with. Tessa Silverman, Brian Jarrod, and Travis Moran. They knew who I was."

Elijah and Molly walked back toward the fair's exit without further conversation. They were just passing a large, bouncing obstacle course when they heard a woman's voice calling their names from off to the right. Both turned their heads at the same time. About thirty feet away, Psychic Cynthia Foster was sitting at her own decorated tarot-reading booth, waving at them.

"Oh, no," Elijah said.

It was too late; they had already acknowledged her. Molly gave Elijah a small push, clearly warmer to the idea of visiting Cynthia than he was. It was as though his new acquaintance could read in his heart the desire to have a mother who would accept him for who he was, even if he was attracted to other boys. Yet Elijah hoped his tears were dry; all he wanted right now was to leave the fair and hide his secret for another day.

Cynthia met them with a positively exuberant smile, as if the Fourth of July fair were her favorite event of the year. "So, you two lovebirds out partying at the fair tonight? You staying for the fireworks?"

At this, Elijah could barely bring himself to look at her. It was almost the exact statement his own mother had made about his new acquaintanceship with Molly.

"We were just leaving," Molly said. "Fireworks don't start for another couple of hours, but I might be coming back with my dad."

"Good girl," Cynthia said, but from the corner of his eyes, Elijah saw that she was really looking at him. "And Mr. Bryce. Are *you* staying for the fireworks tonight?"

He fought his nerves as best he could. "No, I think I'm going in, actually."

Cynthia's eyes fell to the left side of Elijah's forehead. "Oh, dear, honey. Did something happen to your head? It's all swollen!" Whatever pretext with which she had greeted them was now gone; in its place was concern that was positively motherly.

"It's nothing. I'm fine," Elijah lied.

"Tell me what happened," she said, beckoning Elijah to lean forward so she could see. He surprised himself by stepping toward her. The seriousness in her tone made him, for a brief second, want to tell her everything.

Once again, however, it was Molly who piped up. "A boy named Damon Jacoby did it," she said. "He's been bullying Elijah, and tonight, he ambushed us at the bumper cars. He pushed Elijah into the railing and kicked him in the stomach."

"What's *that* boy want with you?" Cynthia asked, suddenly more curious than concerned. She spoke as if Damon were familiar to her.

"He's been making fun of Elijah for—"

Elijah held up his right hand in Molly's face. "Just shut up. Please."

The dark-haired girl retracted herself, taking a step back. Already, guilt weighed on Elijah's shoulders for using such a harsh tone with her, but he was glad Molly had not told Cynthia Foster the reason for Damon's cruelty. The psychic, holding a different deck of tarot cards than the one she had given Elijah's reading from, shuffled while her stare swayed between the two young people in front of her. When her eyes crossed Elijah's, something in them told him a truth that was, however impossible, obvious.

She knows I'm gay.

"Let me tell you something, Elijah Bryce. And yes, I never forget a name, so I hope you haven't been alarmed about why I've remembered yours." Her demeanor was still motherly, but there was something about it that was different, as if she were simply a friend sharing a helpful secret. "I happen to know a thing or two about that boy. He's a hurting unit, let me tell you, and there's more to him than you might think. I'd say that's why he's been picking trouble with you, even if he doesn't realize the depths of it."

Molly stepped forward as if about to speak, then fell back. Elijah turned, and when his gaze met hers, she looked toward the ground. She clearly wanted to say something but was afraid of being shushed again.

"You two better go home," Cynthia said. "Besides, people think I'm giving you a reading, so they're not coming to my booth," she added in a lighter manner. "Lord knows I'm not messing with *you two* again."

Elijah stared at the dirt beneath his feet. Hoping the blush on his face was invisible in the approaching dusk, he turned to leave.

"Hey, wait, you." Cynthia reached for his wrist and pulled it lightly. When Elijah forced himself to look her in the face, he saw that whatever care this woman seemed to have for him was as real as the stars just starting to show in the heavens. "I know you're young and you're not supposed to talk to strangers, but I really would like it if you stopped by my house. I twisted my ankle and need somebody to mow my lawn. I pay the best in the neighborhood, I've heard." She winked at him, and the moment felt perfectly innocent—but innocent as experienced between two adults. Was this the precipice between childhood and growing up?

"I'll think about it," Elijah said.

"Let's say Friday at two o'clock. If the weather's bad, I'll make us tea."

"I'll think about it," he repeated.

With that, he led the way out of the fairgrounds. Molly barely spoke to him on the bike ride back to her house. When she did not invite him to join her and her father for fireworks, Elijah knew he had really messed things up by rudely shushing her.

He rode home under the looming night, sure at least twice that he heard bike pedals following him. Fearing Damon Jacoby really did mean to follow through with his death threat, he pedaled as fast as he could and was home in fifteen minutes.

2038

SHELLY BRYCE DIDN'T YET KNOW why she was driving to the Moon Woods. It was a beautiful day, and what worse way was there to spend it than by snooping around Idle County's notorious, cursed forest? When she reached the end of Hunter Avenue and turned right onto Old Mill Road, circling toward the southern edge of the wood, a tingle of unease ran through her. Victor Zobel owned every inch of land to the left of the cracked pavement, and since all the drama following Jonathan Flite's release two months ago had suddenly put him on the map as a speculated link to the Geneva bombing, the forest now seemed even more imposing than usual. Today, considering Flite's mother was apparently in critical condition because of some new, horrible attack (Shelly had kept her satellite news radio switched off on the drive from Younkers), perhaps the place was about to explode in yet another scandal.

Curiosity crept through Shelly as she approached the southern side of the Moon Woods. She hadn't driven this route in over twenty years—she always took the northern loop of Old Mill Road whenever she needed to go to Blue Hill, and why in her right mind would she ever go southeast to poor, rundown Deadwood? She had, for a period of years following Elijah's disappearance, driven in circles on Old Mill Road to work through her sorrow in silence. Contrary to what people might think now, she *had* grieved over the loss of her son. Their relationship hadn't been perfect, especially after Cynthia Foster had swept in and destroyed it. (If Shelly couldn't be honest about this with herself, what was the point of honesty at all?) At the time, driving this long loop had reminded her of the hope she had felt when Victor Zobel, despite his atheism, had organized searches of the Moon Woods. Never mind that the searches had turned up nothing; they had helped, if only to offer people optimism.

A thin layer of clouds had dimmed the bright August morning just enough to remind Shelly where she was. Regardless of Victor Zobel's now owning this forest, the place would always live in the shade of its dark, quiet history involving that serial-killer priest, Simon Villard, and the cult of men who had venerated him all the way up to 2004. It still sent a shiver down her spine to think that Elijah, her own son, had become intertwined in that decades-old case when he and Molly Butler uncovered the skeleton of Villard's final victim on Spinner's Island. Perhaps she should have moved with Elijah to somewhere bigger after her divorce, somewhere less conducive to interpersonal coincidence. Here she was, seventy-seven years old in her matching denim, and she was still in Idle County, a thankless place that had given her nothing but grief. Perhaps if she had read the signs better, Elijah would still be alive.

A flock of cawing crows dotted the sky in front of Shelly's car, crossing Old Mill Road in a rush toward the Moon Woods. Just as they crossed over the thin layer of trees preceding the Moon Woods' Outer Ring, they spun around in a one-eighty, cawing even louder, as if the forest had outright deflected them.

Maybe people have always been right to avoid this place, Shelly thought. *But why then would Victor Zobel want to own it?*

There it was. The unmarked road to his development at the Moon Woods' center. So far, there wasn't a single reporter loitering at the intersection.

Shelly felt a sudden push to take the left turn, to drive as far into the forest as the dirt road would allow. Zobel had a heavy metal gate in there anyway, according to rumors floating around town. What would be the harm? He lived on that space station for rich tourists, and if anybody were to catch her, she could simply tell the truth. She had met Victor Zobel multiple times in 2010, when he was organizing searches for her lost son and his friends. Shelly was still sharp enough to play the lost, ever-grieving senior citizen if need be.

Do I dare?

Ahead of her, the same flock of crows attempted another flight over the Moon Woods. Again, they were deflected. This time, they continued south after their fluttering one-eighty swerve.

She slowed her car. Considering the media frenzy back in town, this unmarked dirt road looked conspicuously devoid of news vans and reporters. Maybe they were farther in, at the gate. Or maybe the supposed incident that put Jonathan Flite's mother in critical condition had taken the cake for today, and Victor Zobel was no longer at the top of the media's kill list.

No sooner had Shelly chosen to take the turn than she was

questioning it. As Victor Zobel's dirt road crackled under her tires, she felt a heated rush of psychological uncertainty. That this land belonged to such a world-renowned atheist left her feeling both confrontational and barren, as if for all the efforts she had put into her Christian faith since last they spoke, it might all come undone were they somehow to meet again face-to-face.

The Outer Ring was shallower here than in other spots around the Moon Woods. The forest's towering pines, truly staggering as they enveloped her, reminded her of dark walls surrounding some forbidden castle. As the road led her inward, their brown trunks seemed to rise like massive sentinels watching her every move. Were they equipped with cameras? Was she already being monitored by somebody at the rumored mansion inside? Shelly had no way of knowing. She continued on, feeling like a criminal already, her heart rate rising every second. Perhaps this was why people enjoyed being deviant.

A glint of white up ahead caught Shelly's gaze. At first, she thought it might be a massive LED light from a news camera, but as she rounded a slight curve in the dirt road, she saw that it was a car—a sparkling-white Hyundai Flora—parked in front of a tall, gray gate made of thick metal. Standing next to it was a woman with long black hair hanging down her back. When the sound of Shelly's car became obvious and the woman turned, it was clear she was young, not much older than college age. Something about her face immediately twisted Shelly's heart, and without immediately knowing why, Shelly panicked.

It can't be. She had a brain tumor. She would be dead.

Yet the black-haired woman standing in front of her was very much alive, and she was the spitting image of Molly Butler, Elijah's best friend. For a moment, a deep layer of Shelly's psyche leapt upward, into immediate grasp: a sudden, jolting sense of hope that her missing son had somehow been alive all this time. If this young woman was Molly Butler, did it mean Elijah was somewhere nearby? What if they really had been in the Moon Woods all these years, like that Jonathan Flite boy said, living and waiting and wanting to come back and—

This woman standing amid the forest's giant pines was young. Too young. Molly Butler would have been in her mid-forties by now.

Shelly was suddenly fighting tears. Oh, how funny they were, tricks of the mind. When children lost were nothing more than frozen memories, the shatteringly fast span of years could do nothing but preserve them, fledgling, as they were. Even so, a woman here in End Haven could not look so similar to Molly Butler without somehow being related. Andrew Butler had left town a few years after Molly's disappearance, and last Shelly heard, over two decades ago now, he had fathered a daughter with a new wife.

With her delicate, wrinkled hands, Shelly opened the car door. Being careful to balance her gripless flats on the dirt, she eased herself out. For a moment, she stood behind the open door, eyes locked with the young woman as the pines towered around them. A slight breeze had arisen, and Shelly heard the gentle clacking of rustling branches high above.

"You'd think there'd be more reporters here today," the young woman said. "Though I guess Zobel's still up on his space station. Maybe they knew they'd get nothing by being here."

"Clearly the drama must be elsewhere," Shelly said, now aware that the tears still welled in her lower eyelids might be visible. Then, because she couldn't help herself, she said, "I'm sorry, but you look awfully like somebody I once knew. Jesus help me if

I'm going crazy, but are you . . . did you . . . ?" Shelly couldn't finish, and it wasn't for a lack of words. It was the embarrassment over having thought this young stranger was one of the long-lost Idle County Seven.

"Molly Butler," the woman said, and for a moment Shelly's chest seized. Her face must have contorted in pathetic, wrinkled shock, because the woman suddenly shook her head and waved her hands in front of her chest. "No, no . . . I mean, I'm related to Molly Butler, who went missing here in 2010. She was my sister, but before I was born. My dad is Andrew Butler. I'm Kara."

An embarrassing squirm of grief wound through Shelly's chest. How had she been stupid enough to let the very sight of this young woman bring her to tears?

"You knew my sister?" Kara asked quietly.

Shelly eased out from behind the car door, then slammed it. Her feet crunched over the dirt as she approached the young woman. Closer, Kara did look different from Molly—a slightly larger forehead and perhaps a wider mouth. "It's funny that you of all people are here," Shelly said. "My son was Elijah Bryce. He was one of the ones who . . ."

Kara's mouth opened in surprise, as if she were the one suddenly seeing a ghost. The tall pine treetops clacked quietly in the light breeze. From somewhere in the distance came the cawing of crows. Were they trying their flight over the Moon Woods yet again?

"You never found out what happened to them," Kara said. Something about her mannerism changed when she said this, as if she were being extremely careful. Shelly wasn't too decrepit to notice that the young woman had inflected her words as if *she* somehow knew what had happened. "It's funny," Kara continued.

"I decided to book a plane ticket here at the end of June, after everything started going crazy with Jonathan Flite back east. Seemed like it might start getting difficult to visit here soon, so . . ." The young woman stopped, as if catching herself from sharing too much. Rethinking her words, she said, "I flew into Minneapolis last night and drove down just this morning. It's insane timing, considering what happened with Jonathan's mom during that press conference. I'm still shocked at all of it."

There it was again, a reference to the news. Shelly's curiosity was starting to get the best of her, but because she didn't want to appear ignorant, she simply nodded as if she were perfectly aware of what had happened. At least she now knew it had been an explosion at a press conference.

"What a coincidence we came here at the same time," Shelly said. "Can't go anywhere in this town without somebody else knowing about it."

Kara narrowed her eyes but with a smile, as if she weren't quite sure whether Shelly was being friendly. Even Shelly herself didn't have an answer to that. These two chance encounters today—first Eloise Creed and now Kara Butler, this ghost image of Molly—had officially shaken every ounce of closure she had about the Idle County Seven case. Lately, it seemed that each day tore off another peel of that onion, which was now proving to be rancid.

Shelly gestured at the thick, metal gate. "You clearly know who owns this place."

"I do," Kara replied, also looking at the gate, perhaps beyond it. "I'm not sure what exactly I expected to find here. I just wanted to . . . feel how it is, I guess? There's an intercom button or something on the right side of the gate. See it?"

Moving closer to the fence, Shelly focused her eyes and finally noticed the panel on the closest steel support column ten feet to her right. It was basic—a matching gray button and what appeared to be speaker holes. No buttons to dial, nothing that implied possible access for an outsider. Shelly glanced left and right, into the woods. The tall, gray fence continued as far through the trees as she could see in both directions. She suddenly marveled at the fact that her son had once dug up that jawbone in this forest, that it had linked him to Cynthia Foster and, ultimately, to this young woman standing behind her.

Shelly turned and looked at Kara Butler. "We should probably get out of—" she started, but just as a shaft of sunlight fell over the young woman, illuminating a hint of brown in her hair (just like Molly's had been), there came the sound of tires on gravel, from the other side of the gate. Shelly immediately took five steps back to stand next to Kara. Not knowing what else to do, she simply peered through the trees, waiting, until she realized that if the approaching vehicle meant to exit, theirs were in the way.

There came a glint through the trees, then a vision of silver. It was a type of car Shelly didn't recognize. Its logo, a large trident, blazed on its front.

"Why the hell would they be driving a Maserati in Idle County?" Kara said aloud, stepping forward and slightly in front of Shelly in a manner that almost seemed protective.

The car (Shelly had not been able to absorb the brand name Kara had so effortlessly uttered) stopped ten feet behind the gray gate. Shelly couldn't make out the person behind the wheel, but she didn't need to, because Kara Butler, seeming Queen of Knowledge, suddenly stood taller, as if bracing herself. With her gaze glued on the car's windshield, she whispered, "That's Victoria Zobel. Victor Zobel's daughter who had that reality show. *Chick CEO.*"

"The one where they caught her sleeping with what's-his-name?" Shelly asked, unaware until the words were out that she was admitting to watching that sort of drivel.

Kara squinted. "Yeah. That's her. I'm not sure what you're doing here, Ms. Bryce, but I'm about to see how far in I can go. If you want to join me, feel free. I'm not sure what we're going to find."

The words of this younger, newer Miss Butler barely had time to set off warning bells in Shelly's heart, because just then, the gate began sliding open, as if on its own accord. The door of the silver, trident-branded car opened, and a tan, middle-aged woman with severely cropped, peroxide-blond hair stepped out. Even from twenty feet away, Shelly could hear her white heels grinding into the unmarked road's dirt. Her matching white suit, all business except for a skirt that bordered on immodest, made the forest around them look even darker.

"I was expecting reporters today," Victoria Zobel called to them as the gate opened, flashing an array of teeth reminiscent of either a happy greyhound or a shark—it was hard to tell. Shelly didn't have the social experience to gauge people of this sort. The only reason her legs weren't shaking at Victoria's fame was because she had spoken face-to-face with the woman's father, Victor, on enough occasions to call him an acquaintance—even an old one. As the tall woman approached the gate, a particular brand of overconfidence colored her expression in a way that brought back a feeling her father had always instilled in Shelly: that of being a pawn, smiled at and acknowledged on the surface, but cast aside once the exchange was over.

The gate was now fully open, and Victoria Zobel stood directly on its border.

"We were just leaving," Shelly said, stepping forward just far enough to pull lightly on Kara Butler's gray, fitted T-shirt.

"Actually, I wasn't," Kara said. "You're Victoria Zobel, correct?"

Again, the blond, white-suited woman flashed her teeth. "I guess it isn't a secret whose property this is. And yes, I come here from time to time. More often as of late. My father doesn't really touch Earth's surface much anymore, considering it's becoming an overpopulated mess." Victoria said this with a sneering chuckle. Shelly wasn't sure if this was a cordial joke or a snub on everyone who couldn't afford to escape the problems of the world. "We saw you on the security cameras, though, and—"

Shelly turned immediately on her heels and began marching back to her car. "It was a mistake!" she called back over her shoulder. "I turned down this road by mistake. It was very nice to meet you Ms. Zobel, and you as well Ms. Butler, but I must be—"

"Ms. Bryce, I came out here because of *you*," Victoria Zobel called from behind her.

Shelly had just opened her car door and was about to step in, but she stopped, imagining how silly she must look—a gray-haired woman, moving more spryly than her wrinkles and matching denim might suggest be possible. Nervous, nervous, always in a flutter, and now the day had suddenly become surreal. Standing right in front of her was an ex-star of a television show.

"And did I hear her say 'Butler'?" Victoria continued, glancing at Kara. "One can't help hearing that name in these parts and wondering if the person was related to the girl with the tumor. Who disappeared with her friends, I mean."

"We have the same father. Or had, in her case."

"And did you and Ms. Bryce plan to come here together?"

Kara glanced back at Shelly, and despite her solid stance, she looked unnerved. "Coincidence," she said.

Victoria flashed them a sharp grin. "Don't you sometimes wonder if coincidences aren't really coincidences at all?"

Neither Shelly nor Kara said a word.

"What I was *going* to say," Victoria continued, "is that I was videoconferencing with my father—who's up on his little orbiting yacht—when we saw you on the security cameras. The reporters know they're not supposed to cross our property line, so we were curious." She looked directly at Shelly now. "He recognized you, Ms. Bryce. From the days after your son disappeared. He wanted me to offer you lunch, because he's done a terrible job at keeping in touch. Seeing as you both lost loved ones. He's a very busy man, as you know."

Shelly swallowed, keenly aware that her grief over the Idle County Seven's disappearances had rarely extended past her own son; she didn't remember Victor Zobel's stepdaughter, Jillian, in any personal way, other than her rumored abortion. In acknowledgment of Victoria's kind words, however, she said, "Jillian was a decent girl."

"Can I offer you lunch and show you both around?" Victoria said. "I promise that despite what you may have heard in the news recently, my father has nothing to hide here. He simply found it to be a tranquil spot. Hence the home he built here. All the silly things being thrown around on TV about him are just talk of the stupefied masses. He hasn't made a comment, because he doesn't want to lend the rumors credibility. We're both of the mind that people should rise above that sort of nonsense and start caring about improving the state of the world."

Nonsense it might be, Shelly thought, *but I'll never trust an atheist.*

Yet she found herself easing away from the car, about to shut the door in acquiescence. Kara glanced back, saw what could only be curiosity on Shelly's face, and gave her a nod. "I'm game for lunch. I didn't even think I'd get past Old Mill Road."

Shelly swung her purse off her shoulder and dug out her phone. "I suppose it would be unappreciative of me to say no, considering all your father did for us back in the day. Let me just send a quick message to my friend Delia. I was supposed to have lunch with her." This was a lie, but it was for safety, wasn't it? If for some reason Shelly didn't return, Delia would call the police. The text message was a bit long, but Shelly made an effort to hit all the important points.

> *Met Molly Butler's sister, Kara, in the Moon Woods at Victor Zobel's gate. Victoria Zobel is here/saw us on camera. Came out to talk/offered us lunch. Call police if you don't hear from me tonight. You never know these days.*

Delia's response, probably a result of her waiting with bated breath for any developments with the Jonathan Flite drama, came almost instantly.

> *THE Victoria Zobel??? Tell me everything (later).*

Shelly took this as proper confirmation, wanting to roll her eyes at Delia's juvenility but refraining from doing so. She smiled up at Victoria. "All set. Plans changed. But really, I should be home by one."

"Wonderful," the woman said. "Just follow me on in. You can park in the roundabout by the fountain. We'll have to connect my dad on video. He said he'd love to say hello."

Victoria swung around, her heels digging into the dirt, and walked back to her flashy car. A second later, she accelerated without turning around, backing up until the trees engulfed her. The gate remained open.

Kara turned to Shelly with her mouth slightly open and let out a long, tense breath. Once they were completely alone again, she said, "You know what they're saying about Victor Zobel, right?"

"I may be old, but I watch the news," Shelly said.

"I'm here for my own reasons," Kara replied. "I'm going in. I'd be honored to have you join me, but if you don't want to, I completely understand." As if it were a well-calculated afterthought, she said, "I honestly don't think this is safe. At all. That's a serious warning."

It wasn't a challenge by any means, but Shelly suddenly remembered that summer morning in 2005, when she received the call that Elijah was in Saint Mary's Hospital and that he had carried—yes, *carried*—Damon Jacoby's body over the rock bridge linking Spinner's Island to the shore of Spinner's Lake. Despite their troubles, he truly had been a hero that year. Even if it was thirty years late, Shelly supposed she owed it to him to be brave just this once, to satisfy that tiny, devilish inkling of curiosity sparked by Jonathan Flite's claim that the Idle County Seven disappeared here. Who would she be if she turned a blind eye on what could possibly be a clue to Elijah's fate?

"I told my friend Delia where I am," Shelly said. "I'll follow you in."

With that, she embarked after Kara through Victor Zobel's Moon Woods gate, toward the famous compound few in Idle County had ever seen. Whether it was luck, coincidence, or some darker, Godless force shaping her path today, Shelly couldn't discount her own choice to continue down it. If anything, it showed she cared, that she hadn't simply forgotten Elijah and gone on her merry way through life.

Through a break in the trees, she saw what appeared to be another gate, this one an arch carved smoothly out of a fifteen-foot cement wall. Just beyond it lay a clearing in the trees and what appeared to be a home so palatial that Shelly couldn't see where it started or ended. Here was another of Idle County's mysteries, and it had been standing hidden in the trees for almost thirty years, just a few miles from her eyes.

When Shelly pulled into the mansion's roundabout, parked behind Kara, and exited her car, a sudden rush of euphoria overtook her. For a moment, she thought it might be a symptom of the day's heat, which seemed to be increasing, or perhaps an indication that she should have lived a more exciting life before today. Then everything around her seemed to sparkle, but in a way that somehow preceded her physical perceptions, as though God himself were offering her some internal, saintly vision.

Oh my, I never knew how beautiful—

And then her thoughts exploded into a billion different colors and sounds, and everything went white.

2038

WINIFRED FLITE STOOD IN HER KITCHEN, overseeing Gwendolyn, her regular caterer, who was preparing Jonathan's welcome-home dinner of stuffed chicken breasts, parsley buttered red potatoes, almond-infused wild rice, and bacon-wrapped asparagus. So far, Jonathan had been home for four hours, and he had spent the majority of it with his bodyguard, Sounder, and Jimmy Barber—first checking out his new bedroom, which faced the trees on the east side of the mansion, then organizing what little he had to organize, and finally talking with his friends out on the attached deck. Winifred had hoped Sounder would join her in the kitchen so they could at least attempt to break the ice of being both housemates and employer and employee. He had joined Jonathan and Jimmy, however, as if he were just as uncomfortable making this transition as she was.

This of course left Winifred to sip her vodka tonic in the

kitchen with Gwendolyn, who knew Jonathan's story and was walking on eggshells even more than usual. The way she faked politeness as she stuffed the chicken breasts with a mixture of spinach, bacon, and cheese made it obvious she was doing it only for the money. Winifred had always talked down to Gwendolyn, but Gwendolyn kept coming back, because Winifred paid well.

"I appreciate your being here," Winifred said, trying on a new brand of politeness.

Gwendolyn replied with a no-eye-contact half smile. "No problem. You've always been a great client."

"We both know *that's* not the case."

This time, Gwendolyn looked at Winifred for longer than a second, her smile seeming slightly more genuine. "But I appreciate your business just the same. How are you handling all this . . . hoopla?"

Winifred took a longer-than-usual sip of her drink. "Let's just say I'm trying to be a better mother this time around, but I'm pretty sure nobody in this house actually wants me to be here. I guess I do have a friend coming to visit"—she looked at her diamond-studded Cartier watch and sighed—"about ten minutes ago."

"Who's the friend?"

"A psychiatrist from Minnesota who helped Jonathan and me last fall. You know, back when . . ."

"I saw on the news," Gwendolyn said. And after a hint of warmth: "Does it make you nervous? All the attention Jonathan's getting?"

"I can see it makes *you* nervous." Winifred began sliding her drink across the marble countertop, the way she did when her mind was full and her desire to deal with problems had hit a brick wall. Gwendolyn furrowed her eyebrows and didn't reply, and Winifred inwardly kicked herself for her lack of social skills. No wonder Jonathan had turned out the way he did. "Meaning I appreciate you're here at all," she continued. "Sorry. I don't know how to interact with people. My therapist says it's because of all the walls I put up. But . . . I just want you to be comfortable here. And know that you're welcome."

"That's what you pay me for, right?" Gwendolyn said. But she was back to her polite, facade-laced expression. "I'm going to run down to Smith Foods before the chicken goes in. I just realized I forgot the shaved almonds for the wild rice."

With a polite dip of her head meant to be a smile, Winifred acknowledged the subtle abandonment, hoping Gwendolyn wouldn't be swarmed by the reporters and protesters camped down on Wellington Avenue. Four of the reporters had knocked on Winifred's door just two hours ago and asked for an impromptu press conference. As always, she had outright refused, demanding they get off her private property.

She glanced at her watch again. 4:16 p.m. Dr. Thomas Lumen's plane had landed in Providence at 2:50 p.m., which meant, considering plane taxiing and car transportation, he should be arriving any minute. As Winifred watched Gwendolyn exit the house and head briskly toward her electric Ford SUV, she realized, with a bit of comfort, that despite the fact that most people didn't enjoy being around her, Dr. Lumen somehow did. She had faith in him, which was quite possibly a first for her in relation to any other person—at least since her meeting and eventual selfish dumping of Jonathan's father, Dominic Bock.

She sat alone in the kitchen for twelve more minutes before the doorbell rang. Upon hearing it, she jumped off the barstool along the main counter and walked briskly toward the door, trying to wing-clip the butterflies in her stomach. She glanced through the peephole, and her heart leapt with excitement when she saw the gray-haired, small-framed Dr. Lumen. He was wearing the new glasses he had bought in April, which Winifred had seen only during their video conferences in the weeks since. He was also carrying a bottle of wine. She patted the tight bun on top of her head before opening the door.

"Don't kill me for being late," Dr. Lumen immediately said. "The DriveMe car's computer was all off-kilter, and it got lost on the way to the hotel. Then I had to stop at the store for this." He held out the wine and whispered, "Nothing special, but I figure Jonathan and Sounder might not want hard liquor with their dinner."

"As if I don't have *wine*," Winifred snapped, but she did it with a smile, and the psychiatrist gave her a fake scowl. She ushered him into the house.

"Besides, I think we should probably stay soberish," Dr. Lumen said. "It being Jonathan's first night home and all. And Sounder is here, yes?"

"Along with Jimmy Barber."

"The fashionista kid?" Dr. Lumen said. "Are he and Jonathan still a thing?"

"Not a gay thing, but a friend thing," Winifred said. "I'm pretty sure Jimmy has some kind of crush, but not, like, romantic. I haven't even bothered to ask Jonathan what their dynamic is."

"Nice that he has a friend, either way." Dr. Lumen stood as tall as he could for a moment and surveyed Winifred. Only then did she notice he wasn't using his cane. She glanced down at his leg with a raised eyebrow. "Oh, yeah," he said. "Been doing more of the physical therapy I should have been doing all my life. Still limping and always will, but I'd be lying if I said the leg didn't feel stronger. Plus the cane made me feel old."

"Made you look old, too." Winifred ensured her air of insolence was just over the top enough to make the psychiatrist realize it was her version of humor.

"Does Jonathan know I'm coming?"

"No. I figured I'd try to surprise him. Not that it'll make up for all the years of bad parenting."

"I guess we'll find out," Dr. Lumen said, grinning. "But make me a drink first."

Jonathan, Jimmy, and Sounder came downstairs when Winifred sent a text message to Jonathan's new ActoPhone. It had been years since she had experienced any sense of excitement surrounding her status as a mother, but having Dr. Lumen as a surprise guest for Jonathan's welcome-home dinner now brought her stomach butterflies back. Was it because she felt guilty for all the years of maltreatment? Was it for her own emotional benefit? Winifred didn't know, but her desire to make Jonathan happy for his own sake felt genuine. It was new. It was a step in the right direction.

Jonathan and his friends approached the kitchen amid a series of low murmurs that seemed to be a discussion relating to Weston Carrow, the leader of the Children of God. "If he keeps sending you ActoShouts tonight, I want to know," Jonathan was saying. "I know there'll be cops outside for the next few days, but—"

He stopped when he entered the kitchen and saw Dr. Lumen standing behind the marble countertop with his almost-empty glass. For a moment, Winifred thought her son's face was about to contort in anger, but he burst into a smile and reached the psychiatrist in four big steps.

"Wait, what?" Jonathan said. "How the . . . Did you just fly in today?" Behind Jonathan, Sounder was on his phone, discussing Weston Carrow in a hushed voice. A second later, he turned and, still talking, walked toward the front door.

Dr. Lumen grabbed Jonathan into a hug, and they embraced in a way that was a curious blend of mentor, mentee, and adult friendship. For the millionth time that year, Winifred wondered how Jonathan had managed to become a decent human being. Perhaps her legally mandated outsourcing of his teenage years had paid off.

"It's a big day, and it was a good excuse to visit," Dr. Lumen said with a grin, flitting his gaze at Winifred as well.

"Well, you're right on time," Jonathan said. "Sounder just called the police. I'm guessing he went outside to talk to them."

Winifred's thawing heart froze over once again. "What do you mean 'called the police'?"

Jonathan gestured with his neck toward Jimmy Barber, who had already made a wardrobe change since his appearance that morning at the courthouse. "Jimmy's getting a bunch of ActoShouts from that Weston Carrow dude. Like, 'Tell the blasphemer Jonathan Flite that God won't let him live to see another day' and 'It's a matter of cosmic importance that the Children of God execute this Antichrist before day's end.' He sounds insane. Like *really* insane."

"Welcome the hell back," Winifred said, turning to Dr. Lumen, whose smile had disappeared.

The psychiatrist was now leaning over Jimmy's shoulder. "Show me. Who is this person?"

Winifred mixed another drink as Jonathan and Jimmy relayed to Dr. Lumen everything they knew about Weston Carrow. Then they showed him a new string of ActoShouts, the gist of which Winifred picked up from the air of fear darkening the psychiatrist's eyes. "And Jonathan can't leave the state?" he asked, glancing at Winifred.

"Not until he turns nineteen."

"Christ. This guy says he's camped out at the bottom of your hill. He's probably one of the people I passed driving up here. There were at least twenty reporters out there filming all the protesters."

"You want me to go check things out?" Jimmy Barber asked. "I can run down if I change my shoes."

"No more media for you today," Jonathan replied with a strained grin. He then glanced at Dr. Lumen. "I seriously can't even think about it anymore. I felt safer at Crescent. But maybe this is just how it's going to be. If I can't leave the state, I'm going to have to get used to people wanting me dead. I just didn't think it would be this . . . immediate."

"We'll do everything possible to protect you," Dr. Lumen said as he accepted a new drink from Winifred. He didn't sip it. "Could we take you to a hotel in Providence? Or some random one off the highway before the state line? They reprogrammed the geo zones on that chip in your leg, correct?"

"Yeah. But no way in hell am I going anywhere public. I'm not putting anyone else in danger. *You* guys might be better off leaving, though. It's just . . ."

"It's unfair is what it is," Jimmy Barber chimed in, like some best-friend character in a 1960s sitcom.

Jonathan shrugged, but Winifred noticed he was breathing with an open mouth and tilting his head in an unusual way, as though he hadn't yet figured out how to fit this madness into his new, free reality. Whatever Dr. Freede had taught him at Crescent to curb his anxiety seemed to be working, however, because for the first time in months, he wasn't shutting down. "No, not unfair. If

Ellen Graber were still alive, nobody would know about me. And all the stuff in my head would still be a secret. This is all my fault. Don't forget that." With a desperate frown, Jonathan shook his head.

Winifred was again sliding her full glass across the marble countertop, from hand to hand. Kate Crookston's face rose in her mind as her old-fashioned feelings of blame toward Jonathan returned. All those rushes of water under the bridge—they came back on days like this, when Winifred wondered what her life might have been like had she not tricked Dominic Bock into being the father of her child. But choices were choices, and there was no unmaking them. Kate Crookston would say that her feelings of blame toward Jonathan were attempts to offset her own guilt over having made mistakes in raising him, and neither were productive sentiments to dwell on. What she needed to do was use these emotions as arrows to aim her life toward a new trajectory—one on which feelings like that would no longer arise.

"Jonathan, you just have to live now," Dr. Lumen said. "Do your best. It's all you can do. And those of us who care about you will stand by you a hundred percent."

As if on some sickening cue, there came a cadenced, deafening sound from the back patio, beyond the long glass windows lining the dining area just off the kitchen. Before Winifred could register what it was, the glass behind them was shattering, and Dr. Lumen was tumbling toward her and dragging her to the floor. Jonathan and Jimmy were screaming, and through the sudden cacophony that without warning had made the kitchen a war zone, Winifred realized what was happening. Somebody was bullet bombing her house with a machine gun.

PART 4

WE'RE ALL FINE

2038

J IMMY BARBER WAS TOO SHOCKED TO SCREAM, too pumped with adrenaline to cry, and too fueled with the drive to survive to even register the significance of the bullets flying through the windows and hitting the walls, furniture, and house decorations around him. The machine gun's magazine emptied in a matter of seconds, faster than it would have in a movie, but there appeared to be two shooters in the backyard, because just as the first stream of bullets stopped, another began.

"Get behind the counter!" Jonathan screamed. Jimmy had already scrambled there and settled along the dark-stained cupboards underneath the kitchen sink, but Winifred Flite and the psychiatrist from Minnesota, whom Jimmy had first met at Mason Witzel's funeral last December, were on the dining area's side of the long marble counter. They were open to the spray of bullets shattering the back-patio windows. Jonathan was lying with his upper half stretched a foot beyond the kitchen's cooking area, ushering his mother and the doctor into it, along the floor behind the horseshoe-shaped marble counter.

Within five seconds, all four of them were huddled with their hands over their heads. The second machine gun outside had stopped. Jimmy's mind raced toward all possible routes to safety, but seeing as they were blocked into the kitchen's cooking area, the only way out was through its half-loop opening. They would have to crawl across a five-foot stretch of floor shielded only partially by the counter, then into the shaded hallway leading to the house's front door.

"Jesus Christ, we need to get out of here," Winifred said. "Somebody needs to call the po—"

"Sounder was on the phone with them already!" Jonathan whispered. "Quiet!"

Nobody spoke. A shard of glass that had been hanging from one of the demolished patio window frames fell and shattered, but only silence followed. No rush of footsteps. No militant orders between shooters. Nothing.

"Let's get across to the hall," Jimmy whispered, gesturing with his neck toward the opening at the cooking area's entrance. "Do you think they'll see if—"

The machine guns roared back to life. This time, they weren't aimed at the kitchen but at somewhere else outside. *At Sounder in the backyard?* Jimmy wondered.

Just as the weapons' magazines emptied again, he heard sirens approaching from the bottom of Columbus Avenue. It was more than one—Jimmy counted at least four distinct, high-pitched warbles nearing the house.

"Jimmy's right," Jonathan said. "Hallway. Front door. We can't get stuck in the corner like this. They could trap us if they decide to come into the house."

"They're probably not looking for hostages," Dr. Lumen replied in a low voice. "But you're right." He glanced at Winifred. "You go behind me on my left side. Keep low. I'll block you."

"I can't let you—" Winifred started, but Dr. Lumen cut her off in a fierce tone Jimmy would never have thought possible from him.

"*Don't argue. Your safety comes first.*"

"Let me or Jimmy go first so we can check the door," Jonathan said. "There could be other shooters out there—"

More gunshots interrupted him. Still machine guns, but now they were farther behind the house. Jimmy heard yells and footsteps from the front, and a moment later there were more shots, these ones single bursts, closer but aimed away. The front door flew open, and two people Jimmy could make out only as silhouettes against the bright frame of daylight rushed into the house. Within seconds, he heard a woman's voice. "We have two gunmen heading toward Eastnor Road through the backyards off Columbus and Harbor View." It was an officer, an auburn-haired female, yelling into her radio, which Jimmy assumed was connected to a pair of ActoLenses in her eyes. All emergency and law enforcement agencies had their own dedicated Acto networks, which meant somebody somewhere was likely seeing a police-point-of-view video of Jimmy, Jonathan, Winifred, and Dr. Lumen huddled on the kitchen floor.

It took less than half a second for Jimmy to sit up against the cupboard so that he wouldn't look afraid in the video, in the minuscule chance it were ever to stream publicly.

"We're in here," Dr. Lumen yelled, but the two officers were already rushing toward the kitchen.

"Are any of you hurt?" the female officer asked, immediately taking a position at the hallway's kitchen entrance. She was tall but graceful with her movements as she cleared the space, gun drawn and eyes watching the backyard like a hawk. Her hair was pulled back, and her gaze, scanning every visible spot around them, was razor sharp. She gestured toward the dining area and attached living room, which Jimmy assumed were now covered in glass. The second officer, a male, rushed to the far side of the counter and eased toward the shattered windows.

"We're all fine," Winifred said. "Right?"

The male officer crouched to the floor to examine them. "Nobody's hit?"

"All good," Dr. Lumen said, surveying everyone. Jimmy followed his gaze and was relieved not to see any blood coloring the kitchen's floor tiles. But Jonathan's mother looked anything but fine. She was holding her heart, and tears glazed her shocked eyes. She was breathing in short bursts, as if trying to come to grips with everything happening in front of her. Jimmy, who had experienced the life-altering rush of having to dodge bullets during the attack on Jonathan last year, wondered if this might have damaged her irrevocably. Jonathan had told him she was trying to be a better mother, but how could she possibly come through this unscarred?

"This can't be happening," she was saying over and over to the psychiatrist from Minnesota. He had taken her in his arms from behind, and she was hanging onto him so tight that her fingers, gripping his wrists, were white at their knuckles.

Jimmy glanced at Jonathan. His friend was breathing fast, also looking a bit glazed over, but when Jimmy snapped a finger in front of him and said, "Hey, you all right?" he turned and started shaking his head.

"This is going to be a national headline," he replied in a slow, almost drawly voice. "If it was Weston Carrow's people, the media's going to start asking . . ."

Typically, Jimmy's ability to finish people's sentences was second to none, but right now he was unable to predict Jonathan's next words. "Asking what?" he said, suddenly aware of how shaky his own voice sounded, how his words couldn't quite keep up with his brain.

"Why all these religious people think I'm a threat," Jonathan replied. "Once people start focusing on that, I'll have no idea what to say. There's too damned much."

For the first time since Jimmy had known Jonathan, he saw real panic in the young man's eyes. Whether it was simply due to the intensity of that very moment or somehow related to whatever Jonathan thought he knew about the vanished Idle County Seven kids, it seemed to have thoroughly shaken him. Jimmy loved the limelight, the cameras, and the feeling of knowing life could be snatched away at any second. Even now he was relishing the sensation of his racing heart and the memory of that initial explosion of bullets, which had hit their lives like a splintered freight train and forked their roads in what could only be new and more intense life directions. But Jonathan had to be seeing this through different eyes. He was the center of it all.

The kitchen soon swarmed with police officers. When one of them ushered Jimmy to his feet, his legs were numb, and walking with his eyes open felt like walking blindfolded. He had almost just been ripped apart by flying metal bullets, narrowly escaping the act of unbecoming. It was more obvious this time around, in broad daylight, alongside the people whom he now considered his friends. He saw the weight of the situation in their eyes as they stumbled in shock toward the front door. Despite the warm day, Dr. Lumen draped Winifred in a blanket he must have found in one of the other living rooms, and she grabbed it around herself as if it were a cocoon. Jimmy stepped onto the front porch behind Jonathan as a wailing ambulance turned from Columbus Avenue into the driveway. The late afternoon became a mishmash of so many police procedures and questions and speculations that Jimmy fell to his rear on the front steps and stared, for a duration that somehow seemed free of time, at the glistening harbor in the distance.

2038

NICOLAS LEANDRO RIM, killer of Mason Witzel and criminal target of the FBI, sat in front of a dance stage under the dusky, color-gelled lights of Mermaid Corner on Park Street, one of Hartford's prime spots to find beautiful women dancing for keeps. The place smelled musty and musky, as if some of the male patrons hadn't stopped drinking and burping and breathing for days. He was leaning on the black counter lining the stage, sipping on absinthe and analyzing a new, two-inch scratch on his muscled forearm that he hadn't noticed before. It was already scabbed over.

Near the ceiling to the left of the stage hung an old television. Onscreen was its usual news station, once again with a live report from Newport, Rhode Island, where Jonathan Flite had just been attacked on his first day home from juvenile lockup. This was it: the boy had just become an official media buzzword. As of six hours ago, he had broken the barrier between being a local pariah and being a national—possibly international—sensation.

Details were still sketchy, but two men sporting automatic weapons had shot at Jonathan's house around 4:30 p.m. Eastern Standard Time. Both suspects had been shot dead while running from police just minutes later, and now media outlets everywhere had focused their lenses on the small, East Coast city of Newport, Rhode Island. At first, reporters had speculated that the attack had been carried out due to fears over Jonathan's being free to walk the streets. Then, without realizing the ramifications, the Associated Press Television News had interviewed a pale, red-haired man named Weston Carrow, who had been standing amid protesters on the road below the Flite house.

"Jonathan Flite says he has memories of other lives," Carrow had started. "These New Age claims defy God's natural order for spirituality and are a threat to Christ's message for humanity. In this age when God's chosen have had to declare war on those who attempt to undermine Christ—namely scientists like Victor Zobel who defy Biblical truth—blasphemous ideas like reincarnation will only confuse, divide, and inspire people to laugh in the face of death. Last year, we saw the power of Christ at work in the fiery cleansing of Geneva. This year, a new foe is on our very shores. While I wouldn't tempt the wrath of God by applauding an atheist like Victor Zobel, perhaps he was right to try to silence Jonathan Flite last November. The boy's lies, once believed, will become a threat. That threat must be removed."

Carrow's interview was already streaming front and center via national news outlets and had piqued media interest enough to create the most controversial, polarizing headlines about Jonathan Flite yet.

"Boy's Past-Life Claims Invoke Firestorm."

"Christian Fundamentalist Accuses Victor Zobel of Covering Up Threat to Atheism."

"Jonathan Flite: A Menace to Belief?"

Nicolas Rim was almost certain Victor Zobel had ordered last November's botched assassination attempt on Jonathan Flite. The instruction for him to work his way into Paul Simpleton's social circle and bribe him to help kill the boy had come from Larry Kane, CEO of Carey Developments—a subsidiary of Zobel's Grand Natural Development Corporation—during a hushed, face-to-face meeting in January 2037. Nicolas had performed many illegal deeds for Larry Kane since Victor Zobel had arranged for him to be Kane's personal assistant after high school, following his family's sponsored relocation to the United States. Kane's hesitant tone during that January 2037 meeting, however, had implied not malice but fear. He had tossed an array of recent photographs onto his glass-topped desk; they were of Nicolas's sisters, Nora and Luana, and their children, shot with a long lens during their mundane day-to-day activities in Bern, Switzerland. Kane had relayed a threat, assuring Nicolas it wasn't coming from him, that Nora, Luana, and their husbands and children would be "endangered" were he not to follow through on this order. Unspoken in the man's tone was a clear message that Carey Developments, the company itself, would also be under threat if they did not attempt to end Jonathan Flite's life. Suspecting a mandate from Victor Zobel, Nicolas had called the man's son, Revis, whom he had remained friendly with since childhood, and casually asked if his father had any special interest in the Rhode Island boy. Revis Zobel, who had been docked in Naples during a Mediterranean sailing trip, expressed a curious lack of surprise at the idea but assured Nicolas that he hadn't the foggiest notion of any such family interest. Against his heart, Nicolas had followed through with the assassination order as best he could, but of course it had gone terribly awry. Now he was a target himself, and his quality of life was irrevocably lost.

Six hours ago, the minute Nicolas learned of the most recent gun attack on Jonathan Flite, he decided it was time—without wasting another second—to attempt his escape from police surveillance. The heavier the media descended upon Jonathan Flite, the higher the chances that Nicolas's connection to him via Paul Simpleton would squirm its way into the public eye. If that were to happen, there would be no way for Nicolas to end his own life the way he wanted—quietly, privately, and peacefully. The last thing he wanted was to go out in a bath of public humiliation. After writing his suicide note and leaving it on his kitchen table four days ago, he had spent every waking moment figuring out how best to escape the eyes of the Hartford police and FBI. Tonight's assault on Jonathan Flite had been the final word; Nicolas needed to take action before the media got wind of his name. Mermaid Corner, his tenant Aurora Demark's place of employment, was the only starting line he could think of.

He hadn't yet seen Aurora, even though it was Wednesday, one of her usual days. Was she somewhere in the back room? Putting on an outfit just so she could take it off again?

Sitting along the far end of the stage, near the private booths along the back wall, was a white-haired, white-bearded man who was about a foot shorter than Nicolas but just as thick. Nicolas had seen him in four places today: at the public library, at the grocery store, in the Duane Reade, and at the ShopRite on Prospect Avenue. It wasn't obvious whether he was a fed or some task-force member of the Hartford police department, but it didn't matter.

The man was following him. So much for the strip club being a public place of private indecency.

The bar's music was far too loud, and the absinthe had already begun to blur Nicolas's vision. All he needed was to lose the man so he could get to one of his other apartments, probably the one in Westfield. There, he had credit cards, a falsified passport, cash, clothing, and weapons. It would be a risk, of course, because it was quite possible the feds had discovered one or both of his aliases and all properties owned or rented under them. Isn't that what they did? Dug into the gritty details of the depraved to publicly brand them as jailworthy villains? This was the end, as far as Nicolas was concerned. Upon writing his suicide note, he had reflected on the incredible reality that he truly *had* become one of those jail-worthy villains. Tonight was the beginning of what could be his final ride.

With the weight of Aurora's absence sinking in his heart, Nicolas held out a hundred-dollar bill to Shandra, the silver-clad dancer closest to him. She was thin and Asian—a new addition to Mermaid Corner since Nicolas had last been here. Washed under waving pink light, Shandra danced up to him, slowly moving in a way that accentuated what physical curves she had. When she saw Benjamin Franklin's face on the bill Nicolas was holding out, she immediately warmed to him and leaned down to whisper in his ear.

"Nobody in Hartford uses hundreds." She grabbed at the bill, but Nicolas pulled it back.

"Would you do me the honor of a private dance?" he asked. "One of those booths?" It was strange to observe the reality of the situation when his interest had nothing to do with the young woman's body. He saw a sliver of confidence light her eyes before he saw it overtaken by a spark of greed.

"First booth on the left," she said. "I'll be there in five minutes, sexy. Going to change."

"Wait," Nicolas whispered. "A thousand dollars cash if you do two things for me. Let me use your cell phone to order a cab. And let me leave through the dressing room door. I've been back there a hundred times, so I know the way."

For a second, Shandra's expression fluttered with incredulity. She looked Nicolas in the eyes. He raised his brows but didn't smile. "Five minutes," she said before hopping to her feet.

Nicolas stood up from his seat in front of the stage, stretching his arms and taking the opportunity to steal a glimpse at the white-haired man sitting at its opposite end. Had he fluttered a glance left? Nicolas couldn't tell, but he ambled past the man, surprised that he felt more adrenaline now than he did fear. Amazing how quickly a finalized choice to die on his own terms could cleanse a muddied course of action.

It took only three minutes for Shandra to join him in the booth. She had changed into a sparkling red bra and matching panties, but around her torso was a black leather vest. Swiping the private booth's glittering curtain shut, she slinked toward him, digging into the garment's inner left pocket and withdrawing a beat-up ActoPhone that was at least three years old. The screen worked, however, and she held it out to him. He made to grab it, and she pulled it back.

"Ah ah. You promised."

"Oh, yes," Nicolas said, feeling himself blush. Out of his pocket came ten one-hundred-dollar bills. Shandra took the money at the exact moment she released her phone into his hands. "DriveMe app's open," she said. "You can just charge it to my account."

"I need two cabs," Nicolas replied. "Is that all right?"

Shandra narrowed her eyes. "How far do you have to go?"

"Not far. Westfield."

"Why two?"

"First one will be just six blocks or so."

"Why?"

"Have to stop at the liquor store. On Wyllys." Was there even a liquor store on Wyllys Street? He had no idea. But Shandra nodded and tucked the thousand dollars into her vest's inside pocket. It took only two minutes for Nicolas to order himself both cabs—one for the alley entrance outside the dressing-room exit of Mermaid Corner (due in five minutes) and the other for the corner of Wyllys and Lisbon (due in thirty).

Nicolas waited the five minutes, slipping Shandra dollar bills as she twirled her body over him. Suddenly, she stopped, dug into her vest once again, and pulled out her phone, which had lit up with an alert.

"Car's outside," she said.

After sliding another hundred into her vest pocket, Nicolas walked to the curtain and glanced through one of its cracks. The white-haired man was on his phone, looking the other way at one of the topless strippers. It was now or never. Nicolas turned to Shandra. "*Thank you.*"

He slipped out of the private dance booth, turned right, and walked straight for the dressing room—through the curtain and past four girls who were primping themselves, fixing their makeup, and adjusting their scanty outfits in front of mirrors. Nowhere did he glimpse Aurora's Demark's golden hair, and in no way could he tell whether the white-haired man had seen him. All he knew, stepping out into the club's back alley on this warm May evening, was that tonight could be his last chance to maintain control of his own life.

To his left, at the end of the alley and facing south on Washington Street, was his cab, a self-driving Ford Nebula. Nicolas walked briskly toward it and climbed into the back.

"Quick, quick," he said to the navigating computer, knowing the artificial intelligence wouldn't give a damn that he was in a rush. "Override directions. Go down Washington, then left on Jefferson, then straight onto Wyllys. Then right on Groton, and let me out halfway down." The car eased toward the Park Street intersection despite having a green light. "Faster, goddamnit!" Nicolas yelled at the computer, ducking down as the car passed within eyesight of Mermaid Corner's front door. He didn't look to see if the white-haired man (or anyone else) was rushing to a regular car to follow him.

The DriveMe car, despite its inability to break the speed limit, followed Nicolas's directions perfectly. When it pulled to a stop halfway down Groton Street, which was lined with old, three-story brick apartment buildings, Nicolas left the car and bolted across the street without checking for other approaching ones. He disappeared into a black-shadowed driveway between two of the apartment buildings and continued on until he reached their rear garages. Moths fluttered under the light shining above the complex's back door. Nicolas continued out of its way, through the private resident driveways, toward Lisbon Street. He had left his ActoPhone—and all other GPS-activated valuables—at his old unit on Babcock Street. Let the feds seize his property and go through it once he was gone. The thought of simply shrugging off his apartment buildings, his tenants, and his business was positively liberating. All he hoped was that Aurora Demark's three remaining weeks under his landlordship wouldn't be affected too terribly.

Ten minutes. Catching his breath. Realizing he was alone.

Nicolas breathed in his freedom.

When he finally crept through the apartment driveways to Lisbon Street, he glanced left. Idling near the corner was another self-driving taxi, this time a Toyota.

Thank God for small favors, Nicolas thought.

With his first trace of confidence that he might actually live what remained of his life on his own terms, he climbed into the cab and headed toward Westfield, to the closest of his secret apartments, owned (on paper) by a man who didn't exist.

2005

"WELL, WELL, WELL, I didn't think you'd actually show up." Cynthia Foster opened the door for Elijah Bryce, and he stepped inside her house. "And how is your head, dear? Get inside. You're dripping wet."

There was no front foyer in Cynthia's house, just a rug that sat atop her living room's worn beige carpet. It had begun to rain two blocks before Elijah turned onto Cage Street, and now it was pouring. There would be no lawn mowing today, but he had a feeling Cynthia had been expecting that all along. "Head's okay. Just a bruise," he told her, remembering how she had jumped up to examine him when they had crossed paths at the fair. "Haven't seen Damon Jacoby since the Fourth. So, that's good."

He didn't tell Cynthia that he hadn't seen Molly Butler either after rudely shushing her that night. He had, however, received an email from the girl just yesterday regarding a *Circle Gazette* article from 1992 that she had found at the library. She had scanned and attached a copy of it for him, making no mention of the shushing incident at the fair. The article had detailed a story about "the Cage Street house of Elijah Earnshaw" being vandalized with obscene spray-painted marks insinuating he was a homosexual. The article also reported that Earnshaw had been hospitalized "since early August" of 1992 and was "failing in his battle with AIDS." Had it been normal back then for newspapers like the *Circle Gazette* to print such personal things about people? Elijah didn't know much about AIDS, other than that a lot of people in Africa had it—*and* that it was often associated with homosexual people.

He had typed this back to Molly, taking care not to mention his rudeness at the fair and hoping the email exchange meant they were still on good terms. Her response put him in his place, however, perhaps enough to even their score. It was a single block of words with neither an opening nor a closing salutation.

> *Elijah, not everybody in this country who has AIDS is gay. My dad's cousin died from it out in New York before I was born. She got into drugs and stuff after she moved out there. I guess she got it from sticking infected needles in her arm or whatever.*

Elijah had blushed while reading Molly's slight chastisement, even though he had been alone in his bedroom. At the same time, he appreciated her implied defense of homosexual people. It meant he might have a friend in her after all.

His resulting curiosity from the article had led him to Cynthia's house today. If she was indeed his biological mother, and if this Elijah Earnshaw had been his biological father, it seemed they might have had a good reason for putting him up for adoption. Now that the possibility of it had been planted, he couldn't ignore the idea.

Cynthia led him inside. "Do your parents know you're here?" she asked. Already, her teakettle—seemingly heated for his arrival—was beginning to whistle.

"My mom is at work, so I have a babysitter on weekdays. And my dad left when I was three, so he wouldn't care anyway."

Cynthia's back straightened, as if this bit of knowledge struck a deeper chord than the care she already seemed to have for him. She turned, wearing an incredulous glare. "He *left?*"

"Yeah, when I was three," Elijah repeated.

"God almighty," she said. Her eyes were watering.

Elijah stopped in his slow tracks, feeling a sudden and strong sense of self-consciousness. It wasn't the usual kind, not like when those classmates had pointed and laughed at the fair. Cynthia was staring at him, but it didn't seem like an attempt to make him feel awkward. She seemed to be feeling around his psychological edges, as if weighing her thoughts against her own better judgment.

"I thought you'd have known about my dad, being a psychic and all," he tried to joke. Nothing about Cynthia's behavior seemed threatening, but he readied himself to bolt out her front door just in case the visit became uncomfortable. She was still a stranger after all, and he had just broken the cardinal rule of childhood by stepping into her house alone.

Cynthia smiled weakly at his joke. "I'm a pretty pathetic psychic when it comes to things that matter. *Most* of the time, anyway. And I've made a point in life to steer clear of town gossip. It's never good for anyone."

"Well, you sure told me a lot of true stuff when you did my

card reading." Still standing just a few steps past the door, Elijah reached into his left pocket and withdrew Cynthia's Death card. "Here," he said, taking a few steps toward her. "I brought this back for you. My jeans got rained on, so I hope it's not too wet." He held out the card, which was surprisingly dry. "I guess I got a little freaked out when I saw it. It's just . . . creepy."

"A lot of people think that," Cynthia said, meeting him half-way through the living room. With a trickle of hesitation, she accepted the card with two scissorlike fingers. "Again, I shouldn't have done that reading. Especially since I was a stranger."

"It's okay. I'm old enough to handle it."

The teakettle's high-pitched shriek had grown so loud that Elijah's ears were almost screaming at it to stop. Cynthia quickly held the card back out to him. "Here. It's yours. Keep it." He took the card, and she turned and made seven long strides toward the kitchen and removed the teakettle from the stove's left rear burner. Through the doorway, Elijah saw her preparing two cups to take the water.

"What kind of tea do you like?" she called to him.

Elijah had never drunk tea before, and he had no idea what to say. He settled for, "Whatever's good."

"Green jasmine, then, with orange and passion fruit under-tones. It never fails to satisfy."

Elijah shrugged, then turned toward Cynthia's dining room table, the same one where she had performed his tarot reading. She noticed and shook her head. "Oh, not there—that's where I do my psychic stuff. This visit isn't about that. We'll go in the three-season porch. It's here, just through the kitchen. I like hearing the rain while I'm drinking tea. You might, too."

The tea was burning hot, but against the drenching day's

coolness, it was somehow perfect, as if it knew all the secrets to calming anxious hearts.

"So, what made you come here today?" Cynthia asked when they had settled into two wicker chairs on either side of a matching, glass-topped coffee table. "I honestly didn't think you were going to."

Elijah considered first the jawbone buried in the Moon Woods and then the article Molly Butler had emailed to him. "I'm still curious about a few things," he said.

"Before I answer any of your questions—" Cynthia started, then stopped, as if she were thinking better of saying whatever had nearly slipped out of her mouth. "There's something I was curious about as well," she restarted. These words, too, made her wince. "Okay, how about this? Let's play twenty questions. I started. Now it's your turn. You said you were curious. What's your first question?"

Elijah sipped his tea, knowing they were officially entering potentially "inappropriate" territory. Yet Cynthia Foster was treating him like an adult, unlike his mother did, and he appreciated the vote of confidence. He chose his question carefully. "Why did you act all funny when I told you that my dad left when I was little?"

Cynthia sighed and looked out the window while responding. "Because I've purposefully cut myself off from certain people, and as I said, I like to avoid town gossip as much as I can. It wasn't something I expected to hear." The cryptic response made Elijah even more curious. Perhaps this was part of the game. "My turn," Cynthia continued. "Why did you have my address written on your hand when you and your friend Molly stopped in front of my house?"

Elijah thought for a moment. Then: "I wrote it there when I was at the library."

Cynthia smiled. "I see you're going to be just as difficult as I am. Your turn again."

"What *did* you expect to hear when you asked about my parents?"

The woman's smile faded, and an anxious expression replaced it, as if she knew perfectly well that this visit should not be happening at all. Yet there was a longing in her eyes that seemed to be preventing her from ending it. "I expected them to still be together," she replied, barely pausing before asking, "Why did you write down my address at the library?"

With each question, Elijah was stretching further and further from being able to turn back and forget the ashes and jawbone forever. "Because I saw your name in an old phone book. Why would you have expected my parents to still be together?"

"Because I once knew them, and they seemed happy enough. Why were you looking in old phone books?"

"Because I was trying to find out who had the last name 'Earnshaw.'" Cynthia's eyes widened in surprise, but Elijah continued before she could say anything. "When did you know my parents?"

Tears glistened in her lower eyelids now. Elijah saw in her expression what he was feeling inside: a sense that these questions were a race, hand in hand, toward the edge of a cliff, and they were running too fast to stop before the plunge. "I knew them before you were born," Cynthia said. "Why were you curious about the name Earnshaw?"

"Because I saw it written on something I found." He gulped, now fearing the question tightening his throat more than the answers he was giving. "Why did you meet my parents before I was born?"

Cynthia's cracking exterior broke, and her tears fell in silent drops. She buried her quivering lips inside her mouth as if to ward off a crushing blow, then released them to speak. "I was pregnant," she whispered, "and I was trying to find a couple to adopt my baby once he was born."

Elijah froze. He stared at Cynthia Foster, irrevocably sure of the truth. His mind whirled with disbelief and amazement at the series of events that had brought him together with this woman, the one who had given him life before giving him up.

"And what was the thing you found that made you curious about the name Earnshaw?" Cynthia asked, somehow keeping the game alive.

"Some names I saw written down," Elijah said in a low, detached voice. The box, the jar of ashes, and the jawbone no longer mattered at all. This woman, this beautiful, red-haired tarot card reader, was his biological mother. Yet he was unsure how to make sense of the hurricane inside him. Swirling in it was sadness; next to that was anger; but there was also joy. Putting his tea down, he asked in a shaking voice, "Why did you give me away?"

Cynthia jumped up from her chair and threw her arms around Elijah, cradling him in a way he had never been cradled before, not even by his adoptive mother. It took him a moment to lean into her hug, but when he did, he surrendered completely.

"Oh, my sweet, dear boy," Cynthia said, weeping. "So many things happened all at once, and you were a miracle to begin with. A *miracle*. You're *still* a miracle." She was heaving now, and Elijah rode up on her chest with every one of her breaths. "Your father . . . his name was Elijah, too, just like you . . . He wasn't the man I thought he was when I married him, but it wasn't his fault. Not really. I've come to accept that now, and I'm just focused on being healthy. I've been so lucky. But that's something else . . ." Cynthia's cheek pressed against Elijah's forehead, and he felt one of her tears drip down his own face. "Your father did the best he could, Elijah. We were trying for years and years to have kids, but I could never get pregnant. All I wanted in this world was to have a baby, at least one. To see my face in another, you know?"

Despite the feelings storming within him, Elijah smiled.

"Your father was a very depressed man. I always blamed my miscarriages on that. Like maybe his energy wasn't strong enough or something." She chuckled and wiped a tear. "It was kind of ridiculous, but that's what I thought. For whatever reason, I never carried a pregnancy to term until you came. But then . . ." Cynthia gasped for air, as if it were all too much.

Elijah could barely believe he was hearing the story of his birth, the one he had always wondered about in the back of his mind. It was surreal, as if some hand of fate really had brought them together. Could this be the fortune his Death card told?

"When I was two months pregnant with you, he told me he was a homosexual."

For the first time at somebody else's mention of the word, Elijah didn't blush.

"He'd been keeping it from me all those years while having affairs with other men, including one named Samuel Jacoby, whom he'd fallen in love with."

Jacoby.

With a racing heart, Elijah began linking the threads.

"Except Samuel Jacoby had been spending time with other men in New York," Cynthia continued. "He—"

"He got AIDS," Elijah whispered, remembering the old newspaper article Molly had found. He remembered what Damon had told Molly during their bumper car match—that his parents were dead. Now Damon's torture began to make sense. Had he targeted Elijah knowing of their familial connection, or had he simply latched onto the story of Alec Pent's shirtless chest and aimed his hatred at the closest gay person he could find?

Cynthia loosened her hug and pulled back. Confusion had overtaken her tears. "How did you know it was AIDS?"

"And someone vandalized your house once?"

It was as if these memories were breaking Cynthia's heart all over again. She nodded, scrunching her face as more tears came.

"That girl Molly who came here with me last time . . . She's been working in the library, cleaning a bunch of old stuff out, and she found a newspaper article yesterday about it. It was in the *Circle Gazette* back in the nineties."

"God, and it all comes back at once," Cynthia mused.

Elijah shrugged, waiting for her to continue.

"I'm not supposed to be doing this," she said. "I signed things saying I would never try to contact you. My family is dead, and I'm not in touch with any of your father's extended family, because they were always super-religious and embarrassed by me, especially after he died. But I couldn't help myself from getting in touch with you . . . I saw you that day, and once I learned your name, I just *knew*. Except I could get in a lot of trouble for this."

"But didn't *I* get in touch with *you*?" Elijah asked.

"If that'll keep me out of court with your mother, then maybe," Cynthia said.

"Well, I won't tell her."

"I'm afraid one of us is going to have to."

Elijah's heart fell. He had lost track of whose turn it was to ask a question, but one in particular was tugging at his heart. It was a difficult question, one he didn't know how to form into words, because it was all so technical in ways that were too grown-up for him to know about. He had always heard that sex was a way of spreading AIDS, and if Cynthia had gotten pregnant with him after Elijah Earnshaw was infected, there was a good chance that she would have the disease too. But asking her made him feel like a child. He looked out the window as he spoke, dreading her eventual answer.

"But . . . when did my dad get AIDS? And, like, do you—?"

"God, it all happened so fast," Cynthia said. She had deflated completely, as if the pent-up secret she had held around Elijah had lent her, until now, a larger-than-life stature. Seeing her for the grieved woman she was, Elijah couldn't help but feel sorry for her. "He had just started to get sick after I got pregnant with you, and I think he knew what it was even before I made him go see a doctor. He went, and . . . well . . . it all came out the night he got his blood test results back. Everything. And yes, Elijah, he infected me with HIV, too."

Panic suddenly gripped him. "But I saw on a video in school that babies can get it. Did I—"

A fresh set of tears escaped Cynthia's eyes, and she shook her head, sighing. It took Elijah a moment to realize they were tears of relief.

"I told you, you were a miracle, Elijah. My little miracle." She closed her eyes and shook her head. "I was so worried. So ungodly worried. My virus count was so high the month you were born. They told me back then that almost 30 percent of babies who were born to parents with HIV would test positive for the virus, too.

AIDS is actually the disease that comes as a result of the virus, once it overtakes your immune system and makes your body unable to fight against other illnesses. But the doctors at the WHIP Clinic in Wind Prairie gave me as many antiretroviral drugs as they could. Some were brand new at the time. And, by God, you came out completely fine." Cynthia's eyes opened again, but they were lost in her own past. "I knew then, though, that I couldn't raise you myself. If I got any sicker than I already was, what would happen to you? You know? Your father was on his way out, and we didn't have anybody else to help us if I got worse."

For the first time in his life, Elijah understood. "So my own dad was gay," he said. He didn't register that it came out sounding like a relieved admission of his own homosexual feelings.

"He was so scared to tell anybody," Cynthia said. "Minnesota wasn't a good place to grow up if you were a boy who liked other boys. He did everything he could to hide it. Even married me and did his best to do what a husband is supposed to do. But I guess it got to the point where he couldn't pretend anymore. You could say he cheated on me with those other men, Sam Jacoby in particular, but I don't blame him. Even now I don't blame him."

It was the first time Elijah had ever been involved in an adult conversation, face-to-face with someone who would trust him with truths he wasn't guaranteed to understand. He bit his lip and looked at his birth mother's quivering face. "How come you aren't sick?"

She allowed this question with an unfortunate frown. "Like I said, I almost was. My CD4 cells were so low the month you were born that they almost classified me as having AIDS. I'm on something the doctors call ART. Antiretroviral therapy. I take drugs that help corner the HIV virus so that it doesn't get a hold of my system.

I always used to hate using prescription drugs, but now I have my life because of them. So far, my virus count is so low that it's undetectable in my blood. We actually *call* it 'being undetectable.'"

"Well, it's good you're not sick," Elijah said.

"And don't you worry—you're safe here with me, and you won't get HIV just by being around me. A lot of people who don't understand HIV and AIDS think that, your father's ignorant relatives included. But I'll understand if you don't want to see me." She went in for a second hug. It felt right to Elijah, and again, he surrendered to it. After a full, quiet minute, she pushed him off her chest and looked into his eyes. "So, I've answered your question, even though it took a while. But I have another one for you."

"Okay," he said. For a second, he had to remember that they were still playing the question game. He suddenly hoped Cynthia had made the connection between his sexual orientation and Damon Jacoby's bullying. If so, he could finally talk about it. When her question came out, however, it had nothing at all to do with homosexuality.

"You mentioned you saw the name 'Earnshaw' written down somewhere," she said. "Where exactly was it?"

Elijah knew she was expecting the answer even before he said it. When he told her about the wooden box in the Moon Woods, she gave him a slow, understanding nod. Then Cynthia asked the question Elijah had been both fearing and waiting for.

"And did you find the jawbone?"

2010

PALMER, ALASKA, WAS FLATTER than Cynthia Foster had imagined it would be. Located forty-five minutes from Anchorage, it lay in what she quickly learned was the Matanuska Valley, the drive through which was lined on either side by blazing, orange-leafed trees and, farther in the distance, towering, snowcapped mountains. What struck Cynthia immediately upon leaving the airport and journeying northeast on the Glenn Highway was the crispness of the air—made even more appealing by a cloudless sky interrupted only by low strips of mist at the base of the Talkeetna Mountains up ahead. They glowed in the afternoon sun, filling Cynthia with a mixed sense of optimism and freedom that Idle County had never offered her. The beauty was nothing less than majestic—a reminder that life and surroundings could change if a person really wanted them to. She thought back to her husband, her miscarriages, the jawbone, and Elijah.

Perhaps this is why Max Pope moved north, she thought. *To just escape it all.*

Cynthia had walked off the plane with her rowmate Frank, whose last name, she learned at the baggage claim, was Brennin. She had also learned that he was a contractor in Wasilla, that he built homes, and that he was divorced and childless—a life status he thoroughly enjoyed. After lifting her suitcase off the carousel and handing it to her, handle pulled up, he had posed a location for dinner.

"Turkey Red. It's the only decent place to eat in Palmer. How's seven o'clock?"

She had agreed with a blush. Her initial reaction to his seriousness about meeting her for dinner was disbelief—and a presumption that he would end the night by telling her he was just trying to be nice because of her missing biological child. They exchanged phone numbers right there at the baggage claim and then went their separate ways—Cynthia toward the Hertz rental cars and Frank toward the curb outside, where he planned to pick up a cab. Cynthia had almost offered him a ride, but after a few seconds of thinking on it, she thought it might look both desperate and ridiculous. They had parted ways with a firmly shared handshake.

Now Palmer rolled past Cynthia's eyes, and she tried to imagine herself in Max Pope's shoes, arriving in this small, removed town so near the top of the world. Had he chosen isolation with some particular purpose, or had he simply been aiming his trajectory as far away as possible from the civilization that had shunned him? Perhaps the people of Palmer hadn't been aware of the news. Perhaps he had been able to come here unnoticed, with his new, generic name. What else could a disgraced man hope to do?

The first Cynthia she entered was a rather musty one called

the Moosehead Saloon. She approached the bartender through the dim lights, feeling silly for having zero intent whatsoever to order a drink. He was a heavyset man with pale jowls. Cynthia wondered if he had ever made any goals outside of being a bartender in Palmer. "Excuse me," she said, forming fists and resting her knuckles on the wooden bar.

The jowly man glanced her way. "What'll it be?"

"I'm sorry, I'm not actually here to drink. *Yet.*" Cynthia added this last word with a rather desperate smile, as if to throw the bartender a bone. His interest in her had immediately flickered. "I'm wondering if anyone up here follows the news from down south. Regarding seven kids who disappeared in Minnesota? And perhaps a man named Maximilian Pope, going by the name Michael Johnson?"

"Oh, the FBI thing? Sort of." The bartender dried a glass and set it on the rack in front of him. "I heard they were working with the Palmer PD. Were they looking for this Michael Johnson guy or something? I only really heard about it once."

"Do you know anybody who might know him? He moved up here two years ago."

"Not that I can recall," the bartender said.

Conversations like this became a pattern as Cynthia walked around downtown Palmer, from address to address, using the Google maps app on her iPhone to find each new stop. She had performed a search for restaurants and bars, and the crisp, sunny day inspired her to walk between them. After the Moosehead Saloon came the Palmer Bar (more of the same vague familiarity with the Max Pope/Michael Johnson name but no useful knowledge), then Klondike Mike's Saloon and Road House BBQ (also the same), and then the Eagle Hotel Restaurant and Lounge (nothing but cocked heads, furrowed eyebrows, and a polite "No, I'm sorry!" from the makeup-caked woman at the front desk—who didn't even offer to sprinkle Max's names over the other hotel employees to help Cynthia further).

Cynthia left the hotel on South Colony Way and began walking toward Elmwood Avenue, where she had parked her rental car. To her right was a grassy strip of land lined with trees sporting yellowing leaves. A line of railroad tracks cut through it about twenty feet in from the road, but it was quiet and empty. The mountains towering in the distance reminded Cynthia just how small her own personal dramas were. Those jagged outcroppings of rock had been there long before Elijah disappeared and would be there long after the world stopped caring.

She stopped at the Elmwood Avenue intersection. The task she had set for herself burned in her chest like humiliation. Had she really thought it possible that a trip to Palmer might uncover anything new about Max Pope?

To get her money's worth, she left her car on Elmwood and kept walking up South Colony Way. She posed her questions about the disgraced neurologist (and received similar answers) at an auto parts store, a home goods store, a law office, a bookstore, and a Wells Fargo bank before finding a bench and collapsing onto it, in tears. She cried for ten minutes before looking up without thinking, at a perfect angle to see a business sign hanging on a building across the street.

Valley Real Estate.

It was so obvious that Cynthia wanted to smack herself. She had been going door to door at random, asking people if they knew anything about a man who had moved to town two years ago. Not once before flying here had she thought to ask somebody whose business it was to help relocate people. Would there be ethical implications in asking a Realtor to share private information about past clients? It was likely, at least for the Realtor. But there was also no guarantee that this particular office had worked with Max, and it didn't hurt to try.

Wiping her eyes, wondering just how runny her makeup had become, Cynthia stood up from her bench, walked across South Colony Way, and entered Valley Real Estate.

FIVE HOURS LATER, at ten past seven, Frank Brennin was sitting in the far left corner of Turkey Red when Cynthia rushed in. She probably looked like a tornado, because she hadn't had time to check into Alaska Choice Inn, her cheap hotel, even to glance in a mirror. When she sat in the chair opposite his booth seat, however, he grinned.

"You're beaming, Miss Detective."

"You're damned right I'm beaming," Cynthia said. "It turned into a good day."

Frank, still dressed in his Carhartt jacket, folded his hands and twitched his head as he gave her a shy smile. "I wasn't sure how serious you were about dinner. The normal me would have shied away and stayed in. I'm glad I didn't." After a pause, he added, "So, you made progress?" Frank's rough skin and gentle grin made her feel like a character in a movie who was finally getting lucky— good fortune with a quest, a handsome dinner date, and, quite unexpectedly, a bit of happiness.

"You want the full story now?" she asked. "I just have to get to my hotel by midnight."

"I'm all ears," Frank replied.

Cynthia had spent the entire afternoon making progress—*real* progress—tracking down information on Max Pope. One of Valley Real Estate's Realtors, a verging-on-thirty blond named Jessica, had known Max by his new legal name, Michael Johnson, and by the property he had bought. "He was the guy who looked like a movie star," the woman had said. "All the girls talked about him when he came into town, and everyone in the business tried to be his agent. A friend of mine sold him a place up on Wolverine Lake. Kind of removed. You say he's mixed up with that missing kids case?"

Jessica had lit up with gossipy flair when Cynthia explained her relation to Elijah Bryce and the fact that Michael Johnson had not been Max's given name. Out had come Max's story, similar to how it now came out to Frank Brennin—the Rock Shore Nursing Home scandal, Max's connection to the Idle County Seven, and his move to Palmer after the name change. In the discussion with Jessica, Cynthia had left out her suspicions and questions about Rebecca Sparks, the young woman in the wheelchair whom Max had taken an interest in, but now she discussed Rebecca with Frank. His expression became a disconcerted frown when she told him that Rebecca had since fallen off the grid completely.

"But there's more," she continued. "I drove up to Max's little cabin place, which was empty except for some basic furniture—and I *think* a security camera blinking inside on the far wall. I didn't do too much snooping in case somebody ended up being there, but I did go around to his neighbors asking if—"

A bearded male server interrupted Cynthia's unrehearsed monologue to place ice waters on the table. Cynthia sat back politely, glanced at the menu for the first time, and immediately decided she would order the portobello mushroom salad. Frank scanned his menu and then closed it almost as quickly. It took less than a minute for them to order wine, appetizers, and their main courses.

Cynthia resumed her story when the waiter left. "So, anyway, I asked around Max Pope's neighbors a bit. The first few who answered their doors didn't really know anything about him, but then there was one who did. A single guy with a big house down the road a bit. Divorced I think. His name was Chuck, and he said he ran into Max from time to time taking walks out on Wolverine Road, near where they both live. He knew Max only as Michael Johnson and thought he was depressed, because Max kept talking about wanting to just wander into the wilderness someday and not come back. Like, to *die*."

"Like the *Into the Wild* guy?" Frank said. "Jesus."

Cynthia shrugged and shook her head. "I think it was more definite. Like, Max wanted to walk into the mountains and just starve. Let the animals get him or whatever. I had to make Chuck repeat it. He said Max slowly opened up about all this once they got to know each other better. I—" Cynthia stopped and shook her head with an embarrassed chuckle. "I'm sorry. You're a stranger, and I'm talking your ear off with all this insane stuff."

"I really don't mind," Frank said, though his expression remained serious. "But you said Victor Zobel, the big famous author dude, knows this Max Pope guy, right? It stuck out to me, because my brother Kenny's friend who works at the Palmer airport dealt with him during a random visit last year. Apparently he was a huge asshole. It was right after that big Oprah interview in November."

"Which is the *kicker*," Cynthia said, swooshing her pointer finger into Frank's face, aware that it might just seal the deal of her being too over-the-top. "This neighbor, Chuck, said the same thing. He didn't actually meet Victor Zobel, but he said that he went by Max's house one day last November to check on him, because he had been particularly adamant the night before about the whole 'walking into nature to die' thing. He said Max drove an old Ford F150 that always sat in the driveway looking dirty, because it was white. But the day he went to check on Max, there was another car in the driveway. A big black Hummer. He decided not to interrupt Max's visit with whoever it was, but he asked about it the next time he saw Max. Max said it was 'his daughter's stepfather.' That's Victor Zobel. He's been in and out of Idle County since the kids disappeared, heading up all the big searches."

"Seems the police would have looked into this, no?" Frank said.

"I'm guessing yes. Chuck said he talked with a Palmer detective who was doing some neighborhood canvasing. He told them the same thing about Max—that he had talked about 'just disappearing into the mountains.' *That* would be a tough search, though, obviously."

"Quite."

Cynthia shrugged. "I'm guessing Victor came up here to discuss Jillian. My son, Elijah, said he was trying to get custody of her to bring her back to Switzerland, even though they weren't technically related. It seems like Max went off his rocker after the whole nursing home thing. Maybe Victor was just doing his best to see that Jillian was cared for."

"Except Jillian Pope disappeared," Frank said. With a blush, he added, "I actually read up on the Idle County Seven this afternoon after you told me who you were. The whole thing is so weird. And the Dallas factor? Seems like a dead end. I don't blame you for coming up here. I could maybe ask my brother if his friend at the Palmer airport might be willing to talk to you."

Cynthia slowed her investigative enthusiasm down now and stepped outside herself just enough to consider the man in front of her and contemplate what it was he wanted out of this unplanned, fleeting connection. She had of course experienced her share of romantic trysts back in college, including dinner dates with strangers followed by unspeakably pleasurable activities, but she was almost fifty-five years old, and her big bones and questionably constructed left hip—among other more hidden things—didn't exactly make her the biggest catch.

"I'm HIV-positive, undetectable," she said before allowing herself to think further.

Frank sat up straighter, frowned, and then partially nullified the frown with a half smile. "Wow. Okay. Didn't see that one coming. You're a bundle of surprises."

Cynthia put her face in her hands, and the bracelets on her wrists jangled as she shook her head. Just then the bearded server came back with their wine and appetizers. Cynthia waited for him to leave before continuing. "I'm not sure why you agreed to have dinner with me tonight, but if it's for some kind of date or insta-romance fix because I'll only be here for a few days, then you should know my HIV status." With a wince whose actual appearance she didn't want to imagine, Cynthia looked into Frank's eyes and lowered her arms to the table. "And this is completely embarrassing either way, because I might be reading you a hundred percent incorrectly."

"You're not reading me incorrectly," Frank said. He stretched his arms forward over the table. "To be honest, you were a nice surprise today. I decided a few years ago to just live by my instincts.

I realized I like being spontaneous. Since I'm attracted to women who take the initiative, I said yes. Easy as that, really. You're not reading me wrong."

Instincts. It was almost identical to what young Eloise Creed had said that day in the rain, in front of the shuttered Rock Shore Nursing Home.

"I feel crazy being here," Cynthia said.

Frank shrugged. "You're right to feel a little crazy. All this Idle County Seven stuff is pretty nuts. If there's anything I can do to help you up here, please let me know."

"Thank you," Cynthia said, forcing herself to look into his eyes. "Just . . . thank you." She shook her head to thwart impending tears and took a sip of water. "I don't have a lot of friends. My life has been a lot of drama, and I've probably made most of it myself. But I didn't make *this* drama. These kids disappearing, I mean."

"Have you ever considered relocating?" Frank asked. "Starting fresh?"

Now Cynthia wiped one of the tears that had finally made it past her eyes, and she chuckled. "Where? To Palmer?"

"Palmer could work."

Just as Frank smiled at her in a way that somehow made his blue eyes sparkle behind his leathery face, the server appeared with their main courses. As Cynthia began picking at her salad, she watched her dinner date close his eyes, take in the aroma of his grilled salmon, and smile. She liked a man who could appreciate his food.

Dinner continued, and she shared more and more, not just about the Idle County Seven case but also about her own life— about her late, homosexual husband, Elijah Earnshaw, his affair with Samuel Jacoby, and the HIV virus that had made her the last surviving casualty of his secret, extramarital relationship. She then spoke to Frank about Elijah not as a disappeared boy but as the boy he had been, at least during the initial days of his life and then the later years during which she had known him. She wore a guilty but unapologetic smile while relaying the story of the day Elijah came over for tea, when she had explained the circumstances of his birth and ultimately the story of the jawbone from the jewelry box.

At her mention of the jawbone, Frank cocked his head and said, "Wait, *what*?"

Cynthia laughed at the ridiculousness of it all. She considered how naïve she, her husband, and Samuel Jacoby had all been in believing Samuel's game stand manager that the prized jawbone had been "a good luck charm from India." Yet the manager, who had won the jawbone himself in a game of poker, had believed the good-luck-charm story, too. After finally turning the jawbone in to police, Cynthia had taken five long days to gather the courage to call Shelly Bryce, admit her teatime infraction with Elijah, and prepare her for the possibility of his being questioned by police.

Maybe Idle County really was cursed. Looking back on her life now from the high and distant state of Alaska, she realized how small, despite everything, her world there really was. For the first time since July, she saw potential for a happy life beyond the reality of her lost son. As Elijah had told her from his hospital bed in August 2005, mere hours after the final Damon Jacoby incident, there was something wrong with Idle County, with the effect it had on people. Perhaps leaving it once and for all—assuming there really was nothing left for her there—was an idea worth considering.

"How cold does it get up here in the winter?" Cynthia asked, mostly in jest, enjoying the play-out of this fantasy with Frank Brennin, the stranger.

With a flirtatious grin, Frank said, "Cold. Enough to make you wonder why you live here. But then you look out at the mountains and think, 'Oh yeah, that's why.'"

As they ate their Friday-night dinner, allowing themselves to rise to happier and more kittenish banter, Cynthia felt a path solidifying before her. It felt so comfortable and right that she gave very little notice or credibility to the layer of intuition whispering that, if she made the choice to stay here, it would be one of her last.

2005

L IFE WOULD NEVER BE THE SAME. Elijah Bryce was walking toward Windsong Road's dead end, past the newly sold house with the chipped white paint, toward the pile of newspapers he would soon be delivering to the entire street. For the first time ever, he would have welcomed the mindless monotony of delivering newspapers to drown out how crazy his life had become. This morning, however, he was expecting to see Cynthia Foster's story of the jawbone on the *Wind Prairie Tribune*'s front page.

After their visit over tea, she had left him hanging for five days. Finally, last night, she had called his mother. She had confessed all her questionable transgressions—her burial of the ashes and the jawbone, her intersection with Elijah, her sending him the Death card after the tarot reading, and her knowledge of Damon Jacoby's increasingly dangerous bullying (the reason for which

Elijah had shared, with tremors of relief, before leaving her house that rainy day). While Cynthia had kept the reason for the bullying quiet, she did let Shelly know that the police had collected the jawbone and identified its remains, and that the news story would be breaking in the morning.

Elijah had been sitting on the new leather couch when Cynthia's call came in, and it had taken only ten seconds to sense through his mother's silence the sudden emotional friction blooming under their roof. He had walked as quickly and quietly as possible to his bedroom and shut the door.

Twenty minutes later, his mother followed with her usual, loud attempt to walk sure-footedly. She was in tears when she knocked firmly on his door and entered without waiting for his consent. Out came her immediate mandate: to forget Cynthia Foster, to never contact her again, and to answer truthfully any questions the police might have about the jawbone. Despite acknowledging Damon Jacoby's bullying, she made no effort to question the reason for it, nor did she acknowledge the inappropriateness of it. If Cynthia's mention of the bullying had sparked extreme embarrassment in him, his mother's casual dismissal of it felt like outright betrayal. When Elijah had adamantly refused to stop seeing Cynthia, his mother had said, "You don't know the whole truth," and stormed out.

This morning, Elijah was still fuming. He arrived on the street corner to pick up the day's *Wind Prairie Tribune* bundle, almost hoping that whatever story was breaking about Cynthia's jawbone would mention him by name and embarrass his adoptive mother to her very bones. He snapped open the bundle's plastic binding strips, grabbed one of the papers, and, holding his breath, scanned the front page.

Fifty-Year-Old Investigation Reopened
By Deidra Wallace

July 14, 2005—End Haven

For the second time in the span of a year, human remains have been uncovered in Idle County. Newly appointed County Sheriff Kevin Applebee has informed the Wind Prairie Tribune *that an End Haven resident named Cynthia Lynn Foster came forward Monday with evidence in a case that has gone unsolved since 1947.*

Forty-six-year-old Joshua Lucas Grime was reported missing on October 2, 1947, after his wife, Elizabeth, came home from a city function to an empty house. Until this past Monday, police had found no forensic evidence to indicate there had been foul play or an intruder involved with the disappearance, and according to the fifty-eight-year-old case files, there were no signs of a forced entry or a disturbance in the house. Grime had been incapacitated at the time with a broken leg, says Theodore Tarnish of End Haven, who was a family friend. It was thought by some, including his wife, that Grime's disappearance was somehow related to Father Simon Michael Villard, the Catholic priest who went on a killing spree in Idle County between 1942 and 1947, burying his victims near a homemade chapel at the center of the Moon Woods. Villard disappeared later that same year and was never found.

In 2004, the FBI investigated allegations of corruption in the Idle County Sheriff's Department, leading to the exposure of a decades-old cult of men devoted to Villard's legacy and intent on hiding his secret history. Members claimed that, in 1947, Villard crossed from life into death, body intact, and had since been sending directives from "the other side" for them to continue his "study of death." The twenty-three cult members, fourteen of whom worked for the Idle County Sheriff's Department, kept the mass grave site at the center of the Moon Woods a secret for over sixty years.

On Thursday, the department issued a statement regarding Grime's disappearance, claiming that a human jawbone, which had until Monday been in Cynthia Foster's possession, matches the lower half of a dental cast taken of Joshua Grime two years prior to his disappearance. No statement has been made regarding how the End Haven resident came to be in possession of the remains. The sheriff's department will conduct a full investigation into the matter, and Sheriff Applebee hopes "they will find swift, long-awaited closure to this case."

Elizabeth Anne Grime, wife of the deceased, passed away in September of 2004 after what friends called "a lifetime of wondering."

The article calmed Elijah's anger somewhat. Regardless of his mother's anxiety over the situation, it was bringing justice to an old case. The streetlight above him flickered as he ran the names it mentioned through his head. They were familiar, and as their presence rose in his mind, so did the face of Molly Butler.

Joshua Grime.

Elizabeth Anne Grime.

Mrs. Grime, the librarian.

The old woman had been this murdered man's wife. Molly had been friends with her; she had implied as much to Elijah the day they met. He tried to remember Mrs. Grime's face. It had always been bright and sparkling, as if age had never really taken the best of her, the way it did to some people. Yes, her hair had been white, but her wrinkles had been minimal, and her mysterious youth had seemed to make these marks of time almost transparent.

She was dead—gone forever now, according to Victor Zobel's *In God We're Dust*. In her place, however, was this anonymous footprint from her life: the jawbone of her lost husband, Joshua. Elijah had always assumed the old woman was a widow, but he had never known her husband disappeared without a trace. If Joshua Grime had indeed died in 1947, it would mean his jawbone was in circulation almost twenty-five years before Samuel Jacoby's game stand manager took possession of it. Also, if Father Simon Villard really had committed the murder, as authorities seemed to believe, either he had handed off the cleaned-up jawbone himself, or somebody had pulled it from Grime's remains at a later date. Surely it hadn't been an innocent person who initially dispersed it; an innocent person would have reported the remains to the police.

Elijah shivered. It felt strange, almost unearthly, to be the catalyst for this case's unexpected resurfacing. Another inkling of anger pulsed through him as he thought of his own mother's outright dismissal of it all.

The crisp, morning air chilled his neck while he delivered the story to his neighbors. The beginning of the day's light had now crept into the sky, but the street lights were on, and shadows still shrouded the neighborhood. He stepped onto Mrs. Freederman's porch, quietly opened her storm door, and dropped a newspaper between it and the closed main door as swiftly and quietly as he could.

He hiked to the next house, the Billingtons. They had neglected to cut their grass after the rain last week; it was long and sopping wet with dew. The water had already seeped through Elijah's tennis shoes by the time he climbed the steps of their front porch and put a newspaper in their mailbox. When he turned to face the street, however, he stopped.

Somebody was standing in the middle of it, directly facing the Billingtons' front sidewalk. Under the streetlight, the person's face was tipped forward and obscured by darkness. He stood with the slumped and frozen gracelessness of a scarecrow.

Maybe it's the new neighbor, Elijah thought at first. Then his intellect kicked in. He needed to run right now. Possibly through the backyards. If this person was following him, he had to get home immediately. After studying the figure for a moment, however, his eyes caught a glint of recognition. The rickety porch suddenly grabbed his feet like glue.

It was Damon Jacoby. Even through the shadows on his face, the boy's sharp eyes were visible, and they seemed to be glistening with something that was not quite a reflection of the streetlight.

Damon—or the figure that looked exactly like him—didn't advance. Elijah looked left, then right, wondering whether he had time to escape down the Billingtons' front steps or if he should simply hop over the side of their porch. But agility wasn't his strong suit. A horrible vision struck him of landing on his face, newspapers flapping everywhere, and Damon Jacoby descending upon him.

Then he noticed something strange. Damon's lips were moving, but no sound was traveling through the crisp morning air.

Elijah finally allowed himself to close his eyes in a blink that was just long enough to be a mental check on his sanity. In the millisecond of blackness, he willed his feet to move so that he wouldn't have to find out if Damon was about to make true on his death threat.

When Elijah opened his eyes, however, Damon was gone.

A grand tingling sensation took over Elijah's body, and his legs suddenly felt as if they weren't even there. He stepped forward, still on the Billingtons' front porch, and braced himself against its support pillars. His thoughts were broken, and they came in slow succession, their gaps filled by his racing heartbeat.

I saw him. I know I saw him.

He was there.

He disappeared.

If he disappeared, it means either I'm crazy, or he's a—

Anxiety raced in Elijah's chest.

He didn't believe in ghosts. In fact, ever since finishing *In God We're Dust*, he was proud not to believe in them. It felt good to be different than his mother, to be one of the intellectuals who were above that sort of spiritual mumbo jumbo. The book had finally made him feel as if he belonged somewhere.

Except people all over the world had reported experiences like this throughout history—seeing things that weren't there, seeing dead people, having questionable experiences of the mind. Just last year, Elijah had believed wholeheartedly that ghosts might be real. Had *In God We're Dust* really changed him that much? What if Victor Zobel was wrong, and his opinions on ghosts, religion, and belief in an afterlife were simply that—opinions?

Elijah's initial urge was to call 911 so the police could check up on Damon in case he had done something crazy and gotten himself killed. If Damon were to end up alive and fine, however, Elijah would become the butt of even more jokes. Worse yet was the possibility that Elijah himself was the one going crazy. Given his circumstances as of late, it almost seemed more likely.

When a light turned on inside the Billingtons' house and cast a dim glow onto the porch from its windows, Elijah jumped back into reality. He still had a paper route to complete, and Damon Jacoby was nowhere near him.

It was a trick of his mind. It had to be.

Nevertheless, as he continued his job, he was sure that eyes were watching his back. Each time he faced a door or a mailbox or the small slit of a letter slot, he had to confront the throbbing fear of turning toward the street again. But only the brightening neighborhood lay before him. Even dog walkers were out now, and the morning was beginning to feel more alive.

Elijah had just delivered his last newspaper when he remembered his Monopoly game with Molly Butler the day of the tarot reading. What was it she had started to say? That sometimes she thought she saw ghosts?

It was with a mixed sense of fear and guilt that Elijah decided he needed to call her immediately after sunrise. For the first time ever, he was questioning his perception of reality, and Molly was the only person he was free to see who wouldn't call him crazy.

2038

"I FEEL LIKE SOMETHING HORRIBLE is going to happen," Winifred Flite told Kate Crookston on the morning of June 22, 2038. It was Tuesday, and they were sitting in Kate's Zen-green office off of Long Wharf. Today, Kate was wearing blue dolphin-shaped earrings. Winifred glared at them as they jangled from side to side against the woman's cheeks. "I mean, the shooting was bad enough. I can't even describe it. Like, I was almost *calm* during it. I had no idea what was happening. But now I feel like there's more coming. Worse than the shooting. Worse than everything." Winifred wiped a tear from her left eye that she hadn't intended to let loose. "At least the new sheetrock came in yesterday for the bullet holes on the living room wall. That's something good, right? Christ."

"Do you think this sense of danger is based on intuition or just fear?" Kate asked.

Winifred threw her hands up. "How am I supposed to know?

It just feels like none of this is over. I mean, the media stuff hasn't really died down. Reporters are still demanding Craig Graber and I do some face-to-face interview, except now they're twisting the blame to be on Craig for going public with Jonathan's case to begin with. They want a goddamned *showdown*." Winifred glanced at the closed door to Kate's office, wondering what anybody in the world beyond it would think of the problems she was spewing out. At least they could no longer call her spoiled. She had almost been killed—all because she was caught unprotected in this unprecedented hurricane of insanity. "Also, there's something else," she said, fighting the tremor in her heart warning her not to continue. "Jonathan got another letter yesterday."

"I thought he's getting hundreds of letters."

"No, I mean, like, one of the *blue* ones. Here, look." Winifred dug into her purse, found a photo of the letter on her phone, and handed it to Kate. "This is just the last of five. They're all on there."

The familiar blue envelope had been delivered amid a slew of other letters from Jonathan's new supporters and haters. Most of the letters came in white envelopes, and as always, the robin's-egg blue had immediately jumped out. With a quickening heartbeat and sinking feeling in her chest, all rendered inexplicable by her dovetailed mixture of curiosity and utter bafflement, Winifred had run to the kitchen to embrace what was now a familiar routine: latex gloves, a ziplock bag, and her ActoPhone to record her process for immediate video sharing with the FBI. She had finished the process even before calling Jonathan from his sunny, second-floor patio to review it.

The letter's text had jolted her in a way the others hadn't. She hadn't even planned to mention it to Kate, but now, after admitting to her feelings of dread, she couldn't help doing so. As Kate read the letter, Winifred realized that she herself had already more or less memorized what it said.

Dear Jonathan,

People are afraid of growing past their own selfishness and complacency to embrace the challenge of improving our global human experience. Everyone has the ability to make a difference. All that's needed is a spark. Is it really so hard to be the best we can be? The answer is no.

I know the FBI has taken an interest in these letters. All they need to do is investigate events scheduled in Geneva last August 12. They will then realize why ideologies worldwide were about to be reshaped, and why somebody wanted to stop it. Unfortunately, it will likely take much more for them to build a case.

For some people, change is a welcome friend. For others, it is a threat. You, my friend, signed up for this. You just don't realize it yet.

Signed,
Your Spark

"Does Jonathan really know who's sending these?" Kate asked.

Winifred raised her eyebrows. "I think so. He's totally tight-lipped and won't say a thing, even after the shooting. An agent from the Resident Agency in Providence already took it today for analysis. I'm sure they'll love that little comment about Geneva."

"Good to know not everyone has forgotten the bombing so quickly," Kate said. She read the letter over again, then handed Winifred's phone back. "These are some pretty big concepts."

"They're *too* big. Obviously, whoever's sending these letters is some 'higher-road' hoo-hah. It just makes me feel that much worse for being scared of supporting Jonathan publicly. Like, maybe I should be braver or something."

"Do you think that means acquiescing to the media?"

The sigh that escaped Winifred rode a sputter of anxiety that almost brought on more tears. "Weston Carrow is out there trying to rile up every fundamentalist Christian he possibly can to try to kill Jonathan for being some New Age enigma. The police can't arrest him, even though the shooters last month were from his church. But either way, I'm the one who raised Jonathan like shit and caused all this. Shouldn't I be the one to try to fix it?"

"Do you think it would do any good? At least in this case?"

"Maybe. I don't know."

"Okay, then. I think it might help to figure out what you really want. There's no way around the fact that you're going to have to handle all this somehow. Wallowing in shame and thinking catastrophically is only going to make you a deer in the headlights."

"You can say that again."

Kate nodded. "Yeah, so, I'm thinking that trying to reshape your outlook might help. Like, treat all this as an impetus toward positive action—'positive' being whatever would actually make you happy. If you could wake up tomorrow and do anything, what would it be?"

"I'd run away." Winifred ran a hand along the flat, pulled-back stretch of her hair. "I'd give Jonathan enough money to live, and I'd run off to Greece or something. I have a villa I rent. Mykonos."

"So you've said."

What Winifred wasn't telling Kate was that she had already checked flights, already checked the availability of the villa, and already told Jonathan that she might leave. They had been eating takeout last night amid the construction dust and tarps and building supplies now littering her kitchen and living room. Despite outwardly supporting her Mykonos idea 100 percent, for her sake, Jonathan's eyes had flickered with despair when Winifred mentioned it. It was the same look he had tried to hide during childhood every time she had brought him to therapy or given him an exasperated sigh or squashed any mention of his true, peculiar nature.

"I'd be a coward if I left," Winifred said. "Jonathan's a legal adult now, but he needs me. Or at least *somebody*. I guess he has Sounder. And Jimmy. And hell, even Tom Lumen, except he had to leave again for Minnesota on Sunday. He stayed for three weeks after the shooting. It was nice."

"Has your relationship with Jonathan progressed any?"

Looking at her perfectly manicured hands, Winifred thought over the question, seeing once again Jonathan's glimmer of despair from last night. Her guilt at having damaged him so thoroughly had somehow thrust her toward a bona fide sense of motherly love, in whatever way she was capable of feeling such a thing. She glanced up at Kate, trying to hide the trickle of inner pride her answer inspired. "We've been good. Better than I ever expected. If anything, he's protective of me. Something I couldn't deserve any less."

"I can see you'd feel guilty leaving."

"Which is a good thing, isn't it? Somehow, I finally care. Maybe it's progress. Except what if my intuitions are really just leading me to be a bad mother? What would people think of me if I just left Jonathan for the birds? Christ. I should be defending him to every single one of those reporters."

"Could, would, should," Kate said. "Those are other people's measurements of who and how you should be. What are *your* measurements?"

Winifred wanted to purse her lips, but instead, she looked out the window, at the boats docked along the wharf, and felt her face submit to her feelings and loosen. "My measurement is that I messed up. I shouldn't have had Jonathan. I haven't told you this yet, but I had him for a stupid reason. I basically wanted to prove I could do a better job raising a kid than my own parents did. It was very *me, me, me*."

Kate laughed. "So, now we know your major issue. *Kidding*."

"No, you're right," Winifred said, smiling against her will. "I *am* very me, me, me. I think I *had* to be when I was a kid, in certain ways. My parents basically ignored me except for surface, practical ways. My brother, Michael, was the one who acted out and got all the attention. He tried to kill himself in high school, and God— you should have seen it. All the whispers. My parents almost killed each other trying to sling the blame back and forth. But mostly they were embarrassed by Michael for having 'issues.' Could I have been more of a cliché doing the exact same thing with Jonathan without even realizing it?" Winifred shook her head. "I feel like I'm failing some big life test."

"Think of yourself a year ago," Kate said. "How much have you changed?"

"People weren't shooting machine guns through my windows a year ago."

"Fair point."

Winifred shook her head. "The sick thing is that a huge part of me is more worried about people pointing and staring than it is about my own safety. I'm scared I'll never be able to crawl out from under all the attention, especially if all the hoopla Weston Carrow started about Victor Zobel wanting to kill Jonathan doesn't go away. Going on TV to defend Jonathan would make me look like a better mother, but if I tell people why I believe him about his memories, it could make it all way worse." Winifred said. "Just thinking about following my gut and running away terrifies me, though, because I'd probably fall apart knowing people were thinking I was a weak bitch."

"Careful with that fear," Kate said. "What we need to do here is look at your track record and discern what the difference is between fear and intuition. If your intuition is telling you to avoid all this and run, that's significant. At the same time, if it's just outright fear, facing it head-on might help you grow and get over it. If showing people you're a good mother might be productive, that's also significant. Intuition *isn't* fear, though. It's usually something that shows you the right path. You just have to allow yourself to pay attention."

"So, what you're saying is that it's lose-lose, and I'm screwed either way," Winifred said. This time, her shrug at Kate was frantic once again. An intense need for a vodka tonic followed it.

Kate smiled and shook her head. Her dolphin earrings jangled. "I'm saying that your base consideration here is choice. And I'm telling you to be careful of choosing something based on fear rather than intuition. Sometimes the difference is hard to discern."

"And I'm bad at discernment." Winifred flicked her manicured thumbnail across the nail of her pointer finger.

"Think of your deathbed. Looking at your choices now, think

of how you might feel about them then. Which ones wouldn't you regret?"

Winifred sat back on Kate's couch, still and stoic, her hands now in her lap.

Regret. It could undo a person ill-equipped to handle the ramifications of bad decisions. Was she ill-equipped?

It was 3:00 p.m. Time for a drink. Time for life.

The looming sense of dread followed Winifred out of Kate's office, even though the day was perfect—sunny, lightly chopping water, seabirds winding through the salt-dusted air. As she pulled onto America's Cup Avenue, avoiding a group of tourists who were meandering over the crosswalk toward Long Wharf Mall, she thought back on Jonathan's most recent blue-envelope letter.

"Is it really so hard to be the best we can be?" the mystery person had written. The question implied people everywhere could always choose to make their corners of the world better. Is that what Winifred was doing in therapy? Learning how to improve? It felt as though today's session had gone nowhere. Or perhaps it had gone somewhere, but she was simply too slow to catch up.

As she drove down Wellington Avenue, approaching her left turn toward home on Columbus, she passed the ever-present crowd of reporters and protesters. There, same as every day for the past three weeks, was the pale Weston Carrow, holding his sign, which today read "**BATHE HIM IN FIRE.**" He had a crowd of at least twenty supporters on his patch of sidewalk. When the crowd noticed Winifred passing in her car, everyone but Carrow began to scream—the protesters obscenities, the reporters questions. Carrow, however, simply watched Winifred with a trailing gaze, content to escalate her terror with a simple frozen stare.

2005

THURSDAY, JULY 14 WAS APPROACHING HOT but only just. It was a mere six hours since Elijah had awoken to the newspaper headline regarding Joshua Grime's jawbone and seen the inexplicable apparition of Damon Jacoby. Still terrified to admit his confrontation with insanity, he had called Molly Butler at 8:00 a.m. on the dot, first to apologize for having been snippy at the Fourth of July fair and then to see if she wanted to hang out at the Lemon Avenue Library. Molly had accepted his apology with an air so carefree that it almost seemed overdone, as if she were trying to hide from him just how hurt she had really been that night. Before he could mention what he had seen from the Billingtons' front porch, however, she had directed him to turn on the television, because NBC8 was airing the first news report on the reopened jawbone case, anchored by none other than Alice Winterblume, the reporter from Wind Prairie who had covered the Moon Woods cult scandal last year.

"Crazy how real all this is," Molly said through the phone as they both watched the report.

They had then spent the remainder of the morning together, sitting on the library's second floor next to the radiant stained glass window, discussing Joshua Grime's jawbone. Elijah attempted three times to force out the story of his paper-route apparition, but every time his mind analyzed the factor of Damon disappearing, he couldn't work up the courage to tell Molly. What if he were wrong, and she really would think him crazy? Or worse, what if she for some reason were to tell his mother, who would then attribute his vision to the devil and use it to defend her religious hogwash?

Now they were outside, walking up Main Street toward Hunter Avenue under several light clouds gracing the windy sky. The entire afternoon still lay ahead, and they had decided to pass the time by walking around instead of riding their bikes, which they had left parked on the library's rack.

"Let's go to the Bean & Leaf and get something cold," Elijah suggested, hoping the extension of their hangout would lend him some courage. "I just got my paycheck from the *Wind Prairie Tribune*, so I've got some money."

"I brought my wallet, too," Molly said.

Elijah smiled, because he didn't know many girls who carried wallets. Now that he noticed, Molly was almost a tomboy. Not quite, but *almost*. "I'll buy yours. I was a jerk after the fair. I sort of owe you."

"Whatever," Molly said. "My money is just allowance from my dad. But if you really want to . . ."

"My mom would be proud of me for being so nice."

"Which mom?"

Elijah snorted a quick laugh, despite the seriousness that lurked under Molly's joke.

"I seriously think it's so weird that your bio dad had an affair with Damon Jacoby's dad," she continued. "I mean, I guess it makes sense why Damon would hate gay people. And considering how homophobic he is, he's probably too embarrassed to tell people at school the real story. Maybe on some level he secretly knows you're the only one who would really get why he feels the way he does."

"Wouldn't put it past him," Elijah said.

"I'm dying to go back and talk to Cynthia about Mr. Grime's jawbone," Molly continued. "I bet we could find out the name of whoever gave it to Damon's dad."

"My mom will kill me," Elijah said. "She even yelled at me for re-reading the article about it during breakfast. But I cut it out anyway. She was being such a bitch."

They arrived at the corner of Main Street and Hunter Avenue. The breeze floated above them in the blue sky, and the small, recently planted maples lining the sidewalk swayed under its gentle force. It took Elijah a moment to notice the pause in his conversation with Molly. When she didn't respond, he turned his head and saw her staring at the street. When the light turned green, signaling to cross, she didn't even notice.

"Hey, we can go," Elijah said.

Molly snapped herself out of her brief reverie and offered him a reticent smile. "Sorry. I just . . ."

He raised a curious eyebrow. "What are you thinking?"

Another smile, even more strained than the last one.

"Ha. Nothing interesting. Just that my mom died here. Well, at the hospital actually, but this is where she got in her car accident."

Elijah blushed and immediately regretted calling his own living mother a bitch. Molly had told him just this morning that she had yelled at her mother and left for school in a huff the morning of the accident. He should have known better than to act so similarly right in front of her. "I'm sorry. I didn't know it happened here."

Molly gave him a sad twist of a smile. "It's okay. I pass it all the time." She motioned with a pointed finger along Hunter Avenue's stretch of the intersection. "She was crossing this way during a snowstorm last year, and a truck slid through on Main Street coming south. I was in school, and my dad came and picked me up. She was already dead when we got to the hospital. Totally like a TV show."

As angry as he was at his own mother, Elijah could barely imagine losing her—the mere thought was nothing less than a hypothetical nightmare. Heck, now that he knew his birth mother, the thought of her dying was almost just as terrible.

It was now or never.

"Remember the day of the tarot card reading when you told me you thought you saw something in Cynthia's living room? Like a ghost or whatever?"

Molly bristled at the question, and now she was the one blushing. She didn't answer.

Elijah took a deep breath, then continued on the exhale. His heart rattled in his chest. "I'm wondering what you meant by that."

The light turned red again. Three cars passed through the intersection, en route perpendicular to them. A robin bounced along the grassy yard of the office building to their left, pecking the ground for worms.

"Why do you ask?"

Hot tingles rushed through Elijah as he tried to form words that didn't sound ridiculous. "I saw somebody during my paper route today, and then he disappeared right in front of my eyes."

Molly's face glowed under a ray of sun, but she was standing with her weight on one foot, staring at the paved intersection. Her expression seemed caught between two emotions Elijah couldn't pinpoint, almost shaky. Tears lined the lower rims of her eyes. "I've had that happen to me, too," she said, still staring at the pavement.

"I thought it might be a ghost, even though I don't believe in them," Elijah continued. "Except this one looked like Damon Jacoby. Which probably makes me crazy."

Instead of bombarding him with awkward silence, Molly looked straight into Elijah's eyes. For a moment, their heartbeats danced together in a warm, tandem feeling Elijah had never before experienced. Molly suddenly chuckled and shook her head, but not in disbelief. If anything, it appeared to be the opposite.

"I thought I saw him at Cynthia's house that day," she said. "I saw . . . I guess I should say I *started* seeing things last year. Like, ghosts or whatever. I think my mind started opening to them, and now it won't go back." She shook her head yet again. "During the tarot card reading, I thought I saw something right behind Cynthia. Like the shape of a person, and then for a second somebody's face. It looked like Damon, but I only saw him that one time at the library, so I wasn't sure. Didn't you see me staring at the wall?"

"I thought you were staring at *Cynthia*," Elijah said. "But how the heck could Damon be a ghost if he isn't dead? We saw him at the fair after that."

Molly shrugged with an expression that suddenly seemed to be verging on desperate. Elijah, having now experienced the sensation of questioning his own sanity, wondered whether his period of doing so were just beginning. Molly was taking heavy breaths now as if fending off some sort of emotional attack. She closed her eyes and shook her head quickly. "I didn't think we'd ever talk about this. After that day we played Monopoly, I decided never to bring it up." For a moment, it seemed as if she were about to fight tears. "I *do* feel crazy sometimes. I have nobody to talk about it with. My friend Jacob knows I've seen ghosts, but we got kind of distant." Molly opened her mouth as if she meant to continue on this thread, but after a moment, she simply shook her head. "I guess I just feel—"

"Lonely," Elijah finished.

Molly smiled. Instead of avoiding his eyes by staring at the pavement, she was staring at the sky, at the invisible wind. After a moment, she continued. "You know, I have a million different things I could be doing this summer, but I'm stuck on this whole ghost thing. I'm totally going to be one of those weird kids at End Haven Middle School in September."

In a rush of exhilaration he wasn't expecting, Elijah said, "Well, I'm gay, I think, so it's not going to be much better for me." The words felt both foreign and revitalizing as they left his mouth.

Molly looked back at him. If there wasn't understanding in her eyes, there was at least some sort of compassion. "So, you mean Damon really knows that you are?"

"*I* don't even know if I am," Elijah said. "But I was looking at my friend Alec last year when he didn't have a shirt on, and I did kind of feel funny when it happened. And then he saw me looking, and he told his sister and their parents."

"I'm nervous around most boys," Molly said.

"Me too. I've looked up things about being gay on the internet, and it all sort of makes sense. I just hope my mom doesn't see that I've been to those websites."

"My dad told me never to look up anything on the internet that has to do with sex," Molly said, chuckling. "But my friend Jacob did last fall, and he told me all about it on the way home from school. He got grounded though. And besides, we studied all that sex stuff in fifth grade, so I don't see what the big deal is."

Elijah blushed, marveling that he was actually talking about sex with another person. Maybe he wasn't the only person his age who was curious.

"Either way," Molly went on, "if I'm a loner who sees things and you're gay and see things, maybe we can form some sort of Weirdo Group at school this fall."

At that moment, the loose ends of their unexpected connection came together and tied a knot of friendship. The light across Hunter Avenue then turned green for the fourth time since they had arrived at the intersection. Molly gestured toward the Bean & Leaf, which lay on the opposite side of Hunter Avenue and two doors down to the left. They crossed the street, and as they approached the café's front door, Molly said, "You know, you don't have to get freaked out when I mention my mom. If we're going to be friends for real—like, now that we have each other's phone numbers—you're going to have to get used to it."

Elijah's intended frown somehow came out as a smile, yet a question most potent was itching to escape his lips. "But how can you just talk about her like it's no big deal? I don't know what I'd do if my mom was dead."

Molly replied in a businesslike tone, one he wasn't expecting. Pulling the door open, she said, "I just told you I've been seeing ghosts for over a year. Which means I'm lucky enough to know that just because people die, it doesn't mean they're gone forever. No matter how crappy life gets, there's really nothing to worry about, because there's something after."

She held the door for Elijah with a perfectly confident expression. As he slipped through, digging for his wallet so he could pay for both their drinks, he decided Molly was somebody he wanted to keep around. Even if everything she stood for contradicted Victor Zobel's *In God We're Dust*, Elijah didn't care. As of this morning, his own beliefs had begun to sway toward a similar contradiction, even though the very idea of it terrified him. If Damon was indeed alive and well, it didn't necessarily negate what Elijah had seen during his paper route.

What he didn't see behind him now, in the shadow of an alley across Hunter Avenue, very solid and very rooted in the physical world, was Damon Jacoby, standing and watching them enter the Bean & Leaf, as if he had known exactly where they would be. Only later, at the moment of Elijah's own death in 2010, would he understand the raw truth behind Damon's undoing—that it was only temporary, a product of body and mind, and that, like all other tragedies on Earth, it held an intrinsic potential for opportunity.

2038

IT SEEMED IMPOSSIBLE, but Nicolas Leandro Rim was once again experiencing the simple pleasure of freedom. Four weeks had passed since the machine-gun attack on Jonathan Flite, this one with a seemingly legitimate basis in religious fervor. Perhaps inspiring such copycat behavior had been Victor Zobel's whole reason for having Nicolas put the extremist Christian note in Paul Simpleton's breast pocket on that snowy night last November. If so, it had been a brilliant risk that was now paying off.

After his escape from Mermaid Corner four weeks ago, Nicolas had returned to his apartment in Westfield, but only long enough to grab everything important there, in case Shandra the stripper had ratted him out and the FBI was now combing video footage from inside the taxis she had ordered for him. Last year, just two days before his ill-fated assassination attempt on Jonathan Flite, he had prepacked it all: a rolling suitcase of luggage, a small plastic bag with a wallet, thirty thousand dollars cash, six credit cards, and a Swedish passport under the name Asmund Odder Strand. In the small apartment's garage, disconnected from the weathered brick building along the back driveway, was a ten-year-old electric Honda X88. It was a pleasing dark red color and sportier than the white Ford Sanctuary he had driven to Crescent Rehabilitation Center last November. In the rear trunk of the Honda was an assortment of false license plates from multiple states. Some were expired, but at least four were good through late 2038. Next to the plates was a toolbox with all necessary screwdrivers he might need to make quick switches from car to car, to keep him inconspicuous, at least until any police officer found reason to run the numbers. Now he was lodged in a rundown Residence Inn Extended Stay off I-90 in Framingham, Massachusetts. No police. No FBI. No pictures of his face pasted on news websites or television stations. It likely meant they still had nothing on him but suspicion.

Yet the mere fact he had attempted to evade their little task force would make him look unquestionably guilty. Enough to implicate him in terrorist activities? Nicolas had no idea. Innocent people left town all the time. But did they do it by bribing strippers and sneaking out back doors? Did they leave incriminating notes? The beauty of it was that he wasn't even trying to outsmart the police. Not really. It was slowly starting to feel more and more real: the prospect that these would be the last days of his life, and that he would be able to live them as a free man, possibly redeeming himself in the process.

It was 4:06 p.m. and a bright afternoon. His hotel room was comfortable. The bed's mattress was firm; the sheets were clean; the place smelled faintly of eucalyptus. He had even allowed himself to start going to the bathroom without fearing that police might kick his door in while he was doing the deed. Perhaps they'd finally received a warrant to search his apartment in Hartford, seen his note, and presumed he had already killed himself.

For four weeks, Nicolas had been closely monitoring the media's coverage of Jonathan Flite. The shades of the boy's public image had changed conclusively the night of the attack on his mother's house. That morning, he had simply been a nurse killer about to roam free on the streets of Newport, Rhode Island; by nightfall, after surviving his second assassination attempt and sparking the widely circulated interview given by the pale, red-haired religious zealot, Weston Carrow, Jonathan Flite had become a most combustible bit of fuel for social speculation.

The shooters had been identified as thirty-four-year-old Aiden Tate and forty-two-year-old Gregory Waltham, both residents of West Greenwich, Rhode Island, and avid so-called Children of God at Weston Carrow's Heaven Church of Christ, located in the same town. While their attack seemed on the surface to be a stand-alone result of religious mania, the media was finally connecting the dots between Jonathan Flite's Idle County Seven claims and the possibility that people thought the claims might be legitimate—enough to threaten those whose beliefs about life, death, and consciousness swayed heavily toward opposing viewpoints. On top of this being the second attempt on the boy's life, rumors had gone mainstream that the FBI, while investigating the religious-terrorism angle of the attack on Jonathan last November, had somehow found reason to believe his assertions were true. They were, unnamed sources claimed, using his memories of Victor Zobel's stepdaughter, Jillian Pope, to link Victor Zobel to the murders at Crescent Rehabilitation Center and, possibly through that, to last year's nuclear terrorist attack in Geneva.

By Friday, June 4, a generous blogger with the URL Gossip. news had outlined and shared via his ActoHub a rundown of Jonathan Flite's legal history and "paranormal" claims, set against a history of Victor Zobel, the Idle County Seven, and the small Minnesota region itself—including its local forest known as the Moon Woods, where Jonathan Flite said the seven teenagers disappeared in 2010. By Sunday, the post had been shared on various social media networks by thirty thousand people.

What truly cemented the mysterious link between Jonathan Flite and Victor Zobel into the sphere of serious conjecture was a snippet of an article written by esteemed Associated Press reporter and ActoShouter Seth Kelly, republished on over six hundred different news websites on June 6.

> *People have reason to be curious. When you put this crazy Jonathan Flite story together with last year's rumors that Victor Zobel once knew Geneva's psychopath bomber Jean-Claude Apostol, we have global-scale intrigue. And what of the rumors about the FBI taking Jonathan Flite's past-life memory claims seriously, particularly regarding the memories of Jillian Pope, Victor Zobel's stepdaughter and one of the missing Idle County Seven? It sounds ridiculous at first consideration, but one must ask: If these federal police are seriously considering Jonathan Flite's past-life memory claims, did they somehow find reason to believe they are legitimate? If so, what would the implications of this be? If people were to become intrigued enough by Jonathan Flite to start questioning the nature of science and*

*consciousness, it could quite feasibly become Victor
Zobel's worst nightmare. That alone could be reason for him to want Jonathan Flite dead.*

So far, there had been no comment from the seventy-four-year-old billionaire, nor had there been any public reactions from Zobel Enterprises or any of its subsidiary companies. Nicolas Rim watched and waited as the speculation around Jonathan Flite, the Idle County Seven, and Victor Zobel unfolded. How long would it hold the public's attention? The mysterious snippets claiming to connect it all to the Geneva bombing were the parts that made Nicolas worry that the drama had only just begun.

Last year, after surface-level speculation over Geneva had ended with Cardinal Jean-Claude Apostol's religiously fanatical ActoVid post, the media's coverage of it had become dull and repetitive. Major questions were still unanswered, at least publicly, about how the man had acquired a nuclear weapon, smuggled it into France, and then driven it over the open Swiss border into Geneva without being noticed. Until three weeks ago, attention on the increasingly stagnating story had been waning. Now Jonathan Flite, due to his supposed connection to both Victor Zobel and the so-called religious extremist who had targeted him last fall at Crescent Rehabilitation Center, had slowly but surely injected life into the story once again.

If the media were to discover the truth about Nicolas's botched assassination attempt on Jonathan, all these inklings would take a firm, hard stance in the realm of newsworthy fact. Whether Victor Zobel was truly linked to the Geneva bombing didn't matter; he was linked (without a doubt in Nicolas's mind) to last November's fiasco at Crescent, and that would be enough to cause a firestorm of controversy.

Nicolas had purchased a new pair of invisible ActoLenses and their accompanying red transmitter phone, and he was currently sitting on his hotel balcony with the lenses switched off, using the phone's screen to navigate through a slew of ActoHub discussions tagging Jonathan Flite. One of them had gained a prominent following—an exchange between Jonathan's friend Jimmy Barber and the religion-crazed Weston Carrow. It had begun the morning of Jonathan Flite's release hearing in Providence, even before the recording of Carrow's infamous news interview. Now, since Carrow's castigation of Jonathan Flite had gone viral, over ten thousand people had commented on the digital back-and-forth shouting match. It had started with a shout to Jimmy Barber from Weston Carrow, condemning the string-beany teenage boy for supporting "a minion of Satan."

The first response from Jimmy had been sent less than three minutes later.

> *Yes, @WestonCarrow, I support J-Flite. Almost saw him get shot last fall by a religious freak like you. WAS it you??*

Carrow's response had first made Nicolas chuckle, then shake his head.

> *The Lord calls for fire upon blasphemers and those who encourage them.*

This, almost humorously, had prompted a five-shout tirade from young Mr. Barber:

Oh really, @WestonCarrow? Could you please tell me when #TheLord talked to you and told you that?

And BTW, @WestonCarrow, you're delusional. There is no proof to justify any of your beliefs.

@WestonCarrow – If your beliefs are so correct and so strong, why does #JonathanFlite's story threaten you? Because it is ACTUAL PROOF of something that contradicts everything you cling to?

@WestonCarrow – You may want to start assessing WHY you believe what you do and WHY you think your beliefs are air tight and rational. If you're so right, how come you're the one spreading division/ violence and the rest of us are perfectly happy being peaceful?

Time to use your brain and get real, @ WestonCarrow. #Enlightenment.

This last shout at Weston Carrow had been reshouted 6,534 times. Nicolas clicked on Jimmy Barber's ActoProfile and saw a number of shouts aimed at him from all over the United States, and even a few from Europe, Oceania, and Asia. Somebody had grouped all of Jimmy's five-shout tirade into a single video meme that included footage of Weston Carrow's news interview, then shared it with the world. Thousands of people had "liked" the meme, shared it, and then shouted statements at Jimmy concerning Jonathan Flite.

Whoa, @JimmyBarber. You're friends with a killer and don't judge? YOU must be the #Enlightened one.

@JimmyBarber – Very weird story. But anyone who believes in past lives missed the memo: that's #NewAgeHoohahGarbage. #ScienceRules.

So curious, @JimmyBarber – Has JF said anything about what he thinks actually happened to the IC7 kids? Just read about it. Creepy story!!

Nicolas had long since abandoned the ActoProfile through which he had accessed Paul Simpleton's privately broadcasted ActoVids from Crescent last year. Even then, he had used the account only through a quantum key VPN connection, like the one he was currently using. Now, at the top right corner of his ActoPhone's screen, there was a link in glistening pixels that said "Create New Account."

Did he dare?

It was the only way he could think of to get in touch with Jonathan Flite—through Jimmy Barber, anonymously, at least at first, in a way that would provide a buffer between making the choice to help Jonathan and having to accept the possible consequences. When he thought of an account name and tested its availability, it was green. Untaken.

With only a fleeting hint of trepidation, "@FriendOfJF" became Nicolas's new ActoHub alias.

After Nicolas confirmed the account name, he saw in his mind's eye that terrible, dark image of Mason Witzel wriggling and struggling in bed and then exploding under the bullets. Nicolas was probably the furthest he could possibly be from being Jonathan Flite's friend. If he were to redeem himself at all, however, he would have to face the truth that he might die without ever earning Jonathan Flite's forgiveness.

Jimmy Barber was now taking the brunt of Jonathan Flite's media pummeling. Nicolas had waded through a number of online news reports, and not one of them showed Jonathan Flite actually talking to reporters. Young Mr. Barber, however, tackled them with the dramatic precision of an expert actor. He paused at the right moments, withheld the most crucial tidbits of information, and scowled with just enough relish to make a person question his priorities. Even so, and despite his apparent excess willingness to take as many of his friend's media bullets as possible, he truly did appear to be loyal to Jonathan Flite.

Some people might have said Nicolas wasn't aware of what he was doing when he typed his message to Jimmy Barber. They would say he was psychologically disturbed, that it strained both sanity and credibility that, in his guilt, he would reach out to an eighteen-year-old via an anonymous ActoHub account to—what? Apologize? To share information that could help protect Jonathan Flite? To make amends before bowing out of life and all its choice-traps once and for all?

Whether Nicolas sensed it in his gut or whether he was simply enjoying a little daytime fantasy of helping the world toward a positive outcome, he typed a message to Jimmy—a private one so that none of the public trolls could see it.

My guilt is heavy, and I have information that could help protect Jonathan Flite. Will not share with

*media or police. Possible connections regarding
events scheduled in Geneva last August 12. You
seem like a good vehicle for it.*

A good vehicle. It sounded like a silly way to translate his over-all vision for how this might play out.

There were so many things he could say to Jimmy. He had first-hand memories of time spent with Jillian Pope when she had been living in Geneva, Switzerland. If Jonathan could corroborate them and prove his so-called memories were legitimate, what would the implications be? Nicolas shuddered over how he himself might react to proof that Jonathan Flite actually had Jillian Pope's memories. It would be proof not just that consciousness somehow transcended death but also that life wasn't necessarily a one-stop shop. Would knowing this make suicide easier, or would it render the action futile?

Nicolas reviewed his message, then hesitated only a moment before pressing the ActoHub's "shout" icon. When his message fluttered into cyberspace, still hiding his location behind quantum key VPN protection, he sat back and waited for his world to crumble, for his sky to fall.

For just under a minute, nothing happened. Then his ActoShout inbox jingled an alert.

It was a private response from @JimmyBarber. Nicolas opened it.

*Prove you're legitimate and not some creep. Then
we can talk. Thanks.*

Adrenaline poured through Nicolas's body, leaving him in a cold sweat. For a moment, his fingers danced on air over his phone screen's keyboard. There were so many memories of Jillian Pope he could draw upon. The addition his father had built on Victor Zobel and Cassandra Pope's home outside Geneva had lasted over a year. Nicolas and his sisters, Nora and Luana, had played at the house often after the project started, because their mother, Genevieve, had to work into the evening, and their father, Jonas, was in charge of childcare and couldn't afford a babysitter. To help him out, Victor and Cassandra had offered to have their nanny watch the Rim children. The Zobel children, a set of fraternal twins named Victoria and Revis, had become Nicolas's best friends. Jillian, their older, mysterious, radiant, and red-haired half sister (of whom Nicolas always sought glimpses whenever he could) had been a product of Cassandra's first marriage back in America, and she had sometimes babysat the younger children. If Jonathan Flite truly had Jillian's memories, there was one day that would no doubt stand out.

Nicolas typed a new message.

> *Ask JF if he remembers the day Revis stepped on the nail. And who hid behind J. Pope's legs when Victor was screaming at him.*

This time, Nicolas's ActoHub inbox remained empty for well over an hour. He settled into a chair on his hotel balcony and watched a flock of geese fly back and forth over a nearby lake, honking like mad things. When the inbox link on his ActoHub screen jingled once again and gave its pulsing glow, Jimmy Barber's response was shorter but much, much sweeter.

> *I'm listening. JF asks: Are you Little Nick?*

2010

CYNTHIA FOSTER AWOKE TO A BLOOM OF LIGHT coming through Frank Brennin's bedroom window. Though the window was closed, she could hear wind rushing through the autumn-tinted trees outside. It was her fifth morning in Alaska, and for the first time in years, or perhaps ever, she felt as though she were home. No matter all her questions about Max Pope, Jillian Pope, Victor Zobel, and Rebecca Sparks—she was allowing herself to live in the here and now, and it felt divine. The crisp blue sky and the spired, snowy mountains that lay just moments from her eyesight, out Frank's deck window, reminded her that life was short. Happiness, that elusive emotion she had finally glimpsed during those five years with Elijah, now shimmered on her horizon once again.

She and Frank had made love after their third date two nights ago. Cynthia had never been a prude, but even for her, the third date was fast. It had been months for Frank since he last had sex and decades for her, but she had found it to be like riding a bike—something a person learned once and never forgot. Frank had used protection, miraculously unfazed by her HIV-positive status, and the last two days now felt like a good dream.

"We're getting up there in years," he had whispered to her after their fourth round. They had been naked, sweaty, gloriously uncaring that their bodies were both softer and creakier than they had been in more ideal days. "What if you really did just stay up here?"

"Like, forever?"

"Like, for however long you want."

To Cynthia's surprise, her only concern was whether she would have to fly back to Idle County to pack up her house and pick up her cat. Her generous and hands-off landlord, Darius Smith, would deserve to have regular notice and a cleaned, empty house were she to leave. Darius could have sold her house after inheriting it from his late father, but he hadn't. "Just take care of it," he always said whenever they exchanged words. Today, she planned to call him to warn him that she might not be back for a while. If winter were to come early, he would need to turn off the outside water lines.

Waking now, allowing her random, unexpected surroundings to meet her eyes, she felt a rush of adventure, as if she were finally approaching a sense of peace she had waited many years for. If Eloise Creed was a fraud and Elijah were somehow still alive, she would go back to Minnesota immediately—no questions. But until then? Shelly Bryce would likely be glad to have her out of the picture.

Frank's house was quiet. If she remembered correctly, he was out at a scheduled meeting regarding a new apartment complex going up in Anchorage. Cynthia wrapped herself in his bathrobe—left for her on the door hook—upon climbing out of bed. She walked out of the bedroom and down the hallway, loving the feeling of Frank's soft, gray carpet between her toes. To her right were his deck windows and beyond them the mountains; to her left was the kitchen. On Frank's homemade wooden table sat a piece of paper with his scrawled writing. She picked it up.

> *Hello Beautiful. In Anchorage for the morning. Heard back from my brother—his air traffic control friend in Palmer said yes to talking. His number is 907-999-1029. Blake Locklear—he's in the flight services station at the regional airport. Said he remembers Victor Zobel flying in and out.*
>
> *Looking forward to seeing you this afternoon. Hike and then dinner of your choice?*

Cynthia read the phone number over five times. Four nights ago, Frank had called his air-traffic-controller brother, Kenny, whose friend at the Palmer regional airport had mentioned dealing with Victor Zobel when he visited late last November. "He flies in a Bombardier Learjet 40XR," Kenny Brennin told Frank and Cynthia on speakerphone. Frank had rolled his eyes at the unnecessary plane-model detail, but Cynthia smiled. "I know he flew through Palmer though and had some sort of hissy fit," Kenny continued. "My friend Blake dealt with him, and it became kind of a joke afterward. You know, like, rich and famous people thinking they can get anything they want, even clearance to fly into a dangerous storm. But yeah, security is basically nonexistent for private planes at that airport. There wouldn't necessarily be a record of everyone who flew on that plane."

Pondering the implications of this, Cynthia made coffee, ate a slice of Frank's special leftover egg bake from yesterday morning, showered, and took her ART medication before building the courage to call Blake Locklear. She grabbed her phone and Frank's note and walked toward the deck windows. The craggy mountains in the distance, dotted with snow, glowed under the morning sun as she dialed the stranger's number.

It rang four times before a man answered. "This is Blake." He spoke quickly, but in a jovial sort of way, not rushed. Cynthia took a deep breath, introduced herself, and explained the reason for her call. She felt a rush of relief when Blake said, "Heh, this is pretty funny. Like, it's the reason I told Kenny Brennin to have you call me. It's been a story going around the FSS office. Five of us rotate schedules here. Victor Zobel was at the airport that day. No big deal. We get famous people sometimes. But there was, like, a display when he tried to leave."

"A display?"

"Like, *behavior*. We had a blizzard coming in and had to delay the plane after Zobel's pilot checked in about his flight plan before takeoff. It was like, 'Um, nope, you could have maybe made it out two hours ago, but not now.' Major weather system coming down, and Victor Zobel was in the pilot cabin *screaming* about keeping to the schedule. Two of us were working and heard it. He didn't realize how ridiculous he was. Didn't seem human."

"Was anybody with him? Do you know how many people he had flying out?"

"Three others," Blake said. "We saw them when they got off the plane. It was the pilot, some assistant type guy, and that other dude all the ladies around here liked. He moved up here a couple years ago, I think. I let my coworker deal with Victor Zobel and walked outside to check out the Bombardier. The other dude was just pacing back and forth, laughing. I think because the whole thing was so crazy. I even said to him, 'Victor Zobel sure doesn't act like that on TV.' The other guy said, 'No, he sure doesn't.'"

"Did they eventually leave?"

"The next day, my coworker said."

"All three of them?"

"Not sure. I could ask. But we don't usually see who is on a private plane. No real security or official record. This was a weird fluke, though. Again, why I said to call. Thought it was funny you were asking about it."

"One last thing," Cynthia said. "If I were to text you a photo of someone, would you be able to tell me if it was the same guy? The one you talked to, I mean."

"Sure thing. This is my cell number. Text away."

When they hung up, Cynthia opened her iPhone's photo album and pulled up the photo of Max Pope that she had been showing to the residents of Palmer. It took her twenty seconds to send the image to Blake Locklear, who responded almost immediately.

> *That was the guy, only he had a beard. If you need to tell police my info, feel free.*

Cynthia's heart fluttered with a mixture of self-consciousness over having traveled all the way to Palmer and the validation that her unyielding desire for answers had actually turned one up. She found the Idle County Sheriff's Department's number in her phone but hesitated before pressing the green "call" icon on its screen. Would they listen? Would they care?

She called anyway. The phone rang five times before somebody picked up. Her call and the reason she gave for it were short and quick. While she wasn't the legal guardian of Elijah Bryce, one of the Idle County Seven, she was his biological mother, and she quite possibly had new information on the teenagers' disappearances. According to an employee from the Flight Services Station at Palmer Municipal Airport, Max Pope had seemingly left Alaska in late November 2009 on a private plane headed back to Minnesota. Were the police aware? Was there a way for them to confirm?

The woman who answered her call spoke with the blandness of an underpaid administrative assistant. "I'll pass your information along," she said, sounding as if she would do no such thing. Cynthia hung up feeling deflated.

Who next to call? Who would care?

Shelly Bryce. She had spoken to Victor Zobel one-on-one multiple times since Elijah and his friends disappeared. Even so, she had also been rather unplugged from Elijah's life in the years leading up to his disappearance, with a rather glaring amount of resentment toward Cynthia for having earned Elijah's love and trust. He had shared his feelings with Cynthia about school, books, homosexuality, his newfound desire to work out and build muscles—all the things about him that Shelly barely wanted to hear. If Shelly had Victor Zobel's ear, however, she had to know about this. All the Idle County Seven parents did.

When Cynthia called Shelly's number, it went to voice mail after one ring, as if the woman had seen her name on caller ID and denied the call outright. Feeling a shred of unwelcome disappointment, Cynthia left a voice mail detailing what she had learned about Max Pope.

"I hope you'll let anybody who cares know, and please ask Victor Zobel about it next time he's back in town," she said, winding the message down. "I know you don't want me doing any of this, but I care too much. That's all. I hope you're well. I'll continue to respect your space and stay away. I might even relocate. This place is gorgeous."

When she ended the call, Frank's house felt too quiet, as though it were offering a voiceless hint that her quest for answers was about to hit a dead end. Only the sun-glinting mountains, at their distance through the window, seemed to confirm the validity of her efforts.

The thought brought forward a weariness she hated to acknowledge. She had tried her damnedest during this life to make progress, to help people see the world with eyes anew. What had she become as a result? A laughingstock with good intentions and not much more.

Frank Brennin, the man who was either a new, glowing angel in her life or an ephemeral fling, wouldn't be home for another four hours. In the downtime between now and their ongoing formation of a potential relationship, perhaps she could make herself useful to Elijah and his friends, or at least to their families. If Max Pope had truly flown from Alaska to Minnesota on Victor Zobel's private jet, then it was possible there was no record of it, which meant he could secretly have been in Idle County when the seven teenagers disappeared.

Cynthia punched Max's address into her Google Maps app, then clicked "Directions." It was forty-eight minutes away. Did she dare return and take one more look around? Five days ago, all she had done was knock on his door and peek through a few windows, afraid somebody might see her. She hadn't returned for a second look after discussing Victor Zobel's visit with Max's neighbor.

One more try, and then I'll stop playing detective.

Within twenty minutes, she was driving east along South Knik Goose Bay Road, toward the Palmer-Wasilla highway and the end of whatever answers she hoped to uncover here. Then it was on to whatever would come next in her own life—that gray, nebulous cloud of choices and probability.

2005

"OKAY, THIS MIGHT LEAD US SOMEWHERE," Molly Butler said, slowing her internet-browser scrolling and beckoning Elijah to take a look. They had returned to her house after the Bean & Leaf and were taking their first steps in trying to discover who might have given Samuel Jacoby the jawbone back in the 1980s. Molly's living room was spacious but cozy, carpeted white and connected to a dining room that exited onto a deck overlooking the backyard. On the deck lay Sabrina, Molly's babysitter, who was tanning in a hot pink bikini and tapping her feet in rhythm with inaudible music coming from a set of small, white headphones. Elijah had shaken her fingernail-painted hand politely on the way inside, but he was relieved when she went back to tanning without further conversation.

"Here it is," Molly said, pointing at her computer, which sat along the house's west wall, next to a set of wide corner windows.

On its screen was a garishly teal website with a light yellow heading reading "The Idle County Fair: Established in 1918."

Elijah turned from the windows and peered at the monitor. "Let's see. . . . Eighty-seventh annual Idle County Fair, August 10 through the 14. That's in a few weeks."

"Looks like it's at the fairgrounds up near Spinner's Lake, not where the Fourth of July fair was."

"Who are the people in charge?"

Molly continued scrolling. "There's a board of directors here, and a president, vice president, secretary, and treasurer. The president is a guy named Omar Razor. They have his phone number here. Should I call him?"

"The name sounds creepy," Elijah said. "What about someone else?"

"Jane Clemens, vice president? Says she's in charge of organizing all the 4-H activities. Horse shows, baking competitions, things like that. She also manages 'carnival game-stand logistics.' Her number is 237-341-4322."

Elijah was about to give her the go-ahead when he remembered Sabrina, the babysitter. "Is she going to hear us?" he said, pointing at the hot pink bikini.

Molly smirked. "No, she turns her iPod so loud that I sometimes hear it even through the earbuds." She pressed the Speaker button on the desktop telephone sitting next to the computer, then dialed Jane Clemens's number. One ring, two rings, three rings. Then:

"This is Jane Clemens."

The woman's tone was polite but straightforward, like that of a strict but respectable school principal, perhaps in her fifties. For a moment, Molly faltered.

"Hello?" Jane Clemens said.

Elijah gestured, eyes wide, for Molly to hurry up and speak.

"Uh, hello," she finally managed. "My name is Molly Butler, and I found your phone number on the county fair website."

Jane Clemens's voice seemed to soften when she inferred Molly's age. "And what can I help you with, dear?" Elijah listened as Molly succinctly explained the reason for their call. Silence followed for a good five seconds before the woman replied. "You're calling about a jawbone? Is this a prank?"

"No, Ms. Clemens," Molly said in a slight panic, waving her hand at Elijah. "My friend Elijah Bryce and I—"

"Hello," he said, hoping it was the correct move.

"—are on speakerphone here, and we really are trying to track down the name of a man who worked at the fair. We weren't able to speak with the woman who turned the jawbone over to police this week, so we were wondering if you might have any sort of records or know of this person."

"Well, I'm sorry, but I can't possibly know the name of every person who ever worked a game stand for us," Jane Clemens said. "And I've not yet seen today's newspaper. I'm not aware of this issue."

"The man who won this jawbone at the county fair was named Elijah Earnshaw," Molly said. "He was in his early twenties I think, and the man who gave him the jawbone was named—"

"Earnshaw, you said?" Now there was recognition in the woman's stern voice. But again, it had a soft edge.

"That's right, Elijah Earnshaw. He passed away in the early 1990s. So did Samuel Jacoby, I think—the man who was working the game stand."

"You would be correct," Jane Clemens said. "Now, it's funny

that you're calling, bringing up those names. They were two of the few around here who died of AIDS back when doctors were only just figuring out how to slow it down. Word got around, sadly enough."

"Small towns," Molly said with a nervous laugh.

Jane Clemens already seemed far beyond such false pleasantries. "When I say 'word got around,' I mean certain ignorant people in End Haven publicized these people's personal business and dragged their names through the mud. Vandalized their homes, even. I don't know why I'm telling you all this. You sound like children."

"We're both turning thirteen soon," Molly said in a steady voice.

Jane Clemens cleared her throat. "May I ask why you both are so keen on finding out about Sam Jacoby?"

Again, Molly opted for the truth. "Well, again, it's about that jawbone. We're trying to find out how Samuel Jacoby happened to have it at the fair to give away as a prize. It belonged to a man named Joshua Grime who disappeared back in the 1940s, and the sheriff's department just reopened the investigation. I knew Joshua Grime's wife when she was still alive, and I'm curious about doing some investigation stuff myself, with Elijah here."

"I'm sure you'll do a better job than our sheriff's department," Jane Clemens said. "Fairly useless when it comes to those sorts of things, if you ask me. Still trying to pick up the pieces from that cult last summer."

The woman sounded almost defiant through the speaker, as if she had some extra bone to pick with the department. Elijah shrugged at Molly, who shrugged back.

"Anyway," she continued, "I'm going to direct you to a man

named Arthur Brown. He owned the particular game stand you're talking about. I know, because I once rolled five of a kind with those dice and won a giant, stuffed snake. He was there during all those summers when Sam Jacoby was around and might know something that could help you, if he's still lucid enough. He lives here in Idle County, in End Haven." Jane Clemens cleared her throat. "I have to warn you, though; he's getting on in years. I'm not sure how much he'll remember. But he wouldn't hurt a fly. You can quote me on *that*."

ARTHUR BROWN LIVED AT 902 EAST LOVELL ROAD, in the northeast part of End Haven. His phone number at 237-346-6877 rang without answer ten times on Thursday, so on Friday morning, July 15, Elijah and Molly decided to pay him a visit. That morning, there had been a second article about Joshua Grime's jawbone. The Idle County Sheriff, Kevin Applebee, said the department was still "looking into it," but based on how old the case was and how any evidence relating to it was likely long gone, they "weren't making it a high priority." To Molly, this of course amounted to heresy. If she had been determined in tracking the path of Joshua Grime's jawbone before, she was now unshakably resolute in following through with the process. Elijah, welcoming the importance behind her mission, was happy to follow along.

At just past 1:00 p.m., he was waiting outside her house on his bike. Her lawn, which had looked rather straggly yesterday, was freshly mowed. Molly appeared behind her screen door. "I'm going for a bike ride, Sabrina!" she yelled, bursting outside and running down her front steps. A minute later, they were riding toward Main Street, where they would turn right and follow it through the

Hunter Avenue intersection, into the northeast corner of town. "I can't believe that article this morning," Molly said as they reached a good riding pace.

Elijah offered her a condoling grimace. "You really think they're just giving up?"

"Kind of looks like it. And considering Mrs. Grime is dead and nobody needs to care anymore, I wouldn't be surprised."

"But that new sheriff had a point," Elijah said. "Seems like it'll be hard to find any real evidence." When Molly scowled, he added, "But maybe this Arthur Brown dude will know something."

As it turned out, Arthur Brown had already spoken to the police earlier that week. He was sitting on an old, rickety porch swing when they wheeled their bikes up his front sidewalk. Capping his head was a red plaid beret, and his knobby face and wrinkled eyes were focused on somewhere far away, either the trees across the road or somewhere altogether beyond. Even as Elijah and Molly parked and approached the steps wearing cautious expressions, his intrigued but serene gaze didn't shift an inch. He seemed not to have noticed them.

Molly knocked gently on the porch's ledge when she stopped at the top of the stairs. "Mr. Brown?"

He didn't move.

This time, Elijah tried. "Arthur Brown?"

Now, perhaps, a flinch.

"My name is Elijah Bryce, and this is Molly Butler. We're here because Jane Clemens from the Idle County Fair sent us." Molly flashed a look of "*not exactly sent*" to Elijah, but he only shrugged.

The old man remained almost motionless. When Elijah moved closer, however, he saw that Arthur Brown was holding his left palm face up and stroking what appeared to be a small, black pebble with his right index finger. The porch swing squeaked in the day's light wind, as if its sole occupant were light as air.

"Mr. Brown?"

"Such lovely things, the creatures of this Earth," the old man replied with surprising vocal clarity. He appeared to be pushing eighty-five years at least, maybe even ninety, and while his tone was cracked and weakened by age, the words were sharp enough.

Molly moved nearer now. "What do you mean by that?"

"Such lovely things," Arthur said again. "See? Don't you see?"

He held out his hand, continuing to stroke the black pebble. Only when Elijah stepped close enough to touch Arthur's shoulder did he realize that it was not a pebble the man was holding but a fly—medium-sized, nothing special. The moment Elijah leaned forward to see it for sure, it buzzed out of Arthur's hand.

"Oh, racket. He's gone, isn't he?"

A slow, yearning disappointment had woven its way through the old man's statement. His gaze followed the fly, or at least tried to, as the breeze fluttered a loose strand of gray hair peeking out from under his beret.

Elijah exchanged deflated glances with Molly. Jane Clemens hadn't told them Arthur Brown was downright senile.

"We're here to ask you about Sam Jacoby," Elijah said. "He was a man who used to work for you at the county fair, back in the 1980s."

At this, Arthur frowned, as if someone had just trampled on a carefully planted flower. "How come it is that flies are such dirty little creatures, but they can still feel happy in the palm of my hand?"

It took all of Elijah's energy not to grit his teeth; he attempted to hide his frustration with a sigh. "I'm not sure, Mr. Brown. We can leave you alone, if you want. I'm sorry we disturbed your fly."

"No, no," the old man said. "Nobody should feel sorry for a creature doing what it does best. He belonged in the air."

This time, Molly stepped forward. "But he felt comfortable with you, didn't he?"

"I love all of the world's creatures."

"That's very nice," Molly said, smiling.

"So, do you remember working with a man named Sam Jacoby?" Elijah tried again. "He would have been young at the time. In his twenties, I think."

Arthur had made his first bit of sense with them after Elijah's apology about the fly. Now, after Elijah's second attempt at their pressing question, there was a glint of lucidity in his eyes.

"If I recall," he began, "those policemen came here to ask me about Sam and that old jawbone. But it wasn't one of my clear days, so I couldn't remember what I should have to say about any of it."

"So, you remember the jawbone?" Elijah pressed.

"We really appreciate that you're even talking to us," Molly added, seeming already to have a genuine affinity for the old man.

"I only remember my favorite creatures," Arthur said. The clarity from moments before seemed to be leaving him again. "Only the creatures. They're all I have now, you know. Nobody else. Nobody else at all."

"I'm sure you have nice people to come and visit you, right?" Molly offered. For some reason, she seemed to know exactly what to say, because Arthur's tiny flair of intellect came back once more.

"Oh, here and there, but the creatures are the ones I like the most."

"And how come that is, Mr. Brown?"

"The creatures might die, but I can't tell the difference between them, so it doesn't make me sad. There's always one to take another's place."

Elijah listened to this with strangely open ears. Perhaps the man really was making some sort of sense.

"Sam Jacoby died, I remember that much," Arthur said. "He was one of those homosexuals, and a bunch of people threw rocks in his windows. When a broken window got replaced with a new window, someone else would go on by and break it again. But I liked Sam Jacoby. He was a good boy, even if he got that disease."

"That's right," Molly said. "He had AIDS, didn't he, Mr. Brown?"

"I heard it came from monkeys in Africa, but I never quite believed it," he replied. "Monkeys are nice creatures. I've never seen one up close, though." For the first time since their arrival, he turned his head—not to Molly, but to Elijah. "Have you? Have you seen a monkey?"

"Only at the zoo," Elijah said, hoping it was the right thing to say.

"Zoos," Arthur growled in response.

Elijah turned to Molly for help.

She shook her head three times fast, as if recomposing herself, and then asked, "Where did the jawbone come from, Mr. Brown? The one Sam Jacoby gave away at the fair?"

"I always thought it must have come from one of the dead creatures," Arthur said, now in a perfect blend of senescent bliss and analytical nostalgia. "He said it came from India. A good luck charm from India."

"Sam Jacoby said that?"

"No, not Sam Jacoby."

"Then who, Mr. Brown?" Molly pressed. "Did someone else know about the jawbone?"

Now the old man chuckled, but it was an anxious chuckle, clouded by some darker memory. "It wasn't from a creature, that jawbone. Not an animal creature. It was from a man, the police said."

"A man named Josh—" Elijah started, but Molly held up her hand.

He might have known Joshua Grime, her look said. *Don't make him remember.*

Her recovery of the conversation was fast and smooth. "It did come from a man. And the police don't know where the rest of his skeleton is. They're giving up looking. Which is why we want to know where you got that jawbone."

"Poker," the old man said with surprising bluntness.

"Poker?"

"Levi Mariani lost it to me in poker. I had three aces; he had three kings."

Elijah doubted Joshua Grime would ever have guessed that part of his skull would have ended up on a card table. The absurdity of it would have been humorous were it not so morbid.

"Levi Mariani had it for a long time. He didn't want to give it up, because it was good luck, but he had to play the game. We all had to play the game. That was during the time when my beautiful Beverly was very angry with me. She didn't like my gambling."

"And this jawbone," Molly said. "Where did Levi Mariani get it? Who gave it to him?"

"I didn't know Sam was going to give it away as a prize," Arthur said, his attention fading again. "I hid it in my sock drawer after I won it at the poker game, but it started to get in the way. I put it in one of my storage boxes filled with fair supplies. I gave it to Sam when he found it during work one day. He was the type of boy to like a good luck charm."

"But this Levi Mariani," Molly continued, "the man you won the jawbone from in poker. Where is he now? Is he still alive?"

"He smoked."

"You mean cigarettes?"

"And he drank. A lot more than I ever did, didn't he, Beverly?"

Now Arthur turned his head left as if looking at someone next to him on the porch swing, except nobody was there. He smiled, as if Beverly had agreeably said, *"Yes, indeed, dear, he drank like a fish!"*

Elijah turned to Molly quickly and saw that she was already one step ahead. Her sharp eyes were surveying the other side of the porch swing, as if they might be able to see something most other eyes couldn't. But she looked at Elijah and shook her head. *"No ghost,"* she mouthed.

"So, Levi liked to drink?" Elijah continued. Guilt tightened his throat when he realized his conversational tone wasn't as fault-less as Molly's; it was more of a ruse to get this old man to tell them more.

"Oh, he drank all right. Drank lots. At Miller's Tavern in Stone Ridge, near his house. Never did marry, because he could never keep a woman. That crazy Italian." Again, Arthur smiled. "But Beverly here"—he gestured to his right once again—"she tells me you're here to ask about that damned jawbone."

"That's right," Molly replied, taking another glance at the empty half of the porch swing. Elijah looked, too—squinted even—but there appeared to be nothing out of the ordinary. Maybe this ghost really was in Arthur Brown's head. Perhaps the memory of his wife was so painful that he had to imagine her with him, now that he was old and alone.

"That poker game was so long ago," Arthur said. "Levi asked me about that jawbone from time to time, but he died even before I gave it to young Sam."

"Did he ever tell you where he got it?"

"The man in the bar."

"You mean a man he was drinking with?" Elijah asked.

"Yes. 'A man dressed in black' was all Levi ever said. This guy apparently told him he was looking down on his luck. I always guessed Levi was too drunk to really remember right. Hell, he might've even made up the part about the bone coming from India. But it *was* Levi's good luck. For twenty years, it was. And then he bet it in the poker game and lost it to me. Then he got sick. All of God's creatures get sick, you know."

"A man in black," Molly said. She turned to Elijah. "Do you suppose—?"

Elijah nodded. "That priest who killed all those people? Simon Villard or whatever?"

"I don't know about any priest," Arthur Brown said. "But that jawbone wasn't really good luck. I think it made things sour, wherever it was. Because that's when Beverly here got sick. Right before I gave it away to Sam, the homosexual."

"And then he got sick, too," Molly mused.

Elijah stepped closer to Arthur. "So, that's all you know?"

"I'm sure that's all." His eyes had glossed over again, and a moment later, Elijah heard a faint buzzing sound, just before it stopped. Another fly had landed on Arthur Brown's open palm.

"Well, we should get going, Mr. Brown," Molly said. "You have a nice day with your creatures."

"We're all creatures," he replied.

Unfortunately, Elijah and Molly were now creatures up against a brick wall. Both the jawbone and the body it had come from seemed to be slipping into history with every effort they made to uncover them further. All alleys in this investigation pointed toward death.

Just like the tarot, Elijah thought.

On their ride home, all he could think about was Cynthia's card, the one with the skeleton riding the horse. Had that skeleton's jawbone really been shaped like a smile? Or had it simply been a disguise for something worse?

2038

EVERYTHING WAS SPIRALING DOWNWARD. Nine weeks of therapy, and this is what Winifred Flite had to show for herself: a living room crowded by FBI agents, the son who had driven her crazy in the first place, and his *second* ever small-statured friend—one she hoped wouldn't meet the same fate as the first. Thus far, Jimmy Barber had proven to be far more reckless than silent and waifish Mason Witzel, and if today's course of events had proven anything to Winifred, it was that he wasn't helping this situation.

The first ActoHub message from Nicolas Rim, one of the main suspects in last fall's murders at Crescent Rehabilitation Center, had come in at one o'clock. By two o'clock, Jonathan and Jimmy had a chain of messages all but proving it was indeed him and that the memories Jonathan had about Jillian Pope's days growing up in Geneva were legitimate. By three o'clock, because Jonathan had immediately called the FBI, Agent Ethan Prescott and two of his colleagues had appeared at their door. He and one of the others had made the thirty-minute helicopter flight down from Boston and had been joined by an agent from the Providence resident agency.

They had immediately called Jimmy's mother, the pharmaceutically balanced Kendra Barber, and invited her to Winifred's house, where the agents had directed Jimmy to stay. She had arrived in a casual daze, as if whatever painkillers she was on had numbed her to the seriousness of the situation. Jimmy's father, Steven, was in China for a month on business, and it appeared nobody had made any effort to contact him.

In Winifred's house now was Special Agent Ethan Prescott, the chiseled, dark-haired member of the joint terrorism task force squad in Boston. They had met twice last year—first after the Geneva bombing, when his office had received a tip-off to interview Jonathan about Victor Zobel, and then again after the murders at Crescent, when the note found in Paul Simpleton's shirt pocket hinted at upcoming Christian terrorism efforts on US soil.

Today, Agent Prescott had come to the door devoid of his usual air of superiority, because behind him was his squad's supervisory special agent, a middle-aged bombshell of a blond named Janice Hensley. The saturation of her red lipstick had shocked even Winifred, who had always considered her own preferred shade to be the most intimidating one out there.

Last in their line of three had been Special Agent Colleen Casey, an equally fit but round-faced woman with pulled-back brown hair and a placid demeanor. Agent Casey was the senior resident agent at the FBI's satellite office in Providence, and Winifred had met her on five occasions, when she had driven to Newport to collect Jonathan's blue-enveloped letters. What Winifred wondered now was just how special Jonathan's nebulous, parapsychological connections to the Geneva attack had become for them. Was it truly a special case, or were they approaching it in some basic, by-thebook way?

After reviewing Jimmy's phone, they had made a number of calls on their own relating to internet records, phone records, and court orders, then questioned Jimmy, Jonathan, Winifred, Sounder, and even Kendra Barber privately, in separate rooms. Now they were all in Winifred's front living room, which had not been damaged in May's bullet attack. She wondered just how much information the agents would be willing to share. Last year, Agent Prescott had allowed very few details through about the FBI's interest in Victor Zobel, despite her putting up a fight to be placed thoroughly in the loop. Today, Winifred simply accepted her ignorance; she felt limp, like a strung-up puppet dancing in a theater far out of her league.

Agents Prescott and Casey were sitting in two living room chairs opposite Winifred, who was sitting on the couch. Next to her were Jonathan and Sounder, and to their left, on a love seat between the chairs and couch, were Kendra and Jimmy Barber. Jimmy was sitting alert and with perfect posture next to his mother. Behind the chairs, pacing back and forth, was blond Special Agent Hensley, who had already shown while making her phone calls an attitude eerily on par with Winifred's. That the woman had risen to this pinnacle of professional achievement was somehow comforting, as if it proved that even personalities like theirs had places in the world.

"I'm sorry we can't give you as many details as you'd like," Agent Prescott said, looking at all of them one by one. "What we need here is to lock down a location for Nicolas Rim, if he indeed was the one who sent these messages."

"He was," Jonathan said. "Nobody else would have known about Revis Zobel stepping on the nail. I honestly wouldn't have even thought about it if he hadn't brought it up."

"It does seem quite specific."

None of the agents made any effort to glance at each other or give any physical acknowledgment of the glaring elephant in the room: that by being here, they had legitimized Jonathan's naming of the Rim family as being a close Zobel-family connection in Geneva, which in turn insinuated that Jonathan had indeed helped their investigation.

As if to put Winifred's thoughts into words, Kendra Barber leaned forward with a distant, confused look and said, "So, wait— the news people are right? You guys seriously *did* get this guy's name from Jonathan?"

Winifred and Jonathan exchanged the slightest of eye rolls. Upon seeing them do so, Jimmy added his own highly exaggerated one, as if confirming that his mother truly was the type of media bottom feeder they should all be exasperated with. Winifred wondered if the boy realized the incongruity between this and his seemingly intense desire to provide such low-level feed.

Agent Hensley, the blonde, approached the back of the couch her colleagues were sitting on. She put two delicate-looking hands firmly on the top of the plush seat back, looking straight at Kendra. "Quite frankly, Ms. Barber, this current situation has nothing to do with how we received the information identifying Nicolas Rim." She spoke with a stereotypically rude Boston tone. "I need you to understand before this conversation continues that you and your son's lives could be in danger if you blab about this to the media, your friends, or anybody else. Jimmy has become fairly high profile lately due to his friendship with Jonathan. I need you to confirm your understanding that speaking to anybody about this discussion we're having today could put your lives in danger."

Agents Prescott and Casey both readjusted themselves without looking at each other, as if quietly disagreeing with Agent Hensley's intensity. On the love seat, Kendra began forming a rather affronted expression that Winifred herself often inspired in people. The affinity Winifred felt for Agent Hensley grew even stronger.

"I just want to be sure we're all on the same page here," the woman continued. "I realize there are rather interesting implications regarding young Mr. Flite's so-called memories, but they exceed the scope of this discussion. With that understood, I need to know from *all* of you that you won't slip up and get lured by the media people stationed at the bottom of the hill. We already know who let the cat out of the bag about our talking to Jonathan last year."

"You do?" Winifred said. "Who was it?"

"I'm sorry, but I can't share that information. Now, hopefully all those reporters thought we were Jehovah's Witnesses. The reason we didn't drag our entire damned task force here today is because the last thing we want is any further media insinuation that you're working with us. If that occurs, Nicolas Rim may follow through on his promise and disappear. We'd really like to avoid that." The woman stood up straight again, turned her body, but kept her neck tilted toward Winifred. "Ms. Flite, you mentioned that you've been solicited for multiple news interviews regarding Jonathan's release and that you're considering them. I'm wondering where you currently stand on this, as it could affect our efforts one way or another. Also, does anybody outside this room know about the letters Jonathan has been receiving?"

Winifred bristled with self-consciousness. "Dr. Thomas Lumen and Dr. Collin Freede know about the letters." After a moment of hesitation, she added, "And my therapist. Why should it matter?"

Kendra Barber cocked her head in further curiosity. "What letters are we talking about here?" Jimmy immediately waved his hand in front of his mother's face to shush her. Instead of following up on her own curiosity, Kendra seemed passively to accept Jimmy's dismissal of it.

Glancing over his shoulder at Agent Hensley, Agent Prescott said, "The last letter we obtained from Jonathan contained a statement regarding events scheduled in Geneva last August 12. We can tell you that the mailer used proxy mailing services overseas, not unlike the quantum key VPNs Mr. Rim probably used to create this new ActoHub account. We're sharing this information, and wanted you here, Ms. Barber, because we're hoping to plan an operation to apprehend Mr. Rim. The most obvious solution would involve our continuing to use Jimmy here, or at least his ActoHub account, to lure the guy out of hiding, hopefully for a meeting. This isn't exactly a new concept, seeing as police departments around the country have used underage cadets in alcohol stings and things like that. This exact situation is pretty volatile, though, because Rim reached out to Jimmy personally. All we need is a visual on Rim, and if Jimmy can help us flush him out, it could be a huge help. Jimmy's a legal adult, but seeing as he's still on probation, it was necessary to bring you in on this. And again, the confidentiality of this operation cannot be stressed enough."

Jimmy sat up straighter than Winifred had ever seen before,

and the beaming expression on his face made him look twice as big as he was. Next to him, Kendra Barber uncrossed and recrossed her legs, then put a hand on Jimmy's back. "My Jimmy? Like, use him as bait? That sounds like something out of a movie."

"And I would be *honored*," Jimmy said with a glow. The only thing missing was his old-English curtsy.

"This could possibly require more interaction with the man and obviously a very clear plan for apprehension, which we're already working on." Agent Prescott turned his neck around to Agent Hensley. "Do you want to add to this?"

The blond agent walked to the living room's fifteen-thousand-dollar love seat and sat on the armrest. Winifred shuddered at the idea of the furniture piece breaking. "There are a few clear objectives up front," Agent Hensley said to Kendra. "First would be that we'd need full control of Jimmy's ActoHub so we could pose as him, trying to get Rim to agree to meet. We'd need to make him think Jimmy's doing it secretly and without anyone's permission. I don't think that'll be a hard sell."

Jonathan immediately tensed next to Winifred. She didn't have to read his mind to know exactly what he was thinking: Jimmy would do this; Jimmy would *beg* to do this; Jimmy would forever define his life by doing this.

Agent Hensley now addressed Jimmy directly. "This would involve us writing from your account. Ideally we'd make Rim think you're on the fence so that he makes more of an effort to see that you follow through with a meeting. He might then make an effort to help you feel safe; people like him sometimes do stupid things. If he's dumb enough to allow the meeting without first confirming by ActoLens that you're acting alone, we may not need you physically at all. Just your account. At most, we'd have you drive alone while broadcasting video to him through your lenses, so you can look in a mirror and prove you're not with anyone. Obviously we'd have any location completely covered and apprehend him as soon as we have clear line of sight. We have probable cause to make an arrest, based on what he admitted to in these messages today."

"This would be a total sting operation," Jimmy said. Bedazzlement shimmered in his voice.

"Yes, those *do* actually happen, Mr. Barber," Hensley said. "But again, we wouldn't be asking for your cooperation if it didn't have pressing implications on a larger investigation. Twenty years ago, we probably wouldn't have even considered this, but ActoLens technology has opened up some unique possibilities. Agent Casey would be monitoring all activity here in Rhode Island and would also alert any local PDs, assuming we can get Rim to come here. Now, we're considering this guy armed and dangerous, so we'd have a SWAT team on hand as backup, particularly if we end up needing you there in any physical capacity. What we need is to apprehend Mr. Rim without a hitch. If he asks that you wear your ActoLenses, all the better. We could monitor the feed and hopefully get recordings of him admitting his crimes, whether it's the murders at Crescent Rehabilitation Center last year or any covering up of information about the bombing in Geneva. Anything to help us strengthen our case."

"And then there's the blue letter connection," Agent Prescott said. "He's the second person hinting that there's a link between events occurring in Geneva last August 12 and the bombing, relating to motivation Victor Zobel might have had to help plan the attack. If this ends up requiring any sort of video interaction between you, we're hoping you can ask him again about the letters Jonathan has been receiving and whether he knows anything about a woman named Dorothy Garland."

Jimmy snorted a laugh. "Dorothy Garland? Like, as in Judy Gale? Who the hell is that?"

"A theoretical physicist," Agent Prescott said. "She was scheduled to be present at a meeting taking place the morning of the bombing at the European Organization for Nuclear Research in Geneva. CERN, if you've heard of it."

Winifred heard Jonathan's breathing pick up a bit at the agent's mention of Dorothy Garland. The name meant nothing to Winifred, which of course exacerbated the sensation of feeling like a deer in the headlights. Her first thought, however, was that the woman might be the one sending the blue-envelope letters. Was Dorothy Garland somehow related to this unsolved angle of the mystery, or perhaps to Idle County? It still baffled Winifred—and perhaps always would—that the memories in Jonathan's brain were somehow relating him to these foreign people, that foreign place.

She jumped out of her reverie when she noticed Agent Hensley from Boston looking straight at her. "You never answered me about your plans with the media," the woman said. "Where are you with hiring a publicist or doing some sort of press conference?"

"I'm nowhere with that," Winifred barked. "I already told you I'm still—"

"Meaning the media has had nothing new to gush over since the shooting here," the special agent cut in. "Pardon me for sounding crass, but the nature of the media these days is crass. Agent Prescott had the brainchild here that scheduling some live media event at the same time as a possible sting could provide a solid distraction so that Mr. Rim feels he's still in the shadows, and attention from Jonathan and anyone related to him is aimed elsewhere. Even scheduling a press conference so that he sees media reports that it'll be happening could potentially help us. We could obviously orchestrate it so that he thinks Jimmy's using the event as an excuse to escape reporters for a night and meet up in secret. Something like that. We could also spin it as your final public statement on anything related to Jonathan so that the media people get off your back. Kill two birds with one stone."

Almost glaring, Winifred eyed Agent Prescott. "This was *your* idea? Don't you think it'd bring unnecessary attention?"

"We're considering that," Agent Prescott said. "But it's something. The main goal here would be to get a solid visual on Rim if at all possible, and anything more would be a bonus. If some sort of diversion might help him feel less in the spotlight, it could help. You do a press conference here or in Boston, maybe in early August, and our team could carry out the sting in Providence. Possibly with Jimmy via video, if the guy requires proof of his presence. I think all eyes being on you would actually help us. Of course, things can always go wrong."

"You're damned right they can."

"But you'll consider it?"

Before agreeing, Winifred pondered the ever-present array of fear radiating from her chest at every imaginable angle. The sooner people started caring about Jonathan's well-being, the sooner they'd start leaving him alone—which of course would loosen her own media chains. With the FBI's insinuation that her doing a press conference might help them, that they might be able to use her for their own purposes (the way she had used Jonathan, his biological father, Dominic Bock, and virtually everyone else in her life), the decision came with a pressing sense of guilt. Of course she would help them. She owed them that, owed *Jonathan* that.

"I'll consider it," she told the agents. Only then did she feel the trap of duty close in on her fully, the certainty that she would indeed pressure herself to follow through on this endeavor. What terrified her was that Kate Crookston's description of intuition suddenly swarmed in her gut, telling her "*no, no, no,*" that it was folly, and that there would soon be better paths not taken.

S HELLY BRYCE HAD STARTED A VERY BAD DAY on Earth on August 3, 2038, first stuck in her apartment avoiding calls from *WorldLine* and then coincidentally meeting Molly Butler's sister, Kara, at the gate of Victor Zobel's Moon Woods home. Now, however, time was gone, and her mind was consciously untethered from her body. Had she been expecting such a shift of conscious focus upon stepping out of her car in Victor's driveway roundabout, she might have equated the sensation to that of a dream—a seemingly phantom yet immeasurably real experience of the mind.

A ring of light had engulfed her field of vision. It immediately struck her like a gateway. To heaven, perhaps? Except she saw no golden doors and no sign of Saint Peter. From what Shelly could gather, she was alone.

Her first thought (and it was surprising, because no fear

accompanied it) was that her ideas of God and Jesus and heaven and hell were based on nothing more than myths—stories handed down by a good book that had been put together by men who claimed to have had an inspirational portal straight to the Holy Spirit. Yet mankind was flawed, was it not? Wasn't that the entire message behind her precious Christianity? That men could be corrupted by power and worldly lures and the temptation to place themselves in positions of glory? Where in the Bible had it ever explained the physical, psychological, and energetic mechanisms by which she existed and by which her beliefs might somehow be confirmed as universal fact? Now it was as though a veil were pulling up, and she were seeing the true gears of the universe. It was all more vast, glorious, and stimulating to her senses than she had ever imagined.

The fountain at the center of Victor Zobel's roundabout sparkled in the sun, and instead of seeing it, Shelly felt as if her entire being were inside every drop, every molecule of its rainbow mist. She had never considered before what the world was actually made of. What did those physicists say? That it was all tiny particles? Something even smaller? It was clear now that it was all energy, that *she* was energy, and every manifestation of the physical world—every place, every thought, every choice, every movement in her life—had existed beforehand in patterns of energetic potential created by some deeper part of herself.

I'm part of the unified fundamental force, she thought, barely understanding what this meant but tingling under its implications.

Sound was clearer here, too, almost like music. Colors were vibrant. Nowhere was there fear—only reservation about learning more, embracing more, and looking back at the minutiae of her life as Shelly Marie Bryce, born March 16, 1961.

Three minutes old. Opening her eyes for the first time, with hesitation.

Seven months old. Listening to her father, James, scream at her mother and knowing (on levels below language) that he was a selfish man, and that her mother wasn't happy.

Four years old. Pushing her cousin Lance off his yellow, duck-shaped swing.

Seven years old. Attending a bridal shower with her mother and dreaming of the day she, too, might be just as happy as the bride to be, who was glowing under the smiles of the doting lady guests.

Thirteen years old. Sitting in Christ Evangelist Church, for the first time in her life feeling absolutely certain that Christianity was the truth behind everything, even though it was the only point of view she had ever been exposed to.

Seventeen years old. Losing her virginity to Bob Higgins, who was twenty-one and a good Christian. It was something she had never told anyone, partially because Bob had died in a mining accident up north four months later, and to admit having slept with a now-dead man was somehow embarrassing.

Moments, moments, and more moments, all hitting her at once, as if they existed in a tapestry of possibilities whose stitches had always been present. Perhaps she had simply been looking at one thread at a time. So much of who she had become—the seventy-seven-year-old in her matching denim vest and shorts, always lacking a sense of self-satisfaction—hinged on Elijah. He had been her test, one she had failed by her own measure, and she had spent the remainder of her life running from that failure, trying to prove to anyone who cared that she was more than a worthless letdown. The puzzles and games she bought for Common Ties' community area? An effort to gain favor. The sweets she baked for the residents, even the ones who smiled politely at her but glanced uneasily at their friends the next second? A beseechment for approval. The help she offered the facility's cleaning staff? An act of desperation to show someone (anyone) that she had some purpose yet in the world.

It seemed so silly now, in this lively, timeless in-between focus, looking at what had mattered to her in life. From this vantage point, she could see—even experience—how her kindnesses, infractions, and prejudices had made other people feel. So many of the negative experiences she had inflicted on other people had come from her own sense of religious superiority as she pigeonholed people like Cynthia Foster and even Elijah for having different outlooks. Yet these people had embraced a version of life that seemed to align closer with what she was feeling now: a universal sense of belonging, a fearless sense of caring.

Friday, July 15, 2005—during the summer of Cynthia Foster and the jawbone—had been the lowest point of her life. Even now she wanted to take that day back. It had been the week Joshua Grime's unsolved murder had made the front page of the *Wind Prairie Tribune*, just days after Elijah had found his birth mother, talked to her, and *liked* her. Shelly had been working her nursing job at Saint Mary's Hospital all week, trying to suppress the storm of anxiety in her chest over Elijah's transgressions, ignoring completely the severity of the bullying situation with Damon Jacoby and instead demanding he forget his biological mother altogether. Yet he had continued his interest by cutting out newspaper articles about that jawbone. Somehow, it had been those snippets of paper lying on the kitchen counter that had symbolized her loss of control. They had sent her over the edge.

Shelly Bryce now saw that it had been fear sparking her anger. Not just fear that her adopted son would lose his innocence but fear that he had already started to outthink her, to grow past her own ability to reason, and to take control of who he was in a way she didn't have the capacity to dictate.

The sun had set that night, and the sky was black. Shelly Bryce was standing and waiting next to the kitchen sink when Elijah—

2005

—ARRIVED HOME AT 9:00 P.M. He had once again spent the afternoon at Molly Butler's house, only to be invited by her father, Andrew, to stay for a hearty dinner of Sammy's Pizza. It was the best pizza in town, and their meal for three was more fun than Elijah could have hoped for. Watching Molly and her father interact was almost like watching two adults. Andrew Butler never talked down to his daughter, and they seemed to discuss things as equals. She had told Elijah earlier that her father had asked about him—Was he her boyfriend? Did she want to have a boyfriend yet?—but she had told him the truth: "Elijah thinks he might be gay." It was as simple as that, and for the first time since starting down the road to adulthood, Elijah felt he did not have to hide that part of himself, even though Andrew Butler didn't mention it. Nor did they discuss the jawbone or Arthur Brown. His investigation with Molly, for the moment, was still a secret few people knew about.

When he turned toward the kitchen after stepping into his house, he saw his mother, Shelly, standing next to the counter, waiting. She was holding his two clipped newspaper articles about Joshua Grime in her hand.

Elijah had forgotten to put them away after cutting them out. During his day with Molly and their visit with Arthur Brown, it never crossed his mind that the articles were still lying on the counter. That morning, he had assumed he would be home in time to hide them.

"So, what are these?" were Shelly's first words. "You're cutting out articles about this jawbone now?"

He could only stare at her, searching for words.

"I thought I made it clear last week, Elijah," Shelly continued before he took his chance to reply. "I wanted you to forget about this whole thing. About that jawbone, about Cynthia Foster, about all of that."

"Why?" Elijah knew he sounded petulant, but his mother's immediate hostility upon his return home had hit whatever anger remained in him like water hit a sponge. It had begun to swell.

"I thought we went through 'why,'" Shelly said.

"We didn't go through anything."

"I told you to stay away from that woman, because even if she gave birth to you, she has no right to see you. She shouldn't have meddled in your life in the first place."

"*Meddled*?" Elijah yelled. "What are you talking about? I was the one who found the jawbone and ashes and went to visit her! She had nothing to do with it! Only you wouldn't even listen to me the other night!"

He had not been prepared for this sort of confrontation. After such an interesting day and enjoyable evening, it was hitting him like a freak storm.

"Maybe I'll just leave," he said.

"Don't be ridiculous. You're only twelve."

"I'll be thirteen in a month and a half. I can take care of myself!"

"Like you did that night at the fair, huh?" Shelly said, her voice a positive snarl. "Get your face bashed in again?"

Elijah froze in his place.

Tears ran down Shelly's cheeks the moment the words left her mouth. She cupped both hands over her lips. "Oh God!" she whispered. "I'm sorry! Elijah, I'm so sorry! That just slipped! You know I would never mean anything like that!"

She stepped forward as if to comfort him, but Elijah held up his hand. "Don't touch me," he said. It wasn't a request; it was an order. The power he now held over her boiled in his veins. It came on the back of a new type of anger, one that made his chest burst and his body feel like flying. It was beautiful, twisted, and pure, like a vampire waiting silently in the night for its prey. Was this grown-up anger? Was this what it felt like to get older?

"I didn't mean to say it like that!" Shelly said. "Please, believe me!"

Elijah scoffed, standing erect with confidence for what felt like the first time in his life.

"Please! Don't go to your room yet! I didn't mean it. I meant to say that I didn't want you to get hurt again, and—"

"Yeah, right."

"No! Elijah, I'm trying to be honest! It was a slip-up. Even moms make slip-ups, okay?" Shelly seemed to be using all her might to keep from sobbing now, but tears were continuing to break through the barrier. "I've just been so worried about you lately—first with your run-in with Damon Jacoby and then with this whole Cynthia Foster thing. It's too much for you to have to deal with all at once. And you're right to be mad. What I said just now was evil. Downright evil. I was frustrated."

Elijah's mind raced, and his anger was beginning to give way to a feeling of hollow letdown. Maybe nobody ever grew up. "I didn't do anything wrong," he said.

Another rush of pompousness flowed across Shelly's face like moving water. "Look, it *was* wrong," she said. "It *was*. Cynthia Foster has no place in your life. None whatsoever. You always knew you were adopted. We left it at that, and you always seemed to be fine with it. Now you randomly find out who your birth mother is, and you think you can just go visit her? You're still a child! And she's a woman I do *not* want you to be around. Not just because she's a stranger but because I know her values. They have no place in the way I want you raised."

Elijah scoffed again. "How do you know her values? Please. Enlighten me."

"She has *AIDS*, Elijah. I don't want you being around a disease like that. If she so much as cuts a finger, you'd be in danger of getting infected. She's survived this long due to a miracle that never should have happened. That disease is still in her, and it's dangerous."

"We learned about AIDS in fifth grade," he replied. "She has the HIV virus in her system, but it's *undetectable*. It hasn't even turned into AIDS. And you can't just get it by being around a person, even if they *do* cut a finger. That's a stupid reason why I shouldn't see her."

Elijah stared into Shelly's eyes until she looked away. When the woman finally continued, she sounded desperate.

"Elijah, you have to understand something. Cynthia Foster

is a woman who dabbles in evil. It's not just that horrible tarot card business. She's one of those women who is friends with *gays*. Homosexuals. Some of the ladies from Lake Gospel have seen her around town, hanging out with those groups. That agenda is not something I want you to be a part of!"

"What agenda?" he asked.

"The homosexual agenda, Elijah! Those people are choosing a way of life that is sinful and wrong, something totally against what the Lord wants for his sons and daughters! They're trying to do away with religion and normal families by adopting children of their own, and they're telling these kids that it's okay for men to go to bed with other men, and they're—"

"You adopted *me*!" Elijah screamed. "How the hell are they doing anything wrong? If they're trying to make normal families disappear, they might as well look at you for an example! Look how your marriage turned out!"

Shelly's fervent expression flinched as if Elijah had slapped her in the face. This time, it was he who kept talking before she could muster a response.

"You went and adopted me to have a nice little family of your own, and then my fake dad Kevin Bryce leaves us both and divorces you? Do you think *that's* a normal family?" For the first time in his life, he was proving his mother wrong, finding a flaw in her parental logic. It felt both empowering and tragic. He could outmatch her, and he would never look at her with unquestioning eyes again.

"I did my best with you, Elijah," Shelly whispered. "Kevin and I were trying to *save* you from that life! It—God—!" A burst of tears escaped her. She put a hand on her forehead as if to check her own sanity.

Keep going.

Elijah had a feeling that whatever she had been wanting to tell him all along was inching toward her lips. He was waiting, and his mother knew it. It was clear in her eyes. They were far away, lost in some troubling memory that was bubbling its way to the surface of their pleasant little life. "You don't know the whole truth," Shelly said for the second time that summer. Her voice was low, broken.

Say it.

"Your dad and I were hoping we'd never have to tell you this, but after he left, the burden was on me. He never wanted to be involved, and that's why he didn't make it. He never even wanted kids. Even though you were part of his own family."

"What do you mean?" Anxiety had clamped down on Elijah's heart. He was about to hear something that would forever change the way he thought about himself. It was electric in the air between them.

"Your dad . . . Your adoptive dad, I mean . . . was your real dad's cousin. His dad's sister was Elijah Earnshaw's mom, Louise Earnshaw. She was married to a man named Daniel."

The names tingled at the back of Elijah's mind. It took him a moment to place them. Then it clicked. He had seen them in this very house, on the laptop screen in his bedroom, the night he typed their last name into the internet search engine and found their obituaries. Now, in light of the truth Cynthia had also shared with him, the names held meaning. They were his grandparents.

"Elijah Earnshaw went off and married Cynthia Foster, who wouldn't even take his last name, because she was all 'progressive.' I had just gotten married to Kevin Bryce in Wind Prairie when we found out that his cousin had chosen to be homosexual and gotten himself sick."

"He didn't *choose* to be gay," Elijah said, seething.

Shelly gave him a flustered shake of her head. "He *did* choose, even though he was already married to Cynthia. He had already stopped talking to the rest of his family after everyone made it abundantly clear they wouldn't tolerate Cynthia Foster in any of their homes. Even your adoptive dad's Aunt Louise and Uncle Daniel couldn't stand her. She was the daughter of an old town whore, for one thing, and her twin sister died from a drug overdose. She wasn't the type of person we wanted around."

The hatred spewing from Shelly's mouth felt like a meat hook piercing Elijah's heart, then twisting. How had he lived with this woman for so long? How could he continue to?

"Even though your real father was going to bed with other men, he somehow managed to get Cynthia pregnant. They found out just before he started getting sick. It was like clockwork. I heard it all from Kevin's parents."

"I know that part. Cynthia told me that."

"You heard *her* version." Shelly had regained some of her composure, and now it was as though she expected Elijah to fall back in line with her, to accept what she said as fact and continue his existence while shunning the woman who had given birth to him. "She found out that she was sick, too, and then the rest of the family had to step in, because you were at stake. You were innocent, even if your parents weren't, and somebody had to take you. Your biological grandmother already had cancer and couldn't take you, and your grandfather was just starting to go bad with Alzheimer's. Kevin and I were the only ones left to save you."

"To *save* me?"

"Even Cynthia thought you should be with your own flesh and blood if possible, because she didn't think she'd last. She never liked Kevin, because he was Christian, but she already had AIDS, so she had to think fast. They didn't know yet if you had it or not. The doctors said there was a good chance you'd come out with it, too. We had to wait and see."

"You mean you were waiting to see if I was sick before you'd adopt me?" Elijah asked.

Shelly's expression became grave.

Elijah felt the size of a mustard seed, smaller even than when Damon Jacoby had taunted him at the library or pushed him into the guardrail at the Fourth of July fair. It was just as he had always feared, but now it was certain. His mother, his adoptive mother, had never really wanted him.

"I'm leaving," Elijah said.

"No, wait. You didn't let me finish what I—"

"That's because I was stupid enough to think you wanted me here." He had begun to shake from the courage building in his heart. "But now I know it was only because you wanted to *save* me. Well, I guess it didn't work!"

"Honey, we can get *past* this—"

"Damon Jacoby hates me because I don't like girls, Mom!" Elijah screamed. "Because I'm *gay*! He knows I was looking at Alec Pent last summer when he didn't have a shirt on, and Alec told everybody at school, and now they all make fun of me. Either way, you didn't save me. I'm still Cynthia's son, and even Elijah Earnshaw's!"

"You're only twelve years old!" was all Elijah heard his mother say before he turned around and walked back out the front door, into the night.

PART 5

MISTAKES

2038

S HELLY BRYCE AWOKE on a plush white couch in Victor Zobel's
grand living room. A crystal chandelier sparkled over her
eyes. Upon seeing the fixture's hanging, coruscating frag-
ments, her first inclination was that every bit of energy comprising
her existence had suddenly coalesced into something solid, through
what she could only think of as a filter made of perception. Her
experience on the driveway roundabout had come in a grand, glorious wave, and now it was nothing more than a triumphant echo.

"Ms. Bryce? Are you okay? Greta, get some ice."

It was Victoria Zobel's voice—loud, and deep for a woman.
And who was Greta? An assistant of some sort? Most likely.

"Shelly? Can you hear us?" It was Kara Butler speaking now.
Oh, how she sounded like her sister, Molly. It surprised Shelly
when her memories of Elijah's young friend came with a newfound
fondness, as though some cloud of judgment had been lifted.

"I'm here," Shelly said. It was a stupid thing to say, because clearly she hadn't gone anywhere. Against all odds, they were in Victor Zobel's house, probably less than a hundred feet from the roundabout where she had parked. The tan-walled living room was adorned with simple white trim and crystalline objects similar to the chandelier hanging from the ceiling—sparkling-white vases, picture frames, and even a three-foot-tall decorative ship, as though somebody in the Zobel household had a passion for sailing the high seas.

"You went all dizzy when you got out of your car," Kara said, kneeling down, close to Shelly. Behind her was a massive television wall, switched on, appearing to show a live feed from some luxurious office with plum-purple walls. It was empty, as far as Shelly could see, and something about the office windows immediately struck her as slightly off-kilter. Something bright—blue, green, brown, and white—was spinning slowly in and out of view in a way that would have made her sick were she not feeling so refreshed. It now struck her how unlikely all this was, that they were in Victor Zobel's famously discreet Idle County compound at all. She had never heard of the man inviting town residents in for lunch.

Shelly blinked five times. Everything around her was clearer than usual, as though she had donned a new pair of glasses. "Did I fall?"

"No, you just stopped and were staring off into space," Kara said. "I think we should get you to a hospital. I was about to call 911." Shelly saw Kara's gaze flicker toward Victoria Zobel, as if there were some sentiment she wanted to address but consciously held in. They were both leaning over her as somebody reached into view with a glass of sparkling ice water. Greta the assistant, no doubt.

"How long have we been here?" Shelly asked, grabbing the water and allowing Victoria to help her sit up.

"We just got you in the door," Kara said. "Two minutes ago, maybe? Do you want me to call an ambulance?"

"No, no," Shelly said. "Maybe it was the heat. I'm perfectly fine." She realized only after saying this that the day's temperature could not yet have passed seventy-five; there was no heat, just some sun, and then that sudden rush of . . . of what, she couldn't say. But all her woes had suddenly become weightless, as though there would never again be anything to worry about. Even her memory of that night with Elijah, of that horrible fight that had forever severed what healthy strands had existed in their mother-son relationship, now glistened anew in her mind. All those events had been steps along a path, nothing more. Could they have played that night out differently? Yes. Had either of them been capable of knowing that at the time? Maybe. But choices were choices, and "maybe" meant nothing in their wake. When Shelly realized Kara and Victoria were still staring at her, both with differing levels of concern, she added, "It seems so strange you invited us in for lunch. Considering who you are, I mean."

"Even famous people eat," Victoria Zobel said. "Greta, is the kitchen staff ready?"

Greta stepped fully into Shelly's view. She was a short and perky ginger of perhaps twenty-five, possessing large breasts perched with particular zest in a tight, navy-blue dress. Something in Shelly's mind had changed; instead of judging Greta's wardrobial immodesty, she now saw with empathy the young woman's vulnerability, beauty, insecurity, and, yes, even fear. "Short notice, so it's sandwiches," Greta said. "Are you sure we shouldn't call an ambulance? Or maybe one of the doctors—"

"Let Ms. Bryce here decide," Victoria cut in, with more bite in her voice than seemed appropriate. Greta flushed and set off for the kitchen.

"I'm *fine*," Shelly insisted, sitting up and wondering what doctors the assistant had been talking about. She turned to Victoria and immediately read on the woman's face that it wasn't a question worth pursuing. In order to buffer the sudden tension, she continued as if Greta's statement hadn't been uttered at all. "I'm hungry, if that means anything. But really, I find this all a bit strange. Being here, I mean. It's funny to see this place in real life. I can't think of a soul in Idle County who has actually been here."

"Sometimes it's hard to convince people we're actually real," Victoria said, again with her greyhound grin. "Fame has a way of separating a person from the rest of the world. But I assure you, we're just like any other neighbor down the street. And we've had our share of curious gawkers."

Victoria was polite enough not to look at Kara Butler when she said this. Instead, she raised her eyebrows up and down with quick and obvious amusement. "Even so, I'd be lying if I said we were just trying to be polite. When my father saw you on the security cameras, Ms. Bryce, he wanted to speak with you." The woman took Shelly's hand, helping her off the couch. "He's actually connected on camera behind us. We were in the middle of a video conference when you two appeared."

Kara Butler immediately tensed as Victoria gestured toward the massive television wall opposite the white couch. Her eyes began darting around their sockets quickly as she turned to view the screen. The camera on the far end was still sitting motionless, facing the office with the plum-purple walls.

"Looks like he stepped out," Victoria said. "Anyway, that's his office up on Star Island. I still can't fathom how he enjoys looking out at Earth like that. Artificial gravity means the station is always spinning. It's big enough now not to be too awful, but still."

Shelly now noticed what had struck her as peculiar about the video feed a minute ago: the office had one visible window showing, and the bright object spinning beyond it was the planet she herself was living and breathing on. It was surreal to see the Star Island view she had heard so much about on the news and in media gossip columns. No matter how strange it was that she was sitting in Victor Zobel's living room, though, it was as his daughter had said—they really were just people, too—neighbors even. Owning mansions all over the world and a space station was their version of normal.

"Anyway, you're sure you don't need an ambulance?" Victoria said. "At the very least, I'll arrange for drivers to bring you and your car home. I'm not about to let you have another episode behind the wheel."

Eyeing Victoria Zobel, Shelly wondered just how similar she was to her father. Yes, she carried elements of his personality, but there was something more genuine behind her politeness—a subtle sense of humor at the very least. The media had always portrayed her as Victor's lapdog, but today, this didn't necessarily seem true.

Now that Shelly was standing, Kara Butler had ventured back toward the front foyer, near the L-shaped hallway Greta had disappeared down. Shelly glanced at the hallway's other stretch, which lined the open-walled living room. It went deeper into the house, opening up in multiple spots to a lavish dining room. Beyond that, she guessed, was some extravagant kitchen.

"Could I use your restroom?" Kara asked suddenly. "I just

had a green tea at the Bean & Leaf in End Haven. Totally digested faster than I thought it would."

Shelly smiled at Kara's candor, recalling how her sister, Molly, used to be equally straightforward. Victoria, despite saying, "Of course," looked hesitant. She pointed toward the length of hall branching straight off the living room, past the front foyer. "Down there about thirty feet, on your left."

A tremor of upheaving awareness overtook Shelly as Kara disappeared down the hall. Every moment of the day since she woke up five hours ago now felt perfectly orchestrated, as if it were all pasted together by some underlying force that determined the very concept of choice and probability. She was now alone with one of the most famous heiresses in the world, and standing in her living room no less—the most unlikely situation she could ever have dreamed for herself. Victoria simply watched her for a few quiet moments, and contrary to usual expectations, Shelly didn't cower under another person's unflinching eye contact. An intense curiosity burned in the wealthy woman's retinas as she waited with Shelly. Did she somehow know what had just caused the whiteout?

A face hovered into frame on the television wall behind her. It moved with the same surreal flow of serenity still running through Shelly's heart.

There he was, one of the richest and most famous men alive, and here she was, an inconsequential ghost of his past. Victor Zobel's wrinkle-free face was far too tan to be natural on a space station, and his hair was a gentle gray, still with some salted blond. When he exposed his blazing-white teeth in what appeared to be a pasted-on smile, it had the same questionable greyhound look as that of his daughter. With a chuckle at their circumstances, Shelly raised a hand. "Hello, Victor," she said. "Been a while. I'd never have imagined this morning that I'd be talking to you again."

His smile segued into an unconvincing laugh. "I was on a call with my daughter there, and we both saw you on the security cameras with that other young woman, whom I hear is related to Molly Butler? I can't help but be curious how you both ended up there today."

"Honestly, I can't even tell you," Shelly said. "She's visiting from Portland and was curious to see the Moon Woods, I think. It was quite the coincidence."

"Coincidence," Victor repeated, as though unpersuaded. "Not always the easiest concept to swallow."

An hour ago, Shelly would have been quaking in her shoes, both fearing the man's fierce intellect and judging him for his atheistic depravity. Now the transparency she had always sensed in his motives was clearer than ever. He was agitated underneath those smiling white teeth; whatever was bothering him beyond the obvious ruse of pretending to embrace unwelcome guests seemed to be fluttering wordlessly between him and Victoria.

"I believe Kara went to use the restroom," Victoria said, as if to buffer the tension seeping from her father through the television.

Victor's face shifted in hue from orange to near-red as he frowned at his daughter. "Very well. I do hope you showed her to the first-floor powder room. Please go make sure she found her way." He raised his eyebrows, then looked again at Shelly, adopting once again his narrow-eyed smile, the same one that had always made her feel like a pawn. "I'm sorry, Ms. Bryce. It's been a long week. Sometimes up here in space, the weeks seem *extra* long, because you lose track of time." He laughed again with excessive mirth as Victoria left with an awkward smile to fetch Kara from the bathroom. Shelly glanced after her, then back at the screen with a polite expression. "I did want to take this opportunity to speak with you, considering all the new interest in your son's and my stepdaughter's disappearances. May I ask how you're managing with all the press? I did see a number of reports from Idle County, and I fear you must now be seeing these media people the same way I do—as vultures."

Shelly pretended to brush a hair off her denim blouse. "I had to change my phone number," she said. "Of course some of them found me anyway."

"Might I ask who?"

"Oh, just a few here and there. Alice Winterblume, for one. But that's to be expected. She interviewed Elijah back in 2005."

Zobel cleared his throat. "I'm aware."

"Is that why you wanted to speak with me today?"

The man caught himself in a scowl, then forced a joyless grin to take its place. "I wanted to know what the general consensus was with all this new Idle County Seven attention. Between the remaining parents, I mean. What, if anything, you plan to say." After a pause, he added, "That way, I can help if need be. I think it's essential we squash this Jonathan Flite drivel before it causes some sort of misguided spiritual uproar. Human beings get crazy when they find something new to distract them from their lack of education and abilities to think."

Shelly stood as tall as she could. "I honestly haven't talked to anyone from that group in twenty years. I was only ever friendly with Andrew Butler, David Thorsen, and Claire Gilbert. David's wife was always rude to me, so we rarely talked. I haven't heard from them since they moved to San Francisco. Andrew's out in Portland, according to Kara here. Last I heard from Claire Gilbert, she was living with some new husband in Montana."

"I'm sure you'll understand how it could create difficulties for me to talk about Jillian's disappearance now," Victor said, "considering my social status and all the ridiculous things going around about me. The Winterblume woman is even breathing down my neck about the hunting accident in Alaska that killed your son's biological mother, if you can believe that. As if I were somehow involved way back when. Reporters like that will do anything to fabricate a good story."

"I've often thought that myself," Shelly said, noting the man's apparent fervency of opinion. Yet Cynthia Foster's unexpected death in September of 2010 now scratched at her heart. Shelly initially hadn't believed it when it happened and then had been secretly relieved. Looking at herself now and realizing just how much jealousy and resentment she had harbored toward the woman, Shelly was appalled. The world—the universe—was far too beautiful for such nonsense. For *this* nonsense. Victor Zobel seemed to have no idea how transparent he had become. Or was she the one whose perception had changed?

"I'm of the mind that our world should be better than all this media hoopla," the man continued. "Nobody even thinks anymore. Look at what happened last night." This time, the man couldn't even hide the sourness in his expression. "Alice Winterblume and her people have been pursuing an interview with me ever since this ridiculous Jonathan Flite malarkey started happening on the East Coast, and I wanted to impress upon you the importance of avoiding the spotlight on this. Until our society enlightens a bit, it could truly destroy your life and mean you'll never have privacy again. I wanted to make a gesture of good faith to you, even though you and that new-and-improved Butler girl for some reason felt the need to trespass on my private property."

Shelly stiffened at the awkward and sudden contradiction in Zobel's treatment of her, and it came as an immediate push from her intuition: a realization that everything he was, everything he did, was a manipulation to serve his own agenda. Even this gauche lunch invitation into his private Moon Woods compound was a dramatic attempt to learn what she planned to say about him to reporters. Twenty-eight years ago, this tendency toward self-centeredness in Zobel had been just a shadow well-hidden under politeness. Now Shelly saw it for what it was: a true lack of empathy. He didn't even realize his subtle insult about Kara's and her trespassing had just toppled over his intended illusion of civility.

From down the hall came the sound of Victoria Zobel and Kara Butler's voices. The former had retrieved the latter, and it sounded as though Kara, an ever-so-curious young woman, was inquiring about the building of the mansion, which had begun in April 2012. Shelly glanced toward the hallway politely, and then turned back to the television for a final good-bye to Victor. Onscreen, the man had turned his attention to his desk, on which sat a number of opened blue envelopes, some of which looked crumpled and reflattened. It appeared he had forgotten Shelly was even there. She cleared her throat.

"Disconnect," Zobel finally said, and the television went blank.

Shelly's newfound sense of security—and possibly even adventure—rippled through her as Victoria and Kara approached with surprising friendliness, only to see the television wall blank, pending a connection. "Did we miss anything spectacular?" Victoria Zobel asked with a wry smile.

Grinning back at her, Shelly shrugged. Kara shifted from one foot to the other. Lunch awaited.

2005

THE BLACKTOP, illuminated only by the orange streetlights in their regular interludes, passed beneath Elijah's eyes. He pedaled with all his strength toward nowhere in particular. His mother had wanted him only on the condition that he wasn't born HIV-positive, probably because it would have associated him with homosexuals like his biological father. Now he had just told her that he, too, was attracted to other males. Whatever pit he had already dug himself into this summer was now a thousand times deeper.

His mind was a whirl, unraveling, and in his heart was an aching pressure to burst forward, to ride on, into the night, and leave everything in his life behind. How, he had no idea. Where he would go was uncertain. He no longer could tell what was real and what wasn't—both with the relationships in his life and with the very world around him. Moving forward felt like blindly navigating a treacherous darkness, but there was no way he could go back to his old house, his old life, his old misery.

Elijah had already passed the intersection after Windsong Road curved west and became Kendrick Avenue. At the next intersection, he turned north with a half intent to return to Molly Butler's house, which he had left less than an hour ago. When he finally approached it on Exeter Avenue, her lights were on, but a pit of embarrassment formed in his stomach. He couldn't knock on her door again so soon. This was not her fight. He could think of only one other person in End Haven who would lend him her shoulder: Cynthia Foster, the woman he was forbidden to see.

Elijah turned south on Donahue Street, and then right on Lemon Avenue, which would take him west, past the library. Cage Street was another ten blocks past that, and Cynthia's house would then still be another mile north, toward Hunter Avenue.

The streetlights were on; the road was empty. Approaching the library, Elijah looked at its dark windows, its high stone tower. Was there a bell up there? If so, what had it once signaled? Did it matter? Did anything?

A figure was standing in the middle of the street, two hundred feet in front of him.

It's not real. It's just like during the paper route yesterday morning.

Elijah was pedaling as fast as he could, and no, not even another ghost hallucination of Damon Jacoby was going to stop him. As of late, he had been existing in a shroud of fear every single day, and every single day, he had to question why it was he continued to wake up each morning. What did it say that receiving paychecks from his paper route so he could go buy books was the most exciting thing in his life? What would Victor Zobel, the author of *In God We're Dust*, say?

The figure in the street was closer. By God, if God even existed, it looked like Damon Jacoby yet again.

You've lost it. You're seeing things. You're going crazy.

Despite having spent the day with Molly Butler, he had not yet accepted 100 percent that apparitions of this sort were real, and unless Damon Jacoby knew how to disappear, chances were high it was merely a sign that he, Elijah, was the one losing his mind.

He pedaled even faster.

It definitely was the Damon Jacoby figure again. The boy's eyes were visible now, as were his silently moving lips and the hate emanating from his face. Closer, closer, and now pedaling fast, Elijah charged as if on horseback.

"Get—out—of—my—*life!*" he whispered, closing his eyes as he barreled forward on his bike, straight toward this horrific, repeating trick of his mind.

When it happened, it happened swiftly. Elijah felt a sharp slice of pain sear his upper right arm, near his shoulder. Without even opening his eyes, he knew he was bleeding. The pain was so intense that his feet fell from his pedals, and his grip on his handle bars waffled. He opened his eyes as he dragged his feet on the pavement and clenched his brakes. It was like a wasp sting times a thousand, and the pain was rushing across his entire shoulder. He had driven his bike straight through the Damon Jacoby ghost, the trick of his mind, but somehow it had hurt him, had actually been real—

"I knew you'd be riding here tonight," came Damon's voice from behind him. "Back to your precious library."

Elijah heard a rush of bike pedals coming from the left.

"Dude, he was actually right again," somebody whispered. It sounded like Tyler McFadden. "He knew the fag would be here!"

In his daze of pain, Elijah heard Nolan Snagsby respond, "Okay, it's starting to get weird. I don't want to do this, man."

Elijah had just begun to feel faint when he realized what was happening. This time, Damon Jacoby really had been standing in the middle of the road, and Nolan Snagsby and Tyler McFadden were doing his bidding yet again. As Elijah attempted to find his bike pedals with his feet, he glanced back and saw a very corporeal Damon walking toward him. Clutched in his right hand, out to the side, was a small pocket knife with a blade no more than four inches long.

He slashed me, Elijah thought, finding his pedals. He brought his left arm up to his right shoulder and felt the cooling wetness of blood. Nolan and Tyler were now next to him, but when Elijah looked up from his bloody hand, shaking his head in shock, neither of the two boys had on his usual vindictive, follow-the-leader grin. Nolan, his face just visible under the streetlight, was actually frowning.

"Get him off his bike," Damon demanded.

Too shocked to speak, Elijah tried to pedal again, but Tyler grabbed him by the left arm and pulled. Elijah's foot found the pavement, and he was able to shed his tipping bike just before it scraped his leg. They were in the middle of Lemon Avenue, not even a block past the library. The houses around them still had lights on; it wasn't even ten-thirty.

Scream, the smart half of Elijah's mind told him. *Scream as loud as you can, because if anybody sees them, they'll run.* Except screaming would give Damon even more reason to call him a faggot, a pansy, a sissy homo. Every defensive ounce of him wanted to keep Damon from experiencing that pleasure. Perhaps this was it: a final surrender to hopelessness.

Damon had circled to Elijah's rear and grabbed both his arms, taking control from Tyler. The limbs twisted under the bully's strong grip but wouldn't break free. When Damon leaned in toward Elijah's ear, closer than any boy or man had ever leaned in before, his breath was hot and moist. He whispered in a voice so low that even Nolan and Tyler didn't seem to hear. "I saw you in my head. Fighting with your mom who doesn't even want you. She thinks you're a stupid faggot, too."

Elijah shuddered. There was no way Damon could have known about the fight he had just had with his mother. No way at all.

"You don't believe me?" Damon whispered, as though reading his mind. "I know things. I can track you wherever you goddamned go. Because I'm a psychic motherfucker."

Elijah struggled against Damon's hold, but it was impossible to get loose. Now screaming really was his only option. "Somebody help—!" he started, but Damon's powerful hand, still holding the pocket knife, smothered his mouth with one fierce swipe. The blade was now inches from Elijah's eyes.

"You're not going to scream for any help," he whispered, as if reading Elijah's mind. "Faggots like you deserve to die. Everybody thinks it even if they don't say it."

"*I know what happened to your parents!*" Elijah tried to say under the muzzle of Damon's hand, but it came out as a muffled groan.

"And you know what people in the Bible would have done to you? They would have cut off the part that causes problems." Damon let go of Elijah's arms with his left hand, swung the free arm around, and grabbed the flesh between Elijah's legs. If there had been any extra water in him, Elijah would have let it loose onto Damon's hand if it might have given him a chance to wriggle free. Alas, even his own body was trapping him tonight. "Do you get it? We'll *cut it off*," Damon said again.

"Okay, let him go, man," Nolan whispered. "We're right in the middle of the street. If anyone—"

"Ty, unbutton his shorts." Damon's voice, still inches from Elijah's ear, was quivering with rage and excitement.

Tyler shot him a questioning glance. "Huh?"

"We have to be quick. Nolan, come back here and hold the faggot's arms while I cut his dick off. I had a dream about this last night, and I want to do it. I need to."

"Damon, we probably shouldn't—"

But Nolan seemed too afraid to finish. Tyler had undone the button of Elijah's gray shorts and pulled them down, looking away as he did so. Now only a thin pair of boxer shorts hung between Elijah's skin and Damon's blade.

"Come on, Nolan, grab his arms!"

Nolan obeyed Damon, but his softer grip made it clear he was even more reluctant than Tyler. The bully was crazy, and the other two boys now seemed to know it.

Damon moved around to Elijah's front. He brought the blade up, flashing it in front of Elijah's terrified eyes again.

No. No. This can't be happening. Oh God, get me out of this—

Elijah didn't even realize he was praying.

Damon stuck his blade through the slit opening in the front of the boxer shorts. Elijah felt its cold, sharp metal graze his skin.

Oh God, oh God, oh—

Damon turned the blade so that the sharp edge ran against

Elijah's flesh. With the motion came the evening's second burst of sharp pain and then warm blood immediately turning cold on his skin. Damon really was cutting his penis off. He hadn't been kidding, and now—

"Car's coming!" Nolan yelled. He let Elijah's arms go. As he bolted to his bike, he added, "Damon, you're totally messed up!"

As quickly as the three boys had converged upon Elijah for the third time that summer, they scattered in separate directions, as if suddenly repelled by a magnet. A car was indeed approaching, and Elijah was standing in the middle of the street in his boxers, bleeding with his shorts around his ankles.

Go, go, go. Before whoever it is sees.

Blood dropped from his shoulder as he bent down to pull up his shorts. It left dots of black on the glowing-orange pavement. Quietly, sadly, and humiliatingly thankful he hadn't worn a belt that day, Elijah rushed to button the shorts, pick up his bike, and drag it to the side of the street so the car could pass. The driver slowed for him but didn't stop to check if everything—or any-thing—was okay.

When Elijah climbed onto his bike seat, the cut Damon had made inside his boxer shorts stung, and more wet blood trickled down, along his thigh. He began pedaling, riding west on Lemon Avenue, feeling light-headed and wondering just how deep his cuts were. As his bike tires spun and the pavement rushed beneath him, all he could hope was that Damon Jacoby would realize what he had just done and not turn around to resume his chase. Elijah's legs grew heavier and heavier, and by the time he reached Cage Street, he was moving slowly enough to get caught once again.

A turn north. Pedaling feverishly. All he needed now was help.

There, up ahead. Flashing lights. A police car.

It was sitting in front of Cynthia Foster's house, and there the woman herself stood, in her front yard, next to a uniformed deputy who appeared to be the same one from the Fourth of July fair—Deputy Thropp. Elijah should have known his mother, Shelly, would be smart enough to realize he'd head to Cynthia's house, that she would call the police to prevent the woman from taking him in. When he wobbled his bike onto the city sidewalk, diagonally into Cynthia's yard, it took a moment for them to turn and notice. At first it was too dark for the two adults to see that he was bleeding, but then the man shined a blinding flashlight on him. Elijah's attempt to hold back tears only resulted in an explosion of crushing sobs. The woman who loved him came rushing, and even though the sheriff's deputy told her she wasn't allowed, she hugged him, bleeding shoulder and groin and all, and told the man to call an ambulance.

2038

SOMETHING WAS ABOUT TO GO WRONG. Jimmy Barber could feel it. It was now Monday, August 2, two months since Jonathan Flite's release from Crescent Rehabilitation Center, and he was sitting with his friend at the Green Fish, one of Newport's premiere cafés on Thames Street. Sounder had driven them in the new Lexus SE7 that Winifred had purchased to allow Jonathan some mobility, and he was now sitting next to the café's door to give them some space. Outside, a swarm of photographers loomed, snapping images through the restaurant's glass—exactly what the FBI had hoped for in their effort to take all possible attention away from their planned sting for Nicolas Leandro Rim that evening.

Jimmy, having retained access to his ActoHub account so he could continue to post regular updates, had read all the bureau's interactions with the unsavory miscreant as they happened. Rim had bitten their lure too quickly, in Jimmy's opinion, as if he had some ulterior motive for agreeing to meet in Providence—at Swan Point Cemetery, no less, a closed and secluded patch of private property that would be easy for police to monitor. The "meeting" was a farce, of course, and the FBI's use of Jimmy as a decoy, while far from standard procedure considering his age, seemed distastefully sanitized and far too conservative. Jimmy was old enough to be more than just a pawn kept at a safe distance, and something in his gut told him that no matter how guilty Nicolas Rim felt over his crimes, he wasn't stupid enough to walk into a trap so glaringly obvious. The moment he realized Jimmy's on-camera drive to Swan Point Cemetery was simply a measure to draw him out of the shadows and that Jimmy wasn't allowed to leave the car at all, he would likely disappear yet again.

Eight mornings ago, on July 24, Jimmy had watched privately behind his ActoLenses as some special agent or another had fabricated to Rim, via Jimmy's ActoHub account, a legitimate-sounding agreement to go behind Jonathan Flite's back and meet somewhere for an "information exchange." Using language clearly meant to solicit self-incrimination, they had suggested Pana e Vino Ristorante in Providence for a meeting venue so they could set up a sting with armed special agents appearing as patrons. When Rim had immediately opted to meet somewhere less public, the agents in Boston had sent a retort almost just as quickly, again in an amusingly realistic imitation of Jimmy's aloof but desperate-for-grandeur voice.

> *If ur really the murderer from last fall, then stupid to meet somewhere secluded. But I wanna help JF/so do you. He'd kill me (maybe for real, ha) if he knew we're still talking. Also pissed his mom is*

planning to talk to reporters. Could maybe meet whenever she does, so he'd be distracted and no reporters would notice. P.S. Ur dumb for wanting to meet in person. What if I'm lying and police are there?

Almost twelve hours passed before Jimmy, lying in bed and browsing online articles about the seemingly obscure physicist Dorothy Garland, received another message from Rim, which again had been intercepted by the FBI immediately.

I would meet JF directly, but it would draw attention. I will always be armed. Police can kill me if they think I am a threat. No answers for them, then. These are my own terms, by which I plan to end my life. I want to show my face before the end and die without shame. Guilt has consumed me.

Four mornings later, on what seemed like far too obvious of clockwork for Jimmy, Winifred Flite had announced her press conference at the instruction of Agent Prescott, to the immediate thrill and buzz of reporters up and down the East Coast. Within three hours, the Boston FBI task force had sent Rim a short message, again posing as Jimmy, saying that if there was any good time to meet under the radar, it would be during Winifred's event. Finally, yesterday evening, another ActoHub message from Nicolas Rim had jingled into Jimmy's account.

7:00 p.m. during the Flite media event. You will drive alone and walk to H. P. Lovecraft's grave at

Swan Point Cemetery in Providence. Broadcast private ActoVid feed in car mirror to prove it's you and you are alone. What I have to offer is more important than you know. What I'll do if you don't come alone will not be as exciting as you think.

Today, in four hours, Jimmy would be dressing himself in front of a mirror, wearing his ActoLenses and broadcasting their live video feed so that Nicolas Rim could see he wasn't wearing a Kevlar vest or secondary wire. Per the FBI's specific orchestration of the day, Jimmy would then drive alone (but surrounded by a secret entourage of special agents) to Swan Point Cemetery in Providence, where Rim had agreed to meet. Around the same time of his arrival, Winifred Flite would be stepping out onto the front steps of Newport City Hall, making her press conference debut in the chance it might lend the suspect a false sense of security.

Yet it all felt off-kilter. Jimmy's hint of anxiety didn't stem so much from the fact that the sting operation was happening so fast or even that it wasn't playing out with the slick desperation present in his fantasies. Instead, the day felt similar to those moments just before the bullet attack back in May, when the excitement he so craved had been teetering dangerously on the edge of harsh reality. He was again craving something more, at the very least a chance to offer the FBI a truly meaningful contribution in their effort to apprehend Rim, but it was impossible to ignore the actuality that it all might go disastrously wrong.

Across the table from Jimmy now, Jonathan was sitting with as casual a posture as he could, considering the game plan for the day. Since acknowledging Agent Prescott's suggestion that they eat a lounging lunch together somewhere in public, he was by all appearances fairly relaxed despite the media mob outside. His mother would be in front of live television in mere hours; the reporters outside knew it; Jimmy was here, being the good friend. Jonathan was reading, as he often did when Jimmy had things to check on his ActoPhone. The book was *Our Elegant Universe*, his five-hundred-page birthday present. Jonathan had started it two days ago and was already three-fourths of the way through—a clear indicator to the reporters outside that he was an intellectual, not just a murderer. He was flicking his pointer finger over the edge of what appeared to be an unusually large bookmark stuck near the paperback's front, amid the pages already consumed.

"I'm just not sure about today, today," Jimmy finally whispered with a sigh, hoping Jonathan would pick up on his underlying exasperation. The sun outside the café windows was hidden behind clouds, and the restaurant's air-conditioning was thankfully granting them a respite from the day's humidity.

Jonathan looked up from *Our Elegant Universe*. He glanced behind his shoulder, at the black-haired, gaping waiter (who was whispering with the cashier), and then at Sounder (who was reading something on his phone near the door). Looking at Jimmy again, Jonathan said, "You mean the stuff tonight?"

"It just seems so clunky," Jimmy replied.

"It's not a movie. They're working with what they have."

"No, they're playing it safe. If they're going to use me as bait, they might as well go all out. I could do way more than just drive around like some lame-ass—"

"Don't you *dare*," Jonathan whispered, glancing around the café again. "This isn't just you standing in front of a camera. Let them do their job. If anything happens to you, it's on them. And me, actually."

"What do you mean 'you'?"

"Meaning we wouldn't even be here if I hadn't killed Ellen Graber. This is *all* my fault."

"Okay, so?"

"So, I'm just saying that you always seem so excited about the worst parts of my life. Like maybe you're friends with me for all the attention you get. But there's real stuff happening here that could put a lot of people in danger."

Flushing red, Jimmy turned to look at the café's other patrons. An older couple sat near the front window facing Thames Street, seemingly oblivious to the nurse killer's presence in the restaurant. Two young women were sitting near the bar, whispering and gesturing toward the reporters outside. A lone bald man with a surprisingly angular face was sitting two tables behind them, staring at Jonathan as he counted cash for his bill. When Jimmy finally turned back to his friend, wearing as defensive an expression as possible, he whispered in a way that sounded like a hiss. "I'm just saying this could all be handled better." He heard a chair scrape the floor behind them. The angular-faced man passed with hesitant footsteps, heading for the restroom. He turned his head as he walked, giving Jonathan a lingering glare. Jimmy waited for him to disappear down the back hallway before shaking his head and continuing. "I guess I just feel like this is all a shot in the dark. Nobody knows what they're doing or what's really going on. Well, except for maybe you."

Jonathan's flicking finger stopped along his large bookmark. Taking a closer look, Jimmy saw that it appeared to be a folded piece of stationery. When he looked up, the nurse killer was staring right at him.

With an unexpected trip of his heart, Jimmy sat back in his

chair. He suddenly saw what others feared in Jonathan: a level of intellect and unpredictability that was impossible to categorize. It appeared Jonathan was gauging him, either calculating something about Jimmy behind those steely hazel eyes or readying himself to pounce. "There's something I didn't tell you," he finally whispered. "Even Sounder doesn't know."

Jimmy went from cold to hot. "What do you mean?"

"I got another letter ten days ago. The blue-envelope kind. I didn't share it with the FBI. Or my mom."

For a second, all they exchanged was silence. Jimmy was just about to respond when he saw the glaring bald man reenter the restaurant's main dining area. "Hold that thought—bald guy coming back, eleven o'clock," he said to Jonathan in a low, uncertain voice. "He's staring at you. Doesn't look happy."

Jonathan marked his spot in *Our Elegant Universe* with his finger, then braced himself in his chair. Just as the bald man passed their table in what appeared to be a false alarm, he stopped abruptly and turned toward them. He teetered on the edge of words, as if building the gumption to speak his mind. Jimmy, from the corner of his eye, saw Sounder jump up from his chair by the door and start toward them. The bald man took two steps closer to Jonathan and said, "I just want to say something. You deserve everything that's happening to you. Best you get out of Newport while you still can." He turned away just as Sounder reached him, but after a moment of hesitation, he spun around, cleared his throat, and projected a mass of saliva straight onto Jonathan's forehead.

Jonathan sat frozen with shock. Sounder grabbed the man by the shoulders, immediately causing him to start struggling, screaming, and threatening to sue the bodyguard for laying hands on him. As Sounder escorted him out of the restaurant, to the awe of the restaurant's employees and other patrons, Jonathan slowly grabbed his napkin and wiped the spit away. Avoiding eye contact with Jimmy, he whispered, "If this is how life's going to be, I'm not sure I can handle it." His face pulsed with embarrassment. "I'd seriously rather go back to Crescent until full time I can move somewhere out of the way."

Jimmy felt an unexpected wrench of his heart at the thought of Jonathan leaving Newport. "You'll be okay. You just need to get through these first few months. It'll pass."

"Yeah, well, I don't have your people skills."

"You just need to practice!"

"Or maybe I just need to start talking, like this new letter says."

Suddenly remembering what Jonathan had just told him, Jimmy did his best to swallow the ego sting of knowing he had been kept in the dark. It was likely a consequence of his never having asked about the murder of Ellen Graber, or the Idle County Seven, or why exactly Jonathan was convinced his supposed memories were real. Their friendship was all surface and had been for the past nine months, because that was the way Jimmy liked it. Today, however, it was all getting real. If everything went smoothly tonight, they could see Mason Witzel's murderer in federal custody. And then what? Jimmy now realized his anxiety was rooted in something deeper: an underlying fear over what he would do once all this excitement dissipated. "Can I see the letter?" he asked, doing his best to sound cautious. "And weren't you supposed to give them all to the—"

Jonathan held up a hand—the one holding the spit-stained napkin—to shush Jimmy. "This one isn't going to matter to the feds either way, assuming I do what it says to do. I'm still thinking on it." With a subtle glance at the wall of reporters outside, he slowly pulled his large, folded bookmark out of *Our Elegant Universe* and pushed it across the table. Realizing now why the bookmark had appeared so oddly sized, Jimmy grabbed it, unfolded it, and saw a small paragraph typed once again in a dull Courier font.

> *The FBI has what they need. This one is for you. I know that I've finally caused a spark, and that you're considering speaking with Alice Winterblume. When you're ready, access her private ActoHub username "@AWinter." Your memories of Elijah Bryce will prove you're not a liar. She knows I've sent this letter.*
>
> *Most Sincerely,*
> *R. S.*

Jimmy suppressed a shudder.

Alice Winterblume.

Of all television journalists working today, Alice Winterblume was *it*, the cream of the crop. Jimmy's body pulsed with a refreshing burst of adrenaline. "Does this mean you're talking to *WorldLine*?" he said. "Have they tried contacting you?"

"No, not yet," Jonathan replied. "I've been thinking of contacting them, though."

"And why haven't you?"

"Because it'd be a step I couldn't take back."

Jimmy threw his arms up and shook his head. "But it's the *obvious* step. Of all people, Alice Winterblume! And how the hell does she know this 'R. S.' person? Have you known who's been sending these all along?"

"I've had clues," Jonathan said. He grabbed a second napkin, dipped it in his water, and raised it to his forehead for a second round of saliva wiping. "Now I know. It's somebody from Idle County. A woman named Rebecca Sparks. She was Lindsay Thorsen's boyfriend's sister, back in the day. She couldn't talk and was usually in a wheelchair, and she always had to type everything out on a computer thing. It's the same person Agent Prescott mentioned the other week. The physicist. But now she goes by the name Dorothy Garland. I looked her up online."

Jimmy furrowed his eyebrows. "So did I. All I saw were sites talking about her going to UC Santa Cruz and some new theory nobody thought would hold up to academic whatever-the-hell."

"Scrutiny. Yeah, I read that, too," Jonathan said. "But it seems like she's really causing a stir. A lot of scientists are arguing about her ideas."

"Whatever. I barely understand physics forums." Jimmy took a sip of his strawberry-mango smoothie. "What does any of it have to do with you?"

Jonathan took a deep breath. "Well, for one thing, she was supposed to be at CERN in Geneva the day of the bombing, just like Agent Prescott said. If somebody like Victor Zobel wanted to get rid of her and all her supporters, sending a guy like Jean-Claude Apostol in to do it would be the perfect ruse. Losing all those physicists would practically go unnoticed in the grander scheme, right?"

"Seems like a long shot," Jimmy said.

"But a *possible* long shot. And then there's the whole Idle County factor. I have memories of Rebecca. She was special. A lot of stuff happened with her." Jonathan shook his head and looked down at the table, as though he weren't quite sure how to proceed.

By his hushed tone, it seemed he wanted to finish this conversation before Sounder returned. "Her family died in a house explosion. I'm almost sure Victor Zobel was behind it, but there was never any proof." Jonathan looked at Jimmy again, then leaned forward, grabbed the letter, and slid it back into his book. "But that wasn't even the biggest thing. She was disabled, but she was also psychic. Like, the real deal. Proof of stuff a lot of scientists like to ignore. She was missing part of her brain, which made it hard for her to talk or walk. As I said, she had to type everything out on a tablet. Sometimes she'd type stuff right out of people's heads. Like, exactly what they were thinking. It was usually a game. Like, 'tell me what I'm thinking!' and she would. She also talked a lot about life and death, reincarnation, the nature of reality—things like that. I'm not surprised she became a physicist. If she really did have some connection to a higher level of consciousness, she could have insights about the universe that most people don't."

Jimmy felt himself blushing. His high school grades in mathematics and basic physics had been Cs at best, despite Crescent Rehabilitation Center's noble tutorial efforts.

Jonathan set his wet, second napkin on the table, then noticed how over Jimmy's head the conversation was becoming. "Think of it this way," he said. "Physics is the science behind everything. Every other area of science depends on it. Everything you see is made of tiny particles that are either dictated by some invisible wave or not technically there at all until being measured. Even then, everything you observe or think you know is a result of electromagnetic activity in the brain. But projected onto what? Why are we conscious of anything at all?"

Jimmy's day-to-day thoughts consisted of clothing, flashy things, and attention—the physical world. Never in his life had he given more than a moment's thought to concepts like the ones Jonathan apparently spent hours thinking about. Even so, it was the very reason they were here today. They were about to participate in an FBI operation that seemed intertwined with the people moved or shaken by these ideas. This Rebecca Sparks—or Dorothy Garland, whoever she was—now appeared to be the silent nexus linking Idle County, Jonathan Flite, and the bombing in Geneva.

When Jimmy did finally react outwardly to Jonathan's question, it was with a more derisive tone than he intended, as though his ego were unconsciously trying to defend his inability to cope with such big ideas. "So, what happens if you talk to this Rebecca Sparks chick and Alice Winterblume? Do all three of you partner up and change the world?"

"I'm pretty sure that's *exactly* what they want," Jonathan said. "One of the people whose memories I have . . . Elijah Bryce . . . He met Alice Winterblume once. It was a news interview back in Minnesota, before she got super famous. He helped solve a murder from the 1940s. If my memories of that meeting are real, she's going to know it."

A chill ran up the back of Jimmy's neck. He glanced apprehensively around the restaurant, suddenly realizing that believing in Jonathan's mystifying claims would align him with a camp of people no different than Cardinal Jean-Claude Apostol or Weston Carrow—those whose beliefs about the invisible had potential to create chaos. He glanced at the book in Jonathan's hand. *Our Elegant Universe*, the birthday present tome about physics, the cosmos, and all of life's big questions.

Jonathan was watching him closely. "Does it scare you to hear me talk about my memories?"

When Jimmy said "Of course not," he knew immediately

that Jonathan saw right through the lie. For the first time since last fall, he saw the sting of betrayal flicker on his friend's face. It was the same vulnerability he had displayed last November, when Jimmy and Aubrey Carlyle had laughed off his warning about Paul Simpleton, the night guard.

Jonathan stood up, gesturing with his head toward the windows, where the reporters were waiting for his exit. "Time to go fight the vultures. And don't worry about lunch. I'll pay. But one more thing before you go out and do your thing with Little Nick, because I see the doubt on your face."

With a gulp, Jimmy said, "Okay. What?"

Jonathan held up his book. "I'm not pretending to be some expert, but I've read enough to know that the smaller you break our reality down, the crazier it all becomes. And that's science talking, not freaky old me. If you start looking at it all and realizing how much we still don't know about what life even is, it'll scare you even more than I do."

Jonathan walked toward the counter, where the black-haired cashier braced herself before allowing him to scan his ActoPhone for payment. After doing so, he walked straight for the door without waiting for Jimmy, and the reporters outside began flapping their wings.

2005

FOUR WEEKS. Elijah Bryce was grounded for four solid weeks—almost the rest of the summer. Even his bandaged knife wounds wouldn't stick around for that long.

"My mom's acting crazy," he told Molly Butler over the phone the following Monday, after Shelly had left for work and his babysitter, Selma, who was now waiting to find out her GRE scores, had sat down on the couch with a book. "She was watching me like a hawk all weekend and didn't even let me use the phone. Not even my cell phone. She thought I was going to call Cynthia."

On the other end of the line, Molly sighed. "At least you know Cynthia cares about you. That's something."

Conceding to this with a growl, Elijah filled Molly in on all the other grisly details, including the fact that Shelly Bryce had even refused to let Elijah do his paper route, though it had been clear upon his return home the night of Damon's knife attack that it was because she was scared that the bully, free from End Haven's juvenile detention center since Saturday, would track him down. "They had some sort of hearing this morning," Elijah said. "Tyler and Nolan ratted him out. I guess he's going to family court again in four weeks. Probably makes sense that I'm grounded for that long. To keep me safe or whatever."

"At least they caught him," Molly said.

"You should have seen his eyes. They looked . . ." Elijah closed his own, despite the horrible memory it recalled. "They looked *insane.* And he was whispering in my ears, saying he knew I'd be there. That he had a dream about it. I think something's really wrong with him."

Molly remained silent for a moment, then said, "I guess this isn't a good time to tell you there's someone else I want to talk to about the jawbone."

Pangs of enthusiasm and longing tugged at Elijah's heart. Any pursuit of the jawbone mystery would result in disaster now, because his mother hadn't grounded him from anything in particular. It had been a flat-out, across-the-board "You're grounded!" with the single understood parameter that the house was now his prison.

Molly continued without waiting for him to respond. "This guy lives here in town, closer than Arthur Brown, even. Do you remember that first article in the *Tribune*? They quoted a guy named Theodore Tarnish, and I think I met him last year. He drove Mrs. Grime to the cemetery, and I saw them both. I was visiting my mom." Again, Molly spoke of her mother's grave with a fearless, matter-of-fact tone. It crossed Elijah's mind now that she was the bravest person he had ever met. "Anyway," she continued, "he talked in the article about how they always thought that the creepy priest guy from the Moon Woods killed Joshua Grime, but they never had any proof of it. Remember?"

"My mom made me throw away the article, but I think I remember," Elijah said.

"I want to ask Mr. Tarnish about Levi Mariani. What if he knows something about the 'man in black' guy from the bar who gave Levi the jawbone? Like, maybe it really was that priest."

"Well, I'm freakin' grounded until Damon Jacoby's done in court," Elijah said. "I can't go anywhere."

"Well, see if you can swing leaving for a day. I'll wait for you either way."

After they hung up, Elijah felt his house's walls closing in on him. Surviving four weeks of being grounded was one thing, but surviving four weeks of being grounded because going out would mean risking a psychopathic teenager attacking him? That was something else. There was no win in this situation, and the one interesting and unthreatening aspect of this summer had come to a screeching halt because of it.

Selma seemed silently to be feeling his pain, but for three straight weeks, all she mentioned regarding his grounding (between pitying glances) was that they had to follow his mom's rules. She allowed him to talk to Molly on the phone as much as he wanted, and, more often than usual, she posed joint games of Monopoly or Super Smash Brothers.

On Tuesday, August 8, during a tornado watch that amounted to nothing more than a green-tinged sky, Selma dashed for no particular reason into the living room from the kitchen and jumped onto the right side of the new leather couch, opposite Elijah. Today, she was dressed in gray sweatpants and a sky-blue T-shirt sporting a graphic of Tweety Bird. "Hey, bugger," she said. Elijah sighed and turned toward the window. Outside, rain had begun to fall—no tornado sirens yet. He suddenly noticed a small U-Haul in the driveway of the recently sold house at the end of Windsong Road. It looked as though the new neighbor was finally moving in. Considering the size of the U-Haul, he or she didn't seem to have many possessions.

"You doing okay?" Selma tilted her head into Elijah's face.

"'Okay' meaning I'm still grounded for no reason at all? Not really."

"Your mom just wants to keep you safe."

"Did she even tell you what else happened the night of the knife thing?"

"About the fight you two had? Yeah."

Elijah hesitated for a second, then said, "Did she tell you it was about my bio mom? I bet you didn't even know I was adopted."

Selma furrowed her eyebrows, adjusting a strand of hair that had fallen out of her loose bun. "No, I didn't."

"So, she also didn't tell you there was a chance I was going to be sick before I was born. Or at least be HIV-positive." Still looking at the U-Haul in the new neighbor's driveway, Elijah added, "And she wouldn't have adopted me from her husband's cousin if I had been."

Small drops of water raced down the glass in front of him. The weather had left the world outside dark enough for him to see Selma's reflection under the living room light. She stiffened and turned her head to him. "She said that? Seriously?"

Elijah gave Selma a quick but thorough overview of the life story he hadn't known about until this summer.

Selma's posture deflated with a heavy, incredulous sigh. "She told me the fight was because you told her Molly was your girlfriend. That she said you were too young to date anybody, so you got mad and ran out."

"She said *what*?"

"Wait, so Molly *isn't* your girlfriend?" Selma said. "I thought . . . I mean, all this time you've been spending with her—it sort of made sense. But that's cool if she's not, too. Friends are always good either way, right?"

"She isn't my girlfriend at all, because I'm *gay*, just like my bio dad," Elijah said. The words came out with more pride than he had intended.

Selma's expression immediately softened, and within seconds, tears lined her eyes. A drape of newfound closeness settled between them. Fearing it would soon become awkward, Elijah's only choice was to escape once again to his sanctuary of a bedroom. Books and *Star Wars* posters would have to suffice for another day.

Outside, another bolt of lightning brightened the day like a moment of electrified sunlight. Thunder followed.

THE NEXT MORNING, AUGUST 9, Selma returned to babysit as Shelly was leaving for work. Elijah had awoken early, starving for breakfast, just in time to slip awkwardly into the kitchen. Selma, with an unspoken but protective air of a linebacker, took a step toward Elijah as Shelly grabbed her purse and walked toward the garage door. "I don't think Elijah should be grounded," she said suddenly, without any visible provocation.

Next to the door, Shelly froze in her tracks. She turned around, her face growing red.

"He's been miserable for over three weeks," Selma continued with a shaky voice. "You're not even letting him see the only friend he has. And he told me the truth about the fight, and I think it's pretty crappy to keep him locked up. I would have run out, too."

After a razor-sharp moment of silence, Shelly said, "Fine. Let him do whatever he wants. Just don't come crying to me if he gets himself killed." Her purse swung after her as she spun out the door, into the garage. As they heard the garage door open and her Ford Focus start up, Elijah and Selma stared at each other with wide eyes. Elijah's mind was racing—not just with gratitude toward Selma but also with shock over what his mother had said. Did she really care about him that little?

Selma spoke first. "I think she was just embarrassed over being called out for lying. She knows she can't protect you forever."

Elijah waited until ten o'clock to call Molly. While he still felt grounded, his mother had not called to retract what she said. He was free to do what he wanted.

Two hours later, the day was breezy but humid, and low clouds were moving so fast overhead that the sun was barely getting a fighting chance to burn them off. Elijah rode his bike to Molly's house, his T-shirt flapping through the air in sharp, repetitive snaps. Their plan, finally, was to go visit Theodore Tarnish.

"Hey," Molly said, bursting out of her house as usual and pulling up her bike, which lay in the front yard.

Elijah smiled. "Be prepared: it's crazy-windy today. It almost blew me over on my way here."

"Hopefully it'll stay nice out. I forgot to check the weather."

"Same here. Oh well."

They started riding.

"Mr. Tarnish lives on Sebold Avenue," Molly said. "Three

blocks up from the library but west a bit from Main Street. It won't take long to get there."

"If we survive this *wind*," Elijah said. Molly rolled her eyes.

Less than ten minutes later, they were approaching a fair-sized house, light gray and two stories high, complete with a small deck set inward at the center of the second floor. The address numbers would have read "609" had the last number not been hanging upside down from its base, the bottom sinking below the first two.

And they were in luck. Standing alongside the house, left of the front door, was a tall but frail-looking old man. He was wearing a faded blue baseball cap and watering a strip of multi-colored zinnias, appearing careful not to hit a lone white butterfly fluttering above them. It immediately reminded Elijah of the second time he had met Molly, the day he found Cynthia Foster's address. She had been watering flowers at the library.

Elijah stopped next to Molly at the curb as she took a deep breath and said, "Well, here we go. That's him. He definitely looks older this year." They dismounted their bikes and walked slowly up the front sidewalk. Their feet barely made a sound, and Elijah doubted Mr. Tarnish would hear them over the sound of the hose. When they were ten feet away from him, Molly cleared her throat and said with a loud voice, "Mr. Tarnish?"

The old man's fingers wrestled for a moment with the hose nozzle, and then his grip lightened. The water stopped. With his back still slightly bent over, he turned. For a split second, he looked confused, and then he smiled. "Hello there. I know you from the cemetery last year, do I not?"

Molly immediately beamed. "My name is Molly Butler. This is my friend Elijah Bryce."

"Hi," Elijah said with a polite nod.

"Call me Ted," the old man said. "Everyone else does."

Molly offered Ted a courteous smile. "Okay, Ted. I like your flowers. Do you always get white butterflies flying around them like that? I love butterflies."

"This one showed up just now, I think," Ted said. "I suppose I should wait until it leaves to turn the hose back on, huh?" He chuckled. "So, what can I do you for?"

This time, Molly verged on a blush. She turned to Elijah.

"Well," Elijah started, suddenly flummoxed and fighting to find the right words. "We're actually here because of a newspaper article you were quoted in a few weeks ago. The one about Joshua Grime's jawbone."

Ted Tarnish's friendly grin faded into an expression that was almost defensive. "Why would you both be interested in that?"

"I'm the one who dug up the jawbone in the Moon Woods back in June," Elijah said. "My biological mother is Cynthia Foster, the one who buried it. It's kind of a long story how I ended up finding it. Lots of weird coincidences."

Ted's defensive manner had diminished some, and in its place came a deflated look, as if his beautiful morning had been perfect until they came over and brought up Joshua Grime. "Life's full of coincidences," he said in a low voice. "It's been my experience that the longer you live, the more they start seeming like they were part of some big plan all along."

Molly, who was biting her lip with a trace of embarrassment, took a step forward. "We read another article about how the police aren't really spending much time trying to figure out how Mr. Grime's jawbone got out there in the first place." She looked toward the zinnias now, at the white butterfly fluttering among them. "Also, I was friends with Mrs. Grime. She told me last year about her husband disappearing, so I care about this. Especially if the police aren't doing everything possible to find the rest of him."

Ted looked at Elijah. "Were you friends with Elizabeth Grime, too?"

Elijah's face curled with regret. "No, actually. I only ever knew her from the library."

"She did enjoy young people," Ted said. "As did her husband. Joshua was a fine man. A *fine* man. It was awful when he disappeared. All questions and no answers, until now. It's a shame Elizabeth didn't live long enough to find out what happened. Not that any of these recent developments would have pleased her much."

"We tracked the jawbone down to a man named Levi Mariani," Molly said. "A man named Arthur Brown told us. He used to work at the county fair, which is where Elijah Earnshaw—"

"—my real dad—"

"—won it from a guy named Sam Jacoby."

Ted frowned as they finished telling him what they knew about the jawbone's hand-off progression. He took in their words with unflinching attention.

"Arthur Brown is pretty old," Elijah said. "He seemed sort of confused until we brought up the jawbone. His memories of it seemed pretty clear. He said a 'man dressed in black' gave the jawbone to Levi Mariani at a bar in Stone Ridge. Miller's Tavern, I think."

"A man in black, you say?" Ted asked in a low voice. His eyes widened, and whatever memory was playing behind them had turned his face pale.

"We think it was that priest who killed all those people back in the 1940s," Molly said. "The one who built that chapel in the Moon Woods."

Ted Tarnish was already nodding before Molly finished. With a frown, he said, "I have no doubt it *was* Simon Villard who gave this man the jawbone. Levi Mariani, you say? But by *gads,* it's hard to believe he would have gone that far. Removing and cleaning the jawbone, I mean. He and Elizabeth were close when they were younger. Very close."

The two children breathed quietly as Ted took three dry swallows of air, almost looking as if he were about to vomit. Finally, Molly said, "We're sorry to bother you with all this. We just thought you might be able to help us figure out where to go next. Even old photos or something?"

Ted's wrinkled face warped into a half smile. "You know, I do have a photo, I think. Come here." He placed the hose nozzle gently onto the grass and gestured for them to follow him into the house. "It just so happens that I have an old box of them that belonged to Elizabeth. I took them from her attic when she died, and I can't bring myself to get rid of them. Old habits die hard, I guess."

Elijah and Molly exchanged curious glances as they followed Ted through a light, metal door and into a crooked, screened-in porch. The larger wooden door leading inside was already open.

"You two wait here," Ted said. "I have the box upstairs, but you'd best not follow me in too far. An old man loses his ability to keep things clean after a while." A few seconds later, he was out of sight, and the floor above them was creaking with his footsteps.

After a few moments of considerate silence, Molly turned her neck around and looked at Elijah. "They never showed any photos of this priest guy on the news last year. I'm kind of nervous to see what he looked like."

"Especially if he looked *normal*," Elijah replied. "And funny you had the idea about photos. Good thinking."

"It kind of just came to me. Like, you know when you have that little voice in your head telling you what to do?"

With a grin, Elijah said, "Cynthia would call that *intuition*. I'm not sure I have it."

"*Everyone* has it."

They turned quickly when they heard footsteps coming down the stairs. "Here they are," Ted said, carrying a shoebox and beckoning toward the living room with his neck. He reached the main floor, looking particularly colorless in the foyer's low light. "I took a gander and couldn't quite find the one I meant to show you, but I'm sure it's here. Come over by the window."

Ted led them to a bay window in the living room that looked out the west side of the house. The day's sun, which had now successfully burned through the clouds, shone onto a dusty, mustard-colored cushion that lined the window seat. Ted sat down, and Molly followed suit. Elijah remained standing.

"We're looking for a black and white one taken on a lake," the old man said. "I remember, because there was a white boat in the background that looked like one I used to have." He began shuffling through the box, offering Molly large handfuls of pictures to sort through. Elijah tilted his head to see the old photographs. Many of them were colored, but some were old, small and square, showing people who must now be long dead.

Molly stopped at one photo in particular of a man and a woman standing next to a familiar-looking building. "That's Mrs. Grime," she said, almost to herself. With careful examination, Elijah recognized the woman in the photo.

"Ah, yes, and Joshua, at their library," Ted said, pointing at the picture but careful not to touch it, as if he didn't deserve to. "They were good friends of mine. Very good friends."

Molly set the picture aside and continued sifting through the others, handing them off to Elijah with each new handful. He glanced through some to get a better look, but seeing as none of them was the picture Ted had in mind, he simply waited.

A minute passed before Ted spoke again. "Here it is." He handed the picture to Elijah this time.

Sure enough, the picture was one of the old ones, black and white with yellowed edges. It had indeed been taken on a lake; a white boat floated frozen in the background. In the photo was a man in his late twenties. He was extremely handsome, staring into the camera with piercing, dark eyes.

"That's Father Simon Villard," Ted said. "Elizabeth must have taken this on a day out. I never even knew this picture of him existed until after she passed and I found it in her attic. This was before she married Joshua."

Elijah turned the picture over. On the back was a penciled caption in careful, cursive handwriting.

SMV, August 31, 1933. Our spot on the lake.

Elijah handed the picture to Molly, pointing out the caption. "Which lake, do you think?" he said. There were four large lakes surrounding Idle County: Spinner's Lake, Trunk Lake, Blue Lake, and Finger Lake. Boating on them had always been a prevalent pastime for locals.

"Looks like they're standing on rocks or something, looking toward shore," Molly said. "They look pretty far out over the water."

"You know, I never thought about that," Ted Tarnish said, as if suddenly enlightened. He raised his eyebrows for a moment in what Elijah took to be shock. "Never even *thought* about it," he repeated.

"Thought about what?" Elijah asked.

"Spinner's Island."

The words left his mouth with a ghostly weightlessness, as if the very picture they formed hung among the three of them, waiting to be understood.

"That's *right!*" Molly said, squinting closer at the picture. "It is Spinner's Island! Look, you can even see where the shoreline curves down toward End Haven, off to the right there. It opens up in the background, see?"

"By golly, I think you're right. By *golly.*"

Elijah's breath almost caught in his throat. Spinner's Island was a secluded spot on the eastern edge of Spinner's Lake, whose southernmost tip just touched the outlying northern edge of End Haven. It was a large lake, at least a day's bike ride around the jagged perimeter, but Spinner's Island was fairly close, about twelve miles north of End Haven's town center. Elijah had only driven by it once or twice in his life, because it wasn't on the way to anywhere. What made it unique was that a chain of clustered rocks connected it to land, forming a climbable bridge.

"They must have hiked out onto the rocks and hopped across them," Molly said. "Look, the one he's standing on is pretty far above the water."

"Do you think we could make it there today?" Elijah asked.

Molly scrunched her face with uncertainty before nodding. "It'd be pretty far on our bikes, but we could stop and get some food and water somewhere. I have that Velcro bag thingy on the back of my seat."

"The Antler Foods is closer than either of our houses," Elijah replied.

"Hold on, you two, hold on," Ted said. "Now, I'm not too far out of it to know that you're thinking you might find the rest of Joshua Grime out there. But that's a far ride, even for people your age. Not to mention a far-fetched idea."

"We're both almost thirteen," Elijah said, feeling a surge of both rebellion and his regained freedom. "We can handle it, right Molly?"

"I spent most of last summer on my bike," Molly justified, yet her expression wavered a bit, as though she were using the comment to cover some less pleasant truth.

"Fair enough," Ted said, narrowing his eyes. "But how exactly do you think you're going to find what's left of Joshua? Or it is just some summer game you've devised, doing your own investigation?"

Elijah and Molly exchanged glances. The man's assessment was closer to the truth than Elijah wanted to admit. But it wasn't a game. Everything had changed since he found the jawbone, and not all for the better.

"I hope you're both careful, whatever you do," Ted continued after reading the resilience in their eyes. "I suppose you're smart enough not to fall off those rocks."

"We are," Molly said to Ted. "And thanks for your help. I think Mrs. Grime would be happy to know that not everyone is giving up."

Ted tilted his head with a dejected smile. "Elizabeth herself gave up after all those years passed without a clue. But you're right. She'd be glad."

Elijah led the way back outside, and as they stepped off the stairs to the front sidewalk, they turned to bid Ted Tarnish a final wave.

"Be careful," he said again.

They nodded, then headed toward their bikes.

"You really think we can make it?" Molly asked, now with a hint of doubt. It was windy, and the sky was once again laced with low, transparent clouds.

"You're the one making all the plans," Elijah said. "But yeah, I think so. We can stop at Antler Foods, like you said."

Molly took a deep breath, then nodded with determined eyes. "I have twenty bucks. That should be enough to buy some sandwiches and snacks, right?"

It was settled. They would stop at the grocery store, then pedal the long bike ride to Spinner's Lake. The first thing Elijah and Molly forgot, however, was to check the weather report. The second was to inform their babysitters and parents where they were going and why.

2010

CYNTHIA FOSTER STOOD on the front porch of Max Pope's angular, rustic cabin in Palmer, taking in the property's sounds—a constant breeze through the surrounding trees, birds chirping on their branches, a creek rushing with water across the acreage and into the lake behind the house. As each stimulus hit her senses, she considered the trail of events that had led her to this very moment: her meeting Elijah Earnshaw in 1980 at a drumming circle in Wind Prairie; then their marriage, five miscarriages, and fated-to-fail relationship; and finally their beautiful son, whose life in Idle County, like his own father's, had been cut far too short. For reasons disastrously unknown, Elijah had fallen onto death's path, and he hadn't found his way back. Had Cynthia herself thrust him onto it five years ago, that summer of the tarot reading? She wondered now if their first meeting had somehow planted the suggestion of death in him and whether he, like so many children, never escaped that shred of misguided parental influence.

Cynthia looked at her feet—at the varnished wooden porch beneath her scuffed fluorescent green and blue Asics. The boards under them creaked as she shifted her weight. She knocked on the door five separate times before peering into it. Beyond was the living room she had glimpsed before, a cozy-looking space with wooden ceiling beams, a black wood stove along the right-hand wall, and an open kitchen designated to the far left end of the living area. It was small but functional, the perfect home for a man who didn't want to be found. This time, Cynthia took a closer look at the small black device blinking in the right upper corner of the living room. It did indeed look like a security camera, and it was pointing straight at the door.

Good. Maybe he'll recognize me if he sees—

"Can I help you, ma'am?"

Still leaning forward and peering inside at the camera, Cynthia froze when she heard the accented voice. It belonged to a man, possibly a European. Thanking herself for not jumping out of her skin like the near-guilty trespasser she was, she slowly turned, barely acknowledging the falling sensation in her heart when she realized that the voice could not possibly belong to Max Pope.

The man standing ten feet from the porch had salt and pepper hair and was dressed in jeans, flannel, and a jean jacket. Trying to hide her unease behind an embarrassed smile, she quickly cast her gaze to his right, his left, and beyond. The only vehicle on the property was Max Pope's empty, white truck. It had been there when Cynthia arrived, which also meant so had this man. Had somebody seen her on the security camera last time and warned him to come wait for her to return?

"I'm sorry; I was looking for the man who lives here," Cynthia said, trying to suppress the quake in her voice. "He's been going by the name Michael Johnson?"

"I'm Michael Johnson," the man replied, again with his accent.

Cynthia's unease grew cold on the back of her neck. No, this man wasn't Michael Johnson. He wasn't even American. If ever Cynthia had experienced a genuine moment of reading another person's mind, it was now. She could immediately tell this imitator hadn't expected to have to deal with her face-to-face at this very moment, and now he was improvising. Yet he was clearly doing a better job of it; she couldn't even make up a convincing reason for her visit, because the moment she pretended to believe the man, he would know she knew he was lying.

"I'm talking about the other Michael Johnson," she said slowly. "He used to be named Maximilian Pope. He lived in California for a time, and then Minnesota, before moving here."

The shift in the man's act was visible; his face went from faux-curious to deadpan. Cynthia searched it for aggression, only to find herself back in that gray, cloudy muddle of uncertainty. She was alone again with nothing but her wits. She had assumed the white truck in the driveway belonged to Max; his neighbor and friend, Chuck, had given her the make and model about four seconds after looking at the picture of the disgraced neurologist on her iPhone and confirming his identity. She was fifteen feet from the truck now.

"I live here," the man said. "Look." He dug into his jeans' left pocket and pulled out a ring of jangling keys. He gestured toward the door with his head. "May I?"

Cynthia rushed down the porch stairs in three fast steps, then immediately took two large strides forward and to the right. Half expecting the man to cut her off, she felt a rush of adrenaline in her body as he stepped toward the porch and took the first two stairs in one quick hop.

"I'll be going now," Cynthia said. "I think I have the wrong house."

The man had just turned the key and pushed the door of Max's house open. "Might be for the best. Nothing against strangers, mind you, but this is private property."

"I'm very sorry." As she walked backward with a smile that felt like misshaped plaster, she raised a hand in a wave. Her rental car was ten feet behind the white truck.

"You have a good day now," the man said, still watching her. He had not stepped into the empty house.

Cynthia turned her back to him just as she reached the driver's-side door of the truck. Could she have been mistaken? Was this the wrong house, the wrong truck, the entirely wrong situation?

The man on the porch, the apparent Michael Johnson, was still standing stock-still, watching her.

Cynthia slowed, and her gaze flitted toward the truck's interior. She was barely tall enough to see through the driver's-side window. Perhaps a view of the seat or floor might give her the proof she needed that the man on the porch was an imposter, that Max Pope indeed had not simply wandered into the wilderness, the way he had hinted at doing. But no, she could barely even see the steering wheel. The windows were specked with dust anyway, and oh, the man on the porch had just turned his body toward her again, full on, as if he knew—

There.

Hanging over the dashboard from the rear-view mirror.

A dangling photograph.

The girl it depicted was one Cynthia had seen before and even spoken with on multiple occasions. Flowing red hair, gentle but sharp-witted eyes, an innocent smile.

It was Jillian Pope, Elijah's friend and one of the missing.

The man on the porch was walking down the stairs, toward her. His steps were slow, but his eyes hadn't left her. "Is there something keeping you?" he called across the driveway. His voice hit Cynthia like two hands pushing her with fervency toward the rental car, and she suddenly moved as fast as she could without looking back. She grabbed the door handle, pulled it open, and allowed herself to look out the front windshield only once the car was started.

The imposter was three feet from the passenger's side of the car. Cynthia's gaze jolted toward the door-lock button, and her hand followed. She pushed it just as the man leaned down toward the cracked-open passenger's window and held up his left hand. "Wait!" he called. "There's a big rock right behind the front tire on this side. Must have bumped over it when you came in. Can I fix it before you pull out? Don't want you to get a flat."

No. Stupid. He's going to slash the tires. Put the car in reverse!

But the man had already knelt down, next to the front right tire. If she were to pull out now, she could leave him with a broken arm or hand, and if he was innocent (except he couldn't be, because that had been Jillian Pope's face hanging in the white Ford truck) she could get into more trouble than she had bargained for.

The man was up in seconds. In his hands was a large, sharp rock, at least nine inches long and perhaps seven in height. She didn't remember any bump driving in; perhaps she had curved over it just right while parking.

"Have a good day, ma'am," he said, somehow looking victorious.

Cynthia pressed the gas pedal and, a moment later, was backing down the driveway, away from Max Pope's house on Wolverine Lake, free. She dreaded everything that was coming—the fanatical calls she would have to make, the deaf ears her concern would hit, the shame Shelly Bryce would try to inflict on her for caring. Would anyone else care, or was this a dead end? She could think of only one person who might listen: that reporter in Wind Prairie who was covering the Idle County Seven story. She had interviewed Elijah in 2005. Alice Winterblume, her name was. Did her news station have some sort of tip line to call? Cynthia decided right then to check as soon as she arrived back at Frank's house. She would have to think very carefully on what to say, what details to share. If Max Pope really had flown with no record to Minnesota, and if this random, foreign man really was posing as him for no good reason, it meant that everything the police thought was going on might be wrong. That the kids' cars being found outside of Dallas might be a dead end. That Occam's razor had, in the case of the Idle County Seven, been very, very wrong.

2038

I T WAS TIME. Nicolas Leandro Rim was about to call Jimmy
Barber's bluff, or the bluff of the FBI, if they were the ones
forcing the boy to participate in today's meeting. He was sitting with fretful stillness at the new and improved Starbucks on
the third level of Providence Place Mall, near the Macy's entrance,
with his back to the wall. The place was rushing with people—a
gaggle of teen girls ordering complicated frappuccinos, a mother
of three trying to calm down a screaming baby while the older two
children hit each other, and hundreds of others shuffling through
their afternoons. Were any of them following the local Jonathan
Flite saga? Did any of them have their ActoHub accounts scheduled to switch on the live video stream of Winifred Flite's press
conference at seven o'clock, just an hour away?

It seemed every molecule of Nicolas's body was abuzz. His legs
were both cold and hot, and his chest muscles were spasming, even

though his arms resting on the table felt numb and disconnected from his nervous system. His mind was walking a tightrope, barely balancing on the edge of this Monday afternoon. If the evening's charade were truly to become his swan song, he was mere minutes away from plummeting into the realm of nonexistence.

He had almost drowned in the possibilities of how tonight might play out. Amid his general recklessness, desperation, and mental unraveling were shreds of disquieting logic. No matter how desperate for thrills Jimmy Barber was, there was no way he would have been stupid enough to keep today's meeting a secret from the police, not to mention Jonathan Flite. Nicolas had thrown the Swan Point Cemetery location into their conversation to test the waters. Jimmy had agreed to the spot with minimal vacillation, which seemed normal enough, but the scheduling of Winifred Flite's press conference, hinted at by Jimmy also, seemed suspect. Nicolas knew his desire to see Jimmy Barber face-to-face was unnecessary, that it threatened to land him in the hands of police, and that hiding behind a computer would be the smart coward's approach. Every time he considered it, however, all he could see was the face of Cardinal Jean-Claude Apostol last August—that ActoVid transmission of the man's sweaty, jowly, and desperate visage just seconds before he had detonated the nuclear weapon in Geneva. That man had ended his life behind a camera, in shameful darkness, and Nicolas wanted to end his own in the light, tempting redemption.

Now that the moment had arrived, however, it seemed like nothing more than a romantic ideal, a pathetic effort to leave the world with a futile wisp of credibility. Even if he were to escape this evening alive after sharing everything he knew about Victor Zobel, his only subsequent plan was to quietly drive north, into rural

New England, perhaps to Massachusetts or even New Hampshire, where he would find a patch of forest, put a gun in his mouth, and end his fallen existence. His body would become food for the animals—barely a silver lining.

It was now 5:58 p.m., and Jimmy Barber's live, private ActoVid feed showed on Nicolas's lens display. The boy was standing shirtless in front of a long, body-sized mirror—supposedly in his bedroom, which appeared to be decorated with more style than Nicolas had ever perceived in one eyeful. He was wearing a pair of underwear that seemed overly skimpy for an eighteen-year-old, but then again, kids these days were an entirely new breed.

"See? No wire," the boy said. "I mean, if I were really working with the police or whatever, they could just watch my feed and track my phone anyway. You're not really going to get more proof that I'm being legit."

Nicolas, connected by audio only, said, "Get dressed in front of the mirror, and get in your car."

"*Finally*," Jimmy hissed. "And I still don't get why you're doing it this way. You could just tell me everything over ActoVid."

A tangle of lies and truths swirled in Nicolas's heart, and for a second, he didn't know which answer would best satisfy Jimmy's curiosity. "I'm bored. I'm guilty. I'm suicidal. Which answer would you like?"

"I'd like to know if you're planning on killing me."

"I've never desired to kill anyone."

"That doesn't mean you won't, though, right?"

"I'll kill myself before I kill you. I told you that already."

Jimmy straightened his posture. "Sometimes people get cold feet. And Jonathan Flite's friends haven't been so lucky."

Once again: visions.

Mason Witzel, squirming in the dark.

With a racing heart, Nicolas watched and waited as Jimmy left his house, approached his car, and did a three-sixty panorama video spin before climbing into his car. "No cops," he said.

"They could always be following."

"Obviously. But again, it's stupid you're making me do this in person."

"And why *are* you doing it?" Nicolas asked.

"My therapist says it's because I like excitement. I put myself in precarious situations so my life doesn't feel empty. It's weird, but it works."

Excitement.

Nicolas thought back on his life, to his earliest memories. They were mostly blurs, but one that always stuck out to him was chasing sheep with his sisters, Nora and Luana, on their grandmother's small farm outside Interlaken—running and giggling like mad, because Nora and Luana had been goading him to try to touch one of the larger sheep's rear end. Childhood had given him excitement in all the best ways, even as a poor kid in expensive Geneva. His parents Jonas and Genevieve had raised them in a modest flat on Rue des Peupliers, near the Line 12 tram termination point at Moillesulaz. Jonas Rim had been general manager of his own building company, specializing in home renovation and extensions. Somehow, he had won the bid to double the size of Victor Zobel's home in the town of Gland in 2001—something Nicolas always suspected had to do with the full family photo on his father's company ads. There they had all been, the happy Rim family, with three children and of course the beautiful, auburn-haired Genevieve. Jonas had always wanted to have a "family company," and this had been his attempt to make that clear to his clients. What he had done, unknowingly, was sell his wife.

The Rim family had prospered after meeting Victor Zobel, but at a price kept secret from Nicolas for over two decades. Genevieve Rim had caught Victor Zobel's eye, Nicolas had learned many years later. Their sudden good fortune after intersecting with the Zobels—excitement, prestige, a sense of security—had been a sham, a fishhook luring them in. And how many details could Nicolas really tell Jimmy Barber here tonight? That he had once worshipped Victor Zobel, even as the man secretly paid Jonas $100,000 Swiss francs to sleep with Genevieve? That Zobel's setting up Jonas with a construction management job at one of Zobel Enterprises' American subsidiaries had merely been an attempt to buy them off so that reporters wouldn't get wind of the sex deal? Nicolas's sisters had stayed in Switzerland for their education and marriages while he and his parents moved to America, sponsored by Zobel's corporate empire. His English hadn't been as fluent as Nora and Luana's, and New Jersey had struck him as an ugly, unfriendly place upon his arrival. Yet he had still been ignorant of Zobel's treachery at the time and still admired the man blindly. Even after Zobel had ushered Nicolas's father away to Minnesota to build his house in Idle County, which turned into the last job of Jonas Rim's life, Nicolas didn't question the man's integrity. Only after his father's death, when Zobel had arranged for him to be the personal assistant to Larry Kane, CEO of Carey Developments, had Nicolas, under a delusion of excitement that was truly a dissolution of his spirit, jumped down the rabbit hole. Today, after years of doing Zobel and Kane's illegal bidding, this silly, hopeless endeavor with Jimmy Barber had become the end of the road, the chaotic center of a nightmarish maze.

The boy had just exited onto US Route 1 from Route 138 and was heading north toward the Route 4 intersection.

"Map is saying this way is faster," Jimmy said.

Nicolas sighed. "Let me see the rear-view mirror."

The boy complied, looking up at the glass. It appeared to reflect normal evening traffic. The view of Jimmy's ActoVid feed on Nicolas's lens display was shaky but clear enough. As Nicolas watched his little friend's drive toward Providence, what suddenly frightened him more than anything was the possibility that the boy might really be alone, that he might not be working with police, and that their encounter tonight might indeed end quietly. This in turn would allow Nicolas to make that final drive north so he could wrap his lips around a gun barrel. It now seemed like a stark, hopeless prospect.

The clatters and clanks and coffee grinders of Starbucks grated on his consciousness like fingernails on a chalkboard. He was just sitting there, drawing stares as he looked at nothing but the streaming ActoLens video of Jimmy's drive. People knew the blank ActoLens gaze; it was a social phenomenon since the glasses' introduction to the mass market fifteen years ago. Yet it appeared he was conspicuous for other reasons. Was it his size? His muscles? His red, sweating face? Perhaps the dread wrapping like snakes around his heart had finally become visible—like ink scrawling a message of hopelessness across his forehead.

"Just got to Providence," Jimmy said. "Doesn't sound like you're at the cemetery though. Was that a coffee grinder?"

Nicolas jerked back into reality, noticing the whirring Starbucks noises once again and tumbling toward feelings reminiscent of what Jimmy said his own were.

Excitement.

Anticipation.

Horror.

All of Nicolas's possible choices suddenly whirled around his mind, and a new path began to form. One he hadn't considered. It was gray, uncharted.

"Get off at the Providence Place exit," he said. "No more cemetery plan."

Silence for a full ten seconds. Then Jimmy replied with uncharacteristic feebleness. "What do you mean?"

"We're not meeting at the cemetery. Go to the mall." Blood and adrenaline pulsed through Nicolas with more zest than he would have imagined possible. His nightmare was now malleable, and the nebulous array of potential results spun in front of him like a game of Russian roulette. "Once you're there, I'll know. And you'll need to be alone, or I'll also know, and any feds you're working with won't get their answers. Just let them know that Victor Zobel has a very tangled web."

Next to Nicolas, an old woman of perhaps seventy-five, with dyed brown hair and an assemblage of cheap jewels falling over her saggy white blouse, turned and glanced at him. The glance turned into an uneasy stare. Suddenly feeling as if she were seeing right through his skin and into his soul, Nicolas stood up from his table and walked out of Starbucks, into the mall. If Jimmy Barber was truly alone, he would come. If he was with police, the entire mall would be on lockdown within minutes. The little details in between and the choices they'd inspire would settle themselves as circumstances allowed. All Nicolas knew, as he walked toward the food court without a plan in the world, was that this was it, his final chance for redemption.

2005

S PINNER'S ISLAND was just ten miles away, and as the cool air-conditioning of Antler Foods gave way to the day's warmth, it hit Elijah and Molly like a renewed burst of confidence. Freshly stocked up on water and snacks, they biked out of the parking lot, turned down Main Street, then rode for a block before heading west on Hunter Avenue. After ten minutes came a right turn onto Birmingham Road, a wide and freshly paved thorough-fare that ran along the northwest edge of End Haven. It had bike lanes, which made for a much smoother ride than the sidewalks and thin shoulders of End Haven's other roads.

Over the next thirty minutes, the muggy, windy freedom worked wonders on Elijah. The low, wispy clouds were bright in the sky, shimmering under the diffused afternoon sun. After being grounded for so long, he now felt alive with the fresh air and happy to be with a friend. It was all that mattered.

A fair number of oncoming cars passed them going the opposite way; Elijah could see tired, red-faced kids in the back seats wrapped in towels and surrounded by water toys. When they passed End Haven Regional Airport, which lay to their left, no planes were flying in the sky. The road ascended slightly for about a mile longer before it hit a peak, and when they reached it, a blue and white, glistening expanse was visible on the horizon.

"There we go," Molly said. "See? It wasn't that bad of a ride, was it?"

They approached Spinner's Lake on Birmingham Road's last stretch, which ran in a steady but gradual decline. It made a T with the lake's perimeter road, which was in a heavy state of disrepair. Straight ahead was a wide-open green field preceding a small stretch of sandy beach. Red buoys bobbed in and out of the choppy, silvery-blue water, and a fair number of people still populated the field's picnic tables, mostly mothers and children. Midway across the field, a man with peculiarly colored hair—black with two thick strips of white—caught a flock of paper plates flying in the wind and brought them back to a seemingly unrelated party.

Elijah and Molly crossed the perimeter road and stopped at the nearest picnic table to eat their sandwiches. They were large and filling—deli perfection, in Elijah's opinion. Making sure to conserve his bottled water, he finished with a limited but sufficient gulp.

"Hey, look. You can see Spinner's Island there, up the shore on the right." Molly pointed a finger just before putting her water bottle back on the bike's holder. Elijah put a hand to his forehead to shield from the afternoon's diffused light reflecting off the lake. A bright haze had obscured the secluded island almost completely; it appeared as a mere shadow rising out of the water.

They began pedaling the home stretch. Only one car passed them: a rusty, green pickup truck, speeding along as if the driver were in some great hurry. Thankfully, he passed Elijah and Molly with his brakes pressed, as there were no bike lanes and only a faded, dotted yellow line to separate the sides of the street. The truck slowed for a moment even after it had passed, then sped off around the lake.

The last few miles seemed like the longest. They followed the lake's curved edge, which didn't appear to change until Elijah looked off to his left. Through a break in the trees lining the shore, he saw the beach and green park grass behind it, which had taken their place at a distant edge of the lake. It was quiet now; no cars had passed since the green truck, and only pines and shrubbery lined the road on either side. Above them, the sky had grown white with clouds. Perhaps they wouldn't be so lucky with sun.

Ten minutes later, Molly slowed and turned her face toward Elijah. She pointed at the trees along the road's left side. About two hundred feet ahead of them, nestled near a grove of pines preceding the lakeshore, sat the rusty green truck. With a nervous smile, Molly said, "You don't suppose . . ."

Elijah chuckled. "That Damon Jacoby escaped his aunt and stole the family truck?"

Molly shrugged but didn't laugh off the comment. "Do you know if his uncle has a truck? You said yourself he's psychic or whatever."

"No idea," Elijah said, shaking his head. "And I don't care. I'm not going to be paranoid my whole life. Plus he's not supposed to leave his legal guardians. He'd get in a bunch more trouble."

"Makes sense," Molly said. "I just want to make sure we're not being stupid."

"We probably are, but isn't that what they say being a kid is all about?"

"I sometimes think grown-ups aren't much smarter than we are." Molly sighed, then pointed through the trees. "By the way, you can see the rock bridge now. Look."

The pines preceding the water were tall but not very thick. Elijah and Molly easily pedaled through them on a stretch of ground wide enough to be a small driveway, until finally the branches broke to reveal a rocky shoreline. The wind, which seemed to have settled on their ride around the lake, had risen again. It was coming at them from the northwest.

The rocks were high, at least four feet out of the water at the shore. A stretch of them continued off in a bowed tangent, jutting out of the choppy water in a wide curve. At the far end, perhaps five hundred feet away, was Spinner's Island. A mixture of long, slender trees stretched off of it, their tops touching the white haze with ghostly reverence.

"Okay, be careful," Molly said as Elijah hopped the three-foot gap from the shoreline to the first rock in the bridge toward the island. The humid wind was warm on his face.

"It shouldn't be too bad," he said. "We might have to climb up a few rocks before getting to the next ones, but I'm sure it'll be fine."

Progress was slower than he expected, however, and the island was farther away than it looked. Twice, they had to jump from a high rock to the next lower rock around the small waves rolling in from around the island. Just before they reached the last rock facing the island's high south shore, Molly stopped, wiping a wet piece of hair from her face. The moisture was a mixture of sweat and the day's increasing mugginess. "Elijah, look."

Upon turning, it took Elijah a few seconds to realize what

had caught her attention. The view in front of him, looking back toward the mainland, was like looking into Mrs. Grime's old photograph of Father Simon Villard.

"This is the spot," Molly said. For a moment, only the wind responded.

"Weird that a murderer was standing here once," Elijah replied finally. "Do you see any, um . . . ?"

"Ghosts?"

Elijah looked around, feeling a shiver that didn't come from the warm day. What if either that crazy priest or Joshua Grime hadn't left this place?

"Haven't seen anything," Molly said, turning toward Spinner's Island. The rock bridge ended with an easy jump from one high point to another; the last outcropping was a good ten feet above the splashing water, over smaller and sharper rocks, and the beginning of the island met it at equal height. A tall and jagged stone face formed the small cliff's wall, but it was covered on top with damp green grass. It was soft under their feet.

"It's bigger than it looked from the shore," Molly said. "Do you think there are paths or anything?"

"Not much grass trampled down. Looks pretty empty."

"A good spot to hide a body," Molly said with a matter-of-fact nod. "Do you think we should split up? It'd be quicker that way. Cover more ground and see if there's anything weird."

"Sounds good," Elijah said. "Except . . . what about whoever else is here? Do you think they already hiked out to the island? I don't want you to get caught by some creeper."

Molly rolled her eyes. "This island is too small to get caught on. Besides, I'm sure it's just some wind-watcher-nature-lover type. I have my phone either way."

"I have mine, too. Just yell if anything happens."

Molly gave him a *"Yeah, yeah, let's get on with it"* look and started toward the trees. "I'll take the left side of the island. Let's meet on the far end."

"Sounds good."

Elijah started off to the right, into the trees. They appeared to be mostly birch, and a mixture of leaves, grass, and damp soil made for a soft forest floor. The smell of plants, somehow heightened by the humidity, freshened Elijah's nose. It was different from the Moon Woods here; the feeling of being surrounded by water lent this place an even greater sense of isolation.

Yet what were they actually looking for? Would Simon Villard really have left a marking for his victim? If he had wanted Joshua Grime truly to disappear, he would have buried him deep and with care not to make it look conspicuous. And there was also the jawbone to consider. If Simon Villard had given it to Levi Mariani in the bar, that meant he would have had to separate it from the body himself. What other body parts had he felt it necessary to tear off?

Elijah shivered upon realizing that he was trying to think like a killer. It was one thing that they were looking for Joshua Grime's remains, but trying to imagine how and why they might have ended up here left him feeling hollow.

A sudden movement up ahead, and then a noise, caught Elijah's eyes and ears.

He stopped walking and peered through the trees. Yes, up ahead, near a large, chest-height boulder, a person was walking toward the rear side of the island. Still motionless, Elijah listened carefully to the subtle footsteps crunching across the ground. They were muted, growing more distant. If it was just another hiker on the island, Elijah decided it might be best to follow and make himself known. He plodded on toward the large boulder. It was oddly shaped, different than the large rocks that had led to the island. It was almost rounded, similar to some of the boulders scattered around the Moon Woods. He ran a hand over its mossy top as he passed. It, too, was damp in the humidity.

A gust of wind suddenly rushed through the treetops, and somewhere in the distance, Elijah could hear water crashing against rocks. A second later, the faint glow illuminating the birch trees above him died. A cloud had covered what remained of the sun. *It'll be back,* Elijah thought. *But maybe I should find Molly just in case.*

Two minutes passed, however, and the sun did not return.

Careful not to run into any branches, Elijah angled his neck upward as he walked and looked through the swaying treetops. The sky beyond it was less than white now, and if it was going to rain, Elijah doubted they could get off the island and back to End Haven in time. He would have to call Selma and ask her to pick them up.

He looked at his phone clock. It was 3:42 p.m.

"Molly!" Elijah shouted, surprised at how muffled his voice was amid the trees. He was in the middle of a small dip of ground that seemed to be nearing the island's far end. It inclined again about ten feet ahead. Soon after that, he guessed, would be the end of the trees and the wide expanse of Spinner's Lake stretching northwest. "Molly, can you hear me? We should get going!"

But there was no response. Maybe she was nearer to the shore. The waves would surely be drowning out his voice.

"Molly, answer if you can hear me!" he shouted again, climbing quickly up the incline. Sure enough, through the trees about two hundred feet ahead was the sky. It was definitely darker than it had been before. "I'm coming to meet you on the back side of the island! Looks like it might rain!"

Still holding the cell phone, he trudged forth, faster with every step. If they had incorrectly judged the day's weather, they would have to forget Joshua Grime for the time being.

Elijah was about to call Molly's phone when he heard a stifled scream—a girl's.

"*No—*!"

It had come from beyond the trees, now only a hundred feet away.

Elijah pocketed his phone and began to run. The ground became a blur under his feet, but it was now littered with head-sized boulders threatening to trip him.

"Molly! Answer me! Are you okay?"

Still no answer.

Oh God, why would she have screamed? Why the hell *would she have screamed?*

Elijah saw her before the trees ended, and something looked altogether wrong. Someone else was with her, struggling.

"What—? Molly! What's going on—?"

He nearly stumbled on a rock just as the trees ended, but when he looked up after regaining his footing, a nightmare met his eyes. Damon Jacoby, in his Green Bay Packers jersey, was holding Molly from behind with his open pocketknife to her throat. He was glaring at Elijah in the escalating wind, standing against a billowing wall of gray-green thunderclouds.

2038

I T ALWAYS TOOK SMALL LIFE MOMENTS to inspire shreds of self-reflection in Winifred Flite, those instances of space and time between one action and another. Whether they preceded momentous decisions or occurred during fleeting glances of her own troubled eyes in the mirror, they came as flash-seconds when some underlying, gleaming significance about life could be glimpsed. One of those moments in particular had come last August, when she had been watching the news and suddenly seen a burning mushroom cloud from a distance, rising with eerie slowness over the beautiful, waterside city of Geneva, Switzerland. In every memory of that moment since, she had felt a touch of something bigger, a determination to help humanity be better. Even so, all she had to show for it now was this paltry attempt to make up for her past failures.

Tonight was Monday, August 2, a hot and humid summer night in Newport. Winifred was standing in the main-floor bathroom in the city hall building on Spring Street, wanting to lean forward against the sink in an anxious pose, hands on its porcelain sink, like people did in movies. But touching a public sink was disgusting; her hands would get contaminated with all types of germs. Worst of all, her life would be reduced to a Hollywood cliché.

Outside, on the city hall's front sidewalk and lawn, a crowd of reporters was waiting for her. In mere moments, she would walk out in her simple black Chanel dress, Jordan Alexander pearls, and white Manolo Blahniks and begin her FBI charade. The agents had assured her that surrounding them and barricading the protesters (all the usuals, including the gaunt Weston Carrow, she assumed) would be a sufficient number of local police officers. Inside, in the hallway just past the bathroom door, were three casually clad FBI agents she had never met before. Considering the assault on her house eight weeks ago, they had alerted Newport's finest to their presence only as it related to any potential terrorist threats. Winifred's newly hired publicist, Canary Dickens, hadn't questioned their presence at all, which made Winifred wonder if they had debriefed her on their intent behind tonight's operation.

Her ActoPhone rang. Jonathan's ring tone. She answered it with a short, breathy "Hi."

"Hi," he replied. Silence made of unspoken words hovered between them. Finally, Jonathan said, "Maybe disappearing would have been the better option, eh?"

Winifred smoothed her hair bun. "Tell me about it. Jesus."

"The mountains. That's where I'm going after this year in Rhode Island. Maybe Alaska."

Winifred gave her son an anxious chuckle. "Careful. Judge Wallace would be pissed. Unless talking about everything now somehow makes all the reporters shut up."

Sure. Fat chance.

"Any word from the agents about Jimmy?" Jonathan asked.

"Nothing. No idea. The agents know I'm aware of what's going on, but they haven't said a word. Afraid the wrong person might hear, I'm guessing."

Jonathan sighed. "You're sure you don't want me there? I can still leave now and be there in ten minutes. Sounder can drive."

"You don't want to stand next to me. I've been a shit mother to you," Winifred said. The anxiety in her chest made the words flutter as they left her mouth, and suddenly, tears welled in her eyes. Yes, she wanted Jonathan by her side more than anything, seeing as Dr. Thomas Lumen was back in Minnesota for the time being. She had nobody else. Would she ever tell her son this, though? Of course not. In the past two months, despite being generally confined to their house for his own safety, he had proven himself to be more attentive and caring than she had ever been in all of his eighteen years.

"I can stand in the back and at least be nearby," he pressed.

"What, with Weston Carrow and all the other religious lunatics? No, thanks. You're not leaving the house. Make sure Sounder is still with you."

Silence on Jonathan's end of the line. Despite everything, he was listening to her. He didn't have to speak to make it clear he agreed with her rationale.

A knock sounded through the bathroom door.

"Excuse me, Ms. Flite? Special Agent Dennis Knutson. I hate to interrupt, but we have a possible situation happening with Jimmy Barber."

"Hold on, Jonathan," Winifred said. Still holding her phone to her ear, she stood tall, sniffed back her tears, and reached for the door. When she was eye-to-eye with the special agent, she said, "What situation?"

"Looks like things changed. Rim appeared to be bluffing. Sounds like he thought it was a setup."

"And where's Jimmy?"

"Still driving in Providence. We're gauging the situation but just wanted to let you know, in case you want to cancel this. It may not be the distraction we were hoping for. Otherwise, they're ready for you out there." Agent Knutson closed the door, leaving Winifred alone with her phone.

She looked straight at the mirror, into her own tired eyes. It was the escape she had been hoping for. When she heard a rustle on Jonathan's end of the phone—a book page, probably—guilt fell back onto her heart, bringing to mind her typical tendency to choose the easier, less honorable roads. Perhaps Jonathan had heard Agent Knutson through the phone. Perhaps it didn't matter. The event was scheduled, and leaving now would only fan the flames of her humiliation. The fear of how she'd look if she were to cancel was suddenly stronger than her fear of what might happen if she didn't.

What was she going to tell the vultures? That her son had killed Ellen Graber because she herself had ignored his pleas to be heard and taken seriously? That he had become a key resource for the FBI in the worldwide Geneva bombing investigation? That he was proof of some universal psychological force that transcended death? Shaking in her smart black dress, Winifred raised the phone to her ear. "I should have just done this from a feed in our living room," she told Jonathan. Then, almost to herself, she added, "But no, they wanted a spectacle."

Through the phone came her son's sigh. "I'm not even sure the spectacle has started yet. Nobody is asking the right questions."

"Well, what *are* the right questions?" Winifred asked, edging uncomfortably close to one of her old-fashioned snaps. "What should I say to these idiots?"

"Maybe you should just go all out. Shake it all to hell."

Winifred's breath caught in her throat, and a flicker of courage sparked in her heart.

Shake it all to hell.

Without allowing herself to think further, she hung up her call with Jonathan and exited the bathroom. This was about him now. Not about Jimmy, not about the sting. This would be her own attempt to prove she had some gumption, not to mention a shred or two of value as a mother.

As Winifred walked slowly down the corridor toward the city hall's front doors, where she could already see media lights glaring in front of the sunset and through the textured glass windows, the moments passed as if they were all one. Her footsteps, sounding sharp under her white stilettos, resounded through the quiet hall like beats of a metronome measuring phantom shards of time. Just before a special agent named O'Farrell opened the door for her, she had a most potent sensation: that when all was said and done, the grand sum of her life would ultimately be measured not in time but in the things she did or did not do with it.

Unlike the frenzy following Jonathan's release at the Garrahy Judicial Complex in Providence, the reporters here were mostly silent as Winifred made her way outside and down to the second-to-last step from the sidewalk. There, Canary Dickens had constructed a podium for her, complete with a microphone. Two uniformed police officers were flanking it, one on either side, and one of the casually dressed FBI agents walked carefully behind her. Even the protesters, who were corralled on the hall's front lawn toward the street on the left, were conspicuously silent. Winifred scanned the crowd for Weston Carrow, but the lights were too bright for her to easily make out faces behind them. All she could distinguish was a general separation between the religion-based protesters and the ones wanting Jonathan off the streets.

She had prepared notes for a statement on her ActoPhone, which she now dug out of her black Saint Laurent Y Ligne clutch. She glanced down at the phone's screen and saw a paltry nine bullet points—topics she had struggled to come up with. The prospect of constructing an entire speech from them made her wonder why she hadn't run off to her Mykonos villa after all.

I just need to be me, she had to remind herself. *Show my true colors, whatever they are.*

"Good evening," she said.

Cameras flashed; video cameras of all sizes stared at her like black portals; reporters bristled with anticipation. Behind them, one of the protesters booed, and a few thoughtless copycats followed.

Winifred cleared her throat, then was amazed when words came to her almost effortlessly. "I understand my son has become a local sensation in recent years, first because of his juvenile brushes with violence and then because of the break-in and shootings at Crescent Rehabilitation Center last November. Most recently, people have expressed discomfort with his claims relating to a group of teenagers who disappeared in Minnesota in 2010. I'm here tonight to address these issues, and to defend my son."

The crowd of reporters erupted in a barrage of questions. Their rapaciousness hit Winifred with unexpected force, and she had to purse her lips in an attempt to make sense of the madness. She suddenly regretted not having Jonathan next to her. Or even

Jimmy Barber—surely he would have been better equipped to manage this frenzy.

"Excuse me, if you could just—"

They didn't stop. Winifred tried again, this time louder.

"I'm trying to communicate with you, so if you could please save your questions—"

Now the protesters in the back were booing and chanting "*Flite deserves the bite! Flite deservers the bite!*"

"*Will you all please shut up?*" Winifred screamed into the microphone, for the first time all evening harnessing the base reality of her personality. There it was, an optimal sound bite for the world, a perfect reprimand aimed at these gluttons for drama. They had already begun to flutter down to their perches.

"I wanted to take personal responsibility for my son's troubles and tell you all that it was my own oversight of his needs that led him to do the things he did when he was younger. Almost five years of intensive treatment and therapy have made it abundantly clear to me, his judge, and his caregivers that he is ready to integrate back into normal society. What I want to impress upon you today is the—"

"Ms. Flite!" a male reporter in the front row screamed. "Do you really think your son's violent tendencies have passed?"

"Seriously?" Winifred snarled into the microphone, glaring down at the brown-haired man. "You just asked me a question that I answered in my last sentence. Are you people really this stupid?"

Silence followed, and then another reporter, a woman, yelled out. "Winifred, could you please tell us the extent of your son's involvement with the FBI?"

Winifred scoffed, hiding behind her icy exterior just long enough to mentally review the specific lines she had run through with the agents. "You seriously won't get far with that question. It's the goddamned FBI. As far as I know, they simply had to inquire into last year's incident at Crescent Rehabilitation Center, because Paul Simpleton had a note in his pocket threatening more Christian terrorism on US soil. It looked like a copycat of Jean-Claude Apostol."

The answer was woefully incomplete, and the reporters seemed to know it. Some frowned, unsatisfied, and a few others shook their heads. Clamoring her way to the front row was a brown-haired woman in a horribly fitting lime-green suit.

"Winifred, my name is Lydia Clark, and I'm with *Providence Today*. I'm wondering if you can comment on the religious angle to this. Why do you think your son has attracted the attention of these copycat terrorists?"

Winifred had to think on her response, and when it came, her legs began shaking. She gently gripped the podium. "Because of what's in his head. The memories he has would pretty much prove a contradiction to everything these people think they know."

"The memories he *has*?" Lydia Clark continued. "Are you saying you believe his past-life memory claims are legitimate?"

Winifred froze. It was the question she had been dreading, the one whose answer Judge Wallace wanted to be addressed publicly. Even the protesters now seemed to be waiting with bated breath for her answer. And where was Weston Carrow? The answer to Lydia's question was what his two parishioners had bullet-bombed Winifred's house over. Did she dare bring it to the forefront?

Jonathan's words echoed in her mind.

Shake it all to hell.

"I have strong reason to believe my son has been telling the truth," Winifred said. "I didn't believe it until last year, when I was faced with proof I couldn't deny. I think if people were to really start paying attention to this and consider what it would imply about the nature of life, it'd shake things up on a massive scale. I know it did for me."

A sudden flash of red light caught Winifred's gaze. For a split second, it was as though her quivering eyes were looking straight down a blazing crimson shaft.

The reporters grew eerily silent for an unexpected, drawn-out moment, then exploded in an uproar. Some began gasping, and a few were screaming at Winifred, pointing at her chest. Winifred looked down. A small red dot was hovering over her sternum, jerking back and forth.

It was a laser pointer. Somebody was beaming it straight onto her.

At first, Winifred wondered why anybody would be doing something so silly, why they would be acting like some obnoxious university student trying to interrupt a professor's presentation. And then it hit her.

It's a laser sight for a gun.

Only when Special Agent O'Farrell had jumped on her, bringing her to the ground, and the police were running toward the source of the red laser, guns drawn, did Winifred see Weston Carrow. She could just make him out through an opening beyond O'Farrell's protective arm. The man was off to the unpatrolled left, bolting toward the city hall's front lawn from between two news vans parked on Bull Street. He had one arm extended and was carrying what Winifred at first thought must be a wooden crucifix. But something about its shape didn't look right, and the discrepancy shrieked in her mind when she realized his black jacket was far too bulky, as though he were wearing some sort of heavily adorned vest underneath it. Only then did Winifred realize he was holding a detonation device, not a crucifix. With Special Agent O'Farrell on top of her, shielding her head with his arms and holding her neck at the most twisted of angles, she wasn't even able to scream.

PART 6

SUNRISE

2038

J IMMY BARBER'S FOOT FELT LIKE JELLY as he lifted it off his BMW's gas pedal inside the cityside parking structure of Providence Place Mall. This was it, the failure of the FBI's feeble plan for a sting, and here he was, at the forefront of it all. He had indeed been followed into the parking garage by three undercover FBI agents, the same ones who had been driving both in front of him and behind him from Newport to Providence. Jimmy himself had made the executive decision to exit downtown and abandon the Swan Point Cemetery plan, to the dismay of Special Agent Ethan Prescott, who was forcefully feeding instructions through muted silences in his earpiece via a separate audio feed from Nicolas Rim's. Not only had it been clear that Rim had played them, but it was also obvious now that the FBI's plan to use Jimmy only as side bate, not live bate, had been fraught with holes.

"Jimmy, please turn your car around and exit the parking

ramp, or we'll have to stop you for your own safety," Agent Prescott said. "All we needed was a secure location for Rim, and we've isolated possible spots in the mall based on his audio feed. We already have SWAT units at every entrance and exit, and we can't allow you to do anything more." His voice muted yet again.

Jimmy's heart raced as he decided to call the FBI agent's bluff. If they were to apprehend him in the parking garage, it would show on his ActoVid feed and play straight into Nicolas Rim's eyes, giving away the sting completely. If it truly was important that they catch the man, they would let him through the ramp's entrance into Macy's. "You're in the main part of the mall?" Jimmy said aloud, for the agents' sake but also for Nicolas Rim to hear. "Maybe I'll just make it look like I'm doing a little shopping. Jonathan's mom's press thing probably just started."

Rim's deep, accented voice responded quickly through his earpiece, thankfully during a lull in Agent Prescott's audio feed. "You're a brave young man, doing this in the shadows. Pity we aren't meeting again under better circumstances."

"I'm eighteen. I can do whatever I want."

Rim let out a raspy chuckle. "Well, I need a three-sixty camera view before you enter the mall."

"Okay. And I'm near the Macy's entrance." Jimmy opened his BMW's door and stepped out, wondering how much like a movie it was all about to be. Would a band of black-clad SWAT team members rush him, seize him, and give their charade away?

Agent Prescott's voice sounded in his ear. "Jimmy, we're letting you go in. You'll be with three agents who are going to get behind you after you do your three-sixty. Allow them to catch up before you enter the mall. They're parked thirty feet away. We're going with this until there's any hint of where Rim might be, if he's here at all. We can't evacuate the mall, because it'll be too obvious, but we'll be monitoring everyone going in and out. Walk toward Macy's and try to get him to talk. We'll be surrounding you quietly on all sides and will interrupt his video the second it could compromise you. Just be prepared for it to happen fast."

With a faint rush of exuberance over this operation gone awry, Jimmy walked toward the Macy's entrance. To his surprise, Nicolas Rim didn't even need a prompt to start talking.

"Now, where are you, Mr. Barber?"

"Macy's, first floor," Jimmy said. The place was bustling with early-evening summer traffic—moms, babies in strollers, kids, old ladies, and teenagers probably pondering shoplifting the way Jimmy would have three years ago.

"Walk up two levels," Rim said.

Agent Prescott's voice sounded in Jimmy's wireless earpiece. "We've alerted mall security, and they're calling all the stores. Right now they only know it's a man who is illegally armed. We want to keep this quiet if at all possible. Keep walking upstairs so he knows you're coming. You have seven agents surrounding you."

Jimmy glanced around as naturally as possible and saw nobody of interest, not even the agents who had followed him inside. He walked past a middle-aged Macy's saleswoman behind the checkout counter in the kitchenware department. She had a phone pressed to her ear and was staring at Jimmy; her face was contorted in a stock-still grimace.

"Why is that woman staring at you?" Nicolas Rim asked in his ear.

A flutter reverberated from Jimmy's heart into his voice. "Not sure. Probably because I'm famous? I also tried to steal a watch from here once. I got arrested."

"She knew something was going on."

"Juvenile delinquents tend to freak people out."

They need him alive.

Again came Ethan Prescott's voice in Jimmy's ear. "Try to get a lock on Rim and get more info out of him if at all possible. You're still being watched from all sides. Still no visual on him."

"So, where are you?" Jimmy whispered, stepping off the escalator onto the third floor.

"Leave the store. Top floor exit. Back into the mall."

Where the people are.

Knowing this Macy's like the back of his hand, Jimmy spun around and walked toward the third-floor exit. When he stepped under the mall's massive, arched-glass ceiling, Nicolas said, "Continue forward, along the left side of the promenade. Toward the restrooms."

It was like a drug. The excitement. The racing heart. Jimmy was just about to step up his pace when Agent Prescott's voice rang through the earpiece, suddenly sounding even more tense than he had a minute before. "Jimmy, please stop where you are. We're taking you out of this. There's a situation at the press conference."

Jimmy's heart rushed with further adrenaline as he halted in his spot. Mixed with it now was dread. Had Jonathan shown up at the conference for some reason? Had he been hurt or killed?

"This may have just put you at risk," Agent Prescott continued. "We don't know enough details. Please walk straight to the escalator on your right. Follow the other shoppers."

"What do you mean?" Jimmy said aloud. Only after uttering the words did he realize Nicolas Rim could still hear him.

The suspect must have taken Jimmy's question as a delayed response to his directive, because just as Jimmy realized everyone's concentration had faltered, Rim said, "Turn to your right. Look across the railings. I'm sitting at one of the food court tables."

Jimmy stepped backward toward the public restroom entrance to avoid a mother and her three screaming children, who were heading toward the nearby glass elevator.

"Wait, Jimmy. Don't move. We have a visual," Agent Prescott said.

Jimmy saw Nicolas Rim a second after he heard the special agent's words, and just as a series of shrieks arose from a group of nearby mall patrons, a clamber of footsteps raced toward Jimmy from his left, right, and rear. As the swift FBI agents fell around him in a protective line, Jimmy saw others quietly surround Rim. They were holding submachine guns and dressed in olive-green SWAT vests and military helmets. From the fifty-foot distance, the man's appearance seemed strange, off-kilter. Then Jimmy realized why. Rim was indeed sitting at a table, by all standards calmly, except for one key difference. He seemed to be following through on his promise to die on his own terms, because he was holding a gun in his right hand, pointing it straight at his own head.

2005

ELIJAH, MOLLY, AND DAMON were standing at the edge of a cliff that was even higher than the one on the island's southeast side, at least twenty feet off the lake. Damon said nothing, and his eyes were wide, raging, bloodshot. Molly, white as a ghost and now holding her neck as still as possible under the boy's knife, was whimpering with tears in her eyes.

The air went from summery warm to blustery cold. In the distance, the water of Spinner's Lake had taken on a dirty, gray-green hue, and the wind was creating spinning, circular patterns on its surface. In the sky behind Damon and his hostage, the clouds were dark green on the horizon, almost black, blowing in from the northwest at harrowing speed. One raindrop hit Elijah's nose, then another. Lightning snaked across the sky, and its thunderous boom followed almost immediately. To finalize the nightmare, a patch of low gray clouds was already starting to spin over the center of the lake.

A tornado, Elijah thought. *This can't be happening.*

"Don't you remember?" Damon screamed over the wind, his face contorting in so much anger that it looked as if he were about to burst into tears from the weight of it. "*I'm following you in my head*. I knew you were at the grocery store, and I knew you were coming here!"

"Let Molly go right now!" Elijah screamed, stumbling forward. Another bolt of blinding lightning pierced the lake in front of them.

"What, you think you can tell me what to do?" Damon roared. "You're going to get what's been coming to you, faggot! And she's going to get it first, because she got in my way. And I think she even got in my head, because when I look at her I see flashes of all this crazy shit! I can't close anything off anymore!"

"Well, maybe you could try to—"

"Do you realize what's *right under us*?" Damon said. "I've seen it in my dreams. I can't get it out of my head. All because of *you*. I know you've been looking for it!"

Elijah didn't know what Damon meant by this. All he could do was scream and hope the bully would see reason. "We could die out here! That lightning just struck the water, and the storm's coming toward us! Let her go!"

Just then, a tornado siren began wailing in the distance.

"You think I *care*?" Damon said. "You two are going to die no matter what, and if I do, too, nobody'll give a damn. I already snuck away from my aunt and uncle against the judge's orders. I'll be in deep crap for that. But there's something wrong with me anyway. I don't know how to turn it off." The older boy's face had twisted into something so eerily recognizable that Elijah had to blink twice to see it properly. It was agony, so intense that it finally exposed Damon's devilish malice for what it was—a symptom, not a cause.

"Let her go!" Elijah screamed again.

Molly, rigid but motionless in Damon's grip, was staring at Elijah with wide, hopeless eyes. Her gaze flitted to his pocket and back with a motion that would be invisible to Damon.

Your cell phone. Call the police.

But Damon will see me grabbing!

Who cares? Try!

Elijah stood stock-still for a moment, then dug into his pocket with fierce speed. If he could open the flip phone, dial 911, and click "send" before Damon realized what he was doing, there might be a chance.

But Damon had seen it.

"Throw it over the edge, or I'll cut her throat!"

Truth glared in Damon's eyes. Whatever humanity was left in him, it was hiding, perhaps for good. He wouldn't hesitate to kill Molly.

"Fine! Don't hurt her! Take me instead, but let her go!" Elijah threw his cell phone like a baseball, and whatever splash it made in the water below was swallowed by the storm. The raindrops were falling in faster succession now, and the sky was darker than any afternoon Elijah had ever seen. Somewhere in the distance, in End Haven or perhaps at the airport, the tornado siren was blaring, up and down, up and down.

"Ha, now you're screwed," Damon sneered. "And heck, we don't need her anymore—"

For a split second, it seemed as if he were going to let Molly go. Just as he loosened his grip, however, he grabbed her shoulders and spun her around. In one nightmarish movement, he pushed her off the cliff. Elijah's view of Molly as she floated in the air seemed to stop in time. Her head was turned up toward him in a crestfallen expression. Nothing had prepared her for the reality that she might actually die today. With a scream lost on the wind, she fell out of sight, splashing somewhere below them.

"No!" Elijah screamed, lunging at Damon. "There's lightning—!"

But Damon had jumped toward Elijah, his brandished knife dancing with his swiping arm.

"Elijah!" Molly screamed, dreadfully far away, lost in the churning lake. There were waves now, and they were crashing against the side of the island.

Elijah's mind raced. *I've got to go down and help her, or she's going to die. Oh God, this wasn't supposed to happen—*

"It's time for you to die, faggot!" Damon's knife flew with shocking closeness to Elijah's eyes. Elijah ducked out of the way yet again, getting a good handhold against Damon's back. He pushed the bully as hard as he could, using whatever power his foothold lent him. The maddened boy flailed to the ground. "Oh, you're going to get it now," he said, trying to right himself.

They changed places in the scuffle, and now Elijah was only two feet from the cliff's edge. He took these seconds of momentary freedom to look over it, toward Molly's screaming voice. She was floating up and down with the water, doing her best to paddle in the growing waves.

And there it was. Hope.

Twenty feet to the right, cut perfectly into the island's sheer edge, was a cave.

Before he could point to it, Damon was charging.

Go. There's no other option. You'll be dead either way.

Just as a new and horrifically close vine of lightning twirled across the black clouds, Elijah jumped.

The water hit him like an icy slap to the face. There was no time even to judge its temperature; he had to get to Molly, had to get her to the cave before any lightning hit the water. It was their only chance, because now Damon had the high ground. Elijah could only hope the cave had a dry floor inside.

Five feet away, Molly was fighting the water for her own breath. The waves were larger than Elijah had ever seen. He stole a glance toward the horizon, across the raging water. Something was falling slowly from the clouds, something long and gray, picking up water in its spiral.

"Tornado!" Elijah tried to scream at Molly. "We've got to get to that cave! That way!" He bobbed in the water, pointing. Molly nodded, but the water was growing too powerful. She was getting dangerously close to the rocky cliff face. Elijah swam for his life to save Molly's. Each foot he gained on her seemed impossibly stretched out, but after what felt like an eternity, his left hand scrunched her wet T-shirt. He kicked and paddled with his free arm using as much power as he could muster.

The cave was only ten feet away now. With a final burst of adrenaline, Elijah reached its edge and pulled Molly through. The waves were pouring in, and he puffed with relief when the cave's dark ceiling swallowed his view of the rabid sky. His feet had not yet touched the lake's bottom, however, and if he lost strength now, the waves would drown him. "Come on, Molly!" he screamed. "Swim! Go to the back! Get out of the water if you can!"

Ten feet in, Elijah's feet hit ground. His eyes had not yet adjusted to the darkness, and only dim outlines of large stones sitting on the cavern's pale, glistening shoreline were visible. But it was land, and getting out of the water before lightning struck was all that mattered now. He grabbed Molly and pulled.

Just as they cleared the water, a bolt struck at deafeningly close proximity to the cave's mouth. It lit the rear of the small cavern, which was larger than it had first appeared.

"Get back!" Elijah choked, coughing up the last of the water in his lungs. "Get as far from the water as you can!"

"I'm out, I'm out!" Molly said in a weak voice. "God, Elijah, he just came out of *nowhere*. He said he hasn't been able to get this place out of his head—"

"It's okay, it's okay! You're going to be all right!"

Molly nodded, then coughed with a gagging bob of the head. "He snuck up on me from behind and then pushed his hand against my mouth right after I turned around and saw him."

"I heard you scream," Elijah said. "I was in the woods, and I think I saw him. And . . . God . . ." He shook his head at his own stupidity. "I thought he was the person with the green truck. I couldn't see him clearly."

"He *was* the person with the green truck," Molly croaked. "He told me when he was dragging me toward the cliff. He stole it from his uncle. He said he knew exactly where we were going."

"Damn it!" Elijah said. "What the *hell* did we come here for? We should have known to just leave it alone!"

"Quiet!" Molly said. "Stop yelling! The last thing we need is for him to jump in after us. But I think we could take him if he did."

Elijah wiped away water that was dripping from his hair and down his forehead. "He's not going to jump in the water, not with that lightning."

"*You* did, though."

"Yeah, well, *you* could have drowned, and I saw the cave, and Damon was charging me with the knife. We both would have gone over the cliff when he hit me if I hadn't jumped first."

Molly only shivered in response. She grabbed into her pocket and pulled out her cell phone. She flipped it open, but its screen was black, dead from water damage.

Even if the weather were to clear and they could swim out, Damon Jacoby would likely be waiting for them. It was doubtful he would go back to End Haven without making sure they were dead, because it was obvious they would call the police the first chance they got. This had been far worse than the knife assault on Lemon Avenue, and Elijah was sure it could land Damon in juvenile detention for a serious amount of time.

"I left the trail mix in the bag on my bike," was all Molly said next.

Suddenly hungry, Elijah sat back on the dry rocks and closed his eyes. With horror, he saw that the only image his mind could muster was one of Cynthia Foster's Death card, that smiling skeleton riding its terrible horse.

2010

T O WALK IN THE MOUNTAINS: Was there anything better, more freeing? Cynthia Foster thought not. Because she had spent most of her life in Minnesota (and this was the first time she had ever experienced such a walk), the thought was unexpected and new. It was Thursday, September 9, and she was tramping behind Frank Brennin on the Lazy Mountain trail, a hike he promised was short but strenuous—"worth the steep grade and potential heart attack," in his words. The air was cold, in the forties, and clouds had begun rolling in. The forecast had promised snow around nightfall. Cynthia's legs burned from the effort of the hike, and her body was sweating underneath her jacket. Yet the exhilaration of being surrounded by nature—or by God?—made every breath worthwhile.

"Almost a third of the way up," Frank said. "We can rest on that bench. See there?" He pointed upward and ahead, near what appeared to be a break in the trees. "After that it starts getting pretty. You'll be able to see a bunch of different peaks—Matanuska, Pioneer, Twin Peaks. I think you'll like it."

"Do you ever stop noticing how beautiful it all is?" Cynthia said. "I'm starting to think I don't want to go back to flat old Minnesota. I want a place where I can wake up and be excited about life."

"That's what it's all about," Frank said, slowing and turning to wait for Cynthia as they approached the bench. "Enjoying the moment. If you're not doing that, what's the point?" They reached the bench, and the wind was now whipping them through the thinning trees. Up ahead was the dome of a hill and the tease of mountain peaks beyond. "Do you want to sit?" Frank asked.

Cynthia took a long, deep breath of the cool mountain air. Memories from the week sprinkled over her in a way that made her think of raindrops on a watercolor, small drips washing away her life in Idle County. Somehow, on a level of herself she recognized only distantly, this felt acceptable, as though it were a natural progression. Life had never been simple for Cynthia. Even before losing her husband and only son, she had also lost both her notoriously promiscuous mother, Sandra Jean, to a heart attack and her younger sister, Sara, to a heroin overdose. On the day she found Sara dead in bed, drowned in her own vomit, Cynthia had known her family's legacy of being "untouchable" in Idle County would either follow her forever or perhaps chase her out. Only in the past few days had she realized the latter might be a blessing.

"Let's keep on," she said to Frank, gesturing with her head past the bench, toward the break in the trees. They continued hiking. Her heart was beating fast as the trail around her opened up to the rocky tundra, and within minutes, she was surrounded by a whipping, cold wind and snowcapped mountains. September had never been so beautiful.

The trail had lost its steep grade, and now the incline diminished as it grew rockier and the summit neared. To Cynthia's left and right, the mountain dipped downward toward the valley. Far below, Palmer glistened in the last of the afternoon's sun, but a mass of dark gray clouds was approaching from the west, over the valley—the snow scheduled for that evening.

Gunshots came during a silent moment when the only sounds between Frank and Cynthia were crunches of gravel under their feet and the low breath of the wind. At first, when the initial shot rang out, Cynthia didn't know what was happening. A hole appeared in Frank's back, first dry, then bleeding, then gushing with a gory viciousness that looked like something out of a movie. Then came another shot, followed by a sting on the rear side of Cynthia's right shoulder and pain so savage that her only method of coping, all automatic, was to imagine her mind jumping out of her body, to focus on the sudden shock as if she were a spectator. Her point of view hovered between her eyes' view and an outside view as Frank fell in front of her, his heavy boots tipping to the right, off his rocky footing.

He was my angel of death, Cynthia thought to herself, and then she was stumbling toward him as another bullet zipped by her ear, miraculously missing her and zealously bringing to her mind's forefront the knowledge that this was it; this was the end, and somehow it was permissible. Her son, the only family she was lucky enough to have in the last five years, was dead, and this man, Frank Brennin, the only person who had since begun to promise her a life filled with love, was dying in front of her, rolling diagonally off the trail and stopping on the slope of the Lazy Mountain.

Cynthia, somehow still standing (but aware of time beginning to slow), looked down at the exit wound on the top right side of her chest. The vision was explosive to her eyes, a black feast of mutilation and surrender. Somewhere in the mess, her right breast, so recently touched and appreciated by Frank, was blown open and hanging in tatters. She flickered out of her body, seeing herself lurching toward Frank, then flickered back in. Sinking down next to him, she used all her energy to turn him over, into her lap. He was gasping for air, but then he coughed when a spurt of her blood splashed onto his face and into his mouth.

The snow was approaching. The sun had finally disappeared behind the approaching clouds sailing on the wind over Palmer and the Matanuska River below. Every speck of wet blood touching Cynthia's bare skin was freezing.

Through his heaves and coughs, Frank was trying to speak. At first it was gibberish, and he was repeating it over and over. Finally, as her own light-headedness gave way to a feeling of glorious euphoria, she made out the words "*Hunting rifle.*"

It had all happened so fast that none of it yet made any outward sense.

Were we the hunted? Cynthia thought, forcing herself to stay upright, to shift her position so that she wouldn't bleed further onto Frank's face. It was like a movie, except she was the camera, and this was life—the very end of it. The drama of it all, every little moment and interaction and feeling, had mattered in more ways than even the grand, endless universe could contain. She realized now that her life, even the losses and the blunders and the moments spent learning from them, had been of value.

She was holding Frank, forcing herself to remain in her own body until he had left his. She saw him now for everything he was.

On levels of consciousness she was only now beginning to glimpse once again, they had decided upon this series of events. The road of probabilities leading to this particular moment would someday matter; it had been part of their reason for being alive. They had come into the world to help change it, and this very event was their bowing out after a job well done. She could see now that while her call to the Idle County Sheriff's Department about Maximilian Pope would never amount to a thing, her call to Alice Winterblume at WCMP news in Wind Prairie would. Years from now, when this violent death would be forgotten by all but a few, it would matter. It would mean something.

"I love you, even for this little while," Cynthia whispered to Frank over and over as his breath sputtered on his own blood. He was choking on it, but there was nothing she could do but turn him on his side. Blood rushed out of him onto the cold, rough mountainside. The clouds rolled over them, and while Cynthia's physical senses were beginning to combine more potently with what she had always considered during life to be her "deeper senses," she felt the first of the night's snowflakes hit her cheek.

Once Cynthia finally decided to leave her body, it was as easy as blinking. What had once been the sensations of sight, sound, taste, smell, and touch were now single shades of a much wider gamut of experience, one that immediately felt familiar. In an instant, she knew exactly what had happened to lead to her death. She saw all the links in the chain of choices and interactions: her trip to Palmer, the security camera in Max's house, the imposter posing as Max. As of yesterday morning, the man had been equipped (because of her appearance on the security video five days before) with a GPS tracking device in his pocket to place under her rental car if she were to return to the house and he could find a chance. Cynthia had then demanded to drive her rental car to the Lazy Mountain trailhead this morning, in an effort to acclimate herself to Alaska and show Frank she was capable. It was all so silly, because while their deaths would someday look frightfully planned and calculated to outsiders, they were truly now a result of last-minute planning and cunning improvisation, all in a frantic effort to cover up what had happened to the Idle County Seven.

Victor Zobel.

It was all Victor Zobel. He was, Cynthia now saw, a man of many faces.

The game was already in motion, and as measured by earthly experience and history, Cynthia had been a sacrificial pawn well forfeited. When she turned and focused on what came next, she rushed forward without looking back, joyous to be returning home once again.

2038

Nicolas Leandro Rim's mother, Genevieve, sometimes used to say to him, in her native French, "Arrête
tes bêtises!", which translated in English to "Stop this
foolishness!" He had typically been a calm and happy child; that is,
until unexpected aspects of life latched onto his emotions—usually
nebulously developed needs to do certain things or be certain ways
or have certain objects. When these inexplicable emotions developed, he would explode in temper tantrums or become incredibly
sad, feeling as though the world were falling in on his shoulders.
Rarely since transitioning to life in America had happiness balanced these other emotions out. No regular bursts of elation, no
tingles of excitement, no thrill to be alive—only a constant plod
forward through Victor Zobel and Larry Kane's web of crime, toward what had become this inevitable cliff and deadly jump.

Here at Providence Place Mall in Rhode Island, his world was dissolving. It was, quite literally, becoming a veil of reality that filled his five senses but no longer held sway over him, because he was one trigger finger away from bowing out forever and erasing himself from Earth's context. Or was he simply erasing his context from Earth? He had no idea, because life and death were enigmas he had only recently developed a temptation to understand.

"Get these people out of here!" Nicolas yelled as the SWAT team members surrounded him. He pressed the gun's muzzle to his temple, fighting to keep his sweating hand from shaking. "Please. I don't want to hit anybody when I pull the trigger!"

Time had stopped, and Nicolas watched with unexpectedly slow clarity—both through his eyes and through Jimmy Barber's continuing ActoVid feed—as the police scrambled to direct mall traffic toward the escalators and exits with an ear-splitting megaphone. At the same time, they formed a protective barrier around Jimmy Barber, who was simply standing there, watching everything with a dumbfounded expression.

Suddenly, the boy's ActoVid feed went black, causing the video frame to disappear from Nicolas's lens display. Jimmy and the agents were a hundred feet away, across the walkway linking the two sides of the mall's food court area.

Nicolas could almost feel the police weapons trained on his head, neck, and back. He had indeed jumped off the cliff, and now the softness of the fall surrounded him, despite what was sure to be a final crash at the bottom.

Somewhere inside the chaos he had just created, amid the fleeing mall patrons, a male voice was yelling at Nicolas through the megaphone, telling him to drop his weapon, that all these people were indeed federal agents, and that he was now under arrest. Except he wasn't under arrest yet, was he? Because they hadn't said his name aloud, and they hadn't named his crime. It appeared they wanted to keep him a secret from the public, which meant he had at least one important shred of power. He had information these federal agents wanted, and because they hadn't shot him yet, he knew they were aware of his advantage.

The maelstrom of thoughts battering Nicolas's mind failed to throw anything coherent into his consciousness. He was operating on instinct now, trusting that the words forming on his lips were the right ones, that they would lead him in the right direction.

"I want to speak with Jimmy Barber," Nicolas yelled to the agents. "I know you have weapons pointed at me, but I want privacy, or else I'll kill myself now. That means no ActoLenses for Jimmy. I want to help you, but those are my terms." His finger teased the gun's trigger with the slightest bit of pressure, and what shocked him was the lack of sensation in his body—no shivers, no tingles of exhilaration, just a blank feeling of surrender.

He waited. He watched. He saw the FBI agents fit Jimmy with a bulletproof vest and make him extract the ActoLenses from his eyes. Then they surrounded the teenage boy again. Surely they were hiding a microphone on him somewhere or setting up a long-range one to record the exchange. Perhaps it didn't matter. Nicolas could cover his lips from being read, or he could whisper, or he could simply realize he had purposefully walked into a corner with no further choices. Maybe showing himself at face value now was the only way toward that final relief from his life gone so, so wrong.

Footsteps behind Nicolas, falling away.

SWAT team members retreating, giving him space.

"We're sending him to your table," came the FBI voice over the megaphone.

When the comically small Jimmy Barber emerged from the

swarm once again, drowning in his newly donned Kevlar vest, Nicolas's breath caught in his throat. The young man was smaller than some fifteen-year-olds Nicolas had met, and he walked toward the table with less confidence than he conveyed on television. When he was just twenty feet away, Nicolas pushed the gun extra hard against his own head and said, "The excitement you crave—does this qualify?"

Instead of answering the question, Jimmy's first words were: "I didn't have a choice when you first messaged. I was with Jonathan at his house, and he made me call the FBI right away."

"Would it have made a difference if you had kept the messages a secret?"

Jimmy shrugged. "It might have, yeah. But Jonathan's my friend. He comes first."

They sized each other up with red faces and racing hearts. Nicolas could see Jimmy's lips trembling, his skinny cheekbones vibrating, and his entire demeanor adjusting to his choice to approach the table.

"I'm surprised they let you speak with me."

"Like I said, I can do what I want. And I'm pretty sure they'll use anybody they can to get what they need. Did you know Winifred Flite's press conference just got bombed? This all just got way damned bigger."

"It's nowhere near as big as it's going to be," Nicolas whispered. Instead of saying something snarky, Jimmy simply waited for him to continue. The boy was paler than usual, trembling. "Tell me," Nicolas said, "do you believe Jonathan Flite is telling the truth about his memories? And don't lie. You're not a good liar."

Jimmy continued to sit in stone-still silence for five seconds. Hesitation. "I don't know," he finally said. "He knew you were Little Nick."

Nicolas nodded. "That's what Jillian Pope used to call me. In English." Jimmy flinched as Nicolas raised his free hand to remove the headphones from his ears, still holding the gun to his right temple with the other. "Let me ask you this, then, Mr. Barber. If Jonathan Flite's memories are real, who do you think would be most frightened of their implications? As in, that consciousness somehow survives death?"

"Scientists, I guess. The religious whack jobs would probably just say, 'Told you so, fuckers,' and then kill everybody to prove it."

Nicolas couldn't help but grin. This was the Jimmy Barber he had hoped to meet, even though whatever had just happened at the press conference—a bombing, had Jimmy said?—seemed to have shaken him to his very core. How strange it was to think that this was the boy in the third-floor hall who had come out to inspect the commotion at Crescent Rehabilitation Center last November, in the middle of the night, just feet away from Nicolas's flying bullets. Jonathan Flite had screamed for Jimmy to get back to his room, because Nicolas had a gun. The memory played through Nicolas's mind in a shrieking, minor key.

"So, why am I here?" Jimmy asked.

Nicolas's answer began in a whisper but gradually grew louder. "I'm almost a hundred percent certain Victor Zobel is frightened of Jonathan Flite. I also believe he orchestrated an entire terrorist attack in Geneva to cover up one little meeting of physicists. He has a network of contacts at the Grand port maritime de Marseille, which I believe is where Jean-Claude Apostol's nuclear weapon was smuggled into France. I can name two of his contacts there. I don't know the previous path of the weapon, but I do know Victor's network extends to Turkish ports in Istanbul and Iskenderun, one in Zadar, Croatia, and one in Yevpatoriya, Ukraine."

Jimmy's eyes glazed over for a moment, as if he were listening to some directive, and then uncertainty—perhaps even a shred of terror—flickered in his gaze. "Why the hell are you telling me this? What does it all have to do with Jonathan?"

"I think what Jonathan remembers is real. I don't know how, but it is. The thing linking all this together is that place. Idle County."

"Meaning?"

"Meaning Victor Zobel is hiding something there. I know it, because I've run errands in that forest they call the Moon Woods." The gun in Nicolas's hand began trembling again, and from his finger came an involuntary burst of pressure that was almost enough to set off the gun's hammer. A bead of sweat dripped into his eye despite the mall's air-conditioning, and it stung as he tried to blink it away. "There's a house, but there's something else under it," he whispered. "Some sort of research center. I've seen doctors, lab technicians, and a bunch of people on Victor's private payroll who would never admit to being there. I've even driven vans full of Eastern European girls across the country. They think they're coming to America to be brides, but I bring them there, and they disappear."

Jimmy Barber's expression fluttered with an array of emotions he probably hadn't been expecting. Yes, oh yes, it was all much darker than he could possibly know.

"What I mean to say here," Nicolas continued, "is that all this links back to Victor's forest. Whatever he's hiding there, he's been killing people to keep it a secret. And I think that place has been hiding secrets for a very long time."

2005

"E<small>LIJAH, WAKE UP.</small>"

Someone was nudging him.

"Wake up!"

It was Molly Butler's voice. When he opened his eyes, it was unnaturally dark. He shifted his weight, and his clothes were cold on his skin.

The cave.

He was wet, and he was stuck in a cave with Molly.

She was tapping his shoulder with fair force, talking to him in a low voice. "Elijah, come look. Seriously, get up."

He groaned and turned his neck. Thunder rumbled from beyond the cave mouth. "How long has it been?"

"I don't know. My phone is dead. I'm guessing about two hours. I tried to sleep a little, too, but I couldn't tune out the thunder. It's still crazy out there."

"I saw a tornado coming out of the clouds," Elijah said. "Just before we swam into the cave."

Molly nodded, her pale face barely visible in the low light. "We're lucky we didn't get electrocuted. But come here. Come look at this."

Elijah got to his feet, hating the icy feel of wet clothes rubbing his clammy skin. They seemed barely to have dried in the cave's humidity, but at least the ground was far back enough to keep out the blowing rain. His eyes were now adjusting to what light was coming in from outside. "How far back does the cave go?" he asked Molly.

"Farther than it looked at first. And—" She stopped, as if wondering how best to formulate her next words.

"Yeah? What's back there?"

Molly took a deep breath, then shuddered it out. "I think I found a tombstone."

"A *what?*"

"A tombstone," she repeated. "And I think we found Mr. Grime. Damon was right. I think he actually did know. Can you see enough to walk?"

The floor was made mostly of basketball-sized rocks, but their curves were just visible from the light coming through the cave's mouth. "I can see," he said.

Molly was already ten feet ahead of him, barely more than a gray silhouette. They made their way slowly across the gradually ascending ground. "Do you remember reading about the graves they found in the Moon Woods?" she asked. "I saw an article last September saying they were all numbered. Apparently, that Simon Villard priest guy painted numbers on rocks and marked the graves with them. I think he did it here, too."

They had just stepped onto a flat clearing where no rocks lay in the way of their feet. The dirt underneath them was dry and old, barely disturbed. By the look of it, this was the end of the cave. Molly pointed toward the ground. Elijah knelt down and squinted, forcing his eyes to register the large stone that sat in the middle of the clearing. Sure enough, the writing on it was almost bright, considering the darkness of the cave: a large **62** scrawled in chipped white paint. It looked molded with age.

It took a moment for Molly to speak again. "Should we dig?"

Flashes of Damon Jacoby dashed through Elijah's mind, and an unexpected burst of anger flared in his heart. "How can you be ready to start digging for a skeleton?" he said. "You just had a knife held to your throat!" Molly was barely visible, but Elijah saw her face harden. Even so, it didn't stop him from pouring out everything that had been festering during his agitated sleep. "Damon Jacoby might still be up there, and we're stuck in this cave until we can swim out, and even then, we don't have phones to call anyone to pick us up! We almost just died, and you're still thinking about that stupid jawbone!"

"It's *not* just the jawbone!" Molly shouted back, suddenly crying. "I know we almost just died! My dad is probably crazily worried about me by now, because we didn't even tell Sabrina or Selma where we were going! Besides, *you're* the one who found that jawbone and wanted to figure out who it belonged to!"

"Yeah, well—!"

"So, as long as we're stuck here, we might as well dig. That was the whole point of this, so maybe we're lucky Damon followed us!"

"Lucky in a *twisted* way," Elijah said with a cold, angry grunt.

"Well, there's still lightning out there, and I don't know when it's supposed to clear up," Molly snapped. "I'm not just going to sit here and worry. You can either help me or not. I want to find Mr. Grime either way, because he shouldn't still be missing after all these years."

There was a delicacy in Molly's voice Elijah couldn't ignore. She had been friends with Joshua Grime's wife, and knowing that the old woman had suffered the unsolved disappearance of her husband gave Molly reason enough to be emotional about this. But why was he—Elijah Bryce—here? To help Molly make her dear, dead friend happy? After a few seconds of pessimism, however, he considered this: he had risked his life to save Molly. She had become an important enough friend that he hadn't even thought twice. She had, it seemed, helped him grow up.

With a sigh, he said, "Okay, let's dig. If we find anything, we can leave it here for the police, once we get out of here."

Molly knelt beside him almost immediately. "I've already found some flat rocks to help us clear away the dirt."

"You're way too into this," Elijah said with a trace of dark amusement.

Through the darkness, Molly's expression remained flat. There was still shock under the determination on her face. She hadn't forgotten Damon Jacoby's knife. "Come on. Help me," she said.

Elijah started hacking away at the dirt. It was dry only down to five inches. Deeper, it was damp and firmly packed. He wondered what a real found skeleton might look like. Would things have eaten away at it, or would the ground have preserved it?

After just five minutes, his digging stone slid against something long and curved. It loosened a bit in the dirt from the force of his scooping motion. "Molly, I hit something."

"Oh God, where?" she asked, her voice quieter than he would have expected.

Elijah hesitated a moment, then stuck his finger into the dirt. Sure enough, something hard slid along it as he clawed the damp earth away.

"I think it's a bone," he said. A surreal series of thoughts followed. *This used to be a person. A breathing, walking person.*

"You're sure?"

Elijah pressed the rest of his fingers into the dirt and pulled. They hit another foreign object; it, too, slackened with his touch. "Yeah, here's another one. It's got to be a rib. They're curved in rows."

"Oh my God . . ."

"Help me keep digging. Let's find the skull and see if it has a missing jawbone."

Bright and loud cracks of lightning found their way into the cave as Elijah and Molly dug. Outside, pouring drops of rain pummeled the water of Spinner's Lake. It was not letting up, and now the sky appeared to be getting darker.

"You sure I was sleeping for only two hours? It looks like it's getting late already."

"I don't know; I might have fallen asleep, too," Molly replied between heavy plunges into the dirt. They had unearthed the entire rib cage.

"Either that, or the weather is getting worse."

They worked in silence for a long time; at one point, Elijah allowed himself to smile at the ridiculousness of their situation. There they were, two not-even-teenagers stuck in a cave, digging up a long-lost dead body. However fake and crazy all of this seemed, however, Damon Jacoby was as real as ever, and whatever it was about Idle County that made people "see things," it had just driven him insane.

"Look!" Molly called out.

Elijah had become almost hypnotized by the repetitive digging motions. Molly was farther up on her side of the skeleton, and there, the skull was now protruding from the ground. It was smaller than he would have expected, but not altogether different than the human bones he had seen at the Wind Prairie Science Museum.

"Elijah, hurry up! Do your side!"

He upped his pace, and ten minutes later, they had their answer. It was indeed a skull minus a jawbone, like that of a person who once had a giant overbite. Seeing these bones without a true face brought a sudden twist to Elijah's heart. This man had died an awful death, and that psychotic priest had purposefully ripped off his jawbone to play some sick game with the townspeople of Idle County. There was nothing fun or interesting about it, and a desire for justice now drove Elijah. Joshua Grime deserved to be unearthed. His jawless skull stared up at them, unable to smile like the Death card's horse-riding skeleton but still looking unfathomably similar.

Molly broke through his wandering thoughts. "Let's finish digging out the whole thing. That way, the police won't have so much of a job to do."

Trying to flush away the depressing situation Damon had pushed them into, Elijah said, "Yeah, if we ever get out of here."

Out of the corner of his eye, he noticed Molly's spirits sink again. In a quiet voice, she said, "Well, *I'm* going to finish digging."

This time, Elijah didn't object. He walked back over the rocks, toward the faint, greenish opening of the cave mouth. When he reached the darkened shoreline, he sat, hanging his muddy hands over his bent knees.

The lake's seething water gurgled its echoing tales on the cave walls. From the back came the continuous sounds of Molly's digging.

THE HOURS TICKED BY, and the lake outside was still swelling. Waves continued to crash, and as night fell, nearly all illumination dwindled, save for occasional bolts of lightning that were blinding despite being visible only through the cave opening. It seemed as if the storm that rose during their encounter with Damon had only been the first; the weather itself was moving in surges now, as if multiple storm systems were slowly crashing across Idle County, one after another. Elijah's stomach was in pain from hunger.

"We've got to get out of here," he groaned.

Molly, who had finished unearthing Joshua Grime's skeleton, was washing her hands in the lake with ceremonious care. "Yeah, we're going to have to figure something out," she said in a quiet voice, making no effort to speed up her process but being careful to dip her hands in the water only when lightning seemed unlikely. "Since we have to wait, though, can I ask you something?"

"Sure," Elijah muttered.

"Why do you think all this happened? It all just seems so . . ."

"Crazy?"

"Yeah. But at the same time, it seems funny that we found each other and that you've seen things, too. How could it all have worked out this way?" From outside came a burst of lightning and distant thunder. Molly yanked her hands out of the lake.

"Careful," Elijah advised. "And I don't know. I keep thinking about the tarot reading. That Death card sort of came true in a million different ways. Well, except nobody has died, assuming you don't stick your hands in the water at the wrong time."

Molly sighed. "Wasn't fate a part of it?"

Elijah shifted his weight on the uncomfortable rocks. Even so, it was better than lying on the flat dirt next to the skeleton. "That's what Cynthia said in her letter. She said the card meant that I might be tangled up in a 'matter of fate,' or something even bigger. Everything was going to change, apparently."

Molly fanned her hands off in the air and sat next to Elijah. "Do you believe in that type of thing?"

Elijah thought for a moment. "Well, I don't like the idea that something else is controlling everything I do, just so I end up being in the right place at the right time. That's sort of what fate means, right?"

"Yeah, pretty much."

"Then no. I don't. Doesn't make sense. I think we all do whatever we choose to do and then deal with what happens because of it."

"That's how I see it, too," Molly said. "Which is why I'm wondering about the ghosts. That's the part I can't figure out. I don't even know if we'll be *able* to figure it out. Like . . . what any of that stuff has to do with real life or whatever. But I know they're real."

"I would have thought I was crazy without you here to tell me I'm not," Elijah said. "After seeing whatever I saw that morning on the paper route, I'm starting to think maybe whatever's making it happen for us is also doing it to Damon. Maybe he doesn't know how to deal with it either."

"Do you think he's seen things, too?"

"Either that or . . . psychic stuff. Enough to make him think he's crazy."

"Last year, when I saw my first ghost, my mom had just died," Molly said. "It affected *everything*. I really did think I was crazy. I know how that feels."

Elijah shrugged. "Why do you think it happens so much around here?"

"No idea," Molly said. "But all that weird stuff from last summer—like, the priest guy who killed Joshua Grime? Seemed like he had similar stuff going on, too. Too bad nobody studies stuff like that."

Elijah thought of Victor Zobel's *In God We're Dust* and how the man would positively hate anyone who tried to reconcile such pseudoscience with credible scholarship. "I wonder how anybody even could," he said.

Molly remained silent. After watching the darkening cave mouth for nearly five minutes, she said, "Gosh, I need some food." Elijah heard her stomach rumble. The rain had let up only in short intervals, however, and lightning continued to brighten the rocky chamber every few minutes.

Hours passed.

After countless rounds of discussing whether anyone might be looking for them, whether Theodore Tarnish might have somehow alerted their parents to the Spinner's Island trip, and whether Damon Jacoby might still be outside, waiting for them to reemerge, Elijah grabbed a handful of small rocks along the shore and threw them in a wide spread beyond his feet. A hundred tiny splashes echoed throughout the cave. He spoke without looking at Molly. "You sure you didn't find any sort of passage at the back of this stupid cave?"

"This stupid cave probably saved our lives, and we have you to thank for seeing it," Molly said. "But no, I checked. It's totally a dead end. We have to go back into the water. Looked like there was a place off to the right where we could climb back up."

Another handful of rocks from Elijah; another hundred splashes. "So, then, we wait for the lightning to stop."

Molly rubbed her arms, which were exposed by the tank top she was wearing. The blackness began to feel normal. Elijah continuously pictured Joshua Grime's skeleton, lying flat in the rear of the cave, sitting up like a moving cage of bones and turning its jawless skull toward them, laughing in its own morbid mockery. To be stuck in such a dark place with the remains of a dead man—it was something that would haunt him forever.

Intense hunger began to set in, and Elijah soon found himself dreaming of all the wonderful food he had ever been lucky enough to eat. Now all he had were nearby rocks and bones, and his stomach suffered sharp pangs every time he tried to get comfortable.

Molly, however, was faring worse than he. An hour before, she had grown almost delusional, whispering that she was so cold, that it wasn't a normal cold, and that there might be ghosts with them. "And I'm starving," she kept saying. "Whenever I don't eat, my body gets all weird, and I can barely move . . ." She passed out. Whether it was from hunger and exhaustion or general shock, Elijah couldn't tell. He waited in silence, forcing himself to ignore the spinning in his own vision. Afraid he wasn't far behind Molly, he, too, tried to sleep.

At what he guessed might be three in the morning, Elijah opened his eyes. The wind outside had died down, and the waves had settled into low rolls against the cliff face. When he saw a faint flash of lightning, however, his hopes shrank a bit. Yet twenty minutes later, there still hadn't been a follow up. The storm seemed to be moving away.

He nudged Molly. Thankfully, she opened her eyes, and he updated her. "We should wait until we're *sure*," she whispered, fighting to keep her eyes open.

Two hours later, all the more starving, they were sure.

A faint, grayish glow had bloomed beyond the cave mouth.

The water was calm as ever now, back to the simple Spinner's Lake that fishermen and canoe paddlers always loved. Even in the muted cave, the sound of a thousand chirping birds wafted across it. The storm had passed; the regular world had dawned.

"Molly, let's go. Do you think you can handle the water again?"

She propped herself up on an elbow and winced as a sharp rock dug into it. Elijah lent her a hand and pulled her upright. "I'm dizzy. . . ." she said, touching her left temple. She shook her head around, seemingly trying to focus herself. It made the difference, because she suddenly seemed more awake. "Let's do this."

"So, we're turning right when we swim out of the cave?"

"Yeah, I think that's where the spot was."

Elijah put a foot into the cold water, hating the feel of it flooding his shoes. He turned, waiting for Molly, and saw her looking back, toward Joshua Grime's remains. "I'm glad we found him," was all she said before stepping forward, into the water. The drop-off happened within five feet, and moments later, they were swimming out.

"Oh God, it's *cold*," Molly panted.

"You'll get used to it fast. Just keep swimming!" Elijah yelled back, side-stroking ahead of Molly. When he emerged from the cave, the light came like a glorious blessing. Even though the sun hadn't yet risen, he had to squint. Making sure Molly was close in tow, he turned right along the cliff face. Sure enough, up ahead, it was broken and less steep.

"You're doing all right?" he said, moving through the water as best he could. It had taken this extra effort for him to realize just how hungry and weak he really was; his vision had started to spin once again.

"My shoes are heavy," Molly said, still puffing away behind him.

"Mine too. It's not far, though!"

"Not far . . ." she repeated to herself.

It took less than five minutes for them to reach the shoreline and climb out of the water. Its rocks were slippery with algae, but once Elijah had a solid foothold, he was able to hoist Molly upward.

"You go first," he said. "I'll catch you if you fall back. If you see Damon, tell me, and I'll try to get up and charge him."

Molly nodded and began to climb. Elijah followed. Damp yellow lichens detached from the rocks and stuck to his fingers as he heaved himself upward. Once, Molly's foot slipped, and his own instincts surprised him; he caught her foot almost immediately and allowed her to regain balance. Escaping the cave had enlivened him, and even if it was simply a burst of energy to get them both home safely, it was a taste of renewed hope. As they approached the top, he looked down. The cliff really was at least twenty-five feet high and very steep.

"No Damon, I don't think," Molly said when she was at the top, rolling onto flat stone and breathing heavily. "I think we can make a break for it across the island. Get our bikes as soon as possible and get out of here . . ."

Elijah had forgotten that they still had a fifteen-mile bike ride in front of them. Molly had trail mix in her bike bag—hopefully enough to give them some energy. It was all about getting her home now. Elijah had brought her into this mess, and he would get her out.

"You able to run?" he asked, finding secure footing on the cliff edge. He looked at Molly, who was still lying under the soft, gray clouds sweeping overhead in the warm morning wind. Now, in the east, a hint of pink had begun to saturate the sky. Elijah held a hand down to his friend, whose cold, weakened fingers curled over his with hideously depleted strength. He pulled her to her feet. "Okay, don't let go of my hand." He gave hers a squeeze, then said, "You ready?"

Molly nodded.

"Okay, let's go!"

They ran.

Trees whipped past them as they bolted straight across the center of the small island. The sopping underbrush squished under their feet, spraying cold water onto their ankles.

Elijah didn't look back, but he could hear Molly wheezing behind him. "Are you all right?" he asked.

"Yeah . . . keep running. . . ."

There was no sign of Damon Jacoby during their five-minute sprint across the island. They stopped at the edge of the rock bridge to catch their breath. No footsteps sounded behind them, and by the look of it, they were alone. The pinkish sky ahead was growing more and more vivid with each passing second, glowing behind the purple clouds with dazzling morning splendor. The wind was a mere whisper today.

Elijah hopped to the first tall rock. He grabbed Molly by the hand as she, too, made the jump, and they started their trek toward the mainland. It was slower on the way back, partially because rocks they had jumped down before now had to be climbed. In places, they had to plunge halfway into the water to regain their path.

"I'm sick of being wet. . . ." Molly said under her breath. "Sick of it, sick of it, sick of it . . ."

"We're almost at the end of the bigger rocks, and then it's just those smaller ones all the way back to shore," Elijah said, taking a moment atop the next rock to breathe. He helped Molly up, and she stopped as well, bending over and clutching her knees. "Do you think you'll be able to make the bike ride?"

But Molly wasn't responding. Instead, she had frozen in her resting position, staring onward toward the shore. Terror gripped her eyes.

"What is it?" Elijah said, turning. And then he saw it: Ed Jacoby's rusty green pickup truck.

"He moved it," Molly panted. "Elijah, he brought it off the road! He's still—"

"There!" Elijah pointed ahead, just in time for Molly to see Damon Jacoby reach the top of the next large rock, his dark silhouette embossed against the blazing sunrise.

2038

As Nicolas Rim whispered with the gun to his head and the FBI's weapons trained on him, Jimmy Barber finally began to understand why Jonathan Flite, the enigmatic nurse killer of Rhode Island, had begun causing tremors beneath socially accepted ideologies. Something had happened at Winifred's press conference—an explosion—and now everything was spiraling out of control, toward the unknown. Now that the plan to sting Rim at Swan Point Cemetery seemed like a silly mistake made eons ago, Jimmy realized, not without a shred of horror, that everything had somehow veered off course in exactly the direction he had been fantasizing about all summer.

Rim wandered with his words, speaking without organization. Jimmy had no idea how to connect all the threads, but he was beginning to see links—tiny ones, almost phantom ones—between Jonathan, the bombing in Geneva, Victor Zobel, and the long-lost

Idle County Seven. It was the Moon Woods that started it all, Rim said, that strange forest in Minnesota that somehow affected people's minds, made them see things, and made them question what was real and what was not. He recalled his father, Jonas, traveling to the spot to build a home for Victor Zobel in 2012, and then a telephone conversation with the man five months later, the night he claimed to have blacked out while overseeing the building of an elevator shaft into a cavelike area under the property. Except it hadn't been a real blackout, Jonas Rim had insisted while fighting tears and sounding crazy—it had been a whiteout, an out-of-body experience, a confrontation with, in Nicolas Rim's recollected words, "the real nature of life." Three days later, Jonas Rim had died, and while Victor Zobel hadn't provided any explanation, the Idle County medical examiner had deemed the cause of death an aneurysm.

But there was more. Jumping backward, Rim rambled through an account of his childhood in Geneva, how Victor Zobel had "adopted" his family and given them the means to make ends meet and relocate to America. Yet the celebrity ex-neurosurgeon was sour, Rim claimed. He was a manipulator, a wife stealer, a business mastermind, and a killer. His New Naturalism movement was a brand, a moneymaker, a political lobbying power—and there were rumors floating down from Larry Kane, CEO of a company called Carey Developments, that a few particular foreign subsidiaries of their conglomerate umbrella, Zobel Enterprises, were laundering money and dealing illegally with weapons manufacturing, acquisition, and transportation, all in an effort to . . . to what, Rim didn't know.

"I know Victor hates religion, and he would do anything to erase it from the world," Rim now whispered to Jimmy, still holding the gun to his head. His entire arm was now shaking. Jimmy wondered how long he could keep it raised while maintaining his grip. "I remember him telling my father once that religion was the 'cause of all ills' in the world, and that it should be eliminated. My father asked, 'How?' and Victor said, 'By force if necessary.' I didn't know what he meant at the time, and I didn't even know the morning of the bombing in Geneva that he was behind it. But then all the connections with that cardinal started coming up. People said Zobel was raised in the same town where Jean-Claude Apostol used to be a priest. Saint-Paul de Vence. That's in France."

Jimmy listened, rapt, to Nicolas Rim's intertwining account of people, places, and times. Amid its intricacies, a particular continuity seemed to be building—a web of actions and choices that were finally beginning to gel into an alarming yet cohesive story. As the man continued, it became clear just how close to home everything now was.

"It was only three days after the bombing when my boss told me I had to make friends with the security guard at your old juvenile center. So I could gauge him. And then either pay him to kill Jonathan Flite or convince him to help me, if it seemed possible."

"You're talking about Paul the douchebag," Jimmy said.

"Yes, Paul. I followed him for two weeks before introducing myself at a bar in Providence. One of his morning hangouts after the night shift at Crescent. Led him on toward talking about his job and how much he hated it. Hated all of you boys. Said you were 'spoiled little shitheads.'"

In Jimmy's earpiece, invisibly fitted for him by the FBI agents when they were strapping on the bulletproof vest, he heard Agent Prescott say, "You're doing great, Jimmy. Try to get a reason why."

"But why Jonathan?" Jimmy asked. "What did he have to do with anything?"

"Because Zobel believes Jonathan's memories are real. I think it's because of whatever is going on under that forest in Minnesota, and because there's somebody Victor hates who Jonathan would have memories of. A disabled girl who grew up in Idle County and was friends with those kids. She's now a physicist. All I know is that she made a big splash with some new theory recently, and it was starting to polarize scientists. There was a conference scheduled at CERN on August 12, the day of the bombing. There's a link between the physicist and Idle County and whatever Victor is studying there. I know it, because Revis Zobel told me."

Jimmy's center of gravity suddenly shifted. Somehow, he knew this was important even before he heard Agent Prescott speak in his ear. "Jimmy, it's me again. Confirm any details you can about Revis Zobel. This is news to us."

"Revis as in Revis and Victoria, the twins?" Jimmy said. "Victor's son?"

"If Victor is the snake and Victoria is the shark, Revis is the lion," Rim replied. "Soft until threatened." Rim closed his eyes and shook his head. The angle of his gun tilted a bit higher; his grip on it loosened. "We were friends when we were kids in Geneva. Respected each other all these years and stayed in touch. I called Revis before breaking into your juvenile center to ask casually if he knew anything about why his father might care about this nurse killer in Rhode Island. I wanted to see what the connection was to Jonathan Flite. Why it mattered, you know? Revis had an answer right away. He said it was because some physicist was taunting his father. Sending him letters. Basically telling Victor that her new theory was going to turn science on its head and prove that everything he has been standing for all these years was suspect. She was going to bring ideas about consciousness into the mainstream that Victor thought people wouldn't be ready for."

Tingles rushed up Jimmy's spine. This was almost becoming a mirror of his conversation with Jonathan over lunch, earlier that day. "*If you start looking at it all and realizing how much we still don't know about what life even is, it'll scare you even more than I do,*" had been his exact words. They had stuck with Jimmy all afternoon, and now the weight of them felt like a cold promise that this situation's scope was only just beginning to widen.

"We're all so horrified by death," Jimmy said in a low voice. The thought, and his choice to voice it, caught him off guard.

"It's the ultimate escape," Rim replied. "The end of choice."

"And you're saying Victor Zobel is so afraid of these new ideas that he'd bomb a whole damned city?"

Rim shrugged. "Or use one radical Catholic who felt his faith was being threatened to do it for him. It would be a good cover, because it would look like just another fanatic doing insane things in the name of religion."

"*You're* doing crazy things," Jimmy said. His gaze shifted to Rim's gun. "And I'd rather not see you shoot yourself. I don't know if I could handle that."

Rim's expression shuddered, as if he were torn between smiling and bursting into tears. "It would be too exciting for you, then?"

The question brought a dawning light into the man's eyes—either the edge of desperation or perhaps a desire to alter his intended course. Agent Prescott seemed to notice this just as Jimmy did, and he jumped on it through the earpiece. "Jimmy, tell him there are other options. We'd like to use him as an informant. Reduce his sentence. He could seriously help us more with this case."

"They want to use you as a CI," Jimmy said, whipping out a term he had heard on television. "And I think you should do it. You don't have to shoot yourself."

"A child killer as a criminal informant? And you really think they'd let me back out onto the streets to dig up information? Fat chance." Rim laughed now, but tears had formed in his eyes. He shook his head. "I can't give up my freedom."

"Freedom? Since when has that been a thing?" Jimmy asked. "Seems like you've been Victor Zobel's slave for years now, and it made you go completely nuts."

Rim shuddered. "I close my eyes every day and see that boy Mason in his bed. I see his head explode in the dark. I turned away from him as soon as I could that night and didn't look back. I was a coward."

Jimmy knew that Nicolas Rim might pull the trigger any second. Would the bullet rip his whole head open? Would it collapse the skull and make the face sag? Would Jimmy actually see the moment between life and death in the man's eyes?

"*Help them,*" he pleaded, aware now that he was shaking and that his heart and nerves and adrenaline had surpassed any level of comfortable excitement. The prospect of knowing Rim's brain might soon be working one moment and then spattered onto the food court floor the next was almost more than he could handle, but the man's humanity was now screaming in the silences between their words, in the scopes of the weapons aimed at him, and in the sudden vision of heroic glory overtaking Jimmy. What if he could find a silver lining here, a way to both survive the day and save Rim's life?

"Jonathan's judge wants him to talk," Jimmy said. "To reporters, I mean. Like, to seriously blow this story wide open. You could help. You really could."

Tears were streaming down Rim's face. The sudden display of weakness seemed to reaffirm his resolve, however, and he repositioned the gun next to his right temple. "I can't. *I can't.* Zobel would find a way to kill me anyway."

"So why not help put him in jail?" Jimmy said. "There's a whole line of reporters waiting to talk to Jonathan. And now his mom's press conference just got bombed. It's going to be huge. We're talking *international* huge."

Rim trembled, and Jimmy watched his finger lightly run along the gun's trigger. "There is one reporter," the man whispered.

"What do you mean?"

"Revis Zobel said her people were relentless. Calling his father's reps constantly last summer after Geneva. She's planning some big story about Idle County. Revis said it's one of the other reasons his dad was scared of Jonathan Flite. Because *WorldLine* wants to do a series on him—and on those kids who disappeared."

Recalling what he and Jonathan had discussed at the Green Fish earlier that afternoon, Jimmy's blood suddenly rushed with possibilities. Alice Winterblume likely wasn't just curious about Jonathan Flite, the nurse killer. She was likely curious about Jonathan Flite, the secret keeper of the Idle County Seven mystery and the possible silver bullet to Victor Zobel. If Victor Zobel somehow played a part in the teenagers' disappearances, and if Jonathan really did somehow remember their lives, it could be a news scoop explosive enough to both incriminate the man and upend his precious New Naturalism belief system forever.

"Jonathan told me he thinks he could prove his memories are real if he talks to Alice Winterblume," Jimmy said. "He said she once interviewed one of those kids."

Rim nodded, and when he spoke, his voice was stronger—fewer tremors, more hope. "She did meet one of them. . . . Elijah

Bryce. Interviewed him about some jawbone. The video's online if you know where to look."

For a moment, they looked into each other's eyes. Jimmy then raised his hands slowly, placing them on the edge of the food court table. His fingers were cold and trembling, but when he looked up, into Nicolas Rim's eyes, the hollow desperation in them inspired true pity. "It's not my job to convince you not to kill yourself," he continued, "but I also really hope you don't. I'd feel like I helped cause it. And I don't know if this'll make any difference, but I'm almost a hundred percent sure Jonathan would forgive you for what you did to Mason Witzel, especially if you told him all this yourself. Even if he had to come and visit you in prison. If anyone out there is proof that people can swing back around, it's him." Jimmy stood up, and adrenaline pummeled his chest like some invisible hammer. "I'm going now. Thank you for talking to me." With numb legs and a tingling rush down his spine, he turned around and walked toward the FBI agents on the far side of the mall's median walkway. Above him, the last of the day's sun was shining through the building's colossal glass ceiling. Jimmy was ten feet from safety, and his heartbeat was just beginning to slow, when a single gunshot rang out. From behind him came the sound of a body slumping downward, onto the food court table.

2005

Elijah Bryce and Molly Butler stood head-to-head with Damon Jacoby. The two friends were on one tall outcropping of rock, and the bully was on the other, separated by a thirty-foot stretch of smaller boulders.

"No," Molly whispered. "Elijah, we can't turn back . . . I need to get home . . ."

Blood tore through Elijah's veins at a ferocious speed. What could they do? Damon was blocking the way forward, but the only other option was to turn around and climb back toward the island.

"You guys made it!" Damon screamed from his rock. For a single moment, it seemed as if he were glad to see them, that he had experienced a change of heart since yesterday's storm. But something in his voice sounded off-kilter—a trace of the same derangement he had exuded while holding the knife to Molly's throat.

"Don't do anything," Elijah said, holding Molly by the arm. "Let him come to us."

"I can't, Elijah. I *can't!*" Molly whispered. "I have to get home!" Panic had mixed with her exhaustion, and now she wasn't thinking straight.

"I thought for sure you died, faggot!" Damon screamed. "I waited all night. Was just about to leave when I saw you climbing back. You just won't leave me alone!"

"Elijah, watch out! He's throwing rocks!"

Elijah grabbed Molly out of the way just as one stone and then another smashed against the jagged outcropping beneath their feet. As he tried to balance their intertwined bodies, he felt his center of gravity shift. He swung quickly back, holding Molly beside him and narrowly avoiding a tumble onto the sharp rocks below.

"Molly, find your footing—"

But Elijah heard a sickening, blunt crack.

"Oh—!" Molly shrank in his arms, unconscious. A stream of blood ran down her face from the center of her head.

"No!" Elijah screamed, enraged. He turned around just in time to see another stone flying in his direction. With sudden and instinctive force, he batted it out of the way with his open hand, and it hurled downward and ricocheted off another rock, into the water. "You bastard!" he screamed, torn between jumping off the rock to pursue Damon and staying to shield Molly's defenseless body from further harm.

But Damon had already jumped off his own rock. He was charging across the lower ones, his glinting knife in hand, leaping with sickening ease toward them. Making a final series of leaps onto Elijah and Molly's rock, he stood tall before them, no more than five feet away.

"You just—don't—die!"

He pounced at Elijah, brandishing the sharp, silver blade in a vicious downward arc. Elijah ducked out of the way and to the side, twirling in a frightful dance at the edge of the crag. His gaze whirled over the smaller rocks below.

With miraculous luck, he regained his balance and lunged at Damon. They collided over the unconscious Molly. Elijah grabbed Damon's arm before the older boy could swing the knife into him, and they twisted together. As Damon circled around Elijah's back, Elijah twisted the boy's hand, forcing the knife to drop. It clanked against the rock and landed near Molly's motionless leg. Elijah was still in the losing position, however; if he were to let go of Damon's arm, Damon would regain a full advantage.

"What do you *want?*" Elijah screamed. "What did I ever do to you?"

"*You're inside my fucking head!*"

"I never did anything!"

Damon seethed into his ear. "You tried to put me in jail. No cops to save you this time!"

"But you're going to be a murderer!" Elijah wailed. "They're going to know who did it and put you in jail for even longer!"

His grip on Damon was faltering.

"You don't get it, do you?" the boy whispered, hot with madness. He raised his voice in boiling rage. "I don't care what I do, because I'm gonna kill myself anyway! I can't handle it anymore."

It took Elijah a moment to register the sudden weakness in Damon's arm hold, the cracking in his voice. The veil of rage had pulled back to reveal his underlying grief. In the space of a second, Elijah anchored his foot against an edge in the rock, pushed backward, and twisted.

"What the—"

Elijah righted himself just in time to meet Damon's fist in mid-air. His head rattled with the blast, and for a moment, his vision waved in and out. Damon was lunging for Molly, for the knife—

"No!" Elijah rushed forward and kicked Damon with all his might. His tennis shoe hit the deranged teenager square in the jaw. Damon flew backward, toward the end of the rock, and landed on his back.

"Stop!" Elijah screamed at him. "Just stop! You don't really want to kill yourself!"

"I have to!" Damon shrieked. "I've seen things that nobody will believe. *Nobody will believe.*"

He was down. Elijah safely grabbed the knife, then glanced quickly at Molly, whose arm was now moving toward her head.

"What happened . . . ?" she whispered.

Elijah stepped between Molly and Damon. "Molly, hold your head! You're bleeding! And Damon, we *already* believe you! We've seen stuff just like you have. Let us go, though. Please."

Now the sick teenager laughed. "You're not understanding. You're not listening. I want to take you with me. I want to see if you cross over, too. There's something in this place that makes it all clear, and I want to prove it. Don't you feel it? *It's right there.*"

Adrenaline rushed through Elijah's body. The arm that held Damon's knife was pulsing with heat and passion. Behind his feet, Molly moved into a sitting position, holding her head.

"I don't care who dies, because we're *all* going to die," Damon said, still laughing. His hair was backlit by the golden sunrise. "There's something past all this! I've seen it! So why the hell would we wait through all the shit of life? It's not worth it. Nobody stops to think about that! Our stupid faggot dads were lucky. They fucking killed themselves and got to escape."

Elijah was silent for a moment. It was his first confirmation that Damon knew of their preexisting connection.

"It was an accident," he finally whispered. "Your dad got HIV in New York. He didn't know he was spreading it to my dad."

"They were both stupid faggots. Just like you. Only they realized it was just easier to die. Don't you see that I'm just trying to show you they were right? That dying is easier, because none of this is real?" Damon gestured toward the rock, the sky, and the very morning around them. His expression broke into a jagged exchange of misery and humor, as if he were trying to reconcile his treatment of Elijah with the true reason for it—one Elijah himself could now validate.

"Just because you've seen things doesn't mean all this isn't real," Elijah said, tightening his grip on the knife.

Damon shook his head with a grimace. "Then I really am the crazy one." He rose slowly to his feet, inches from the knife blade. Elijah didn't move a muscle. Damon took a step back with a broken smile on his face. "Tell them all I said good-bye."

He leaned backward.

"No!" Elijah rushed toward him, screaming so hard that his voice seemed to rip through his throat.

The bully tumbled off the rock, headfirst. A sickening thump sounded on the sharp stones below.

"Damon, no!" Elijah fell to his knees on the rock's edge and looked over. Damon's neck was twisted inexplicably, and blood was draining around the jagged stones, into the water. "No!" Elijah said again as time seemed to stop. Impossible moments—amalgams of horror and fear and yes, even love—passed before his eyes until he realized that Damon wasn't moving. He began climbing down.

"Elijah . . ." Above him, Molly was crawling forward.

"Molly, his neck—oh God, his head! I think . . ." Damon wasn't moving, and Elijah, still holding the knife in case it was a farce, pressed two fingers to the boy's neck. He had learned in gym class how to take a pulse, but now he struggled to find Damon's.

"Is he all right?" Molly wailed from above, still holding a hand to her head.

The back of Damon's head had cracked open against one of the sharp stone's ridges, and Elijah saw bits of white. His skull? His brain?

"Oh my God, Elijah, he's bleeding all over!"

"Damn it, there's no pulse, I don't think! Wait—here—" Elijah grabbed his wet shirt and pulled it off his back. He folded it over to form a long strip to tie around Damon's bleeding head.

"Don't touch his neck!" Molly screamed. "I've see it on TV! You're not supposed to move him if his neck is broken!"

"But I don't think he's even alive!" Elijah screamed, turning toward Molly, his eyes wide with an entirely new kind of terror. It was the Death card come true, but not the way he had anticipated. Molly was sobbing now; her eyes blazed over the mess. Their bad dream had turned into a nightmare, and the blood rushing from the back of Damon's head was making it glare a brilliant red. Elijah took a chance and lifted it, gently turning his neck.

"Elijah, no—!"

"I don't think it matters now," he said in a quiet voice. Tears ran down his face in slow lines.

Peering over the edge of the tall outcropping, Molly pressed her lips together and shut her eyes so hard that her entire face warped with grief and disbelief. Tears dropped from her cheeks, ten feet above him. They found their place in a small pool at the center of a rock cluster sticking out of the lake. "What do we do?" she whispered.

A minute ago, Elijah's mind had been racing, but ever since feeling that final surge of compassion for Damon, his mind was hollow and empty. There was nothing now but the face of a dead teenager looking into the breezy morning sky. Whatever life had been struggling to stay inside Damon's body, it was gone. The truth of it hit Elijah with a numb sense of revulsion and sorrow, and somehow, none of the things Damon had done since learning about the Alec Pent incident seemed to matter anymore. He was dead, and Elijah had watched it happen. For the first time in his life, he realized how precious everything in it was. Now even the horrible skirmishes they had shared together glistened with the value of experience.

UNDER THE GOLDEN MORNING LIGHT, Elijah and Molly carefully wrapped Damon's gashed head with the wet T-shirt. With an effort beyond any he had ever known, Elijah hoisted the boy's body up and pulled it over his back.

"We're going," he said to Molly, already out of breath.

She climbed off the rock without a word, solemn in the quiet morning.

They resumed their trek toward shore, this time at an even more laborious pace. Molly, as hungry and exhausted as she clearly was, supported Damon's body where and when she could. It was a blessing when they were able to circumvent the final tall rock— the same one Damon had been standing on not twenty minutes before—by balancing around a lower edge near its base. Joshua Grime's skeleton, lying exposed in the cave on the far side of Spinner's Island, now seemed like a distant memory.

The shore was just twenty feet away. Ed Jacoby's battered green truck, parked along the edge of the trees, seemed to look at them with dumb surprise as they stumbled over the last few steps of the stone bridge.

"Our bikes!" Molly cried as she jumped onto the rocky beach.

Elijah, barely able to feel his legs under the strain on his back, could scarcely muster the energy to look up. All that mattered was getting Damon into the back of the truck. With any luck, he would have a working phone in there; all he'd had in his pockets were his wallet and the car keys. When Elijah finally looked up and saw their bikes, he was too relieved to be on shore to care that they were destroyed, bent out of shape in front of the truck. Damon had clearly done a thorough job in making sure they would remain trapped.

"It doesn't matter. We'll get them later."

"But—if he doesn't have a phone in there—"

"I'll drive," Elijah said. "As long as it doesn't have a stick shift, I'll be fine."

Molly looked at him with wide eyes. They weren't even thirteen, and the idea of driving a truck on a real road, possibly with other cars, was as unfathomable as it was exciting. Except there was one more thing to think about. "Help me open the back," Elijah said. "We've got to get Damon in there."

Still too dazed to react with her usual swiftness, Molly rolled her head around with an almost comical, gangly posture. She found her feet and moved around the truck. Elijah followed with heavy steps.

Molly stopped for a split second by the window. "It's an automatic, not a stick. I don't see a phone, though."

Damon's body was too heavy for Elijah to feel any relief. The last ten steps were the shortest and worst. His heart pounded, his stomach raged with hunger, and his vision was now waving in and out with regular explosions of stars.

"Turn around. Let me get his head," Molly said before Elijah even realized he was close enough to the truck's rear hatch to set the body down. "In here . . . Okay, I've got him. . . ." The girl—almost a young woman, Elijah realized—cradled Damon's wrapped head with one arm and lifted his torso with another. This last burst of real strength, as impossible as it seemed, was almost automatic.

And then it was done.

Elijah collapsed against the unhinged hatch, shaking as he tried to hold himself up. It was no use. He stumbled back onto the old dirt driveway and lay down on his back, breathing heavily, unaware of time. The drive loomed ahead. While looking at the clouds and their brightening blue sky above, all he could think about was whether he would really be able to figure out the truck. He had seen his mother drive their automatic transmission car many times, but he was going to have to back up, turn around, and drive out to the Spinner's Lake perimeter road without any real knowledge of—

"I have food," Molly said. "It didn't get too messed up in my bike bag. Eat some before you do anything. My water bottle was okay, too, but yours was ruined. . . ." She pulled Elijah upward and shoved a bag of trail mix in his face. It was a moment from heaven, and for a second, he simply stared at it. "*Eat!*" Molly insisted again through her own mouthful.

Ten minutes later, Elijah's head was clearer. As if to punctuate the reality of it, he saw Damon's foot hanging over the truck's open back end. "Help me move his legs," he said to Molly. "We have to close the hatch."

Molly climbed into the truck's rear and pulled Damon's

body farther in. She was already thinking ahead, too, because her hand delved into his pocket a moment later. Elijah heard the faint jingling of keys. "Here," the girl said, handing them over before jumping back to the ground.

Maneuvering the truck wasn't all that different from maneuvering a bumper car. The small clearing was large enough to back it up and turn it around, and when Elijah shifted into drive, they were off.

The trip back to End Haven took twenty-five minutes. Elijah drove slowly enough to avoid any bumps, out of respect for Damon's body. It would have been exhilarating to be driving under any other circumstances, and when Molly opened her window, the sensation of speed and regained control over their circumstances was almost enough to make him smile. Out of the corner of his eye, however, he saw that Molly was leaning her head out, her expressionless face seeking some sort of solace in the wind.

When they turned from Birmingham Road onto Main Street, it occurred to Elijah that there had been a tornado the previous night. An uprooted tree was blocking half the road at Kettering Street, and a downed power line and a bustle of city workers diverted them at Dale. Saint Mary's Hospital would now be one block west and another six blocks south.

"I hope people's houses didn't get damaged," was all Molly said as they drove.

Some hadn't been so lucky, however. On one street, shingles were sprawled all over the road. At least seven houses were missing sections of their roofing, and their owners were out in their yards, inspecting the damage. Strangely enough, nobody noticed the two underage drivers hauling a young teenager's body toward the hospital. Not once did Elijah consider stopping to ask for help.

Finally, they reached the intersection of Orchard Street and

Hunter Avenue. Elijah curved into the front emergency drop-off zone of Saint Mary's Hospital.

Both he and Molly were too shocked to realize how strange it looked when they stumbled out of the rusty, green truck. They both turned in slow unison toward its rear and eased the hatch open. Neither saw the nurse running out of the hospital's automatic front doors, nor did they object when more medics rolled three stretchers out to meet them. Three people, two impossibly young but alive and matured, one impossibly young and forever lost, were ushered under the hospital's fluorescent lights.

PART 7

IN THE NEWS

∞

THE EXPLOSION HAD HAPPENED IN SLOW MOTION, and Winifred Flite now stood outside her own body, watching calmly as the living rushed to deal with what had just become Newport, Rhode Island's first-ever religious terrorist attack. Special Agent O'Farrell had been blown right off her body and now lay seven feet away, charred black in spots and bleeding from a hundred shrapnel wounds. Weston Carrow was now nothing more than a bloody, burned array of flesh strewn over the entire front yard of Newport City Hall. Analyzing the situation from without, Winifred now saw that Carrow had been shot by police about fifteen feet from the podium before pressing his detonator as he fell. The bomb had been small and homemade, but the blast overpressure wave had been enough to damage her internally. And the red laser beam? It had been a decoy, a cheap laser pointer, used by one of Carrow's parishioners from afar, to draw attention away from the actual bomb. They had once seen the gimmick on television, and tonight, it had worked like a fiery charm.

Winifred had seen a ring of light when the bomb went off, then moved through it almost instantaneously, as if it were a portal to relief that had been there all along. She had a very strong sense that she was still in control of her living body—and that on some level of consciousness she was actually *creating* it—but to survive now necessitated this change of focus. All the dramas that had originated with her son were now on a time line she was no longer plugged into. The blast, the immediate sweep by the closest surviving police officer to check the vicinity for more bombs, the rushing in of emergency medical personnel—it was all happening in a dimension that, from this vantage point, didn't seem to matter anymore.

Winifred relived her life in what seemed like a perpetual instant: her snowy birthday on February 28, 1992, in Bedford, New York; her near-billionaire parents' money squabbles, materialism, and countless affairs; the childhood social rejection from her brother, Michael; and, later, his family-shaming depression and suicide attempts. Winifred had grown up under a banner of American opulence, and within this cocoon of loneliness, she had built her emotional walls. All those afternoons alone in the backyard gazebo playing with her toy tea set (wishing she had more friends while listening to her parents scream at each other) had taught her to ignore the inklings of her heart—those little whispers of joy and hope and love that seemed so good and natural. Both Stanley and Julietta Flite had spent Winifred's childhood belittling everything and everyone she was enthusiastic about, resulting in her long-term fear of such negative acknowledgment. Even her pursuit of a career in interior design had been overrun by this; it had been easier to rely on her parents' money than to pursue her dream, because running with ambition and courting the possibility of failure was a threat to the Flite family reputation. Her one attempt to prove herself—having Jonathan—had literally just blown up in her face. She now remembered with sympathetic clarity the unfortunate morning in 2033 when she whispered to Delilah Hensel that she wished her troublesome son had never been born. Of course he had been standing right there, in the kitchen doorway, listening to every word and probably feeling the exact same rejection her own parents had always instilled in her. That was when he had snapped, shattered her favorite crystal vase, and run up to his bedroom with one of the shards to cut a long slit into his lower left arm. That night, still wrapped in bandages and in a fit of agitation, he had strangled Ellen Graber.

The memories came back to Winifred as sights, sounds, textures, smells, and tastes, but with them came a burst of potent insight. All these sensory experiences creating the very nature of life as she knew it were merely translations for some deeper level of experience.

Winifred found she could wander. The body she now walked in felt like some energetically charged blueprint of the one she had recently been operating in Newport—separate but related, as if one were a shadow of the other. Time was gone.

HERE. COLUMBUS AVENUE. The building she called her home, recently damaged and recently patched up—not too different from her own life as of late. How had it all happened? How had her comfortable American existence become a war zone?

It was Jonathan: her boy, now nearly a man, the one she had

failed on all counts to love. He was sitting on the couch in her newly remodeled living room off the kitchen, staring at the television wall as it showed the press conference's cataclysmic aftermath. In the dimming evening, he was more desperate and alone than ever before. He was wishing someone were there next to him— Mason Witzel, Jimmy Barber, Dr. Lumen, or even Sounder (who was outside, speaking with police, making sure the house was safe and not yet again a target in some larger assassination plot). With a bit of extra focus, Winifred found that she could glimpse Jonathan's mind. It showed the truth of him, the part nobody could physically see, the shining essence she now realized had been there all along, hiding underneath the turmoils of his life. She hovered in the corner of the living room, watching him now as he trembled, cried, and ran his fingers over his ActoPhone screen, teetering on the brink of contacting someone he had not yet told her about. A reporter. The famous one from *WorldLine*—Alice Winterblume. She had once interviewed Elijah Bryce, one of Jonathan's vanished Idle County Seven, and he was confident he could prove to her his memories were real. To do so would catapult him toward a level of fame he might not be ready for. But what was the alternative? To forever remain a figure of gossip and social mystery?

He had received another blue-enveloped letter. A secret one he hadn't shared with her or the FBI. It was from the same person who had written the others (someone from Idle County, Winifred now saw—a physicist in a wheelchair), and she had given Jonathan a direct line to Alice Winterblume. There were countless moving pieces at play here, ones Winifred could only now begin to fathom. The more she allowed herself to focus on Jonathan's mind, the more she understood the reason for his turbulence. His Idle County Seven memories were real, jumbled in his head both as layers and as one big storm, clear as day in some parts and frightfully muddled in others. Inside the memories were images, feelings, implications—all things he had never truly been able to share as a child, no matter how many crayon drawings he made, stories he told, or mysterious French phrases he uttered. For the first time in her life (but now in her possible death), Winifred appreciated her son, loved him, and saw his potential. It burst forth from her like a ray of light she had no control over.

Jonathan bolted upright on the couch. He stifled a sob as he looked around the room, as if sensing her presence. This was enough for Winifred. She had succeeded. He knew she was there, and he knew she would condone his contacting Alice Winterblume at *WorldLine*. This was his chance to finally take Judge Barry Wallace's mandate seriously, to share his story with the world. With ease, Winifred bowed out of the living room so that Jonathan could make his choice without distraction.

WINIFRED THOUGHT OF YOUNG JIMMY BARBER, Jonathan's fashionista friend, and in no time at all, she was hovering next to him at Providence Place Mall as he leaned in shock against a balcony railing near the food court.

The sting with Nicolas Leandro Rim had, miraculously, worked out for the best. When it failed to go as planned, Jimmy had forced his hand on both the criminal and the FBI, blazing a trail toward success that few people were likely ever to find out about. After speaking face-to-face with Rim, who was holding a gun to his own head the entire time, Jimmy had, quite unexpectedly and due to a surge of unexpected empathy for the man, outlined for him a possible path toward redemption. Rim had slowly begun tilting the gun's handle downward, grazing his temple lightly as the muzzle slowly angled up, toward the mall's glass ceiling. He had finally pulled the trigger, but only once the gun was aimed vertically enough to miss his skull. Jimmy had ducked when he heard the shot, then spun around just after the man dropped the weapon and collapsed forward, onto the table. At first, Jimmy had expected to see the man's head gone or some other gruesome display, but Rim had simply lain there with his massive hands outstretched and moving slightly, rolling at the wrists, waiting for handcuffs.

Jimmy had made a difference. He had talked Nicolas Rim down. He had given the FBI their prized criminal informant, all in the name of some vague agenda he wasn't even sure of. Helping Jonathan Flite? Experiencing some excitement? Perhaps both, on Jimmy's part, but Winifred knew the FBI had its own motive involving Victor Zobel. Jimmy's part in their game, it seemed, was now complete.

As Winifred pulsed with appreciation for the quirky young man, she saw him shiver. He looked over his shoulder, as if searching for the source of a cold breeze, then turned back to watch the FBI agents handcuff Nicolas Rim and lead him toward the mall's exit.

WINIFRED WAS SUDDENLY IN MINNESOTA, standing over Dr. Thomas Lumen's shoulder as he furiously booked a plane ticket to Rhode Island on his ActoPhone. He hadn't even attempted to call the hospital or Jonathan; he would be there for her as soon as he could, no matter what. It was love, the type Winifred was only now beginning to understand.

NEXT CAME HER SEVENTY-SIX-YEAR-OLD FATHER, Stanley, on his Mediterranean yacht. He was sleeping, unaware of the catastrophe his only daughter had just been through. Were he awake, would he care? It didn't matter. Winifred did all she could to convey a sense of love to him. In bed, waking up only enough to form the faintest of memories, he touched the back of his neck, as if someone had caressed it.

HER BROTHER, MICHAEL. He was alone in his yurt in Washington State, on the Olympic Peninsula, completely unaware of Winifred's life dramas. This was how he preferred his family life to be—non-existent. Just as Winifred chose to continue on, she sensed in him a sudden, inexplicable burst of loneliness. He thought on it long into the night, and the next morning, upon finally checking his email for the first time that week, he would learn of his sister's condition and immediately book a plane ticket to the East Coast.

BEDFORD, NEW YORK. Winifred looked in on her old childhood home, the mansion whose backyard tea parties had been her only refuge. Here sat her seventy-year-old mother, Julietta Flite, whose severely cropped gray hair reminded Winifred of her own harsher edges. Julietta was at the kitchen counter, sliding a low-ball glass back and forth across the marble, just as Winifred often did. Tonight's drink, however, was only carbonated water and a semi-sweet raspberry syrup—no alcohol. Winifred needed only to wonder about her mother's condition to become aware of it. She was trying very hard, for what seemed like the thousandth time in her life, to give up drinking for good. It was easier said than done, of course, but when her husband, Stanley, wasn't present (which was most of the time, because he preferred to spend his time sailing with younger mistresses), it was easier for Julietta to clean up her act and be the woman she wanted to be, without feeling his antagonistic eyes staring down the back of her neck. It was a step, and tonight, having seen her daughter—her own flesh and blood—suffer an explosion from a suicide bomb on live television, Julietta knew it was time to be stronger, to face her fears, and to be the mother she always should have been. While she would never let Winifred or her grandson Jonathan know just how closely she had been following their dramas in Newport, she was now waiting for a car to pick her up and drive her to the Rhode Island Hospital in Providence. It was the best trauma and burn unit in the state, and if Winifred would have any chance of survival at all, it would be there.

Winifred felt a sudden burst of gratitude and compassion for her mother. As if on cue, the woman sat up straighter, in the middle of a sip. Because she had never before considered the possibility that life might somehow transcend death, Julietta Flite felt first an unsettling sense of fear and then an unexpected tease of comfort, as if the feelings were letting her in on a big secret—that there really was nothing to fear, even in the direst of circumstances.

LAST CAME THE ONLY OTHER PERSON Winifred could think of who mattered: Dominic Bock, Jonathan's biological father. He was now retired from the US Navy and living in Corpus Christi, Texas, working as an engineer at WaveForm Electric, one of the most prominent wave energy companies in the country. In the peace of her newfound state of consciousness, Winifred needed only to focus on the memory of their first meeting at O'Brien's Pub in Newport to be directed right to him. In what seemed like no time at all, she was outside Dominic's modest family home, half a country away, knowing that her look in on him would be fast—nothing that would infringe too much on his privacy. No matter how she had treated him during life, she had always cared about him. She simply hadn't known how to show it.

Now he had a wife. Three daughters. A satisfying job.

Dominic was sitting on his couch, tan and muscular and still as handsome as ever with his Roman nose and perpetually gentle expression. He was nearing forty-seven, but one would never know it, except perhaps for the few flecks of gray in his otherwise dirty-blond hair. His steely hazel eyes, just like Jonathan's, were red with tears as he watched the CNN news report about the bombing. Winifred aimed all the comfort she could at him, only to realize it wasn't just her possible death that was troubling him.

It was Jonathan. He knew he was the boy's father.

He had found out the truth in 2026 while visiting Newport for department head school at the navy base. Despite having actively avoided anything that might intersect him with Winifred Flite during that trip, he had nonetheless seen her while parking his car on Thames Street, just prior to meeting his friend Burt for drinks. She had by that time begun wearing her long, dark hair in a tight bun, and she had been dragging her hesitant-looking son into Benjamin's Restaurant. Even then, Jonathan's features had been unmistakable—his dirty-blond hair, his Roman nose, his way of carrying himself—and to Dominic, it was like looking through a time-traveling mirror into his own childhood. Based on the boy's apparent age, the timing was obvious. Winifred must have ended their relationship while pregnant. Dominic had never been one to shirk responsibility, but considering both the woman's family money and her previous demand for him to stay away, he hadn't mentioned the boy to anyone over the years—not even his wife, Carolyn. Guilt had been clamping his heart ever since, and now it was time to let it go.

Winifred did her best to send Dominic a rush of comfort as Carolyn approached him and asked, "Honey, what's the matter?" He sat on the couch, staring at the television, finally readying himself to tell her that he had a son, and that this son was Rhode Island's famous nurse killer. The discussion Dominic and Carolyn were about to have would keep them awake long into the night, because Dominic was feeling the urge to travel to Newport, to introduce himself to Jonathan, and to be there for him in a way he should have been since the beginning.

He still cared, despite the way Winifred had treated him. He was still a man of honor, and she counted herself lucky to have known him. At the very moment she attempted to envelop him with this gratitude, he turned to his wife and began to talk.

ALONE.

Winifred was walking down a beautiful driveway, toward a distant mansion that sparkled white, even under the approaching sunset. Flowering cherry blossoms lined the driveway's right side, and on its left was an expansive field carpeted with something gold and soft—wheat, perhaps. She felt perfectly healthy and better than she ever had before, and the crisp environment around her was so vibrant that she doubted her injured, bleeding brain could have generated it. Her awareness hadn't ended after the bombing; if anything, it had expanded outward from her physical brain's perception of space and time. She knew this without having to question it.

A light breeze pushed against Winifred, inspiring her to turn around. Behind her was an equally long stretch of driveway. At its far end (the one from which she had made her approach), there was another mansion almost identical to the glowing one she had been walking toward. It was surrounded by scaffolding, however, either still being built or in the process of a remodel. Perhaps both.

"You always have a choice," came a voice from somewhere nearby, a place she wasn't quite ready to acknowledge.

Winifred stood between the two mansions until she saw a bench sitting about fifty feet farther down the driveway, under the cherry trees along its right side. As the petals from their blossoms fell around her, she walked to the bench and sat down. Glancing left, she noticed just how far away the mansion with the scaffolding seemed. Only a few of its windows were lit; all its other corners were dark.

You always have a choice.

Right now her choice was to sit. To ignore her broken body in Newport. To ignore Jonathan's mysterious connection to those Idle County Seven kids. To ignore all the challenges she knew would come if she chose to return.

2005

ELIJAH BRYCE OPENED HIS EYES at 11:24 a.m. on August 10. The sun was high in the sky, as bright as it should be on any normal summer day. No more chilling water, no more pink and gold sunrise, no more rocks covered by blood—

"He's awake!"

"I'll get the nurse."

It was his mother's voice, followed by another that sounded equally familiar. Elijah tilted his head forward just in time to see Shelly Bryce rush to the side of his bed. As if by instinct, he looked down at his body to make sure it was all in one piece. There was an IV tube sticking out of his forearm, but by the look of it, he was otherwise fine and had only been resting.

He suddenly remembered the rest of that morning and bolted upright in the bed. "Where's Molly? She got hit on the head!"

Shelly, gently shushing him, ran a hand over his buzzed, blond hair. "Shhh, it's okay, honey. She's okay, they think, but she has a concussion. Whatever she was doing, she shouldn't have been out and about walking like that. They're going to keep her here overnight, just in case."

"And what about—?"

Two women entered the room before he could get the words out. One was a dark-haired nurse. The other had blazing red hair—Cynthia Foster. Suddenly, he had a vague recollection of whispering to her in his broken sleep, half in a dream. Something about Idle County being a strange place that affected people's minds.

"Hello, Elijah," she said, looking down at him with a hundred shades of relief on her face. Was his adoptive mother wearing the same expression? Did it matter anymore?

"How come you're both here?" Elijah asked. "I thought—"

Shelly Bryce pursed her lips. She did nothing more to acknowledge his biological mother.

"Your mother called me when she got home from work last night," Cynthia said. "Your babysitter hadn't heard from you all day, and she thought you might have come to my house to hide out."

"That's not what happened! I—"

Shelly tensed as she removed her hand from his head and checked his IV. "It doesn't matter now, honey," she said. "But the police are here, too. They need to know what happened to Damon Jacoby. You and Molly, driving his uncle's truck . . . ?"

"They were about to wake you up anyway," the nurse said as she checked Elijah's pulse. Her fingers on his neck rendered a sudden mental flash from that morning—his own fingers on Damon Jacoby's neck, with bloody white flecks on the rock below the teenage boy's head. Agitated, Elijah suddenly ducked away from all the hands.

"What's wrong, honey?" Shelly said.

"I need to talk to the police," he replied. "There's still . . . I mean . . . Damon came after us out on Spinner's Island, and he pushed Molly into the water during a lightning storm, so I jumped in after her, and—"

"Whoa, whoa, what? You guys drove out to Spinner's Island?" Shelly said, closing her eyes and shaking her head. Cynthia simply stared at him in utter disbelief.

"Molly and I rode our bikes there yesterday," Elijah said. "Damon was out there with his uncle's truck."

"Your mother and I spoke with Marion Jacoby last night, after we called the police about you guys not coming home," Cynthia said. "The tornadoes were ripping through—"

"Four separate ones," Shelly added. "We were so worried. *So* worried. Officer Thropp knew your history with Damon, so when Marion reported their truck missing, he put the pieces together. But really, Elijah, what on earth made you guys ride out to Spinner's Island, of all places?"

Another mental flash—his hands digging into the cold dirt and his fingers running along the curved edge of a buried rib cage. "I have to talk to the police," Elijah repeated. "They need to go out to Spinner's Island."

It took over two hours for the police to get their answers. They would be contacting him if they had further questions about his statement, they said, and that was that. As horrific as the morning had been, Elijah found it surprisingly easy to keep a level head during the questioning. Whatever part of him had grown up overnight now seemed to be holding him by the shoulders, making sure he didn't falter. But the tears, the nightmares, and the shock? They would come. He was old enough now to be sure of that.

2038

Nicolas Rim sat at a metal table under a row of flat LED lights. He was in a small, white-walled interrogation room on the US Navy base in Newport, Rhode Island, across from two FBI agents—one a male whose first name he only remembered as Ethan and the other a blond female with red lipstick whose last name was Hensley. They had apprehended him as quietly as possible in Providence Place Mall and led him out through the nearest parking garage exit. There, an unmarked white SUV had been waiting, and they had whisked him off in a blur. Through the shaded van windows had passed the world: Providence, its streets, its cars, its people as they lived their lives. Perhaps some had been aware of the "gunman scare" and evacuation at the mall, but the farther they drove away from the complex, toward Newport, the more mundane it all seemed. Everything passed before Nicolas's eyes with a glorious sense of relief. He had escaped the world he knew, but not in the way he had so dreaded. He was still alive, now behind the glass of the law. Admitting his crimes would surely result in a lifelong prison sentence, but he would never again have to face the crazy, painful, and cruel world.

While Nicolas had been informed of his Miranda rights, he had neither demanded an attorney nor seen any sign of one. The situation wasn't like ones he had seen on television, and it made him nervous. He had heard the agents talking, and they had thrown around the terms "HIG" and "CIA" and "Department of Defense." It was obvious he wasn't being immediately funneled into the usual criminal justice process. Was this irregular? Was it secret government behavior? He had no idea. Perhaps he didn't have to care.

"We have a pretty good laundry list of federal crimes you've committed," Agent Hensley said, leaning over the table and looking into his eyes. "Based on statements already obtained, including your little goodbye note, we have you for domestic terrorism threats, bribery of Paul Simpleton, conspiracy, credit fraud, identity fraud . . . These don't even include the crimes under local Rhode Island jurisdiction—the murder of Mason Witzel being the big one. Do you want me to continue?"

"I admit to it all," Nicolas said, shaking his head. "This is my recorded confession. You also have your recording from the mall, I'm sure. Use that in court."

"What we want here is to help you," the agent named Ethan said. "We want information about Victor Zobel, and you claim to want to take him down. Your compliance with us thus far is already a huge help, and we're hoping not to have to draw this process out."

"What, no torture?" Nicolas said, half smiling. "I wouldn't care if you pushed needles into my fingertips, you know. I'm done caring."

"Unfortunately, this isn't a movie," the male agent said. "In our business, it's all about gathering information to help us build a case. We have bits and pieces from what you told Jimmy Barber earlier tonight, but what we're going to do here is start at the beginning. Ask you everything."

"May I ask you one question first?" Nicolas said.

"Sure," Ethan said.

Nicolas closed his eyes, and an anxious nightmare of possibilities painted the backs of their lids—the prospect of leaving the security of detainment, going back out on the streets, and doing the FBI's secret bidding. "Little Jimmy Barber mentioned you wanted to use me as a CI. I'm smart enough to know what that means. Are you going to make me go back out there?"

Agent Hensley shrugged. "It isn't out of the realm of possibility. Being a criminal informant could reduce your charges or improve your sentence. That said, we would need a clear plan of action and full confidence that you'd bring in useful information and not be a threat to others. It's a process we'd have to hammer out with the Federal Prosecutor's Office and a review committee in our Boston field office. If you end up giving us information now that helps build our case against Victor Zobel, it might not be necessary."

"And if it *does* become necessary?"

"Then we'd hope you choose to save lives," Agent Hensley said.

Save lives. It came as a shock to Nicolas that the idea of doing this, of stepping into a guiltless life, seemed to shine a ray of invisible light on his heart. All the fear he had been living under, all the anxiety and tears, those considerations of his own undoing, had now transformed into a path he could, going forward, be proud of.

He sat back in his chair, glancing at the camera setup on a tripod behind the agents.

"What do you want to know?" he finally said.

The special agents glanced at each other. Then it began: a jump down the rabbit hole, into a game of connecting the dots, all the way from his childhood and resettlement in the United States to his assassination attempt on Jonathan Flite last November. There were holes, many of them, but he could tell by the expressions on the exhausted FBI agents' faces that he was telling them more than they had expected to hear: how his first-ever committed murder, that of Larry Kane's cocaine dealer, had been a slick aconite poisoning at the Canaan Tavern in West Hartford; and then how Kane had used that murder to blackmail him into killing a prostitute and disposing of her body on a piece of country property in Connecticut owned by Carey Developments. It was the same property where, last fall, he had ditched the white Ford Sanctuary after attacking Jonathan Flite. He then described the bonuses from Larry Kane, the resulting material comforts, the starting of his own apartment rental business, and his first and only attempt at love—Aurora Demark, the stripper tenant he would never see again.

After what seemed like hours, Agent Hensley said, "Tell us about your relationship with Revis Zobel."

Memories of Victor Zobel's family during their shared days in Geneva ran through Nicolas's mind. The warmth they inspired reminded him just how far he had come since his innocent childhood. "Revis," he said with a ruminative chortle. "Well, we played together as children in Geneva."

"Tell us about that."

"Not much of it matters. Probably just what I mentioned

before. The incident with the nail. We were playing once at their house, where my father was building an addition. Revis's sister, Victoria, pushed him onto the construction site, and a nail went through his foot. Victor was home, and instead of taking Revis to the hospital, he just stood there, screaming at him for being so stupid. It was finally his mother, Cassandra, who took him. I guess I was too young to realize just how bad things in that family really were." Nicolas sighed and danced his fingertips over the cold, metal table in front of him. The agents waited in silence. "We've stayed friendly, Revis and me, but only over a distance. Phone calls. Texts. Emails. Things like that. Mostly inconsequential."

The agents accepted this with constrained nods. It seemed they were holding something back from Nicolas. He didn't ask what.

More talk about Geneva. More questions. More memories Nicolas wouldn't have expected to remember. When they finally circled back to the topic of Jonathan Flite, Nicolas looked at the ceiling and shook his head. "It was Victor Zobel who wanted him dead. I'm almost sure of it. Like I said at the mall, it's because of what he's hiding on that land in Minnesota."

"And what is that?" the agent named Ethan said.

"Proof."

"Proof?"

"That everything he stands for is based on false presumptions," Nicolas said. "I heard once from Revis Zobel that his father was doing 'tests on consciousness.' Those girls I told Jimmy Barber about—the mail-order brides I sometimes brought there? I don't think Revis ever knew about them, but I do think they were part of those tests. He only knew Victor was studying how the brain functions during death. I think they've found evidence that it doesn't all just go black when we die. Jonathan Flite and his memories tie into that, too, and that's why Victor wanted him dead."

"And the note you left in Paul Simpleton's pocket that night?"

"A directive. I think it was Victor Zobel trying to pose the guy as a religious fanatic, because every time a person like that makes the news, people start abandoning religion in search of science and neutrality. I think that's what Victor Zobel has always wanted."

Agent Hensley gave Nicolas a tired, incredulous grimace. "Even if he kills people to make it happen?"

"Well, yes. But you're forgetting one thing."

"Yeah? What's that?"

"Victor Zobel is a goddamned psychopath."

2005

WHAT Elijah Bryce wasn't expecting after the deadly skirmish on Spinner's Island was to have newspaper and television reporters show up at his front door. Shortly after arriving home from the hospital that afternoon, the first of them knocked—a ravishing yet cordial woman dressed in a blazing red skirt suit and matching high heels. Elijah recognized her immediately as Alice Winterblume, one of the well-known reporters from WCMP news in Wind Prairie. She had reported on last year's excavation of human remains in the Moon Woods and also this year on Joshua Grime's recently uncovered jawbone.

Shelly Bryce, having stayed close to Elijah's side all day, surveyed Alice Winterblume with distrustful eyes. Because Elijah liked the reporter's respectful demeanor, however, he answered her questions as truthfully as he could. Her cameraman recorded his answers about the jawbone, Spinner's Island, and the confrontation with Damon Jacoby. The only unpleasant thing about the interview for Elijah was the camera's glaring LED light shining straight into his eyes.

Alice asked her last three questions once the camera and microphones were turned off. Her cameraman was loading the news van, and Shelly was in the kitchen fixing refreshments she had pressured herself into offering. With a scrunched forehead and a manner that suggested genuine concern, Alice glanced quickly at Shelly and then back at Elijah. "Tell me one more thing," she said. "Just between us and not for the news, because I'm curious. Do you think Damon Jacoby deserved what happened to him?"

At first, Elijah frowned at the question. "Deserved to die?" A rush of conflict colored his heart, and he shook his head. "I don't think death is about deserving it or not. He had a lot going on in his head."

"'A lot going on in his head.' What do you mean by that?"

Elijah closed his eyes, took a deep breath, and said, "I don't know why, but a lot of people see stuff around here. Even Molly and I have had some weird experiences."

"Like what?"

"Like . . ." Elijah considered the morning he had seen Damon Jacoby's apparition during his paper route, and then Molly's claim to have started seeing ghosts last summer. "Maybe it's all those rumors about this place being haunted," he finally said. "I think they're true. Except I don't think anyone really knows what that means."

Alice's beautiful, made-up lips bent into a most curious smile.

2038

SHELLY BRYCE WAS SITTING in her living room, agape and staring at her television, on which Kara Butler's private ActoVid account was streaming a steady recording of their joint venture into Victor Zobel's Idle County home. Shelly hadn't known it, but Kara had been wearing invisible ActoLenses—part of her ulterior motive for trespassing on the private Moon Woods property. After Shelly's unexpected whiteout experience in the mansion's circular driveway, the coincidence of their meeting today hadn't seemed to be a coincidence at all. She now felt without a shaking doubt that some underlying intuition had pushed her toward the Moon Woods this morning, that somehow the circumstances of the week (particularly the media storm following the attack on Jonathan Flite's mother last night) had become a signal to rekindle her drive to find answers about Elijah's disappearance in 2010. Hints that Victor Zobel had known more than he let on had been there all along. He had funded and led all major local searches for the Idle County Seven. He had quietly purchased the Moon Woods land in 2011. He had conveniently ignored the teenagers' disappearances as his celebrity and wealth exponentially grew in the decades since.

Kara's video footage was fairly smooth due to her ActoLenses' built-in stabilization system, and Shelly now saw on camera just what exactly had happened earlier today, when she stepped out of her car in Victor Zobel's driveway. Her gaze had gone completely blank, as if some inner thought had suddenly demanded her entire conscious focus, yet she had retained her balance, and the expression on her face had been serene, almost rapturous.

"Okay, now watch this, coming up right here," Kara said. "The camera sensor did something weird."

Shelly watched herself on the television, seeing Victoria Zobel approach from the rear side of the car and Kara's point of view coming at her from the front. Both Kara and Victoria had noticed she was suddenly staring off into space, and they had extended their hands to her shoulders to make sure she wasn't about to fall, and then—

Her body flickered white in the picture, blurred with what appeared to be digital noise where her clothes should have been. She then appeared normal again for about three seconds. She flickered a second time and then, for a period of nearly three seconds, seemed to disappear entirely.

"Now, seriously, what the *hell* is that?" Kara said, sounding almost panicked. "You were normal looking the whole time, obviously, so why on earth would the camera sensor mess up just on you?"

"I don't know how technology works," Shelly said slowly,

staring at the footage as Kara rewound it, then played it back again. "I'm also not sure it was legal for you to be recording that on Victor's property."

"Definitely might not have been," Kara said, grimacing and pushing a lock of black hair behind her ear. "But I've heard stuff about that place and wanted to try."

"What do you mean 'heard stuff'?"

Kara shifted in her seat and then offered Shelly a tepid shrug. "I've talked with some people from Idle County, and I keep getting the feeling that not everyone here agrees on what's real and what's not."

Shelly thought back to that peculiar feeling of oneness with each water molecule of Victor Zobel's fountain. She had no idea how to explain it.

"I got a taste of that weirdness when you showed up at the gate today," Kara continued. "Like, of all people, the mother of one of my sister's friends. Granted, the bombing last night is probably making everyone curious about the Moon Woods."

Kara played the ActoLens footage again and again, and each time, Shelly flickered white in the midst of her euphoria, as though something about her peculiar experience had affected the camera. They watched it repeatedly in silence. Shelly's heart was racing. On any other day, it would have been fear coursing through her, but today, it was excitement. Everything had seemed so vivid during her mental episode, as though it were all more real than everything she knew in her daily life. Those colors, those sounds, that sense of unity with everything—had they all been a trick of her brain, or was this video somehow proof that they weren't?

Shelly sat up straight and put her hands flat on her lap, one on each thigh. "Alice Winterblume is doing a piece on Idle County," she told Kara in a low voice. "She called me this morning, but I said I didn't want to talk."

Kara made fleeting, hesitant eye contact with Shelly. "I know. We've spoken, actually."

Shelly's heartbeat quickened. "You and Alice herself?"

"In the flesh. She came out to interview my dad about Molly back in May. It's part of the reason I came here. Let's just say that if I get charged with trespassing, I'll have her lawyers behind me. She's on full charge to do this story on Idle County."

"You mean you recorded this for *WorldLine*?" A rush of tingles ran down Shelly's spine. "All this footage of me—?"

"It's already uploaded on a shared server," Kara said. "I didn't have a good chance to ask for your consent, but I'm sure *WorldLine* will give you a choice. They're reporters, though, so who knows. Alice Winterblume's been trying to get Victor Zobel to do an interview since last year. When he declined, she apparently went on the offensive."

Shelly glanced around her small living room. She and Kara Butler were on the same couch she had been sitting on this morning when the call from Clovia Bell at *WorldLine* had come in. Now that the afternoon light had shifted toward the windows and the room was brighter, everything looked fresh. New. Possible.

"Do you think Alice has a good reason to be investigating Victor Zobel?" Shelly asked.

Kara took a short breath and glanced out the window. "I do." After a pause, she added, "There's something about this place that affects people. I'm pretty sure that's what Victor Zobel is trying to cover up. Alice even says the death of Cynthia Foster, your son's biological mother, was part of it. A murder. She has what she calls 'near-conclusive proof.' She's even trying to court Victor's son,

Revis, for an interview but so far hasn't had a response. Apparently his friends have said he hates his dad, though, and that he'd take Victor down if he could."

Kara continued to stare out the window with an uncertain grimace, at the bright green trees fluttering in the afternoon breeze. Once again, for a fleeting moment, she reminded Shelly of young Molly Butler back in the early 2000s. The girl had been one of the main catalysts for Elijah's development, and today, for the first time, Shelly realized what a great gift that had been to him. Even their discovery and befriending of the late Cynthia Foster had been a blessing. Today, Shelly's fears of the past, present, and future had disappeared, and where this morning she had seen a threat to her comfort and ideology, she now saw opportunity. Again watching the peculiar glitch in Kara Butler's ActoLens footage, she thought of Victor Zobel's expression earlier this afternoon, when it became clear she wasn't going to serve his agenda. Yes, he looked young for his age, but there seemed to have been in his eyes an ancient-looking madness.

"I think I'll speak with Alice Winterblume after all," Shelly said, sitting straight up and offering Kara an expression of emboldened resolve. Their eyes locked, as if finally recognizing their shared path. They both smiled.

2005

At 6:00 P.M. following Elijah Bryce's interview with Alice Winterblume, his home phone rang. It was another reporter, this one from a national news network, wondering whether it was true Elijah had carried the dead body of a sworn enemy over a treacherous path of rocks in an attempt to get him to a hospital. Yes, it was true, Shelly Bryce answered for him, but he would not be speaking to any more reporters that evening. He was perfectly comfortable lying on the brown leather couch, with bare feet, not talking at all.

For a few hours, he slept.

At 9:01 p.m., the phone rang again. This time, it was Andrew Butler, calling to tell them that Molly was awake and okay, and she wanted to speak with Elijah if possible.

He grabbed the phone from his mother. "Hello?"

"You're all over the TV!" Molly said, unable to hide a trickle of excitement. It was subdued excitement, however, because the gruesome death they had witnessed at sunrise was like an invisible spear running through both their hearts.

"I talked to Alice Winterblume," he said. "I just wanted people to know what happened, because . . ."

"I know," Molly said. "I'm scared they're going to think we did something wrong."

"Exactly."

"But we didn't."

"We couldn't have."

Molly paused, then said in a whisper, "I didn't tell anybody about Damon. About his psychic stuff, I mean. Or that we've both seen things."

Elijah, still lying on the leather couch in the living room, glanced toward the kitchen, where his mother was washing dishes in the sink. He thought back to what he had said to Alice Winterblume about Idle County being haunted, and how nobody seemed to know what that actually meant. "I didn't say much either," he told Molly. "I think we should be careful who we tell."

"Do you think you'll keep seeing stuff?" Molly asked in a whisper, as if her father were hovering just outside her hospital room.

Elijah turned the question over in his mind before answering. "I'm not sure. I keep thinking maybe the thing during the paper route was all in my head."

"I thought that when it started for me, too. But it still doesn't explain why I saw Damon at Cynthia's house during the tarot reading." Molly paused, hesitated for a moment, and then sighed. "I guess I'm just a little bit worried."

"About what?"

"Well . . . that you're going to start second-guessing every-thing, and you won't want to hang out with me once school starts."

The caution in her tone made Elijah's heart flutter with some-thing that felt like love. Not the boy-girl type of love his mother might want him to have, but something warm and unconditional just the same. "Don't worry," he said. "You're my only friend. And I'm not going to forget what happened."

Molly's sigh of relief was so loud that Elijah almost laughed. "I don't know what I'd do without you as a friend," she said. "Nobody else is going to understand what really happened."

"We're starting our Weirdo Group, remember?" Elijah said. "You said so that day we went to the Bean & Leaf."

"True," Molly said. She gave him a dazed-sounding chuckle. "Okay, I'm tired, though. I just wanted to call and tell you that you were on the news."

"Well, thanks for the warning."

"Bye, Elijah."

"See you later, Molly."

That night, his dreams were agitated and repetitive but about nothing in particular. He kept waking up, worrying that Molly wouldn't want to be his friend and that everybody would now treat him even more awkwardly because he had achieved a bit of local fame. At one point, surrounded by darkness, he woke up and saw Damon Jacoby standing at the foot of his bed. Whether it was a dream or a ghost, he didn't know. In the morning, he didn't re-member the apparition at all.

2038

STUPIDITY. It was a trait particularly human. People these days were perfectly happy ignoring the calamities of Earth as long as they had nice houses, decent jobs, and entertainment to divert their attention. So few were capable of caring about anything beyond themselves without first being told to do so, and those who could were left with the challenge of corralling the masses and encouraging them to consume the lifesaving elixir of independent thought. Anyone who actively opposed this mission of human enlightenment was, in Victor Zobel's opinion, worth more dead than alive. He wondered: Was he the only living human who had the intellectual capacity to see the light?

Earth spun below him outside Star Island's twirling luxury housing wheel. Victor was on his office treadmill, and he had set the belt speed to be faster than usual. What was he trying to outrun? The ever-present murmur of anxiety in his heart whispering that all his efforts might soon go up in smoke? The prospect of Earth's blithering idiots looking at him only as a news headline or sound bite or laughingstock instead of recognizing the true value of his goals?

"Dad, you're going to give yourself a heart attack."

Victor jolted in surprise, almost tripping on his treadmill.

Revis.

How could his son have entered? Victor had demanded Revis's retinal scan data be removed from the apartment's entry system almost a year ago. Whoever had failed to do that task—or relay the order—was about to become jobless. Victor wondered if anyone down on Earth would miss the grown-up boy were he to mysteriously vanish out an airlock door. It would sure make both their lives easier.

"I'm busy," Victor told Revis, whose graying brown hair looked mussed from the stylish, tourism-grade space suit he had clearly just climbed out of. "Please knock when you come in. You'd think a person your age would know how rude it is to invade another person's space."

"Invade your space? Please. You have two thousand square feet of this thing, and I'm your only visitor. Victoria sure as hell isn't coming up after last time."

"That's asinine. It was just a shuttle glitch. She was fine."

"A glitch. Right. She almost burned up on her way down."

"Human error," Victor said. "Some fool who didn't replace the silica thermal protection coating properly. But you know that." He continued running, regaining his footing, his confidence. "I wasn't expecting you. I was hoping for some peace and quiet today."

"Can't get more peace and quiet than you have up here every day," Revis said, picking a piece of dust off his sweater. "I came up because you need to do some massive PR control. You're being eaten alive down there. Everyone thinks you somehow supplied Jean-Claude Apostol with a nuclear weapon last year."

"I said I want to be alone!" Victor screamed. For a second, his son exuded the pathetic, submissive fear he had always succumbed to as a child. Those big green eyes, always staring up at Victor in terror, always acknowledging who was in control. It was just like the time Revis stupidly stepped on the nail in Geneva and delayed Victor's business meeting. The boy had learned his place that day and for the next few decades, but recently, he had begun to talk back.

Victor turned the treadmill up one kilometer per hour faster.

"No, you're not going to ignore this, because Victoria and I are the ones having to deal with it," Revis replied, quivering slightly, the way he always did after Victor berated him. The boy-man stepped toward Victor's desk and glanced down at an open magazine—the July issue of *Physical Review Today*, surely something beyond his mental scope. "Guess who called me last night?" he continued. "Little Nick Rim from Geneva. Haven't heard from him since last year, when he asked me why you might be interested in that Jonathan Flite kid from Rhode Island. The one who's saying all that stuff about the Moon Woods."

Victor remained silent.

"Except now Nick tells me you tried to have the kid killed. He says he needs to know if I knew about it."

Victor remained silent.

"If that's true, you're fucked."

Victor remained silent.

"Jesus Christ, Dad!" His son's voice had risen in both anxiety and anger. Perhaps he had finally realized how steep a spiral downward it would be if authorities were to find enough evidence to build a case against the Zobel family. "I had to come up and ask you in person in case our ActoHubs are being monitored," Revis continued. "I didn't want to accuse you of anything, even though you're a prick. But this . . . Damn, dude. If it's true, you're not getting out of it."

Victor continued to run, but he eyed his desk. Was there anything sharp on it? Yes, a letter opener—the solid, pure silver kind, the same one he used to open the sickening taunts sent in the robin's-egg-blue envelopes. The letter opener could still stab Revis through his shirt, could it not?

"Okay, whatever. Do your ignoring thing again. I'll just sit here and wait. Because I need to know what the *fuck* you have been doing."

The treadmill cruised in place. Victor's feet pounded, pounded, pounded. Earth passed by the window to his right. The problem with Revis was that, even though his old-fashioned fear sometimes shone through out of habit, he had identified methods of social strategy in Victor that Victor himself hadn't been aware of. The boy always claimed his useless degrees in psychology were a result of his father's abusiveness, but that was a joke. Victor's money had kept Revis wealthy and happy. The family wealth he had access to paid for his vacations, his yacht, his women, his general life enjoyment. The boy had never been a businessperson like his twin sister; he was the one Victor paid to distract. Yet now he wasn't distracted. He was seeing the cracks in their family's facade.

Victor pressed the Stop button on the treadmill. It slowed, and his feet slowed with it. He eyed the letter opener. Three, two, one, and here was an opportunity. Victor stepped off the treadmill and walked ten feet forward, toward his desk.

To his left, behind it, were the stars. Then Earth. Then the stars again. No, he wouldn't be going back down there to face the wrath of reporters, the law, and all those stupid people who had no respect for his efforts to remove from culture the most harmful of human tendencies.

Breathing heavily but feeling vivacious (considering his seventy-four years), Victor picked up the week's stack of mail, which his assistant Simone had brought to him earlier that day before taking the afternoon off. Under a ruse of doing the mundane, he grabbed the letter opener from his pen holder.

Revis approached him from behind. "You're going to talk to me right now," he said. "I always thought you had some shady shit going on, but this is—"

Victor spun around toward his son, bringing the letter opener in a fast arc toward his chest. There were no other choices; this was impulse. This was how animals survived.

Revis jumped backward far faster than Victor anticipated. "Dude, what the—?"

With a whining, guttural scream, Victor lunged at his son again, and once more, Revis evaded him. Now he was chuckling. *Chuckling.* How could he show such insolence?

"You're going to stab me? Seriously?"

Victor attacked again. This time, Revis didn't jump back. He grabbed his father by the arm and twisted it behind the man's back, holding him in a lock. The letter opener fell from Victor's fingers to the floor. A moment later, his son's moist breath warmed his right ear.

"You listen to me, you sick old man. You think I wouldn't have learned to defend myself after growing up with you? You're a joke now. And you're about to fall very hard. So if you don't kill yourself up here, which by the way would be a goddamned blessing to the world, you should get ready for a rude awakening." Victor felt a knee on his back, and then a thrust. He flew uncontrollably toward his desk. The squared edge of it struck his side as he twirled to avoid having it hit him in the gut. He fell to the floor, and in a tilted view, he saw Revis's sneaker-clad feet approaching. The boy, now a man, leaned over and hissed, "You mean nothing to me."

A foot pounded Victor's abdomen. Pain exploded in him.

With a frightfully blank expression, Revis leaned toward the desk, grabbed the folded-open issue of *Physical Review Today*, and threw it down, onto the floor in front of Victor's face. "Looks like your little physicist friend is winning. Way to go. You're about to become old news." Surely ignorant of the physics paper's greater implications, Revis stormed out of the office and back through Victor's Star Island living quarters. A second later, the apartment door opened, then slammed shut.

Just inches from Victor's eyes was last month's article about the physicist, Dorothy Garland—whose name had been Rebecca Sparks back in Idle County, before he had tried to kill her. Before Maximilian Pope helped her go into hiding. Before everything began falling apart.

The headline burned into his eyes for the millionth time.

Mind Over Matter? American Physicist
Poses Orchestrated Objective Reduction in a
Holographic Multiverse, Opens New Paths
Toward Consciousness Studies

A week ago, the day of Winifred Flite's failure of a press conference, the telepathic Idle County native had sent a copy of the scientific journal to *Star Island* in yet another bird's-egg-blue envelope, this time a large one. She wasn't even bothering to remain anonymous with her taunts anymore.

Victor lay alone on his floor. Instead of screaming and putting himself in a position of humiliation, he waited for the pain to diminish. He would blame any bruises on a fall off his treadmill. He would admit to no one that his forty-year-old son had just beaten him, because that would bring questions about their past—not just about Victor's relationship with his children but also about their mother, Cassandra Pope; her daughter, Jillian; and the latter two's untimely deaths. That of course would lead to questions about Cassandra's first husband, Max, who had acted as Rebecca Sparks's goddamned savior. So much of what he had worked for in life now seemed to be crumbling.

Yet he would stay silent. He would breathe. He had to, because he had other seeds of rage already planted on that horrible globe below him, already waiting in the shadows for the time when their fires would bloom. Rage, he had learned, was a most useful tool, especially when it was the only one left to use.

2038

S TILLNESS. Always a symptom of catastrophe, but in the aftermath—a calm respite, a hush-down period in which people allowed the trauma in question to numb them, shake them, and change them. The assimilation of such experiences, whether intimate or globally experienced through a media lens, always resulted in a new definition of the collective social psyche.

The people of small and provincial Newport, Rhode Island, had reacted to the August 2 bombing at their city hall with adrenaline, sadness, anger, and myriad emotions in between. Winifred Flite, up until that point, had been the frowned-upon mother of their small city's famous nurse killer, so it came as a surprise after Weston Carrow's suicide bomb that many people's attitudes toward the Flites seemed to shift. Carrow had attacked their stomping ground; he had put many local lives in danger; he had, unwittingly, put Winifred Flite and her son Jonathan on the side of the people.

Now those same people's sole concern was to protect their city from further terror. In the days following the blast, while still pondering the shock of it all, many Newport residents began adjusting their views of the Flites toward sympathy. Perhaps Jonathan really had been misunderstood his whole life, and perhaps Winifred's mistakes in raising him—considering his peculiarity—were on some level forgivable. Regardless, the majority of people agreed that neither had deserved to become victims of such violent religious madmen.

On a broader scale, those who had not yet followed the Jonathan Flite story closely—those who knew him only as "the nurse killer" and nothing more—now began to take note. In all countries touched by the United States' mass media, people began noticing the details in the shadows, the unlikely web of reasons this "mentally ill" young man had become a threat to religious extremists. That he claimed to have memories of seven teenagers who went missing in 2010 left chills on the backs of many people's necks. For most of them, it was their first exposure to evidence that life was more than what it appeared to be on the surface. Even those hesitant to use the term "reincarnation" while speculating about the nature of Jonathan Flite's peculiar claims had to wonder if there might be some credibility to the idea after all. How else could anybody have memories of other lives?

There were, of course, a few people scattered about the world who observed all this with a bit of humor. They were the ones who had the capacity to think critically about human behavior, who had witnessed over the course of their lives mankind's tendency to attach particular ideas to the human experience—always creating or adopting answers about what it all meant without possessing any solid information about how or why it existed at all.

Alice Winterblume, star anchor of CBS's streaming newsmagazine *WorldLine*, was one of these people. Her fame rivaled Victor Zobel's, and her ability to influence was only just beginning to reach its peak. She was a powerful ally for anybody who needed a voice, and she had just picked the next person to whom she would lend her cameras and credibility: the troubled nurse killer, Jonathan Flite.

AS THE WORLD SLOWLY NUMBED ITSELF to this third attack on Jonathan and his loved ones, *WorldLine* began its effort to elevate the quality of streaming journalism yet again. The most curious piece of evidence accentuating the young man's story was something Alice had been sitting on for almost thirty years, since her reporting days at WCMP news in Wind Prairie, Minnesota.

On September 8, 2010, her department had received a message on their tip line from a woman named Cynthia Foster, who claimed to be the biological mother of the recently vanished Elijah Bryce. Calling from Palmer, Alaska, she had asked to speak with Alice personally about some alarming information she had uncovered regarding Victor Zobel and Maximilian Pope—two people intimately intertwined with the Idle County Seven mystery. The police had ignored her call, Cynthia said, and she hadn't known where else to turn.

A day later, Cynthia had been killed alongside a man named Frank Brennin in what had been deemed a freak hunting accident. The hunter, a Croatian man named Luka Filipović (who was living in the United States on a green card), had come forward to Palmer police that very night, by all appearances shocked and shaken over what he had done while dall sheep hunting. Because he claimed his rifle had accidentally misfired three times from a distance (and because there hadn't been enough evidence to prove otherwise), he was ultimately found guilty on two counts of negligent homicide. This had resulted in a single, year-long prison sentence.

Cynthia Foster, apart from being a woman of questionable repute, had been neither Elijah Bryce's legal parent nor an official link to the Idle County Seven case, so her death made very few airwaves. The coincidence of her phone call the day before always struck Alice as odd, however, so Alice had followed up on it in the years since and uncovered some questionable facts.

First, Luka Filipović, the Croatian hunter, had been sponsored for his green card by a New Jersey weapons manufacturing company called TEKK Group, which was a wholly owned subsidiary of Advanced Defense Machining, whose majority shareholder was none other than Victor Zobel.

Second, Filipović's wife and two sons, who were very poor residents of Croatia when he came to the United States in 2008, mysteriously moved into a beautiful home along the Mediterranean coast in Zadar following the hunting accident. Where their newfound fortune came from, nobody could say.

And third, after serving his one-year prison sentence for negligent homicide, Filipović had immediately returned to Croatia to join his family, where he worked in Zadar as a seaport manager.

Coincidences all around.

Or maybe not at all.

WHEN ALICE WINTERBLUME MET JONATHAN FLITE on August 9, 2038, it was a hushed affair for a Monday morning, taking place at the Renaissance Providence Hotel in Rhode Island. Outside and surrounding the hotel were eight policemen, and in the lobby was a team of security guards hired personally by the *WorldLine* anchor herself. Alice stood in the hallway with her crew, waiting with both simmering intrigue and a hint of trepidation for Jonathan to walk around the corner. She had a surprise guest waiting for him, one whose reveal, once caught on camera and shown in context to the world, would likely become one of the most powerful moments in journalism history. She would interview Jonathan first, get as many corroborative Idle County Seven memories from him as she could, and then stage the big meeting, which would—if his memories were legitimate—feel like a reunion.

When Jonathan finally approached Alice and her crew in the hallway, he reached out politely to shake her hand. Careful not to show any visible signs of hesitation, Alice looked straight into his piercing hazel eyes and accepted his gesture with a firm grip. She immediately felt in her bones that this young man, for all his past psychological troubles, was special in a way people might not be ready for.

Jonathan had been escorted to the hotel by his three closest friends: the twiglike, walking fashion accessory known as Jimmy Barber, a gently graying psychiatrist named Thomas Lumen, and a simply clad (and armed) man they all called Sounder (whose real name, Halstrom Olson, came out over a chuckled introduction). Behind Alice, standing stiffly alongside the two camera operators and hiding both her racing heart and her immediate rush of attraction upon seeing Jonathan Flite, was a young woman named Clovia Bell. Clovia had started as an intern at *WorldLine* during an unfinished stint at New York University, then quickly gained favor with Alice Winterblume before ascending to the prestigious title of producer's assistant. Standing in the hallway with this unlikely group of people, thinking back on her middle-class upbringing in Nyack, New York, Clovia Bell felt an inkling that, somehow, all was right with her world, and she was exactly where she needed to be.

The group of eight stepped into their reserved suite, where Jimmy and Clovia found space to socialize in the lounge while Alice, Jonathan, Dr. Lumen, and Sounder stepped into the large bedroom, where two couches sat facing each other. Sounder stood by the door, quiet as ever, leaving the three as alone as possible. The *WorldLine* anchor began with a simple question for Jonathan: "How are you?"

The young man's eyes grew heavy with tears, and he tried to wipe his emotions away with a fast shake of his head. On impulse, Alice braced herself. After all, this was Rhode Island's famous nurse killer. Yet Jonathan showed no signs of violence or aggression, just grief and exhaustion. His mother was in a coma, and he had just chosen to dive headfirst into an even deeper fishbowl of national attention and speculation. With the subject broached, and with a head nod from the friendly psychiatrist Dr. Lumen, Alice began asking Jonathan questions through which he could validate his Idle County Seven claims.

What did Elijah Bryce's house look like in 2005?

How about his street?

What was she wearing the day Elijah met her, and what had Alice asked the boy in their private exchange after the interview ended?

The answers seemed to come to Jonathan first as emotions, and then as translations into words and images and other sensory experiences. The details were accurate enough to make Alice's ankles shake.

This was her next big story; it had to be. It would be the biggest one of the decade.

When Jonathan Flite began speaking about July 4, 2010—the night the Idle County Seven vanished—Alice Winterblume felt that old, familiar rush, the same one she had felt in 2004 upon receiving the news call regarding the FBI's discovery of a mass grave site in the Moon Woods. It wasn't until now, over three decades later, that the weight of the place's dysfunctions began to make sense. Its secrets were finally taking shape, all because of this misunderstood young man, who had been plagued by their truth his entire life.

Then it was time. Alice nodded to her assistant, Clovia, who walked back to the lounge and through an unobtrusive wooden door linking to the adjacent suite. Jonathan, who had leaned forward with his elbows on his knees and his forehead in his hands, seemed not to notice or care when the low whirring of an electric wheelchair entered their suite. Almost twenty seconds passed before he looked up over their ensuing silence.

When he finally saw Rebecca Sparks, the round-faced physicist who now went by the name Dorothy Garland, his face first went ashen. It then warmed with the most tentative, delicate smile anyone in the room had ever seen on him. The disabled woman was middle-aged and wearing light makeup for the cameras, but her dyed-blond hair was pulled back around her heart-shaped face in the same, simple way she always wore it. Her eyes locked on Jonathan's with recognition so electric that all others in the room felt it as a shared rush of tingles down their spines.

As if by magic (though obviously via a brain-connected computerized device), a message typed in the dullest of Courier fonts appeared on a flat tablet mounted on the Rebecca's wheelchair.

Here we finally are. I've been waiting for this for a long time. Are you finally ready to shake it all to hell?

Jonathan Flite looked down at Rebecca's words, then back up, into her eyes. His expression wavered between awe, euphoria, and a most desperate sense of curiosity. For a few quiet moments, the implications of their meeting today—and the resulting tremors of potential—radiated throughout the room. Alice Winterblume's cameras, the only neutral observers present, had no way to record the truth about how or why the vanished Idle County Seven had thrown this small group of individuals onto a common path; they had no way to record the possibilities of what lay ahead. They simply documented this pivotal gathering—unaware that everyone involved was feeling a concurrent inclination to act, to let the truth out, and to face the consequences of whatever results would come. This, they would all soon know, was the only way forward.

ACKNOWLEDGMENTS

THIS BOOK IS A DIRECT RESULT of the fact that *The Confessions of Jonathan Flite*, its prequel, actually saw the light of day to begin with. The only reason I was able to finish "JF1" (as I call it) was because my dear friend Mike Shay gifted me with time—an entire year of rent-free living that allowed me to spend the majority of my days doing what I loved most: writing, researching, and drinking tea. Apart from allowing me to get this series off the ground, Mike's gift of time also gave me the chance to re-aim my life trajectory and move to the San Francisco Bay Area, which has since become the home I've always wanted. Mike, thank you a million times over. I'll never forget our friendly debates about science, consciousness, and #hope.

I must next thank my soulmate and sister, Mara, who, apart from providing essential critical feedback, keeps me afloat with encouragement at all times. Novel writing is a solitary endeavor, and having somebody there who understands my story and has faith in my overall vision (both for this book series and for life) is invaluable.

Further thanks is due to the rest of my family for their continued support—my brother, Joe; my sister, Amy; my brother-in-law, Steffen; my nephew, Lukas; my nieces Isabel, Carina, and Aurelia; and of course my parents, Walt and Ana.

Next up for thanks is Frank Gelat, who graciously listened to all my fretting about this book (and everything else) throughout the writing process. Frank, life is weird, isn't it?

Sheridan Sperry comes next. Sheridan, your friendship has been a huge gift to me since my move to Marin County, and who would have thought? You've been my biggest fan and most enthusiastic beta reader, and for that, I thank you dearly. Your feedback has made a huge difference.

Thank you next to my glorious proofreader Christine Zuchora-Walske and other trusted early readers: Sarah Koenig, Jacquie Jones, Jill Potts, Chad Aldrich, and Claudio Ramos.

Thank you also to Brendan Kramp, who introduced me to the indispensable Seth Material produced by Jane Roberts and Robert Butts. Apart from quite possibly saving my life when I was at a low point, those books helped flesh out the thought framework for these books.

Next up, thanks to everyone (dead or alive) who helped me with scientific or legal research, idea development, or anything else: Marcio Fonseca, Audrey Sederberg, Anna Sederberg, Brenda Sederberg, Leah Graf, Ed Hernandez, Nathan Casper, Adam Shucard, Philip Maret, JD Olson, John Brimble, Manina Harris, Leah Gift, Katy Hooks, Brian Greene, Brian Weiss, Michael Newton, and the late Jane Roberts and Robert Butts.

Thanks as always to my life inspirations: J. K. Rowling, Stephen King, Kazuo Ishiguro, Michael Crichton, Audrey Niffenegger, Suzanne Collins, Phillip Pullman, Chris Carter, George Lucas, Michael Bay, Steven Spielberg, David Yates, Peter Jackson, Fran Walsh, Philippa Boyens, Alan Ball, Pink, Lady Gaga, Sia, Kelly Clarkson, James Newton Howard, and all the other brilliant composers and musicians whose music I listened to while writing this book.

Finally, thank you, reader, for giving me and my work the time of day. It would be meaningless without you.

ABOUT THE AUTHOR

Matthew J. Beier is a novelist, screenwriter, video producer, and visual artist based in the San Francisco Bay Area. In 2012, Matthew published his first novel, *The Breeders*, and in 2014, he began publishing his seven-book Jonathan Flite series, which thus far includes *The Confessions of Jonathan Flite*, *The Release of Jonathan Flite*, and *The Rise of Jonathan Flite*. In 2003, he attended film school at Chapman University, where he studied screenwriting, film production, and English before spending a final semester abroad at Victoria University in Wellington, New Zealand. When Matthew isn't working, he enjoys drinking tea, exercising, watching films and streaming television shows, and spending time with his friends and family. He's currently hard at work on the last four books of the Jonathan Flite series, along with multiple TV and film scripts. He would love to hear from you via email at info@matthewbeier.com, on his Facebook author page, on Twitter @MatthewBeier, or on Instagram @matthewjbeier. You can also join Matthew's exclusive Patreon fan community at www.patreon.com/matthewjbeier.